Above the center of the Well of Eternity, the Demon Soul flared bright. Within the abyss formed by the Sargeras's spell, forces set in play by both the Soul and the Well churned, slowly building up into the creation of a stable portal. From his monstrous realm, the lord of the Legion prepared for his entrance into this latest prize. Soon, so very soon, he would eradicate all life, all existence, from it . . . and then he would go on to the next ripe world.

But there were others waiting in growing expectation, others with dire dreams far older than even that of the demon lord. They had waited for so very long for the means to escape, the means to reclaim what had once been theirs. Each step of success by Sargeras toward strengthening his portal was a step of success for them. With the Well, with the Demon Soul, and with the lord of the Legion's might, they would open up a window into their eternal prison.

And once open, there would be no sealing it again.

The Old Gods waited. They had done so for so very long, they could wait a little longer.

But only a little . . .

WARCRAFT

WAR OF THE ANCIENTS
TRILOGY

BOOK THREE

THE SUNDERING

RICHARD A. KNAAK

POCKET STAR BOOKS
New York   London   Toronto   Sydney

This book is a work of fiction. Names, characters, places and incidents are products of the author's imagination or are used fictitiously. Any resemblance to actual events or locales or persons, living or dead, is entirely coincidental.

An *Original* Publication of POCKET BOOKS

 A Pocket Star Book published by
POCKET BOOKS, a division of Simon & Schuster, Inc.
1230 Avenue of the Americas, New York, NY 10020

ISBN-13: 978-0-7434-7121-3
ISBN-10:   0-7434-7121-0

First Pocket Books printing August 2005

10   9   8   7

POCKET STAR BOOKS and colophon are registered trademarks of Simon & Schuster, Inc.

Cover art by Bill Petras

Manufactured in the United States of America

For information regarding special discounts for bulk purchases, please contact Simon & Schuster Special Sales at 1-800-456-6798 or business@simonandschuster.com.

To my nephew, Brandon

THE SUNDERING

PROLOGUE

A primal fury raged all about him, relentlessly ripping at him from all sides. Fire, water, earth, and air—all tinged with raw, uncontrolled magic—spun around him in madcap fashion. The strain to simply remain in one place threatened to tear him asunder, yet he held. He could do no less.

Past his gaze soared countless scenes, countless objects. An endless, wild panorama of time assailed his senses. There were landscapes, battles, and creatures even he could not name. He heard the voices of every being who had, did, and would exist. Every noise ever caused thundered in his ears. Colors unbelievable blinded his eyes.

And most unsettling, throughout it all, he saw himself, himself in each moment of existence, stretching forth from almost the birth of time to beyond its death. He might have taken heart from that save that every aspect of him was posed in the same contorted manner as he was. Every existence of him struggled to keep not just his world—but all reality—from collapsing into chaos.

Nozdormu shook his head and roared his agony and frustration.

He wore the form of a dragon—a huge, golden-bronze leviathan who seemed as much made of the sands of time as he was scaled flesh. His eyes were gleaming gemstones the color of the sun. His claws were glittering diamonds. He was the Aspect of Time, one of the five great entities who watched over the world of Azeroth, keeping it in balance and protecting it from danger within and without. Those who had formed the world had created him and his counterparts, and of Nozdormu, they had granted particular powers. He could see the myriad paths of the future and delve into the intricacies of the past. He swam the river of time as others did the air.

Yet, now Nozdormu barely held disaster in check, even though he had the aid of himself countless times over.

Where does it lie? the Aspect asked of himself not for the first time. *Where is the cause?* He had some general notion, but still not any specifics. When Nozdormu had sensed the unraveling of reality, he had come to this place to investigate, only to discover that he had barely arrived in time to prevent the destruction of everything. However, once caught up in that task, the Aspect realized that he could do no more on his own.

To that end, the behemoth had turned to one who whose power he dwarfed a thousandfold, but whose ingenuity and dedication had proven him as able as any of the great five. Nozdormu had contacted the red dragon, Korialstrasz, consort of the Aspect of Life, Alexstrasza, in a fragmented vision. He had managed to send the other leviathan—who wore the guise of the wizard, Krasus—to investigate one of the outward signs of the growing catastrophe and perhaps find a way to reverse the terrible situation.

But the anomaly that Korialstrasz and his human protege, Rhonin, had searched for in the eastern mountains had instead engulfed them. Sensing their sudden nearness, Nozdormu had cast them into the time period from which he suspected the cause. He knew that they survived, but, beyond that, what success they had managed appeared negligible.

And so, while the Aspect hoped for their quest, he still searched as best he could himself. Straining his powers to their limits, the massive dragon continued to follow every manifestation of the chaos. He fought past the swirling visions of orcs on the rampage, kingdoms rising and declining, violent volcanic upheavals, but still could find no clue—

No! There was at last something different . . . something that seemed to be influencing the madness. Power subtilely radiating from a nexus far, far from him. Nozdormu pursued the faint trace as a shark would its prey, his senses diving through the monstrous maelstrom of time. More than once, he thought he had lost it, but somehow managed to pick up the trail again.

Then, slowly, a vague force coalesced before him. There was a familiar sense to it, one that almost made him reject the truth when at last it was revealed. Nozdormu hesitated, certain that he had to be mistaken. The source could not be this. Such a thing could not be possible!

Before Nozdormu emanated a vision of the Well of Eternity.

The black lake churned with as much turmoil as the rest of the Aspect's surroundings. Violent flashes of pure magic battled over its dark waters.

And then he heard the whispering voices.

At first Nozdormu took them for the voices of demons, the voices of the Burning Legion, but he was well familiar with such and quickly dismissed that line of reasoning. No, the evil he felt dripping from these whisperers was more ancient, more malevolent . . .

The primal forces continued to rip at his very being, but Nozdormu ignored his pain, caught up in his discovery. Here, at last, Nozdormu believed, the key to the catastrophe lay. Whether or not it was still within his power to affect matters, he could not say, but at least if he was able to discover the truth, there might be a chance for Korialstrasz to yet succeed.

Nozdormu probed the lake further. He was better aware than most that what appeared a body of water was, in fact, so many things more. Mortal creatures could not comprehend the full scope of it. Even his fellow Aspects likely did not understand the waters as well as Nozdormu did and he knew that there were secrets hidden to him.

Visually, it was as if he flew over the black depths. In actuality, however, Nozdormu's mind plied a different realm. He battled a labyrinth of interlocking forces that shielded the core of that which was called the Well from revelation. Almost it was as if either the waters themselves were alive or something had so insinuated itself into the Well that it now was part of it.

Again, Nozdormu thought of the demons—the Burning Legion—and their desire to use the Well of Eternity's power to open the way and eradicate all life on Azeroth. Yet, this was too shrewd for them . . . even their master, Sargeras.

A sense of unease swelled within him as he wound his way through. Several times, the Aspect almost became trapped. There were false paths, alluring trails, all designed to forever bind him to the Well and devour his power, his essence. Nozdormu moved with utmost caution. To become trapped would not only mean his demise, but perhaps also the end of *all* things.

Deeper and deeper he dove. The intensity of the forces making up the Well astounded him. The power the dragon sensed brought back memories of the creators, whose ancient glory made Nozdormu the equivalent of slug climbing out of the mud. Were they somehow tied to the Well's secrets?

The visual image still remained of him hovering just above the shadowed surface. Only he and the Well had any stability in this place beyond the mortal plane. The waters floated in space, a bottomless lake stretching worlds across.

He drew closer to the violent surface. On the mortal plane, it should have reflected at least some of his image, but all Nozdormu saw was blackness. His mind reached deeper yet, burrowing along, closing in on the core . . . and the truth.

And then tendrils of inky water stretched up and seized his wings, limbs, and neck.

The Aspect barely reacted in time to keep himself from being dragged under. He struggled against the watery tentacles, but they held him fast. All four limbs were trapped and the tentacle around his throat tightened, cutting off his breath. Nozdormu understood that these perceptions were only illusion, but they were powerful ones representing the truth. His mind had been snared by that which lurked in the Well. If he did not free himself quickly, he would be just as dead as if the illusions were real.

Nozdormu exhaled—and a stream of sand turned the Well into a glittering display. The tentacles jerked, slackened. They withered, the magic that had created them worn and old.

But as they collapsed, others darted forth. Expecting this, Nozdormu flapped hard, rising swiftly. Four black limbs slashed futilely, then sank.

But the dragon suddenly jerked, his tail snagged by a tendril from behind. As Nozdormu turned to deal with it, more shot out. They jutted up from every direction, this time so many that the Aspect could not avoid them all.

He swatted away one, then another, then another—and then became trapped by more than a dozen, each binding him with monstrous strength. The dragon was inexorably drawn toward the swirling Well.

A maelstrom formed beneath him. Nozdormu felt its horrific suction even from above. The gap between the Aspect and the waters narrowed.

Then, the maelstrom changed. The waves rushing around its edges grew jagged, then hardened. The center deepened, yet from it issued forth what at first appeared another, albeit different, tendril. It was long, sinewy, and as it rose up toward him, its tip blossomed into three sharpened points.

A mouth.

Nozdormu's golden eyes widened. His struggles grew more adamant.

The demonic maw opened hungrily as the tentacles forced him toward it. The "tongue" lashed at his muzzle, its very touch searing harshly his hide.

And the whispers from within the Well grew more virulent, more eager. Distinctive voices that sent a chill through the Aspect. Yes, these were more than demons . . .

Again, he breathed the sands of time upon the tendrils, but now they cascaded off the black limbs as if simple dust. Nozdormu twisted, attempting to get even one of the tendrils loose, but, they held onto him with a vampiric passion.

This did not sit well with the Aspect. As the essence of Time, he had been granted by his creators with the knowledge of his own demise. That had been given as a lesson, so that he would never think his power so great and terrible that he had to answer to no other. Nozdormu knew exactly how he would perish and when—and this was not that moment.

But he could not free himself.

The "tongue" coiled around his muzzle, tightening its grip so much that Nozdormu felt as if his jawbones were cracking. Again, he reminded himself that this was all illusion, but knowing that did nothing to stop either the agony or the anxiety, the latter eating away within him in a manner he had never experienced.

He was almost at the teeth. They gnashed together, clearly in part to unnerve him—and succeeding. The strain of also holding together the bonds of reality put further stress to his thoughts. How much more simple just to let the Well take him and be done with all the effort—

No! Nozdormu suddenly thought. A notion came to him, a desperate one. He did not know if he had the power to make it pass, but there was little other choice.

The Aspect's body shimmered. He seemed to withdraw into himself.

The scene turned backward. Every motion made reversed itself. The "tongue" unrolled from his muzzle. He inhaled the sands, the tendrils undid themselves, drawing back into the black waters—

And the moment that happened, Nozdormu halted the reversal, then immediately withdrew his mind from the Well.

Once more, he floated in the river of time, barely keeping reality cohesive. The titanic effort took even more of a toll now that he had expended himself in his disastrous search, but somehow the Aspect found the strength to continue. He had touched upon the evil corrupting the Well and knew more than ever that failure would bring worse than destruction.

Nozdormu now recognized them for what they were. Even the horrific fury of the entire Burning Legion paled in comparison.

And there was nothing the Aspect could do to stop their intentions. He barely could keep the chaos in check. He no longer even had the will to reach out to the others, assuming he could have even done so.

There was no other hope, then. Only the same one as ever and yet that seemed so slight, so insignificant now, that Nozdormu could barely take heart in it.

It is all up to them . . . he thought as the raw forces tore at him. *It is all up to Korialstrasz and his human . . .*

ONE

They could smell the stench in the distance and it was difficult to say which was strongest, the acrid smoke rising from the burning landscape or the incessant, almost sweet odor of the slowly-decaying dead lying sprawled by the hundreds across it.

The night elves had managed to stem the latest assault by the Burning Legion, but had lost more ground again. Lord Desdel Stareye proclaimed it a retrenching maneuver enabling the host to better gauge the Legion's weaknesses, but among Malfurion Stormrage and his friends, the truth was known. Stareye was an aristocrat with no true concept of strategy and he surrounded himself with the like.

With the assassination of Lord Ravencrest, there had been no one willing to stand up to the slim, influential noble. Other than Ravencrest, few night elves truly had experience in warfare and with the dead commander the last of his line, his House could present no one to take his place. Stareye clearly had ambitions, but his ineptitude would see those ambitions crushed along with his people if something did not happen.

But Malfurion's thoughts were not simply concerned

with the precarious future of the host. Another, overriding matter ever caused him to look in the direction of distant Zin-Azshari, once the glittering capital of the night elves' realm. Even as the dim hint of light to the east presaged the cloud-enshrouded day, he went over and over again his failures.

Went over and over again the loss of the two that mattered most to him—fair Tyrande and his twin brother, Illidan.

Night elves aged very slowly, but the young Malfurion looked much older than his few decades. He still stood as tall as any of his people—roughly seven feet—and had their slim build and dark purple complexions. However, his slanted, silver eyes—eyes without pupils—had a maturity and bitterness cast in them that most night elves lacked even under such diversity. Malfurion's features were also more lupine than most, matching only his brother's.

More startling was his mane of hair, shoulder-length and of a unique, dark green—not the midnight blue even his twin had. People were always eyeing the hair just as they had once always eyed the plain garments to which his tastes turned. As a student of the druidic arts, Malfurion did not wear the garish, flamboyant robes and outfits considered normal clothing by his race. Instead, he preferred a simple, cloth tunic, plain leather jerkin and pants, and knee-high boots, also of leather. The extravagant garb worn by his people had been a telling sign of their jaded lives, their innate arrogance—something against his nature. Of course, now, though, most night elves save Lord Stareye and his ilk wandered as ragged refugees in muddied, blood-soaked clothes. More to the point, instead of looking down their noses at the peculiar young scholar, they now eyed the green-haired druid with desperate hope, aware that most of them lived because of his actions.

But what were those actions leading him toward? Not success, so far. Worse, and certainly more disconcerting, Malfurion had discovered that his delving into the natural powers of the living world had begun a physical change.

He rubbed his upper head, where one of the two tiny nubs lay hidden under his hair. They had sprouted but a few days ago, yet had already doubled in size. The two tiny horns chilled Malfurion, for they reminded him much too much of the beginning of a satyr's. That, in turn, reminded him too much of Xavius, the queen's counselor who had come back from the dead and, before Malfurion had finally dealt with him, sent Tyrande into the clutches of the Burning Legion's masters.

"You've got to stop thinking about her," someone coming up behind him urged.

Malfurion glanced without surprise at his companion, although most others in the host would have stared even harder at the newcomer than they did the druid. There was no creature in all Kalimdor like Rhonin.

The hooded figure draped in dark blue robes, under which could be seen similarly-colored shirt and pants, stood more than a head shorter than Malfurion even despite boots. But it was neither his height nor his garments that raised eyes and comments. Rather, it was the fiery, shoulder-length hair spilling out from the hood, the rounder, very pale features—especially the nose that bent slightly to one side—that so unsettled other night elves. The eyes were even more startling, for they were a bright emerald green with utterly black pupils.

Despite his comparative shortness, Rhonin was built stronger than Malfurion. He looked very capable of handling himself in combat—which he had—an unusual ability for one who had proven himself quite versed in the magical arts. Rhonin called himself a "human," a race of which no one had heard. Yet, if the crimson-tressed traveler was an example, Malfurion wished that the host had a thousand more just like him. Whereas his own people's sorcery, so dependent upon the Well of Eternity, now often failed, Rhonin wielded his own power as if the offspring of a demigod.

"How can I stop? How do I dare?" Malfurion demanded, suddenly growing angry at one he knew did not deserve such malice. "Tyrande has been their prisoner for too long and I've failed over and over again to even see within the palace's walls!"

In the past, Malfurion had used the training he had received from his mentor—the demigod, Cenarius—to walk a realm called the Emerald Dream. The Emerald Dream was a place where the world looked as it would have had there been neither civilization or even animal life. Through it, one's dream form could quickly reach locations all across the world. It had enabled him to pass through the magical barriers surrounding Queen Azshara's citadel and spy upon her Highborne and the commanders of the Burning Legion. He had used it to disrupt the plans of Xavius, the queen's counselor, and, after a harrowing imprisonment, temporarily destroy the portal and the tower containing it.

Now, however, the great demon, Archimonde, had strengthened those barriers, cutting off even the Emerald Dream. Malfurion had continued to try to pierce the barriers, but he might as well have been physically battering himself against a real wall.

It did not help that, in addition to awareness that Tyrande was within, the druid also suspected that Illidan might be.

"Elune will watch over her," Rhonin replied steadfastly. "She seems very much a favorite of the Mother Moon."

Malfurion could not argue with that reasoning. But a

short time ago, Tyrande had been a young novice in the service of the lunar goddess. Yet, the coming of the Legion seemed to have precipitated in her a transformation as great as in him, if not more so. Her powers had grown strong and, to her immense surprise, when the high priestess had been mortally wounded in battle, she had chosen Tyrande as her successor over many much more experienced and high-ranking sisters. Regrettably, that newfound status had ultimately led to her kidnapping by a transformed Xavius and his satyrs. Xavius had finally paid the price for his actions, but that had not saved Tyrande.

"Can even Elune stand up to the darkness of Sargeras?"

Rhonin's thick brow arched. "Talk like that won't help any, Malfurion," He glanced behind himself. ". . . and I'd especially appreciate it if you'd not speak so around our new friends."

For a moment, the druid forgot his misery as the shadowed forms rose up from the direction the wizard had come. Immediately it was clear that they were of more than one race, for some dwarfed the night elf in both height and girth while others came up short even to Rhonin. Yet all who strode up to where the pair stood moved with determination and a sense of strength that Malfurion had to admit his own people had just begun to find.

A musky scent wafted past his nose and he immediately tensed. A furred figure clad in loincloth and wielding a massive spear paused to gaze down at the night elf. The giant's breath came in heavy snorts which caused the ring through his nose to jingle slightly. His muzzle was more than a foot long and at the skull met two deeply-entrenched, black eyes that burned with determination. Above the harsh, wrinkled brow, a pair of treacherous-looking horns thrust ahead of the muzzle.

A tauren . . .

"This is—" Rhonin began.

"Know that Huln Highmountain stands before you, night elf," rumbled the shaggy, bull-headed creature. "Huln of the eagle spear!" He raised the weapon, displaying the sharp, curved end forged to resemble the raptor's beak. From the lower end of the metal head to the bottom tip of the shaft, a tightly-bound skin had been wrapped, upon it markings in the language of Huln's people. Malfurion knew just enough about the tauren to understand that here was marked the history of the weapon, from its forging through the epic feats of its owners. "Huln, who speaks for all the tribes gathered."

The bull nodded his head brusquely, accenting his words with his gestures. His coat had more than two dozen braids in it, most of them dangling from under his jaw. Each was recognition of a kill in battle.

The squat but muscular figure below the tauren's right arm snorted. Vaguely, he looked like some kin of Rhonin's, at least in features. However, there any resemblance ended. His build made it seem as if some powerful force—perhaps either the tauren or the ursine brute behind him—had taken a war hammer and pounded the heavily-bearded figure flat.

More astounding, he was made of stone, not flesh.

His rough-hewn skin appeared to be a gray granite, his squinting eyes glittering diamonds. The beard was actually an intricate series of mineral growths that even made it look as if the figure was graying with age.

The dwarf—for that was as Malfurion knew his kind—reached into one of his many belt pouches and removed a clay pipe and tinder box. As he lit the pipe, the fire briefly outlined the grizzled face, especially the huge, round nose. Whether or not the "gray" in the beard marked advanced age, he showed no infirmity. Despite being of stone, the dwarf wore a hooded outfit, wide, flat boots, and had the pants and shirt a miner might wear. Across his back hung an ax nearly as big as him with one extremely sharp edge.

"Dungard Ironcutter, speaking for the clans of the Earthen," was all he said, dwarves not much on conversation.

The Earthen. Malfurion made certain to remember the last. "Dwarf" was a night elven word, a derogatory one at that.

The bearlike thing behind Dungard suddenly growled. Neither the dwarf nor the tauren paid the fearsome utterance much attention, but Malfurion instinctively backed up a step.

The creature lumbered forward. It resembled a bear, yet moved more like a man. In some ways it reminded Malfurion of the twin gods, Ursoc and Ursol, but was clearly a primitive creature. It wore a pale, brown loincloth and a necklace made of claws. The three-toed beastman raised a club in one hand. The other four-fingered paw formed a fist.

The creature roared again, its tone slightly different from the first time.

"The furbolg Unng Ak says that he speaks for the packs," Rhonin translated readily.

There were others behind them, but they did not choose at this time to step forth. Malfurion gazed at the unique gathering and eyed Rhonin with some admiration. "You convinced all of them to come . . ."

"Brox and I helped, but it was mostly Krasus."

Malfurion looked among the throng of creatures, but did not see Rhonin's mentor. Taken at a glance, the tall figure in the cowled, gray robes looked the most like a night elf of any of the outsiders. Certainly much more than

Brox, the hulking, green-skinned warrior who called himself an orc. Yes, Krasus could have passed for a night elf—but one long dead, for his skin was very, very pale and much of his hair was a brilliant silver. The mage's features were also more hawklike than any of Malfurion's kind. In addition, his eyes somewhat resembled Rhonin's, but were long and narrowed and held in their dark pupils a fire borne of ancient wisdom.

The ancient wisdom of a being who was in truth a *dragon*.

A figure stalked toward them. Not Krasus, but Brox. The orc looked weary but defiant, as he always did. Brox was a warrior who had battled all his life. The tusked orc had scars everywhere. He vied with the tauren in musculature. Lord Stareye dismissed Brox as a beast no better than Huln or the furbolg. Yet, everyone respected the orc's arm, especially when he wielded the enchanted wooden ax Cenarius and Malfurion had created just for him.

The druid continued to seek out Krasus, but the latter was nowhere to be found. Malfurion did not like that. "Where is he?"

Pursing his lips, Rhonin sourly answered, "He said he had something else that had to be done quickly, regardless of the consequences."

"And that means?"

"I've no idea, Malfurion. In many matters, Krasus trusts only himself."

"We need him . . . *I* need him . . ."

Rhonin put a hand on the night elf's shoulder. "I promise you . . . we'll rescue her."

Malfurion was not so convinced, just as he was still not convinced that Lord Stareye would accept such allies as these. The mission that Rhonin and his companions had undertaken had not been sanctioned by the host's commander, but Krasus had been convinced that once the noble was confronted with such aid, he would see reason. But convincing Desdel Stareye would be a much more difficult quest than talking sense to furbolgs.

The druid finally surrendered to the fact that there would be no new and immediate attempt to rescue Tyrande. In truth, they had already tried everything they could, at least for now. Still, even as he turned again to the matter of the new arrivals, Malfurion's thoughts ever worked to devise some manner by which to save his childhood friend . . . and, at the same time, discover the truth concerning Illidan's fate.

The dwarf puffed stolidly on his pipe, while Huln waited with a patience belying his brutish form. Unng Ak sniffed the air, taking in the different scents and clutching the club tight.

Rhonin, eyeing their potential allies, remarked, "Of course, damned if I wouldn't prefer Krasus here right now myself. I can hardly wait to see Stareye's face when this bunch stands before him . . ."

The noble's jaw dropped. His eyes bulged as much as was possible for his kind. The pinch of snuff almost to his nostril crumbled to the floor of the tent like ash as his fingers twitched.

"You have brought *what* into our midst?"

Rhonin's expression remained calm. "The one chance we have left of staving the losses and perhaps even winning."

Lord Stareye angrily flung aside his richly embroidered cloak. A flurry of intertwining green, orange, and purple lines marked its passage. In contrast, his armor was the more subdued gray-green common among the night elves, although its breast plate was decorated in the center by his House symbol, a multitude of tiny, gem-encrusted stars in the center of each of which a golden orb had been set. Lying on a table used for mapping out strategy was his similarly-decorated helm.

The haughty night elf stared down his lengthy, pointed nose. "You have disobeyed a direct order, yes! I shall have you clapped in irons and—"

"And I'll dissolve them before they lock. Then, I'll leave the host, as, I suspect, will some of my friends."

It was simply stated, but all there understood the threat. Stareye stared at the three other nobles who had been with him when Rhonin and Malfurion had come to announce the arrival of allies. They returned his stare blankly. None wanted to take the responsibility of urging the commander to rid his force of its most prominent fighters.

The senior night elf suddenly smiled. Malfurion resisted shuddering at that smile.

"Forgive me, Master Rhonin! I speak in haste, yes, in haste! Certainly I would not wish to offend you and yours . . ." He reached into the pouch, removed some more of the white powder, and inhaled it in one nostril. "We are all reasonable. We shall deal with this in a reasonable manner, however unjustly it was thrust upon some of us." He gave a negligent gesture toward the tent's flap. "By all means, show the—them in."

Rhonin went to the entrance and called out. Two soldiers stepped through, followed by an officer very familiar to Malfurion. Jarod Shadowsong had been a captain in the Suramar Guard when he had had the misfortune to take as a prisoner Krasus. In the ensuing events, he had become a reluctant part of their band and had even been placed in charge of keeping watch over them by the late Ravencrest. Stareye had left Jarod in such a role even though it had long become clear that no one could keep the band in one place, especially the elder mage.

In Jarod's wake came Huln, the furbolg, and Dungard. Behind the trio rushed in a full dozen more soldiers, who quickly took up strategic positions in order to protect their commander.

Stareye's nose wrinkled. He did little to hide his contempt. Huln stood as if a rock. Unng Ak grinned, showing many sharp teeth.

Dungard smoked his pipe.

"I would prefer that you douse that instrument," the noble commented.

In response, the dwarf took another puff.

"Insolent! You see what beasts and refuse you expect us to ally ourselves with?" Stareye growled, already forgetting his words to Rhonin. "Our people will never stand for it!"

"As commander, you must make them understand," the wizard calmly returned. "Just as these three and those representing the others had to do so with their own kind."

"You prissy night elves need some folks who know how to fight," Dungard abruptly muttered, the pipe still in the corner of his mouth. "Someone to teach you real livin' . . ."

Unng Ak let out with a loud bark. It took Malfurion a moment to realize that the furbolg had laughed.

"At least we understand the intricacies of civilization," another noble snapped back. "Such as bathing and grooming."

"Maybe the demons'll let you live to be their handmaidens."

The night elf drew his sword, his companions following suit. Dungard had his ax out so swiftly that the movement was but a blur. Huln gripped his spear and snorted. Unng Ak swung his club once in challenge.

A flash of blue light abruptly burst to life in the center of the tent. Both sides forgot their argument as they attempted to shield their eyes. Malfurion turned away to protect himself, noticing only then that Rhonin was unaffected by it all.

The human stepped between the parties. "Enough of this! The fate of Kalimdor, of your loved ones—" He hesitated a moment, his eyes looking into the distance. "Of your loved ones . . . depends on overcoming your petty prejudices!"

Rhonin glanced at at Huln and his companions, then at Stareye's nobles. Neither side seemed inclined to have him repeat his blinding display of power.

He vehemently nodded. "Good, then! Now that we understand, I think it's time to talk . . ."

Krasus struck the floor of the icy cavern with a painful thud.

He lay there gasping. The spell to transport him here had been a chancy one, especially considering his condition. The cavern was far, far away from where the elven host lay—almost half a world away. Yet, he had dared risk the spell, knowing not only what it might do to him but also that it might already be too late to do what he desired.

He had dared not tell even Rhonin of his intentions. At the very least, the wizard would have demanded he accompany him, but one of the pair had to maintain control over the situation with the night elves' potential allies. Krasus had full faith in the human, who had proven himself more adaptable, more trustworthy, than nearly any one else the former had known in his long, so very long life.

His breathing stable, Krasus pushed himself up. In the chill cavern, his breath came out in narrow clouds that drifted slowly up to the high, toothy ceiling. Stalactites vied with jagged ice formations and frost covered the rocky floor.

The mage mentally probed the immediate area, but found no trace of another presence. The news did not encourage him, but neither did it surprise Krasus. He had been there to witness the catastrophe first hand, the vision of Neltharion the Earth Warder—the great black dragon—in his madness turning upon his race still seared into Krasus's memory. Every one of the four other flights had suffered, but the inhabitants of this cavern had paid for their resistance most of all.

The children of Malygos had been slaughtered to a one, their lord cast far away. All this by the power of the Earth Warder's treacherous creation, which the dragons themselves had imbued with power.

The Dragon Soul . . . known better to him as the *Demon Soul*.

"Malygos . . ." Krasus called, the name echoing through the glittering chamber. Once, despite its chill, it had been a place of merriment, for the blue flight were creatures of pure magic and reveled in it. How hollow the cavern was now, how dead.

When he had waited long enough for the great Aspect to respond, Krasus strode cautiously over the slippery, uneven ground. He, too, was a dragon, but of the red flight of Alexstrasza, the Mother of Life. There had never existed animosities between the blues and reds, but, nonetheless, he took no chances. Should Malygos dwell somewhere deeper within the cavern system, there was no telling how the ancient guardian would react. The shock of seeing his kind decimated would throw him over the edge into madness from which it would take centuries to recover.

All this Krasus knew because he had *lived* those future centuries. He had struggled through the betrayal of Neltharion, who would later be called—more appropriately—*Deathwing*. He had watched as the dragons had fallen into ruin, their numbers dwindling and those of his own kind, including his queen, forced to be the beasts of the orcs for decades.

The dragon mage again probed with his higher senses, reaching deeper and deeper into the caverns. Everywhere he sought, Krasus found only emptiness, an emptiness too reminiscent of a vast tomb. No significant aura of life greeted his search and he began to despair that his sudden urge to come here had been all for naught.

Then . . . very, very deep in the bowels of Malygos's sanctum, he noted a vague life force. It was so faint that Krasus almost dismissed it as a figment of his own desire, but then he sensed another, similar presence near it.

The cowled figure wended his way through the treacherous, dark passages. Several times Krasus had to steady himself as the path turned precarious. This was a realm used by creatures a hundredfold larger than he presently was and their massive paws easily spread across cracks and ravines he had to climb through.

Had it been his choice, Krasus would have transformed, but, in this time period, that option was not available. He and a younger version of himself existed here simultaneously. It had enabled the pair to accomplish great things together against the Burning Legion, but demanded also limitations. Neither could transform from the shapes they wore and, until recently, both had been vastly weaker when away from the other. While that latter problem had been solved—for the most part—Krasus was condemned to remain in his mortal body.

A shriek overhead made him press against the wall. A huge, leathery form fluttered past, a wolf-sized bat with a feline face, thick fur, and incisors as long as a finger. The creature spun around for a second dive at the mage, but Krasus already had one hand up.

A ball of flame met the beast in mid-air. The bat flew directly into it.

The fiery sphere swelled, then quickly imploded.

Cinders—the only remnants of the creature—briefly showered Krasus. That he had not sensed the bat perplexed him. He caught a few of the ashes and probed them with his senses. They revealed that the beast had been a construct, not a true living thing. A sentinel, then, of the Master of Magic.

Wiping away the last of the bat, Krasus continued his daunting trek. It had cost him heavily to transport himself by spell to such a faraway place, but for this task, no effort was too great.

Then, to his surprise, he was suddenly greeted by a warmth from ahead. It grew as he continued on, but not to the levels that the dragon mage would have expected. A deeper frown cut into his narrow features as he neared what looked to be a second major cavern. By his calculations, the level of heat should have been several times what it was.

A faint, blue radiance from the cavern illuminated the last bit of passage. Krasus blinked once in order to adjust his eyes, then entered.

The eggs sat nestled everywhere. Hundreds of blue-white eggs of varying size, from as small as his fist to almost as large as him. He let out an involuntary gasp, having not expected such a bounty.

But no sooner had Krasus's hopes risen, then they crashed hard. A more detailed examination revealed the awful truth. Savage cracks lined many, but they were signs of decay, not birth. Krasus placed a gloved hand atop one larger egg and sensed no movement inside.

He went along from clutch to clutch, and as he did, the dragon grew more bitter. History appeared destined to repeat itself regardless of his decision to so flagrantly defy it. The future of the blue dragon flight lay spread before him, but it was a future as devoid of hope as originally. In the time line of which Krasus was familiar, Malygos had been unable to rouse himself from the catatonic state Neltharion had left him until after the magic maintaining the egg chamber—magic bound to the great Aspect—had long failed. Unprotected from the cold, the eggs had perished, and, with them, all hope. In the far future, Alexstrasza had offered to aid Malygos in slowly recreating his flight, but even at the time of Krasus's departure into the past, that plan had barely even begun.

Now, despite everything he had initially preached to Rhonin, Krasus had been attempting perhaps the most precarious change yet to the future of his world. He had hoped to salvage the clutches and bring them to a place of safety, but the constant battle against the demons and the need to force allies onto the foolishly-reluctant night elves had delayed him too much.

Or had it? Krasus paused hopefully over a half-developed egg. Life still yet grew within it. A bit sluggishly, but well enough so that the mage felt certain that new warmth would keep it going.

He checked another and found it, too, a viable candidate. Eagerly, Krasus moved on, but the next several eggs revealed no aura. Gritting his teeth, the robed figure rushed to the next clutch.

He discovered four more salvageable eggs. With one finger, he marked each of those and the ones discovered earlier with a soft, golden glow before continuing his survey.

By the end, there were far fewer eggs than Krasus had hoped to find, but more than he deserved. The dragon mage eyed the ones marked, their glow letting them stand out wherever they were in the vast chamber. He knew with absolute certainty that there were no more. Now, though, what mattered was keeping the select few from perishing as the rest had.

The other dragons, even his beloved Alexstrasza, were invisible to his senses. He could only conclude that they had secluded themselves somewhere in an attempt to recover from Demon Soul's horrific power. His own memories of this period were scattered, the result of his journey and his injuries. Eventually, the other flights would return to the battle, but, by that time, it would be too late for Malygos's kind. Even his younger self was not available to him. Korialstrasz, badly beaten in his heroic struggle to distract Neltharion, had gone to find out what had happened to the other leviathans.

And so it was left to Krasus to decide what to do. Even before he had left for Malygos's lair, he had tried to think of a place he considered secure enough for dragon eggs. Nothing satisfied him. Even the grove of the demigod, Cenarius, had proven unworthy in his eyes. True, the antlered deity was the trusted mentor of Malfurion Stormrage and might very well be the offspring of the dragon, Ysera, but Krasus knew that Cenarius had far too many matters with which to deal already.

"So be it, then," the cowled spellcaster murmured.

With one gloved finger, Krasus drew a circle in the air. Golden sparks accented the tracing his finger made. The circle was perfect and looked as if it had been cut into the very atmosphere itself.

Touching his fingertips to the center, the dragon mage *removed* the circle. A white gap floated before him, one reaching beyond the mortal plane.

Krasus muttered under his breath, The circle's outline flared red. There was a moan from within it and small, loose stones began rolling toward the gap. Krasus muttered more, and, although the suction grew more intense, the stones slowed to a halt. Instead, the eggs began to shake slightly, as if even in the cold, dead ones, something moved.

But it was not so. One of the viable eggs nearest to Krasus's creation suddenly rose. It drifted almost serenely toward the small gap. A second marked egg did likewise, then the rest followed. The dead eggs continued to quiver, but remained where they were.

And as he watched, the future of Malygos's flight lined up before the hole and started to enter.

Curiously, as each egg approached, it seemed to shrink just enough to fit through. One by one, in constant succession, Krasus's valuable find disappeared into the gap.

When the last had vanished, the cowled spellcaster sealed the opening. There was a brief, golden spark, and then all trace of the gap vanished.

"Enough to survive, but not enough to thrive," Krasus muttered. It would take centuries for the blues to reach secure numbers. Even supposing every egg hatched, there would still not be that many blue dragons even by the time period from which he had come.

Still, some were better than none.

A sudden wave of nausea and exhaustion overtook Krasus. He barely prevented himself from falling. Despite having for the most part solved the puzzle of the original malady striking him when he had entered the past—that being that both he and his younger self had to share their life force—there were limits yet.

But he could not rest. The eggs were secure, placed in a pocket universe where time ran so slow as to be negligible. Long enough to pass them on to one he could trust . . . assuming he survived the war.

Thinking of that war, Krasus began mustering his strength. Whatever his confidence in Rhonin and Malfurion, there were too many question marks about the certainty of the outcome. The time line had forever shifted; it was possible that the Burning Legion, who had originally lost this struggle, would triumph. Whatever his own meddling with the line, Krasus was well aware that now he had to do everything he could to assist the night elves and the rest. All that mattered now was that there *had* to be a future.

As he began the spell that would carry him back to the host, Krasus eyed the scores of dead eggs. There would also be a future if the demons won. This would be it. Cold, dark, no life. An eternity of emptiness.

The dragon mage hissed vehemently and vanished.

TWO

Zin-Azshari. Once the glorious epitome of the night elf civilization. A sprawling city at the edge of the basis of the night elves' power, the Well. The home of the revered queen, Azshara, for whom her adoring subjects had renamed the capital.

Zin-Azshari . . . a ruined graveyard, the launching point of the Burning Legion.

Lupine felbeasts sniffed through the rubble, ever seeking the unmistakable smell of life and magic. Twin tentacles jutting up from near their furred shoulders darted around as if with minds of their own. The toothy suckers at the end of each opened and closed hungrily. Felbeasts savored draining a sorcerer dry of both his power and his life, but the rows of sharp teeth displayed in the scaly monsters' mouths gave warning that flesh was a tasty tidbit to them, too.

Two demonic hounds rummaging through the collapsed wreckage of what had once been a five-story tree home quickly gazed up at the sound of marching feet and the clatter of arms and armor. Rows upon rows of fierce warriors churned past, their destination the night elven defenders days away. The Fel Guard were the backbone of the invaders, their numbers dwarfing all the rest combined. They stood nine feet high, but while broad at the shoulder and chest, were oddly narrow, even gaunt, in their midsection. A pair of huge, curled horns thrust up from their almost fleshless heads. Their bloodred eyes warily watched the devastated landscape. Although they marched with precision, there was a general impatience among the Fel Guard, for they lived only for carnage. Now and then, one of the fanged warriors would jostle another and the threat of anarchy would break out.

But a quick flash of whip from above ever kept the warriors in line. Fiery-winged Doomguard fluttered above the ranks of every regiment, watching for disorder. Slightly taller, they differed little else from their brethren below, save in their lesser numbers and greater intelligence.

Though a dread mist covered Zin-Azshari now, the monstrous armies had no difficulty maneuvering through it. The mist was as much a part of them as the swords, axes, and lances they wielded. Its sickly green tint matched exactly the color of the fearsome flames that radiated from each demon.

The skulls of night elves watched mournfully from the ruins as the Burning Legion marched. They and countless others like them had perished early on, betrayed by the very queen they worshipped. The only night elves still alive in the capital were the Highborne, the servants of the queen. Their secluded quarter of the city, surrounded by gargantuan walls, kept the visions of the slaughter from their delicate sensibilities. Clad in the garish, multicolored robes of their elite rank, they tended to their needs while awaiting the commands of Azshara.

The warriors of the palace guard still lined the walls, their eyes filled with a fanatic glare worthy of the Legion. They were commanded by Captain Varo'then—more a general these days than a simple officer, despite his title—who acted as the eyes and mouth of his monarch when she could not be troubled from her recreation. Given the order, the soldiers would have stood side by side with the demons against their own people. They had already watched without emotion the massacre of the city's inhabitants. As with most all within the palace, they were both Azshara's creatures and servants to the lord of the Burning Legion.

Sargeras.

One who was neither the queen's nor the demon's puppet hung in a cell deep beneath the palace, trying to stifle the gnawing fear in her gut by constant prayer to her goddess.

Tyrande Whisperwind had woken to a nightmare. The last that she could recall, the priestess of Elune—the Mother Moon—had been in the middle of a terrible battle. Tossed from her dying mount, she had struck her head. Malfurion had dragged her to safety . . . and then from there everything had turned muddled. Vaguely, Tyrande recalled horrific images and sounds. Goatlike creatures with leering mouths. Clawed, furred hands clutching her. Malfurion's desperate voice and then—

And then the priestess had awakened here.

Long, elegant eyes of silver surveyed her prison for the thousandth time. Graceful lips parted in regret and grim acknowledgment of her situation. She shook her head, her long, dusky blue hair—the silver streaks in it more prominent now that she did not wear her war helmet—flowing in waves with each change of direction. Nothing had altered since last Tyrande had looked around. Had she really expected anything to do so?

Chains did not bind her wrists and ankles, but she might as well have been held by such. A shimmering, green sphere floating a foot or so above the dank, stone floor surrounded her from head to toe. In it, she stood with arms stretched over her head and her legs sealed tightly together. Try as she might, the recently-anointed high priestess could not separate her limbs. The magic of the great demon, Archimonde, ever proved too powerful in that regard.

But if his magic had imprisoned Tyrande utterly, Archimonde had failed in his ultimate intention. There had been no doubt as to his desire to torture her, to bend her to his will and, thus, to that of his own master. At his hand, Archimonde had not only had his own terrifying imagination, but the dire skills of the Highborne and the sadistic satyrs.

Yet, the moment that the demon had attempted to harm her physically, a faint aura the color of moonlight had draped around Elune's acolyte. Nothing Archimonde or his minions could do could penetrate it. Against such evil effort, the plated armor surrounding her lithe form would have proven as useful as the thin, silver cloak that they had ripped from her early on, but the transparent aura acted like an iron wall a mile thick. Archimonde had battered himself against it time and time again to no avail. In his rage, the giant, tattooed figure had finally seized an unsuspecting fel guard by the neck, crushing in the other demon's throat without the least effort.

Since then, they had left her alone, their efforts to eradicate the night elf host more important than a lone priestess. That did not mean that they did not have future intentions for her, for the satyrs who had carried her through the magical portal at the battle site had informed their master that she was close to one whom Archimonde had marked . . . Malfurion. At the very least, they would use Tyrande against him, and that was the basis for much of her present fear.

Tyrande did not want to be the cause of Malfurion's downfall.

Marching feet alerted her to newcomers in the dungeon corridors. She glanced up in apprehension just as someone unlocked the door. As it swung open, a figure she dreaded at least as much as Archimonde stepped inside. The scarred officer wore armor of a glittering emerald green with a bright pattern of golden sunbursts across the chest. Behind him fluttered a flowing cape that matched the sunbursts in color. His narrow eyes never seemed to blink and when they alighted on her, their intensity was such that Tyrande could not look directly into them.

"She is conscious," Captain Varo'then remarked to someone behind him.

"Then, by all means," responded a languid, feminine voice. "Let us see what Lord Archimonde so prizes . . ."

With a bow, Varo'then swept aside for the speaker. Tyrande bit back a gasp, even though she had expected who it was.

Queen Azshara was as beautiful, as perfect, as the storytellers said. Luxurious silver hair cascaded down her back. Her eyes were golden and half-veiled, her lips full and seductive. She wore a silken gown that matched her hair, one so thin that it gave ample hint of the sleek form beneath. Jeweled bracelets hung on each wrist and matching earrings hung almost all the way to her exquisite, bare shoulders. The arched tiara in her hair held a ruby that reflected the dull light from the torch a guard carried to almost blinding effect.

Behind her followed another female, one who would have also been considered quite beautiful, but who, in the presence of Azshara, paled in comparison. The handmaiden dressed in garments similar to her mistress, save that their quality was more than a step below. She also wore her hair as much like the queen as possible, although the silver in it had clearly come from a dye and did not even approach the intensity of Azshara's mane. In truth, the only thing that stood out were her eyes—silver as with most night elves, but with an exotic, feline curve to them.

"*This* is her?" the queen asked with unconcealed disappointment as she studied the captive.

In truth, in Azshara's presence, Tyrande felt even mousier than the handmaiden. She wanted to at least wipe the grime and blood away from her face and form, but could not. Even aware that the queen had betrayed her people, the priestess felt the desire to kneel at Azshara's slim, sandaled feet, so charismatic was the monarch.

"She's not to be underestimated, Light of Lights," the captain replied. When his eyes fixed upon Azshara, they did so with burning desire. "She appears favored by Elune."

The queen did not find this at all impressive. Perfect nose wrinkling, she asked, "What is Elune to the great Sargeras?"

"Spoken so wisely, your majesty."

Azshara approached closely. Even her least movement appeared calculated for maximum impact on her audience. Tyrande again felt the urge to kneel before her.

"Pretty, in a coarse way," the silver-tressed figure added offhandedly. "Perhaps worthy to be a handmaiden. Would you like that—what was her name again, captain?"

"Tyrande," Varo'then replied with a brief bow.

"Tyrande . . . would you like to be my handmaiden? Live in the palace? Be a favored of mine and my lord? Mmm?"

The other female started at this suggestion, the feline eyes seeming to flay the priestess. There was no attempt to hide intense jealousy.

Gritting her teeth, the young night elf gasped, "I am

sworn to the Mother Moon, my life and my heart hers . . ."

The queen's beauty was suddenly marred by a brief look that rivaled Captain Varo'then's for its evil. "Ungrateful little trollop! And such a liar, too! Your heart you actually give rather easily, don't you? First to one brother, then another brother! Are there others besides?" When Tyrande did not respond, Azshara continued, "Are males not delightful to play with? It is so fun to have lovers fight over you, isn't it? So tasty to see them draw blood in your name! Actually, I must commend you! Brothers—especially *twins*—are such a splendid touch! Peeling away their familial bonds until they wish to rip out each other's throats, betray each other . . . all for your favor!"

Varo'then chuckled. The handmaiden smiled darkly. Tyrande felt a tear slip from her eye and silently cursed her emotions.

"Oh, dear! Have I brought up tender subjects? I do apologize! Poor Malfurion and Illidan . . . those were their names, weren't they? Poor Illidan, most of all. Such a tragedy, what happened to him. Small wonder he chose to do what he did!"

Despite herself, Tyrande blurted, "What about Illidan? What do you mean?"

But Azshara had turned back to Varo'then and the handmaiden. "She needs her rest, don't you agree, captain? Come, Lady Vashj! Let us see if there is any progress on the portal! I want to be ready when Sargeras crosses over . . ." The queen practically preened at mention of the demon's name. "I want to look my best for him . . ."

The guards stepped aside as Captain Varo'then led Azshara and the Lady Vashj to the door. Just out in the hall, the ruler of the night elves glanced over her shoulder at the captive priestess. "You really should reconsider whether to be my handmaiden, dear girl! You could have had *both* of them alive and yours to play with . . . after I'd grown tired of them, of course."

The slamming of the iron door echoed the dying of Tyrande's hopes. She saw in her mind both Malfurion and Illidan. Malfurion had been there when she had been kidnapped and Tyrande knew that he was grief-stricken by his failure to protect her. She feared that such emotions would make him reckless, an easy target for the demons.

And then there was Illidan. Just before the last battle, he had discovered which direction her feelings lay and had not taken it well. Although Azshara's remarks had certainly been designed to further cut down her resolve, Tyrande could not help put some credence to them. She knew Illidan well and knew how wild he could become. Had that streak, fueled by her rejection, made him do something terrible?

"Elune, Mother Moon, watch over them both," she whispered. Tyrande could not deny that she was concerned most of all for Malfurion, but she still cared for his twin. The priestess also knew how horrible Malfurion would feel if anything befell his brother.

Thinking of that, Tyrande added, "Mother Moon, whatever fate should take me, please save Illidan, at least for Malfurion! Give them one another! Let not Illidan—"

And at that moment, she sensed another presence near her, one certainly within the castle walls, so close it felt. The encounter was brief, so very brief, yet, for all that, the priestess knew exactly who she had sensed.

Illidan! Illidan in Zin-Azshari . . . in the palace!

The discovery shook her to the bone. She imagined him a prisoner, tortured horribly since he did not have the miraculous love of Elune protecting him as it did her. Tyrande saw him screaming as the demons flayed him alive, their magic ensuring that he remained fully conscious through each agonizing moment. They would torture him not just because of what he had done against the Legion, but also for Malfurion's efforts, too.

She tried again to touch his thoughts, but to no avail. Yet, as she made the attempt, something about the brief contact began to bother her. Tyrande puzzled over it, delving deep within herself. She had sensed something about Illidan's emotions that did not sit well, something very wrong—

When she realized just what it was, Tyrande grew cold with dread. It could not be! Not from Illidan, whatever the past!

"He would not become so . . ." Tyrande insisted to herself. "Not for any reason . . ."

Now she understood some of what the queen had said. Illidan—as impossible as it was to believe—had come to Zin-Azshari of his own desire.

He wanted to *serve* the lord of the Burning Legion.

The southernmost tower of Azshara's palace was ablaze in sorcerous energies, be it day or night the work of the Highborne never ceasing. Sentries on duty nearby tried not to stare in the direction of the tall structure for fear that the powerful magicks might somehow engulf them.

Within, the Highborne, their hooded, elegantly-embroidered robes of turquoise hanging on their gaunt forms, stood alternating with sinister, horned figures whose lower halves resembled that of goats. Once, they, too, had been night elves, and even though their upper torsos still showed some indication of that, through guile and witchery they had become something more. Something that was now a part of the Burning Legion, not the world of Azeroth.

Satyrs.

But even the satyrs looked weary as they struggled with their former brethren on the spell taking place within the hexagonal pattern. Floating eye-level over the design, the fiery mass had as its center a darkness that seemed to go on forever, giving witness to how far beyond their plane of existence the spellcasters had reached. They delved beyond the edge of reason, beyond the limits of order . . . and into the chaos from which the demons had come.

Into the realm of Sargeras, lord of the Legion.

A huge shadow loomed over the sweating spellcasters. The winged monstrosity moved on four tree-trunk legs. His froglike face included great tusks. Beneath a thick brow ridge, blazing orbs glared at the tinier figures. The top of his scaly head nearly scraped the ceiling.

His massive tail sliding back and forth across the floor, Mannoroth rumbled, "Keep it stabilized! I'll rip off your heads and drink your blood from your necks if it fails!"

Despite his words, however, he sweated as much as the rest. They had attempted a new spell in the hopes of making the portal larger and stronger—enough so that Sargeras himself could enter through it—but had, instead, nearly lost control. Such a failure would mean execution of some of the sorcerers, but it also might mean Mannoroth's own horrific demise. Archimonde brooked no more mistakes.

"If I might be permitted?" asked a voice from near the chamber entrance.

With a snarl, Mannoroth glanced at the puny night elf. His unsettling amber eyes aside, he saw little of interest in this distrusted newcomer called Illidan Stormrage. Archimonde suffered the creature to live because of some potential he sensed, but Mannoroth would have preferred nothing more than to hang the arrogant ant by hooks through his eyes, then slowly dismember him a limb at a time. It would be some vengeance against Illidan's brother, the druid who had caused Mannoroth so much disaster and shame.

But such entertainment would have to wait. For no reason other than to perhaps watch Illidan fail miserably, Mannoroth indicated with one huge, taloned paw that the night elf should proceed. Illidan, clad in black leather jerkin and pants and with his hair bound tight in a tail, strode past the great demon with utter disregard as to Mannoroth's station. It was worse than dealing with Azshara's pet soldier, Varo'then.

Illidan stopped at the circle, surveying the work. He nodded after a moment, then, with a relaxed wave of his hand, opened up a space for himself between a startled satyr and a Highborne.

The portal rippled. Mannoroth ground his yellowed fangs. If the night elf caused the portal to fail, Archimonde could not fault his second in command for splattering the culprit against the wall.

Illidan made a single gesture toward the fiery gap—and it suddenly held. The fraying that the demon had sensed vanished. If anything, the portal was now stronger than before.

Mannoroth's green brow furrowed. Could this puny creature have the power to—

Before he could follow the notion further, a presence suddenly filled the chamber, a presence whose point of origin lay far, far inside the portal.

"To your knees!" the four-legged demon quickly roared.

Everyone—spellcasters and guards alike—immediately dropped.

Everyone . . . save Illidan.

He calmly stood before the portal despite it being impossible that he did not sense the overwhelming presence reaching out from it. Illidan stared into the blackness, almost expectant.

You are the one . . . came the voice of Sargeras.

The torches flickered wildly. In the dancing shadows they caused, one almost appeared more alive than the rest. It rose not only to the ceiling, but across it, coming to a head exactly above the fiery gap.

Illidan noted the manifestation with the same seeming indifference he had all else. Mannoroth could only mark him as the biggest fool the demon had ever encountered.

You are the one who has done what others could not . . .

Finally, the night elf showed some sense by lowering his head slightly in deference to the voice. "I deemed it necessary to act."

You are strong . . . Sargeras said from the beyond. There was a moment of silence, then, *but not strong enough . . .*

Meaning that, despite his power, Illidan did not possess the wherewithal to enable the portal to allow the lord of the Legion through to the mortal plane. Mannoroth found his own thoughts in conflict, frustrated that the way was still not open for Sargeras, but pleased that the night elf had come up lacking.

"I might know of a method, though," Illidan unexpectedly remarked.

Again, there was complete silence. Mannoroth grew troubled as it stretched long, for he had never witnessed Sargeras so quiet.

Finally . . . *Speak.*

Illidan held up his left palm. In it, the illusion of an object formed. Mannoroth stretched up so as to better view it. He felt quite disappointed. Instead of some intricate amulet or blazing crystal, all the night elf revealed was a rather plain golden disk whose greatest aspect was that it filled the palm.

Had the actual piece lain before him, the winged behemoth would have trampled right over it without pause.

He expected Sargeras to punish Illidan for wasting his time, but instead, the lord of the Legion responded with obvious interest. *Explain . . .*

Without preamble, the renegade sorcerer said, "This is the key. This has the power. This is the *Dragon Soul*."

Now Mannoroth and the others paid much more attention. They had all witnessed its fury, felt its overwhelming power. With it, the black dragon had slaughtered demons and night elves alike by the hundreds. He had churned up the earth for miles around and even cast out the other dragons when they had sought to stop him.

All this from so humble-looking a piece.

"You have seen it, even from where you wait," Illidan went on. "You've sensed its glorious might and you rightly hunger for it to be yours."

Yes . . .

"It could slay thousands simply through your will. It could sweep clear a land of all resisting life . . . all life, period."

Yes . . .

"But you didn't consider that it might be the source of power you need to reach this world, did you?"

Sargeras did not answer, which was answer enough. Mannoroth grunted. The night elf was too clever for his own good. The Burning Legion coveted the artifact, but it was still in the possession of the black dragon. Eventually, the demons would have the strength and resources to hunt the beast, but not while they had Illidan's people to still slaughter.

It has the power, the lord of the Legion at last declared. *It could open the way . . . if it was ours . . .*

"I have the means by which to track its location, to know where the dragon's hidden it."

Another telling pause, then, *the black beast has shielded himself well . . .* Sargeras responded. *Even from me . . .*

Illidan nodded, the smile on his face one that, had it been on anyone else's, the lord of the Legion would surely have ripped it—and every bit of flesh and sinew attached—off even from the beyond.

"But he's not shielded from me . . . because I know how to track him . . . with this."

The night elf gestured and in his left hand there suddenly appeared an almost triangular, ebony plate the size of his head. Mannoroth leaned forward. At first he believed it a small piece of armor from one of the world's defenders, but then he saw that it was not metal.

A dragon's scale.

The black dragon's scale.

"A very tiny bit, easily missed by so large a beast," Illidan remarked, turning it over. "He was struck several times in the combat with the red. I knew there had to be at least one broken scale . . . and so I rode out and searched for it. Once I found what I wanted, I then continued on to here."

Mannoroth glared. Was there no end to the sorcerer's audacity? Unable to keep silent any longer, he growled, "Why? Why not bring it back to your friends? Your brother?"

The night elf looked over his shoulder. "Because I deserve power, reward."

The demon expected more, but Illidan was finished. The sorcerer turned back to the portal.

"I need unrestricted access to the Well's energies. The dragon is mighty, especially with the artifact. But, with the Well to fuel me, I'll find him no matter where he is!"

"And then you'll just take it from him, mortal?" The

tusked demon sneered. "Or will he simply give it to you?"

"I'll relieve the beast of it one way or another," Illidan casually replied, still staring into the raging abyss. "And bring it here."

Mannoroth started to laugh—then cut off as a pressure tightened around his throat. It vanished almost immediately after, but the message was clear. Whatever the winged demon's own thoughts, the lord of the Legion was interested in the miscreant's words.

You would bring the dragon's creation to me, Sargeras declared to Illidan.

"Yes."

And you will be rewarded greatly for your efforts, should you succeed.

The night elf bowed his head. "Nothing would please me more than to stand before you with the Dragon Soul in my hand."

Sargeras seemed to chuckle. *Such loyalty deserves a mark of favor, a mark that will at the same time aid in the fulfillment of your quest, night elf . . .*

Illidan looked up. For the first time, the barest hint of uncertainty graced his narrow features. "My Lord Sargeras, your crossing to Azeroth will be favor enough and I need no other aid in my—"

But . . . I insist.

And from out of the portal shot forth twin tentacles of dark green flame.

Mannoroth immediately shielded his eyes. Illidan—the focus of Sargeras's spellwork—had no such opportunity, not that it would have done him any good to do so.

The flames poured into his eyes.

The soft tissue was seared instantly. Illidan's scream echoed throughout the chamber and likely well beyond the palace walls. All trace of arrogance had left his expression. There was only agony, pure and unadulterated.

The flames intensified. Arms spread wide, Illidan was dragged up above the floor. He arched backward, nearly breaking in two. Supernatural fire continued to pour into his blackened sockets even after the last bit of the eyes had long burned away.

The Highborne and satyrs dared not leave their task, but they cringed and tried to shy away from the struggling night elf as much as they could. Even the guards shifted a step or two further back.

Then, as suddenly as they had shot forth, the flames withdrew.

Illidan fell to the hard stone floor, somehow managing to land on his hands and knees. His breath came out in pained gasps. His head hung nearly to the floor. There remained, at least outwardly, no hint of his earlier brashness.

The voice of Sargeras filled the minds of everyone there. *Look up, my faithful servant . . .*

Illidan obeyed.

There was no sign of the eyes. Only the sockets remained, sockets scorched black and fleshless. Around the rims could be seen parts of the skull itself, so absolutely had Sargeras removed the orbs.

But if he had taken away the night elf's eyes, the lord of the Legion had replaced them with something else. There now burned within twin flames, fiery balls the same vicious hue as that which had wreaked such havoc on the sorcerer. The fires burned wildly for several more seconds . . . then faded until they seemed but smoky remnants. The smoke, however, remained, neither dwindling away nor growing stronger.

Your eyes are now my eyes, night elf, their gifts to serve me as well as you . . .

Illidan said nothing, clearly too distraught from pain.

Sargeras suddenly reached out to Mannoroth in particular. *Send him to his rest. When he is recovered, he will set forth to prove his devotion to me . . . and seize the artifact . . .*

At Mannoroth's gesture, two Fel Guard strode up and seized the shaking Illidan. They all but dragged him out of the chamber to his quarters.

The moment the night elf was out of earshot, Sargeras's lieutenant rumbled, "It's a mistake to leave this mortal to his own devices, even so humbled!"

He will not journey alone . . . there will be another. The night elf called Varo'then may be spared for this.

The demon's broad wings flexed at this news. Mannoroth grinned, a macabre sight at best. "Varo'then?"

Azshara's hound will keep good watch on the sorcerer. If Illidan Stormrage fulfills his promise, the sorcerer will be granted a place among us . . .

Such an elevation Mannoroth disliked. "And if the sorcerer proves treacherous?"

Then Varo'then will instead be granted the favor I would bestow upon the druid's twin . . . once the captain has delivered onto me the dragon's creation . . . and Illidan Stormrage's beating heart . . .

Mannoroth's grin grew wider.

THREE

The Burning Legion renewed its attack with undiminished fury. While the defenders ever needed to sleep and eat, the demons did not have any such weaknesses. They fought night and day until cut down, only retreating when the odds were too great. Even then, they did so making each foot of land retaken paid with much blood.

But now they again found their adversaries refreshed. Now, instead of merely the night elf host, there were others who fought. Almost doubling the host's strength, the tauren, dwarves, and other races added a new and desperately-needed edge to the defenders' strength. For the first time in days, it was the Legion that failed, pushed back within a night's ride of ruined Suramar.

Yet, despite this success, Malfurion felt little renewed hope. It was not just that he had come to see his devastated home as the constant barometer of victory and defeat, the battle continuously ebbing and flowing within sight of the once-beautiful settlement. Rather, it was the very core of the host's new power that bothered him. True, Rhonin had managed to force upon Lord Stareye the new allies, but the prejudiced noble had made what should have been a common cause a reluctant truce. The night elves did not truly fight alongside the others. Stareye kept his people to the left and middle flanks, the others to the right. There was little communication and almost no interaction between the various groups. Night elves dealt only with night elves, dwarves with dwarves, and so on.

Such an alliance, if it could laughingly be called that, was surely doomed to defeat. The demons would compensate for the new numbers and attack harder than ever.

What coordination there had to be had been foisted upon the unfortunate Jarod Shadowsong. The druid wondered that the guard captain did not hate the outsiders, for they had brought him nothing but calamity. Yet, Jarod took on his new tasks with the dour dedication that he had the previous ones, for which Malfurion had to admire him. In truth, whatever the benefit of Rhonin's, Brox's, or Malfurion's presence, Jarod's work matched it. He coordinated all matters between the factions—by necessity filtering out dangerous arguments and slurs—and creating something cohesive. In truth, the captain now had at least as much to do with the host's strategy as the pompous Stareye.

Malfurion only prayed that the noble would never realize all this. Ironically, it appeared Captain Shadowsong certainly didn't. In his mind, he was merely obeying orders.

Rhonin, who had been resting atop a rock overseeing the battlefield, abruptly straightened. "They're coming again!"

Brox leapt to his feet with a grace his hulking form belied. The graying orc swung his ax once, twice, then started for the front line. Malfurion leapt atop his night saber, one of the huge, tusked panthers used by his people for travel and war.

Horns sounded. The weary host stiffened in readiness.

Different notes echoed along the ranks as the various factions prepared.

And moments later, the battle was again joined.

The defenders and the demons collided with an audible crash. Instantly, grunts and cries filled the air. Roaring a challenge, Brox severed the head of a Fel Guard, then shoved the quivering torso into the demon behind. The orc cut a bloody swathe, quickly leaving more than half a dozen demons dead or dying.

Atop another night saber, Rhonin also battled. He did not merely cast spells, although, like Malfurion, he constantly kept watch for the Eredar, the Legion's warlocks. The Eredar had suffered badly during past campaigns, but they were ever a threat, striking when least expected.

For now, however, Rhonin utilized his magic in conjunction with his combat skills. Astride the night saber, the human wielded twin blades created solely from magic. The blue streams of energy stretched more than a yard each and when the wizard brought them into play, they wreaked havoc on a scale with the orc. Demon armor made for no resistance; Fel Guard weapons broke as if fragile glass against them. Rhonin fought with a passion that Malfurion could well understand, for the red-haired figure had let slip of a mate and coming children whose fate also rested in defeating the legion. As Malfurion was with Tyrande and Illidan, so, too, was Rhonin with his faraway family.

The druid fought no less powerfully, even though his spells sought communion with nature. From one of the many pouches on his belt, he brought forth several spiny seeds, the type that clung to one's garments when passing among the plants. Holding his filled palm up, he blew gently on the seeds.

They rushed forward into the air as if taken by a wind of

hurricane strength. Their numbers multiplied a thousand-fold as they spread out over the oncoming demons, almost turning into a dust storm.

Roaring, the horrific warriors plowed through the cloud without care, their only interest the blood of the defenders. However, only a few steps later, the first of the demons suddenly stumbled, then clutched his stomach. Another imitated him, then another. Several dropped their weapons and were immediately cut down by eager night elves.

Those who were not suddenly grew extremely bloated. Their stomachs and chests expanded well beyond proportion. Several of the tusked figures fell to the ground, writhing.

From inside one still standing, scores of sharp, daggerlike points burst through flesh and armor. Ichor drenched the screaming demon's form. He spun around once, then collapsed, dead. His body lay pincushioned . . . all from the swelling seeds within.

And around him, others fell, dozens at a time. All suffering the same dire fate. Malfurion felt some queasiness when he saw the results, but then considered the merciless evil of the enemy. He could ill afford any compassion for those who lived only for mayhem and terror. It was kill or be killed.

But despite the many demons who perished, there were always more. The night elves' lines began to give in as they were especially hammered. They had fought longest against the Burning Legion and so were most weary. Archimonde was too clever not to make use of the weak point. More and more tusked warriors poured into the crumbling area. Felbeasts harried the lines and from above the Doomguard dropped down on distracted soldiers, crushing in skulls or burying lances in chests and backs. Oft times, they would take a night elf or two, drag them up high, then drop the helpless figures among the host. Falling among their fellows, the soldiers became missiles slaying those on the ground as well as themselves.

An explosion threw several night elves yards into the air. From the gaping crater arose a blazing Infernal. Powerful of body but weak of mind, the demon lived only to crush anything in its path. It barreled into a line of soldiers, tossing them aside like leaves.

Before Malfurion could act, Brox met the Infernal head on. It seemed impossible that even the orc could hold back such a giant, but somehow Brox did. The Infernal came to a dead stop and, from his roar, the demon found this quite frustrating. He raised a fiery fist and tried to pound the orc's skull into his rib cage, but Brox held the staff of his ax up, the thin handle somehow blocking the deadly blow without cracking. Then, moving faster than the Infernal, Brox shoved aside the demon's hand and jammed the ax head into his adversary's chest.

For all his vaunted might, the Infernal was no less protected against the magical weapon than his comrades. The blade sank in several inches. From out of the gaping wound, green flames shot out. Brox grunted as he shifted to avoid the flames, then removed the ax for another strike.

Although wavering, the Infernal was not yet defeated. Roaring, he slammed both fists together, then struck the earth with them. The thundering smash sent tremors toward Brox, throwing him off his feet.

Immediately the demon charged, intent on trampling the orc to death. But as he neared, Brox, who had managed to keep his weapon, positioned it against the ground like a pike.

The Infernal impaled himself. He struggled to reach Brox, but the veteran warrior kept his position. In his fury, the Infernal only worsened matters. The ax sank deeper, causing a new gush of fire that came within an inch or two of the orc.

With a shudder, the huge demon finally stilled.

But despite such personal victories, the Burning Legion relentlessly pushed forward. Malfurion tried to summon up some of the emotion that had enabled him to push back the horde in the past, but could not. Tyrande's kidnapping had left that part of him drained.

He saw Lord Stareye far to the left, the noble berating the struggling soldiers there. Stareye was a far contrast to his predecessor. Ravencrest would have been as blood- and grime-soaked as his troops, but Stareye looked immaculate. He was surrounded by his personal guard, who let nothing unseemly near him even at such a critical moment.

Then, to the druid's surprise, a shaggy figure charged past him, heading for the near-breach. Another and another followed, gargantuan tauren moving up to the weakened line and adding their astounding strength. With a gusto worthy of Brox, they attacked the demons, cutting down several of the tusked warriors in the first strike. Among them, Malfurion made out Huln at the head, his eagle spear impaling one Fel Guard with such force the tip broke through the back. Huln shook off the dead demon with ease, then parried a wild swing by another. The lead tauren grinned wide.

And with the tauren came an unlikely figure. Jarod Shadowsong, blade already blooded, shouted to the huge beastmen with him. To Malfurion's surprise, the group shifted as if obeying some command. They spread out, enabling the night elves to rebuild their own lines and come to the aid of their rescuers.

Priestesses of Elune also materialized, the warrior maidens a striking group, especially in contrast to their peaceful ways before the coming of the Legion. Their appearance stung Malfurion, though, for it increased again his guilt that he had not managed to keep Tyrande out of the demons' clutches.

Astride their animals, the priestesses used sword and bow against the enemy. However, among those most proficient was one not truly a priestess. Shorter than the rest, young Shandris Feathermoon lacked a summer or two before she should have been officially able to become a novice. But drastic times demanded drastic measures. Marinda, the sister acting in Tyrande's absence, had granted Shandris a place in their depleted ranks. Now, clad in slightly-oversize armor taken from a fallen compatriot, the newest of the Mother Moon's daughters fired off three bolts, all of which scored perfect strikes in the throats of demons.

The Legion's progress halted. The defenders began to push back. Malfurion and Rhonin added their powers to the task and the night elves retook ground.

In the midst of the sisterhood, there was a sudden shriek. Two of the armored priestesses fell, their bodies contorted and crushed by their very armor. Even dead, their expressions revealed the agony that the compressing metal had put them through.

Malfurion's eyes narrowed and he gasped. One of them was *Marinda*.

"Eredar!" snarled Rhonin. He raised a hand toward the northwest.

But before the wizard could strike back, a fount of flame erupted from that very direction. Malfurion sensed the distant warlock's own agony as the flames engulfed him.

"My sincere regrets for so delayed a return," muttered Krasus, the source of that retribution. The dragon mage stood a short distance behind the pair. "I was forced to make the return in stages," he added with bitterness.

No one condemned him, not after all he had done. Still, it was clear that Krasus would not so easily forgive himself.

"We've pushed them back again," declared Rhonin. There was no enthusiasm in his words. "Just like we did the time before and the time before . . ."

The battle retreated from them. Now that matters were once more in the hands of the defenders, the sisters of Elune turned to their true vocation—dealing with the wounded. They moved among the soldiers and a few even went to tend the tauren, albeit with some clear reservations.

Battle horns made the trio look to where Lord Stareye rode. The noble waved his sword around, then pointed at the Burning Legion. It was clear that he was taking full credit for the host's latest advance.

Krasus shook his head. "Would that Brox had reached Ravencrest in time."

"He did his best, I'm sure," Malfurion responded.

"I have no quarrel with the orc concerning his effort, young one. It is fate with whom I ever battle. Come, let us take this reprieve to see if we can aid the sisterhood. There are plenty of wounded to go around."

There were, indeed. Malfurion put to good use another aspect of his training. Cenarius had taught him much concerning those plants and other life that could ease pain and heal wounds. His talents were not so proficient as that of most of the priestesses, but he left his charges in much better condition than he found them.

Among the wounded, they located Jarod. The captain sat near his resting night saber as a sister looked to a long gash in the officer's arm.

"I've tried to convince her it's nothing," he remarked sourly as they approached. "The armor protected me fairly well."

"The Burning Legion's weapons are often poisoned," Krasus explained. "Even a slight wound might prove treacherous." The pale mage dipped his head toward the officer. "Quick thinking out there. You saved the situation."

"I only pleaded with the tauren, Huln, to give me a few of his people to save mine, then asked the dwarves to make sure I hadn't weakened the tauren lines."

"As I said, quick thinking. The night elves and the bullmen fought well together, when it came to it. Would that our erstwhile commander saw that. The moment I arrived, I perceived that there was no true cohesion among the allies."

Rhonin smirked. "Could you expect any better from Lord Stareye?"

"Alas, no."

They were interrupted by the arrival of a senior priestess. She was tall and moved like a night saber herself. Her face was not unattractive, but her expression was severe. The sister's skin was a shade paler than most of her people. For some reason, despite that, she reminded Malfurion of someone.

"They said they saw you," she commented blandly to Jarod.

He looked at her blankly, as if not certain she actually stood there. "Maiev . . ."

"It's been long since we saw one another, little brother."

Now the physical resemblance became more apparent. The captain disengaged himself from the other priestess's efforts and stood to face his sibling. Even though he stood taller than her, somehow Jarod seemed to look up at Maiev.

"Since you entered the moon goddess's service and chose the temple in Hajiri as the place for your studies."

"It's where Kalo'thera ascended to the stars," Maiev countered, referring to a celebrated high priestess from centuries past. Many in the sisterhood considered Kalo'thera almost a demigoddess.

"It was far from home." Jarod suddenly seemed to recall the others. He looked to them, saying, "This is my older sister, Maiev. Maiev, these are—"

The senior priestess all but ignored Malfurion and Rhonin, her gaze strictly on Krasus. Like the rest of the sisterhood, she evidently saw that he was special, even if she did not understand why. Maiev went down on one knee before Jarod could continue, declaring, "I am honored in your presence, elder one."

Expressionless, Krasus answered, "There is no need to kneel before me. Rise, sister, and be welcome among us. You and yours were timely in your appearance today."

Jarod's sibling stood with pride. "The Mother Moon guided us well, even if it meant the sacrifice of Marinda and some others. We saw the line breaking. We would've arrived before the bullmen if not for the greater distance we had to cover." She glanced in the direction the tauren had gone. "Adept reaction for their kind."

"It is your brother who coordinated all," the mage explained. "It is Jarod who may have saved the host."

"Jarod?" Maiev's tone indicated some disbelief, but when Krasus nodded, she buried that disbelief and tipped her head to the captain. "A simple officer of the city guard playing commander! Fortune was with you this time, brother."

He simply nodded, his eyes cast to the side.

Rhonin, however, did not let Maiev's slight pass. "Fortune? Good, common sense, is what it was!"

The priestess shrugged off the incident. "Little brother, you were introducing us . . ."

"Forgive me! Maiev, the elder mage is Krasus. To his side is the wizard, Rhonin—"

"Such illustrious visitors are welcome in this time," she interrupted. "May the blessing of Elune be upon you."

"And this," the captain continued, "is Malfurion Stormrage, the—"

Maiev's eyes burned into the druid's. "Yes . . . you were known to one of our sisters, Tyrande Whisperwind."

Considering that Tyrande had become high priestess, albeit for only a short period before her kidnapping, the remark was not one Malfurion found respectful. "Yes, we grew up together."

"We mourn our loss. I fear her inexperience betrayed her. It would've been better for her if her predecessor had chosen one more . . . seasoned." There was a subtle implication that Maiev referred to herself.

Biting back his anger, Malfurion said, "There was no fault by her. The battle had spread everywhere. She came to my defense, but was injured. Unconscious. During the chaos that followed, servants of the demons took her." He met the other priestess's steely gaze. "And we *will* get her back."

Jarod's sister nodded. "I will pray to Elune that it is so." She looked to the captain. "I'm glad you weren't injured too badly, little brother. Now, if you'll forgive me, I must attend to the other sisters. Marinda's loss means we must quickly decide on a new leader. She had not yet chosen one herself." With a bow that extended mostly to Krasus, Maiev ended, "Again, may the blessings of Elune be upon you."

When she was far away, Rhonin grunted and said, "A cheerful, friendly sort, your sister."

"She's very dedicated to the traditional teachings of Elune," Jarod responded defensively. "She's always been very serious."

"One cannot fault her for her dedication," Krasus remarked. "Providing it does not blind her to the paths taken by others."

Jarod was saved from further defense of Maiev by Brox's return. The orc had a satisfied grin on his wide face.

"Good battle! Many deaths to sing of! Many warriors to praise for the blood they've spilled!"

"How lovely," muttered Rhonin.

"Tauren're good fighters. Welcome comrades in any war." The hulking, green warrior came to a halt, resting his ax on the ground. "Not as good as orcs . . . but almost."

Krasus eyed the direction of the battle. "Another temporary reprieve, at best, even with the joining of the other races. This cannot continue. We must turn the tide once and for all!"

"But that would mean the dragons . . ." his former protege interjected. "And they don't dare do anything, not so long as Deathwing has the Demon Soul." Rhonin saw no reason to call the black dragon by his original name, Neltharion, anymore.

"No, I fear they dare not. We saw what happened when the blue dragons tried."

Malfurion frowned. He thought of Tyrande. Nothing could truly be done for her unless the Burning Legion was thwarted and they would need everyone, especially the dragons, to accomplish that. But the dragons could not face the Demon Soul, so that meant—

"Then, we've got to take it from the black," he suddenly announced.

Even from Brox, ever willing to leap into any battle, the druid received a wide stare. Jarod shook his head in dismay and Rhonin eyed Malfurion as if he had gone completely mad.

Yet, Krasus, after his initial surprise, gave the night elf a speculative look.

"Malfurion is correct, I am afraid. We must do it."

"Krasus, you can't be serious—"

The dragon mage cut off the wizard. "I am. I had already vaguely considered it myself."

"But we don't even know where Deathwing is. He's shielded himself even better than the other dragons."

"That is true. I have considered some ancient spells, but none so far that I believe will have much success. I will attempt them, and if they fail, I will then have to—"

"I think I can do it," Malfurion interrupted. "I think I can find him through the Emerald Dream. I don't believe he's sealed himself off from it as the palace has done."

Krasus looked quite impressed by the druid. "You may very well be right, young one . . ." He considered further. "But even if he has made such an error, there is, of course, the danger that Neltharion will still sense you. He did, as you mentioned earlier, try to track you inside the Dream."

"I've learned to be more careful. I'll do it. It's the only way to save her—to save us."

The cowled figure placed a gloved hand on Malfurion's shoulder. "We will do what we can for her, too."

"I'll start immediately."

"No! You need rest first. For her sake as well as yours, you need to be at your best. If you make a mistake or are discovered by him, all will be lost."

Malfurion nodded, but in his disappointment, there was now some hope, however slight. True, Neltharion might be prepared, but the dragon was obsessive, single-minded. His megalomania might work against him.

"I'll do as you say," he told the mage. "But there's also one other thing I've got to do, then. There's someone I need to speak with who may better my chances."

Krasus bowed his head in agreement and understanding. "Cenarius. You need to speak with the forest lord."

FOUR

She had not been fed, but Tyrande did not yet feel hunger. Elune still filled her with the moon goddess's love, nourishment enough for anyone. How long that would last, however, was an important question. The dire forces raised by the demons and the Highborne grew with every passing moment and, in addition, the priestess sensed some other, darker presence as well. It did not seem a part of the Burning Legion's plan, but worked alongside it.

Perhaps such a notion was only the first sign of coming madness, but Tyrande could not help wondering if the demons were being manipulated just as they were manipulating the queen.

Someone worked on the door. Tyrande's brow furrowed. She had heard no marching. Whoever was out in the corridor had come in utter silence. Moreover, she realized that the guards had grown extremely quiet over the past several minutes.

The door slid open. Tyrande tried to think who would come in such secrecy.

Illidan?

But it was not Malfurion's brother who slipped inside.

Rather, it was the noble who acted as Azshara's chief hand-maiden. The other night elf glanced up with guarded eyes at the captive, then turned to make certain that the door closed without a sound. As she did, Tyrande could not but help notice no guards visible outside. Were they simply out of sight or entirely gone?

Looking at her, the handmaiden smiled. If it was meant to comfort Tyrande, it did not entirely succeed.

"I am Lady Vashj," the newcomer reminded her. "You are a priestess of Elune."

"I am Tyrande Whisperwind."

Vashj nodded absently. "I have come to help you escape."

Tyrande instinctively thanked the Mother Moon. She had misjudged Vashj, thinking her a jealous sycophant of the queen.

Stepping as close as she could, Vashj continued, "I've taken a talisman that can open the sphere around you and release you from the demon's spell. You can also use it to ward off their notice, as I have."

"I . . . am . . . grateful. But why risk this?"

"You are a priestess of Elune," returned the other female. "How could I do otherwise?" Vashj revealed the talisman. It was a grotesque, black circle with tiny, cruel skulls lining the edge. From the center thrust up a six-inch point with ebony jewels at the base.

Tyrande sensed both its magic and its evil.

"Be prepared," the handmaiden commanded. "Obey me in all things if you hope to no longer be the demons' pris-oner."

She reached up and touched the point to the green sphere.

The jewels flashed. The diminutive skulls opened their macabre jaws and hissed.

The sphere was sucked into the tiny maws.

Tyrande felt the spell holding her dissipate. She suddenly had to twist in the air to keep from falling face first. The priestess landed on the stone floor in a crouched position. To her surprise, Tyrande felt no pain from the landing, Elune's touch still protecting her.

Vashj glanced with frustration at her. With the sphere gone, Tyrande now faintly glowed with moonlight arising from *within*. The handmaiden shook her head.

"You must not remain like that! It will give you away once out of this cell!"

Closing her eyes, Tyrande prayed to her goddess, thanking the Mother Moon for her protection but assuring her that this was now for the best. At first, however, it seemed as if Elune paid her no mind, for she felt the protective spell remain fixed.

"Hurry!" Lady Vashj urged.

Eyes still shut, Tyrande tried again. Surely the Mother Moon understood that now the very gift she had bestowed upon her servant risked the priestess.

At last, Elune's presence began to recede—

And a sense of imminent threat overwhelmed Tyrande.

She opened her eyes to see Vashj thrusting at her throat with the sinister talisman. The daggerlike protrusion would have ripped a wide, lethal gap—if not for the war training all priestesses received. Tyrande's hand came up just in time to shove the point aside. She felt a stinging on her skin, but had managed to keep Vashj from even drawing blood.

Azshara's servant, her expression as monstrous as those of the skulls, sought to tear out Tyrande's eyes with her free hand. The priestess raised her armored knee, catching Vashj in the stomach. With a gasp, the other night elf fell back, the talisman rolling to the side.

Tyrande leapt at her, but Vashj was also swift. She rolled over to where the talisman had landed. Tyrande, crouching, tried to pull her back, but the treacherous handmaiden already had the demonic artifact in her clutches.

She spewed unintelligible words of an overt dark tone as she pointed the talisman.

The sphere suddenly reformed around Tyrande. At the same time, the priestess felt Elune's protection return, though small good it did to help her escape the bubble. Tyrande beat against the sphere, but to no avail.

Rising, Lady Vashj glared bitterly at her nemesis. "It would have been better for you if you had taken the point! You will never be *Her* most favored! I am and always will be!"

"I don't want to be favored by the queen!"

But Vashj seemed not to understand this. Eyes on the talisman, she hissed, "I thought this would work, but I will have to think of something else! Perhaps words in the Light of Light's ear, convince her that you are not to be trusted! Yes, that might do the trick!"

Tyrande ceased trying to convince the handmaiden of her lack of desire to serve Azshara. Clearly, Vashj was quite mad and would hear nothing that contradicted her notions.

A sound from without made Vashj spin to the door. "The guards! They will be back from their 'distraction'!" Looking back at the prisoner, she pointed the talisman again. "Everything must be as it was!"

Once more, Tyrande's arms rose, invisibly binding at the wrist. Her feet clamped tight together.

"Would that I knew more about this piece!" Vashj spat. "I know it could likely slay you with but the right command . . ."

The sounds without drew nearer. Secreting the talisman in a fold in her garments, Azshara's attendant made for the door. As she slipped out, she looked one last time at Tyrande.

"Never hers!" And with that, Vashj vanished into the hall.

The guards reappeared barely moments later. One peered through the mesh grate in the door and eyed her for far longer than necessary. What she could make of his expression indicated that he was disturbed by her presence. Vashj had clearly not acted alone.

As for Tyrande, she could do nothing but berate herself for a chance lost. It should have been obvious to her that Vashj could not be trusted, but Elune had taught that one should look for the best in others. Yet, if Tyrande had acted with more caution, perhaps she could have caught the handmaiden off-guard. Instead of being again trapped here, at least then the priestess could have tried to sneak out of the palace.

"Mother Moon, what do I do?" She was aware that there were limits to the goddess's ability to intervene. It was miracle enough that Elune had protected her so.

Malfurion's visage came to mind, both comforting Tyrande and making her fret. He would *not* give up trying to save her. He would come for her, regardless of the danger to himself. In fact, she was well aware that Malfurion would be willing to sacrifice himself if it meant her freedom.

And it seemed, Tyrande Whisperwind thought with growing despair, that there would be *nothing* she in turn could do to prevent him from doing so.

The small copse of woods was the best Malfurion could do in terms of finding a peaceful place from which to try to reach Cenarius. The druid sat cross-legged on the ground, glancing again at the pitiful foliage around him. The Burning Legion had not reached this place, but their taint had stretched for enough to affect the life here. The trees already sensed the doom approaching and slowly prepared for it. Most of the wildlife had fled. Silence reigned.

Trying to ignore all that, Malfurion shut his eyes and fixed on the demigod. He reached out, calling to Cenarius and trying to picture the deity in his thoughts.

And to his surprise, the demigod responded immediately. An image formed of the forest lord, a huge figure who towered over night elves, tauren, furbolgs, and even the demons. At first glance, he had some similarity to Malfurion, for his face and torso were like those of a night elf, albeit much brawnier and more weathered. Yet, beyond that, Cenarius was a creature like none other. Below his waist, he had the body of a gigantic, magnificent stag. Four strong legs ending in hooves supported his ten-foot frame. They gave him the speed of the wind and a nimbleness no animal could match.

Cenarius had eyes of pure gold and a moss-green mane flowing down his shoulders. In both it and his full beard grew twigs and leaves. Atop his head—and exactly, Malfurion noted with a start, where his own nubs grew—the forest lord had a glorious pair of antlers.

I know why you've summoned me, the demigod said.

Is there anything I can do to counteract and outmaneuver the black dragon's magic?

He is cunning, insanely so, Cenarius replied, his mouth never moving. He was but an vision upon which the druid could focus, nothing more. The true forest lord was miles away. *But there are things I know of dragonkind that he may not realize.*

Malfurion did not press on how Cenarius might know these things. From what he had learned, the deity was likely the offspring of the green dragon, Ysera—She of the Dreaming—whose kind most inhabited the Emerald Dream.

That the great Aspect might have taught her son its inner-most secrets would not have surprised the night elf.

The Emerald Dream has layers, Malfurion. Levels upon levels. She of the Dreaming discovered these through experience. The Earth Warder likely will not know of them. You may be able to use such a path to circumvent his defenses and keep from his attention for a time.

This was something unexpected. Malfurion's hopes rose. Should he succeed in this, perhaps he could use such a method to infiltrate the palace.

But he had to concentrate on one matter at a time. While his heart yearned to rescue Tyrande, the fate of all his peo-ple—and the tauren, Earthen, and others—was of far more consequence. She would have been the first to tell him so.

It did not make his feeling of guilt any less.

Can I learn quickly how to do this? he asked of the demigod.

You, yes. It is all only a matter of perspective . . . see . . .

The image gestured . . . and around the pair an idyllic landscape appeared. It was without imperfection. Malfurion recognized hills and valleys that in the mortal plane had been ravaged beyond recognition by the Burning Legion. The Emerald Dream was as the world had been upon its creation.

The druid looked, but saw nothing he had not already ex-perienced previous.

You note the culmination, but even perfection comes in stages. Behold . . .

Cenarius reached down, his hand gigantic as it touched the pristine world. The forest lord seized a bit of field—and seemed to flip the entire landscape over.

It vanished as he released his grip and in its place was again a primitive Kalimdor, but a Kalimdor in which some new, subtle differences from the previous landcape could be seen. Hills were not as large in some places and a river Malfurion knew did not flow into quite the same region as before. There was a small mountain chain where plains should have existed.

Before the creation, there was the growth, the testing, the earlier stages. This is one.

It was and was not the Emerald Dream. The druid recognized immediately that this was a place of limited scope—and, therefore, use—a Kalimdor that would not enable him to reach every location existing on the mortal plane.

Yet . . . Cenarius believed it could help him with the black dragon.

The looming figure of the woodland deity pointed off in the distance. *Walk it as you would the other, Malfurion, but remain clear of its edges. It is an incomplete place and to wander off it could mean being lost in an endless limbo. I speak of this from dread experience.*

Cenarius said no more, but his meaning was clear. If Malfurion lost his way, there would be no rescue.

Despite that dread knowledge, the night elf was determined to continue on. *How do I return?*

As you always have. Seek to follow your way back to your physical self. The path will become known to you.

All so simple . . . providing one had the training as he did.

Cenarius's image began to fade. Malfurion stopped him.

The others, he said, referring to the forest lord's fellow demigods. *Have you been able to convince them?*

Aviana has spoken alongside me. The die is cast. We must now only decide how.

Malfurion barely checked his disappointment. He had been pressing for the demigods to take a more active part in the host's desperate efforts and, while Cenarius had just indicated that his fellows had agree to do so, now they would debate the manner. With such beings, that debate might last long past the struggle. Kalimdor could be an empty, dead shell before then.

Fear not, Malfurion, the forest lord said, smiling knowingly. *I shall endeavor to hasten their decision.*

The druid had left open his innermost thoughts, a beginner's mistake. *Forgive me! I meant no disrespect! I—*

Cenarius, already fading, shook his antlered head. He pointed a finger—a finger which ended in a gnarled talon of wood—and concluded, *There is no disrespect in trying to urge those suffering from sloth to fulfill their duties . . .*

With that, the stag god vanished.

The druid had expected to return to his body and inform the others of what he had learned, but the unfinished landscape Cenarius had revealed to him already lay open. Malfurion feared that if he took the time to first return to the mortal plane, it might prove more difficult than the demigod believed for him to find his way back to this version of early Kalimdor.

Unwilling to check his impulse any longer, he leapt. As with the path Malfurion usually took, the hazy, emerald light still pervaded everything. In truth, he could not tell any difference between one place and another save for the occasional variation in features.

Over hills and valleys and plains, Malfurion flew. From Krasus he knew the general direction where the dragons tended to live. Obviously, the Earth Warder would not maintain his sanctum so near the others, but Krasus had assured him that the ancient race were creatures of habit. If the druid began his hunt near the ancestral grounds, there was a good chance he might discover something.

The land below became more mountainous, yet, these peaks were neither the perfectly pointed ones of his past journeys into the dream realm nor were they the weathered ones of the mortal plane. Instead, they were, as Cenarius had hinted, *unfinished*. One peak literally lacked its northern face, the earth and rock looking as if some great knife had sheered it off. Malfurion could see the veins of minerals and bits of cavern within. Another peak had a peculiar crown that made it appear as if someone had been molding it like clay but had lost interest.

Tearing his eyes from such fascinating displays, the druid inspected the area as a whole. This was definitely part of the dragon lands. Now all he had to do was find some trace of Neltharion.

As with from the other level, Malfurion probed with his senses for the black dragon's particular trace. He detected others and quickly identified Ysera and one he believed to be Alexstrasza. Other, fainter traces Malfurion determined to be from lesser dragons and, therefore, not of interest.

Moving slowly along, the druid searched in every direction. With each failure, he began to wonder if perhaps Neltharion had not been so naive after all. Perhaps, the black leviathan was more familiar with this plane than Cenarius knew and had shielded himself. If so, Malfurion could wander forever and not find a single hint.

He suddenly halted. A trace that he had offhandedly rejected as belonging to a minor dragon suddenly caught his attention again. It had a familiarity to it that should not have been possible. Malfurion focused on it . . .

The facade peeled away almost immediately. Neltharion's trace lay revealed to the druid. Spells that likely would have kept the Earth Warder hidden from anyone on either the mortal plane or even in the Emerald Dream had proven almost laughably weak here. However, Malfurion tried not to grow overconfident. It was one thing to track the black dragon, another to keep from his notice no matter on what plane. The madness inflicting Neltharion had given him an extreme paranoia that had augmented his higher senses. Even the slightest mistake by the druid might mean discovery.

With the need for utmost caution in mind, Malfurion followed the trace. It took him further on, toward a region where the landscape became more vague, more undefined. Recalling Cenarius's warnings concerning the edges, the druid slowed.

The black dragon was near. Malfurion sensed him just where the mountains began to blur. He also sensed something else, a foul taint that permeated the region and felt far older than anything else. It reminded the druid of what he had felt when probing deep into the Demon Soul. It had not only been imbued with Neltharion's madness, but something more sinister. Then, though, it had only been a trace and he had thought little of it.

What could it be?

Deciding that he could not worry about it now, Malfurion ventured closer. The landscape rippled—and suddenly his dream form reentered the mortal plane.

The huge cavern surrounding him was like a scene out of some nightmare. Noxious-looking clouds of green-gray gas shot up from huge, molten pits dotting the floor. The pits bubbled and hissed and now and then their steaming contents boiled over, spilling across the already-scorched stone. The volcanic activity filled the cavern with a fiery, bloody light and created macabre, dancing shadows. Truly a fitting home for the beast that had slaughtered so may with so little regard.

Malfurion suddenly realized that, in addition to the bubbling and hissing, another sound constantly ranged in the background. Hammering. The more he concentrated, the more the druid realized that it was not simply one hammer, but many, and that there were other sounds of activity as well. Voices, constantly-jabbering voices.

Drawn by it, Malfurion's dream form flew through solid rock yards thick. The sounds reverberated through the mountain. It became an incessant barrage of work-related noises, as if a huge smithy existed within the mountain.

Then the rock gave way to a scene that made the volcanic pits tranquil in comparison.

Goblins. The wiry creatures ran about everywhere. Some worked at huge vats and ovens, pouring steaming, liquid metal into massive, rectangular molds. Others beat with well-worn hammers on hot plates that looked almost like armor for some gargantuan warrior. Scores more hammered out huge bolts. All the while, they all jabbered with one another. Everywhere Malfurion looked, goblins worked on some project or another. A few in grimy smocks wandered about, directing efforts and now and then urging on the slothful with flat-handed slaps on the back of their green, pointy-eared heads.

Aware that this could not be a task with good intentions behind it, he floated closer. Yet, despite what he saw, Malfurion could not figure out what the goblins planned.

"Meklo!" roared a thunderous voice suddenly. "Meklo! Attend me!"

The druid froze in mid-air, briefly overcome by panic. He knew well that voice, as did anyone who had survived the first use of the Demon Soul.

And a moment later, from another cavern corridor, the black dragon himself emerged.

Malfurion quickly moved behind one of the ovens. While he should have been invisible even to Neltharion, past experience had proven that the mad beast could still sense him at times. The path Cenarius had shown Malfurion had enabled the druid to slip past Neltharion's protective spells as planned, but in order to properly search for the artifact, the night elf unfortunately had to stay as close to the mortal plane as possible.

After a brief hesitation, the goblins continued their work, albeit with not quite so much chattering. Neltharion surveyed the area, seeking out the "Meklo" he desired to see.

If anything, the leviathan looked even more monstrous than when he had flown from the scene of destruction. His body was distorted, bloated, and his eyes held a more horrible madness than ever. More shocking, the rips and tears in his scaled flesh had only grown, fire and molten fluids constantly gushing from each pulsating wound. It almost looked as if eventually Neltharion's body would tear itself apart.

But all thought of the terrifying transformation wrought upon the black dragon vanished from Malfurion's thoughts when he saw what the giant held tight in one huge paw.

The Demon Soul . . .

Malfurion wanted to fly up to the dragon and steal away the golden disk, but that would not only have been impossible, it would also have been suicidal. All he could do for the moment was watch and wait.

"Meklo!" Neltharion roared again. His tail came down with a massive thump, causing several of the goblins to jump in fright.

But one who appeared unperturbed by this display was a spindly, elder goblin with a tuft of gray fur atop his head and an extremely distracted expression. As he passed where Malfurion hid, the druid could hear him muttering about measurements and calculations. The goblin nearly walked up to Neltharion's lowered head before finally glancing at his master.

"Yes, my Lord Neltharion, yes?"

"Meklo! My body screams! It cannot contain my glory by itself anymore! When will you be ready?"

"I have had to recalculate, recalibrate, and reconsider every aspect of what you need, my lord! This will require much caution, or we may bring further disaster upon you!"

The dragon's snout thrust against the goblin, almost bowling Meklo over. "I want it ready! Now!"

"By all means, by all means!" Meklo stepped out of biting range. "Please let me look over the latest plate—" The goblin squinted, gazing at Neltharion's paw. "But, my lord! I did warn you, I did, that holding the disk while in this present state amplifies the effect on you! You really need to put it elsewhere until we've made you over!"

"Never! I'll never let it leave me!"

Meklo stood his ground. "My lord, if you don't put it aside, your present condition will consume you and then *anyone* could take it from your burnt bones."

His words finally registered with the dragon. Neltharion snarled . . . then reluctantly nodded. "Very well . . . but the plates had better be ready, goblin . . . or I'll be having a snack!"

His head bobbing up and down quickly, Meklo blurted, "Most assuredly, Lord Neltharion, most assuredly!" Daring his master's further wrath, he added, "Remember! It must remain on the mortal plane! Your initial use of it unbound the spells more than we expected! The new spellwork needs several more days to bind to the physical shell before we can guarantee that such a thing will never happen again!"

"I understand, gnat . . . I understand . . ." With a hiss, the black leviathan angrily turned about and headed back into the corridor.

Malfurion tensed. The dragon was going to secrete the

Demon Soul somewhere. Now was the druid's opportunity to discover the location.

Ignoring the goblins, Malfurion carefully drifted after the Earth Warder. Neltharion's great girth filled the tunnel, allowing the druid no manner by which to see what might lay ahead unless he chose to fly around or through the dragon. Aware of the risks in that, the night elf forced himself to be patient.

That patience wore thin as Neltharion wended his way through a labyrinth of tunnels. The sense of ancient evil the druid had earlier felt only increased as they journeyed. Where Neltharion went was clearly shunned by others. Only once did the Earth Warder pass one of his own flight, that much smaller dragon prostrating himself before his master. Beyond that, no life, not even an earthworm, appeared. The Earth Warder was taking no chances. His obsession with the Demon Soul included distrust of even his own followers—not entirely surprising considering the power the disk granted its wielder.

Malfurion gradually moved nearer, finally ending up just above the dragon's sweeping tail. He all but urged the leviathan to haste.

The giant abruptly paused, his head twisting to look over his shoulders. Malfurion instinctively flew into the nearest wall, sinking deep into the stone. He waited for several seconds, then, dropping to a lower point, thrust his head out to look.

Neltharion was already on his way. Cursing his overreaction, the druid gave chase.

Scarcely had he caught up when the Earth Warder suddenly veered into a narrow cavern. It was all Neltharion could do just to fit into it, the sides of his huge torso scraping the walls.

"Here . . ." he muttered, apparently speaking to his creation. "You'll be safe here."

The sense of dread had grown more so, but Malfurion fought down the desire to flee. He almost knew where and how the dragon hid the Demon Soul.

With great delicacy, Neltharion reached up and took hold of a tiny outcropping. As he did, it flashed—and the piece he removed left behind in its wake a gap clearly gouged out by some great creature, likely the dragon himself.

Neltharion eyed the Demon Soul. Then, with much hesitation, he gently set it into the hole. The moment he had, he thrust the false rock back in front.

Again, there was a flash and now the area looked completely normal. Had he floated directly in front of it, Malfurion could have never guessed that it was not. The false covering had fashioned itself perfectly to fit its surroundings.

Of more interest than even that, however, was that Malfurion could now not sense the disk. Its foul energies were invisible to even the most careful search. The dragon might not have been able to hide it beyond the mortal plane, but clearly had devised the next best thing.

Neltharion paused, eyes still fixed on the spot where he had secreted the Demon Soul. One great paw reached up again, the sharp claws but inches from the false front.

With another frustrated hiss, the black leviathan suddenly lowered his paw and began backing out of the cavern.

The druid sank into the stone again, waiting until he was certain that he had given Neltharion enough time to depart. Seconds passed like hours. Finally satisfied that the dragon had to be gone, the night elf peered out. Seeing that the cavern was empty, Malfurion then drifted toward where the Demon Soul lay.

Even almost pressed up against the false front, he felt nothing. Despite his desire to be away from this cursed place, Malfurion decided to take one look at the disk to make certain that he knew everything necessary concerning it and its whereabouts. Krasus would have questions.

He leaned forward, his dream form slipping through Neltharion's camouflaged vault.

A savage roar filled the cavern.

The Demon Soul forgotten, Malfurion flung himself deep into the walls, soaring several yards through before daring to pause.

He felt an intense, monstrous force probe the area, seeking whatever did not belong. Though it had not so far touched Malfurion, the night elf already recognized the black dragon as its source.

Neltharion had evidently detected something amiss. However, from the vague, sweeping movement of his search, he did not know what it was. The druid stood frozen, uncertain whether it was better to try to leave or to remain where he floated.

The magical probe swept closer, but again passed the night elf by. Malfurion started to relax—then suddenly felt the dragon reaching out directly at him.

The druid immediately pulled back farther. Neltharion's search retreated. The dragon had again missed him.

But the night elf dared not risk himself anymore. He had discovered the whereabouts of the disk. As for the Earth Warder, he might be suspicious, but it was doubtful that he realized someone had actually been nearby.

Malfurion retreated from the caverns, from the mountains. As he left the latter, he sought for the unfinished world within the Emerald Dream. Only when he had reentered it did the druid feel any sense of security.

That sense of security vanished as he once again felt Neltharion's overwhelming presence.

The dragon knew of the Dream realm's layers . . .

The night elf desperately concentrated, focusing all his will on his mortal shell. He imagined returning to it even as he felt the Earth Warder reach out his direction—

And just when he thought the mad beast had him . . . Malfurion awoke.

"He's shaking!" Rhonin blurted from the night elf's left. "And drenched with sweat!"

"Malfurion!" Krasus filled the druid's gaze. "What ails you? Speak!"

"I—I'm all right . . ." He paused to catch his breath. "Neltharion—he—he almost noticed me, but I evaded him."

"You have already gone in search of him? You were not to do that!"

"The—the opportunity arose . . ."

"Now, he'll be warned," Rhonin muttered.

"Perhaps, perhaps not," the human's former mentor returned. "More likely, he will chalk it up to the many shadows he thinks surround him." To Malfurion, the mage asked, "Did you discover the Demon Soul?"

"Yes . . . I know where it is." The druid managed to answer. He saw again Neltharion, the savage draconian face giving him chills. "I'm only afraid that we might not be able to take it from him."

"But we have to," Krasus said, nodding understanding over Malfurion's concern. "But we have to . . . no matter what the cost."

FIVE

Soft hands touched Illidan's face as they washed his burnt, wasted flesh. The scent of lilies and other flowers wafted over his nostrils. He began to stir at last, rising up from the self-induced coma he had used to escape his pain. The latter had finally subsided to something tolerable, but Malfurion's brother doubted that it would ever completely fade.

But as full consciousness returned, his world was suddenly filled with a maddening display of colors and violent energies. The sorcerer gasped and put his arms across where his eyes had been, for there were now barely even lids to cover them. Even that, though, did nothing to keep the swirling energies and constantly-shifting colors from almost driving him mad. This was Sargeras's gift to him, a demonic, magical view of the world.

Then, Illidan Stormrage recalled the words of Rhonin, the human wizard. *Focus,* the powerful spellcaster had so often insisted to him. *Focus and it all comes together. That's the key . . .*

Forcing back his initial shock, Illidan tried to follow through. It was nigh impossible, at first, for there seemed an endless chaos, much too much for a mere mortal like him to control.

But, with the same resolution that had propelled him up so quickly among the Moon Guard, Illidan forced order upon matters. The colors began to organize, the energy to flow with regularity and purpose. Shapes began to form from the natural energies inherent in all things, alive or inanimate.

He realized at last that he lay upon a stuffed couch, its fabric so smooth and soft it was almost sensual. There were three figures standing nearby—all female, Illidan belatedly realized. The more the twin focused, the more he could detail features. Night elves all, they were young, exquisite, and clad in rich but alluring gowns.

More distinctions appeared as he fixed on the one who had been washing his injuries. Illidan sensed the silver coloring of her hair—silver that was not natural—and the feline appearance of her eyes. In truth, his perceptions were more acute than ever. The sorcerer could read minute variations in strands of hair. He could sense the level of power each of these Highborne wielded—and knew that, of all three, the one cleaning his wounds was by far the strongest. Even then, though, her skills were nothing in comparison to his.

The lead handmaiden recovered first. Putting aside the damp cloth, she brought forth what, through the energies surrounding it, Illidan knew was a silken scarf the color of amber.

The color of his lost eyes.

"This is for you, lord sorcerer . . ."

He understood exactly what it was for. This new, sharper sense of sight had momentarily made him forget how he must look to others. With the sort of bow he would have given Lord Ravencrest, Illidan accepted the scarf and wrapped it over where his eyes had been. Not at all to his surprise, the scarf in no manner inhibited his new abilities.

"So much better," murmured the female. "You should look your best for the queen—"

"Thank you, Vashj . . ." came Azshara's voice suddenly. "You and the rest may retire for now."

Vashj clamped her mouth shut, then bowed as she and the other two retreated from the chamber.

Illidan caught his breath as he turned his senses to the queen. A brilliant radiance surrounded Azshara, a silver glow he finally recognized as indication of the power she wielded. Illidan would have blinked if he could. Although Azshara had been beloved by all her people, some, such as him, had assumed that her skills in the arts were negligible. He had always believed that she had required the might of the Highborne for the casting of spells. Illidan wondered if even the late Lord Xavius or the erstwhile Captain Varo'then had ever understood just how accomplished their monarch was.

"Your majesty." Moving from the couch, the sorcerer went down on one knee.

"Please . . . rise up. There is no need for such formality in private." Somehow she moved right up to him without Illidan noticing her do so. The queen guided him back to the couch. "Let us be more comfortable, my darling sorcerer."

As they sat, Azshara leaned toward Malfurion's twin. Her touch set his soul on fire. Her very presence felt almost hypnotic.

Hypnotic? Illidan studied her.

The glow around Azshara had intensified, so much so that it even overlapped him. How Illidan had missed it revealed much about the queen's control.

Even with that knowledge, it was all he could do from being overwhelmed by her.

"I've been most impressed by you, Illidan Stormrage! So very clever, so very powerful! Even our Lord Sargeras sees that or else why would he grant you such a precious gift?" Long, tapering fingers caressed the scarf. "Such a shame to lose the beautiful amber eyes, though . . . I know it hurts much . . ."

Her face was enticingly close to his and, at the moment, it was impossible not to want it closer. "I—I endured it, your majesty."

"Please! For you, I'm merely Azshara . . ." Her fingers ran from his eye sockets to the rest of his face. "Such a hand- some face!" She touched his shoulder, pushing aside part of his clothing. "So strong, too . . . and with the mark of the Great One there as well!"

Frowning, Illidan glanced down to where her hand lay.

An intricate pattern of dark tattoos enshrouded his shoulder. Beneath them and well-shielded, the night elf sensed an unearthly magic—the magic of Sargeras—that permeated his flesh. That he had not felt any of it until now stunned Illidan. With a quick glance to his other side, the sorcerer saw that a similar pattern marked his body there. Sargeras had truly claimed Illidan as a creature of the Legion.

Ignoring the queen for a moment, Malfurion's brother gingerly touched one. Immediately he felt a surge of power. It coursed through him. His body radiated primal energy that he knew took as its source that which fed the Well. He realized that the demon lord had amplified his abilities by marking him so.

"Truly you are favored by him . . . and, thus, favored by me," Queen Azshara whispered, drawing close again. "And there are many favors I can grant you, which even he cannot—"

"Forgive this untimely intrusion, Light of Lights," a figure at the door almost growled.

Illidan tensed, but Azshara coolly straightened, brushing back her luxurious hair and eyeing the newcomer with misleading, languid eyes. "What is it, dear captain?"

In contrast to the seductive brilliance surrounding the queen, Captain Varo'then emitted a darkness that reminded Illidan of the demons. He had only a hint of ability in the sorcerous arts, but Illidan already understood that the soldier was possibly as deadly in his own way as Mannoroth.

Perhaps deadlier at times, at least where it concerned his jealousy against real and imagined rivals for his queen. Varo'then all but seethed as he took in the sight of Azshara and Illidan on the couch. She did not help matters by reaching out and caressing the sorcerer's cheek as she rose.

"I've come for *him,* your majesty. This one's made promises and our lord expects those promises fulfilled."

"And I *will,*" Illidan returned strongly, staring back at the officer despite the scarf. Varo'then's eyes narrowed dangerously, but he nodded.

"Then, by all means," Azshara interjected, coming between the pair and glancing at both coyly. "I'm certain between the two of you that no *dragon* stands a chance! I very much look forward to hearing of your exploits—" She ran a hand across the captain's breast plate, causing his eyes to light up in lust. "—*both* of your exploits, that is!" the queen added, doing the same over Illidan's bare chest.

Despite knowing that she played games with the pair of them, the sorcerer could not help reacting slightly. Steeling himself against her wiles, he replied, "I will not disappoint you . . . Azshara."

His use of her name without any title before or after it—and the close familiarity such use hinted at—did not sit well with the soldier. Varo'then's hand slipped to the hilt of his sword, but he wisely let it pass without actually gripping the blade.

"We must first find the beast—which you claim you can do."

Illidan took hold of the dragon scale. "I make no claim; I speak the truth."

"Then, there is no need to wait. It is nearly nightfall."

Turning to the queen, Illidan executed the sort of bow he had witnessed in Black Rook Hold. "With your permission . . ."

She gave him a regal smile. "And you may go, too, dear captain."

"Most gracious, Light of Lights, Flower of the Moon . . ." Varo'then also bowed, his action crisp and military. He then indicated the doorway to Illidan. "After you, master sorcerer."

Without a word to the armored figure, Illidan marched out. He sensed Varo'then follow right behind him. It would not have surprised Malfurion's twin if the captain tried to knife him in the back, but Varo'then evidently had more control than that.

"Where do we go?" he asked his escort.

"You can do your casting once we're away from Zin-Azshari. Our Lord Sargeras wishes this mission to be finished as soon as possible. He itches to set his feet upon Azeroth's soil and give our world his blessing."

"Fortunate is Azeroth."

Varo'then eyed him for a moment, trying to find fault with his answer. Unable to do so, he finally nodded, "Aye, fortunate is Azeroth."

The captain led him through the palace, eventually descending. As they neared the stables, Illidan asked, "So you're to be my companion throughout all this?"

"You should have someone to watch your back."

"I'm gratified."

"Our great lord puts much stock into this notion of the disk fulfilling his needs. He will have it."

"I welcome your company," the sorcerer remarked. At that moment, however, they entered the stables. What Illidan saw there made him stop dead. "And what's this?"

A dozen Fel Guard stood waiting near the night sabers, their monstrous faces eager for bloodshed. Two Doomguard flanked them, clearly there to keep order on their wingless brethren. Another pair of Fel Guard kept tight rein over a slavering felbeast.

"As I've said," Captain Varo'then answered with possibly a hint of sarcasm. "You should have someone to watch your back. These . . ." He indicated the fiendish warriors. ". . . will watch you very carefully. Of that, I make my utmost promise, sorcerer."

Illidan nodded and said nothing.

"We will make haste, I promise you, Rhonin."

"Promise me nothing, Krasus," the human returned. "Just be careful. And don't worry about Stareye. I'll deal with him."

"He is the least of our worries. I trust you and the good Captain Shadowsong to keep the host together."

"Me?" Jarod shook his head. "Master Krasus, you've got much too much confidence in me! I'm a Guard officer, nothing more! It's as Maiev said, fortune smiled on me! I'm no more a commander than—than—"

"Than Stareye?" smirked Rhonin.

"I am afraid we must count on you, Jarod Shadowsong. The tauren and the others, they see the respect you give them and give it back in turn. There may come another time when, as you did earlier, you must make a decision to act. For the sake of your people, I might add."

The night elf's shoulders slumped in defeat. "I'll do what I can, Master Krasus. That's all I can say."

The mage nodded. "And that is all we ask of you, good captain."

"Now that we have that little matter settled," the human commented. "How do you plan to reach the lair?"

"The gryphons are no longer available to us. We shall have to take night sabers and urge them to their swiftest."

"But that'll take too long! Worse, it'll leave you more vulnerable to the Burning Legion's assassins!"

Archimonde had demons constantly shadowing the host, seeking to slay Krasus and his band. Malfurion had been especially marked by Archimonde after the druid's astounding reversal of certain Legion victory, but the dragon mage had no doubt that he was also high on the demon's list.

"A spell would be too risky a manner by which to travel to where Deathwing awaits," Krasus returned. "I have no doubt that he is on guard for such things. We must journey by physical means."

"I still don't like it."

"Nor do I, but it must be so." He looked to his companions for the trek. "Are you prepared to depart?"

Malfurion nodded. Brox replied with an impatient grunt. While it was true that between the druid and the mage they had exceptional abilities at their disposal, Krasus understood the need for the company of a skilled warrior such as the orc. Spellcasters could be incapacitated in many ways. Brox had also proven himself a trustworthy ally.

"Give us an hour before alerting Lord Stareye," Krasus reminded the human as he mounted.

"I'll give you two."

Seeing that the druid and the orc had also mounted, Krasus urged his beast forward. The graceful cat quickly picked up speed, the mounts of the mage's companions right behind. It did not take long for the animals to leave the night elven host far, far behind.

No one spoke as they rode, all three riders intent not only on the path ahead, but any sign of threat lurking around them. However, the night passed without any danger and they made good distance. When the sun began to rise, Krasus finally called for a halt.

"We rest here for a time," he decided, eyeing the sparsely-wooded hills ahead. "I would prefer to enter those when we are more recuperated."

"You think we might be in danger there?" asked Malfurion.

"Perhaps. While the woods are thin, the hills themselves offer many crevices and such for possible ambushes."

Brox nodded his agreement. "Would use hill to north for that. Best view of path. We should avoid that one when riding."

"And with that expert opinion, I agree." The mage looked around. "This area here by these two tall rocks is best-suited for our camp, I think. We shall have a good view of the surroundings while giving ourselves some protection."

They tethered the night sabers to a crooked tree nearby. Bred for generations, the cats obeyed every command immediately and without argument. Brox volunteered to feed the animals from the supplies they had brought with them. There would be enough for three days, but after that they would have to let the cats hunt. Krasus hoped that by then the party would be in a better location, wildlife clearly sparse here.

The trio ate from their own rations. To a dragon like Krasus, eating salted, dried meat was hardly satisfying, but he had long ago steeled himself to such necessities. Malfurion ate some fruit—also dried—and nuts, while Brox ate the same as Krasus, albeit with more gusto. Orcs were not discriminating when it came to food.

"The cats are already at rest," Krasus declared after their meal. "I suggest we do the same."

"I take first watch," Brox offered.

With Malfurion volunteering for the second, the matter of security was quickly settled. Krasus and the druid found places to rest near the taller of the two stones. Brox, proving more agile than his frame suggested, easily climbed up to the top of the steeper rock and sat. Ax resting in his lap, he surveyed the landscape like a hungry carrion bird.

Despite intending to only allow himself to doze, the dragon mage fell deep asleep. He had pushed himself far beyond his limits. What little rest he had gotten earlier was not enough to make up for so much strain.

Dragons dream and Krasus was no exception. For him, it was the everpresent desire to fly free again, to spread the wings he did not have and take to the air. Here, he was once more Korialstrasz. A creature of the sky, he chafed at being bound to the earth. The dragon had always been comfortable in his mortal form, but that had been when he had understood that with a single thought he could transform to his true self. With that taken from him, he often found himself frustrated with the frailty of his present shape.

And in his dream, that curse suddenly took hold, the weaker mortal flesh binding to his body, squeezing him into a smaller and smaller shape. His wings were crushed into his back and his tail severed. His long, toothy maw was shoved into his skull, replaced by the insignificant little nub of a nose he wore in the guise of a spellcaster. Korialstrasz became again Krasus, who plunged earthward—

And who woke up bathed in sweat.

Krasus half expected to discover that the party was under some attack, but the day was silent save for Malfurion's rhythmic breathing. He rose and saw that Brox continued vigilant watch. The mage gazed at the sun, estimating the time. Brox had gone long past his appointed watch. It was nearly Krasus's turn.

Leaving the druid to sleep, the slim, robed figure grabbed hold of the rock and quickly scurried up in the fashion of a lizard. As he reached the top, Brox leapt to his feet and, with reflexes worthy of the dragon, readied his ax.

"You," the orc grunted, helping him up. Both sat atop the rock, watching while they talked. "Thought you asleep, Master Krasus."

"As *you* should be, Brox. You need rest as much as either of us."

The green-skinned warrior shrugged. "An orc warrior can sleep with eyes open and weapon ready. No need to wake the night elf. He must sleep more. Against the dragon, he'll be more use than this old fighter."

Krasus eyed the orc. "An old fighter worth twenty young ones."

The veteran warrior looked pleased with the compliment, but said, "The day of glory is past for this one. There will be no more tales of Broxigar the Red Ax."

"I have lived longer than you, Brox; I know, therefore, of what I speak. There is much glory left in you, much heroic battle. New tales of Broxigar the Red Ax are still to come, even if I must tell them myself."

The orc's cheek's darkened and he suddenly bowed his head low. "Honored by your words I am, venerable one."

Like Malfurion, Brox had learned the truth concerning Krasus's identity. To the dragon's own surprise, the tusked warrior had already long known. As an orc who had learned some of the shamanistic traditions, Brox had sensed the incredible power and age of his companion and, watching Krasus deal with dragons, had come to the logical conclusion that so escaped most others. That Krasus and the red dragon Korialstrasz were one and the same had been beyond him, but even that the orc had accepted with but a mild furrowing of his brow.

"And speaking as a 'venerable one'," Krasus returned. "I will insist that you go and take your turn in slumber. I will watch for the rest of Malfurion's time—however little left there is—and then my own."

"Would be better if you—"

Krasus stared into the orc's eyes. "I assure you, my stamina is far greater than yours. I need no more sleep."

Seeing that he would lose any further argument, Brox grunted and rose. But as he did, Krasus, glancing past the hulking warrior, stiffened.

"Doomguard . . ." he whispered.

Brox immediately dropped flat. They watched as three fiery-winged demons slowly headed toward the hills. The demons were armed with long, wicked blades. The Doomguard watched the vicinity with equal wariness, but clearly had not noticed the party so far.

"They're heading toward where we must pass," Krasus realized.

"Should stop them now."

The mage nodded agreement, but added, "We need to know if there are more. We dare not take these three if it means giving warning to others in the area. Let me try to discover the truth, first."

Shutting his eyes, Krasus let his senses spread out toward the demons. Immediately he felt the darkness radiating from each, a darkness so repulsive that even the dragon was affected. Nonetheless, Krasus did not hesitate to delve deeper. The truth had to be known.

He saw within each the savageness and chaos that he had felt during previous incursions. That such evil could exist in any creature the mage still found hard to believe. It was a madness of sorts on par with that which had taken the once noble Neltharion and had created of him the foul Deathwing.

In the monstrous thoughts of the creatures he finally found what he needed to know. The three were scouts out on their own, seeking places of weakness of which the Legion might make use. They intended to not just confine the war to the battlefield, but also create fear behind the defenders.

Such tactics did not at all surprise Krasus. He was certain that Archimonde already had other plans in motion, which was why the quest to seize the Demon Soul was so important.

He scanned the area for other warriors, but found no trace. Satisfied Krasus ceased his probing.

"They are alone," he announced to Brox. "We will deal with them, but I think it best done with magic, this time."

The orc grunted in satisfaction. Krasus slipped down to wake Malfurion.

"What—" the night elf began. Krasus signaled him to silence.

"Three of the Doomguard," the elder mage whispered. "They are alone. I intend to take them, with your help."

Malfurion nodded. He followed Krasus around the stones to where they could see the hovering demons inspecting the hills.

"What should we do?" the druid asked.

"It would be best if I struck down all three simultaneously. However, their constant maneuvering means I might miscalculate. I leave it to you to deal with any who escapes me."

"All right." Taking a deep breath, Malfurion prepared. Krasus watched the Doomguard, waiting for the moment when they were nearest to one another.

Two of the demons paused to relate information to one another, but the third continued his observations. The mage silently swore, aware that he now had the best opportunity to destroy the pair. Yet, the third was so far away, Krasus feared that his attack would enable that one to flee.

Malfurion must have sensed his hesitation. "I won't let him escape, Master Krasus."

His words brought the mage much relief. Krasus nodded, concentrating.

Unlike Illidan—and even Rhonin at times—he had lived too long to waste effort creating elaborate displays out of his spellwork. The Doomguard were a threat and had to be dealt with. That was all. Thus it was that first one, then the other winged demon just *exploded*, their remnants quickly raining down on the landscape.

But as he had feared, the third escaped his trap. However, the demon's reprieve proved short-lived. As what was left of the first two creatures plummeted, Malfurion held up a single leaf and muttered to the wind. An intense breeze suddenly arose near the druid, a breeze that quickly took up the single leaf and carried it unerringly toward the remaining Doomguard.

The leaf suddenly became many leaves, hundreds of them. They whirled around in the wind, spinning faster and faster. They closed on the already-fleeing demon.

As each touched the Doomguard, they adhered to him. Scores and scores soon clung tightly to the demon, yet the numbers still swirling about looked no less. The horned warrior fought against the wind, but the ever-increasing weight upon him made his efforts falter.

In but seconds, the demon became a mummy wrapped in green. The wings slowed, unable to battle against that which so weighed them down.

Finally, the last of the Doomguard dropped like a rock.

Malfurion did not watch the demon strike the hard ground. He had done what had needed to be done, but never savored it.

"The way is clear," proclaimed Krasus. "But we must hurry, for it will take long to traverse the hills—"

From atop the rock, Brox suddenly called, "Something else in the sky! Above us!"

And mere seconds later, a shadow briefly covered them . . . a shadow sweeping over the entire area. The winged form moved so fast that it was lost among the clouds before any could identify it. The orc held his ax ready, while Krasus and Malfurion prepared spells.

Then the gargantuan form burst into the open again, diving directly for the trio. Its huge, leathery wings beat easily as it descended.

Krasus exhaled, his generally-somber expression breaking into a brief grin. "I should have known! I should have felt it!"

Korialstrasz had returned.

The mage's younger self landed just before the trio. The red dragon was magnificent to behold. His crest ran all the way to his tail. He was large enough to have swallowed the trio in one gulp, yet, despite his toothy maw, one had only to look into his eyes to see his intelligence and compassion.

Perhaps it was a bit narcissistic of Krasus to admire his earlier incarnation, but he could not help it. Korialstrasz had proven himself much more adept than the elder version ever remembered being. It was as if that they were two distinct creatures despite being one and the same.

Letting the dust settle, Korialstrasz greeted the three with a nod of his huge head. His eyes focused most on Krasus.

"A stroke of luck that I sensed some spellwork as I passed near," he rumbled. "My thoughts have been so caught up in other matters, I otherwise would not have noted your presence." To the mage, he added, "Not even yours."

That did not bode well. "You speak of your search for the others?"

"Yes . . . and I found them. They are seeking some manner by which to evade or deal with the Earth Warder's foul disk, but have not come up with any answer as of yet. Even my queen dares not face Neltharion unless they have some defense. You saw what happened to the blues! Slaughtered to extinction!"

Krasus thought of the eggs he had salvaged, but decided that this was not the time to deal with that matter. "Alexstrasza's concern has merit. There is no honor or purpose in flying out to simply be destroyed."

"But if we dragons do not aid the mortal races, there will be no hope for any of us!"

"There may be hope, though. You have not asked why we are to be found here." Krasus indicated the druid. "Young Malfurion has located the Earth Warder's hidden lair and knows where the Demon Soul is."

The crimson giant's reptilian eyes widened. "This is true? Perhaps an all-out assault while he slumbers—"

"Nay! This must be done with secrecy, cunning. We hope to slip in and steal the disk. Otherwise, Neltharion may take it first and then we are all dead."

Korialstrasz saw the wisdom of this, despite the perils inherent in the plan. "Where must you go?"

Malfurion described what he had seen in the Emerald Dream. Krasus had vaguely recognized the region and so it came as no surprise that his younger self did, also.

"I know it! A foul place! There is an evil there older than dragons, although what it might be I cannot say!"

"That is of no consequence at the moment. Only the Demon Soul is." The tall, pale figure eyed the hills. "And if we hope to even have an opportunity to steal it, we had best begin our journey. It will take the night sabers some time to traverse those hills."

"The night sabers?" Korialstrasz looked bewildered. "Why should you need them now that you have *me?*"

"You face the greatest risk of all," Krasus pointed out to the dragon. "You cannot change shape; therefore you remain a very visible target. More to the point, you are very susceptible to the Demon Soul. With one whim, the black could make you his slave."

"Nevertheless, I will do what I can. You need to reach his lair in a timely manner. The cats are not swift enough and you dare not attempt it by spell."

Arguing with oneself was pointless, Krasus saw. Korialstrasz would indeed enable them to reach their goal much sooner. However, once there, Krasus would insist that his younger version leave and leave quickly.

"Very well. Brox, prepare to turn the night sabers out. I will prepare a short missive for mine to carry. They will return to the host on their own and, hopefully, Rhonin will receive my word of our progress. Take what we can carry. No more."

It did not take them long to shift their belongings to the massive red. After the mage had secured the message to his cat, they sent the animals away. Krasus and his companions then mounted near the dragon's shoulders. Once they were all aboard, Korialstrasz shifted back and forth to make certain that his passengers were secure, then spread his wings.

"I will make haste . . . but with care," he promised them.

As they rose into the sky, Krasus grimly eyed the landscape ahead. Korialstrasz was a boon to them, but the success of their quest was in no manner assured now. Neltharion—Deathwing—would be on the watch for enemies, imagined or otherwise. The party would have to watch their every step once they reached his domain. Still, at least there was one thing in their favor.

So close to the dread one's lair, they certainly would not have to worry about any more demons.

SIX

L ord Desdel Stareye had a wonderful plan.

That was how he stated it to all concerned. He had designed it all himself, so it was foolproof. Most of his fellow nobles nodded eagerly and cheered him with goblets of wine held high while the rest simply kept their peace. The soldiers on the lines were too weary to worry and the refugees only cared about surviving. The few critics Stareye might have had now numbered but a handful, Rhonin chief among them. Unfortunately, the constant departures of Krasus had made even the commander's healthy fear of the outsiders dwindle. The moment it had even appeared that the human had been about to find fault with the grand design, Stareye had politely suggested that the council could manage its own efforts and that the wizard had other duties to which he should be attending. He had also doubled the guards in the tent, making it clear that, should Rhonin refuse his suggestion, they would act.

Not desiring a confrontation that would only threaten the stability of the host, Rhonin abandoned the tent. Jarod met him near where the tauren camped, Huln walking with the officer.

The night elf read his expression. "Something bad . . ."

"Maybe . . . or maybe I've just become too cynical where that pampered aristocrat is concerned. The overview of his plan sounds too simple to work . . ."

"Simple can be good," offered Huln, "if it is drawn from reason."

"Somehow, I doubt Stareye has reason. I don't understand why Ravencrest and he got along so well."

Jarod shrugged. "They are of the same caste."

"Oh, it all makes so much sense, then." When the night elf failed to note his sarcasm, Rhonin shook his head. "Never mind. We'll just have to watch out and hope for the best . . ."

They did not have to wait long. Stareye set his plan into motion before the sun set. The night elves redistributed their forces, creating three wedges. Following their lead, the tauren and other races did the same. The noble pulled back much of his cavalry, sending them around to the left flank. There they waited a short distance from the main host.

The front of each wedge was made up of pikes, followed by swords and other hand weapons. Behind those and protected from all angles were archers. Each wedge also included evenly-distributed members of the Moon Guard. The sorcerers were there to protect against the Eredar and other magic wielders.

The wedges were to drive forward as hard as they could, cutting into the Burning Legion's lines like teeth. Those demons caught between the wedges were to be the focus of the archers and sword wielders. The night elves were to move in concert, no wedge outreaching another. The cavalry were held in reserve to cover any weak points that developed.

There was some skepticism among the Earthen and the tauren, but, having no experience with large-scale military strategy themselves, they bowed to what they assumed was the night elves' superior knowledge.

Jarod rode beside Rhonin as the host moved forward. The demons had been uncommonly hesitant, an action that Stareye took as a good omen, but that the other two believed meant a need for more caution.

"I've talked to the Moon Guard," the wizard informed his companion. "We've a few tricks in mind that may make certain his lordship's plan comes to fruition. I'll be coordinating them."

"Huln promises that there will be no weakening from the tauren and I *think* the furbolg indicated something of the same," the captain replied. "I worry, though, if Dungard Ironcutter's people are enough to hold his part of the line."

"If they fight anything like a dwarf I know called Falstad did," commented Rhonin, thinking back. "They'll be the least of our problems."

At that moment, the battle horns sounded. The soldiers ahead immediately steeled themselves, increasing their pace.

"Be ready!" shouted the wizard, his cat picking up the pace.

"I wish I was back in Suramar before all this . . ."

The landscape ahead sloped downward, finally giving them a clear view of what lay ahead.

A sea of demons stretched all the way back to the horizon.

"Mother Moon!" Jarod gasped.

"Keep a grip on yourself!"

A trumpeter signaled the attack. With a lusty cry, the night elves started running. Deep roars from the right marked the tauren and furbolgs. A curious, wailing blast noted the Earthen's advance.

The battle was joined.

The Legion's front line almost immediately buckled under the intense assault. The wedges drove right into the demons. Scores of horned warriors fell to the pikes.

Jarod grew excited. "We're doing it!"

"We've got momentum, but it'll slow!"

Sure enough, after several yards in, the Burning Legion began to get its bearings. They did not completely stop the onslaught, but every new foot was bought slowly, painfully.

And yet, the night elves did continue to move forward.

That was not to say that there were not dangers or bad losses even in the beginning. A few Doomguard fluttered overhead, trying to get past the pikes and strike the archers. Some were brought down by their very targets, but others managed to keep aloft over the defenders. Armed with long maces and other weapons, they dove down, smashing skulls or gutting night elves occupied with other shots. However, under the onslaught of the archers and Moon Guard, they soon retreated.

At another point, the demon lines opened up to unleash a pair of Infernals against the wedge there. The soldiers attempting to block them were crushed and the wedge blunted, almost inverting. One Infernal was brought down by the Moon Guard, albeit not before several archers had perished. The other continued to wreak havoc among the night elves even after they managed to seal the break behind him.

Rhonin tried to focus on the lone demon, but there were too many soldiers around the creature. Every time the wizard thought that he could cast a spell, he took a risk of slaying several night elves.

From nowhere came three of the Earthen. The dwarves barreled their way through the ranks until they came upon the Infernal. Each of the squat but muscular figures carried war hammers with huge, steel heads.

The Infernal made a lunge, but missed. One dwarf slipped under and battered the stone monster's legs. Another came at the demon from the side. The Infernal managed a back-handed slap at his second attacker, but what would have killed a night elf, shattering his bones in the process, only shook the Earthen for a moment. The Infernal had finally come up against creatures with as hard a skin as his.

Now all three dwarves brought their hammers into play. Wherever they struck the demon, the heavy weapons left cracks and fissures. The left leg collapsed, forcing the Infernal down on one knee.

And the last Rhonin saw of the demon was all three Earthen bringing their hammers down on his head.

The wizard noticed Jarod Shadowsong riding back to him. Rhonin had not even known that the captain had disappeared. "Did you summon them?"

"I thought that they might have a better chance!"

Rhonin nodded his approval, then surveyed the battle again. Recovering from their brief setback, the host was once more pushing the Burning Legion back. The demons maintained a defiant look despite their forced retreat, but everything they did only briefly halted the night elves' determined progress.

"The damned thing's working after all," muttered the spellcaster. "Looks like I've underestimated his lordship."

"A good thing, Master Rhonin! I shudder to think what might've happened if it had failed!"

"There is that—" Rhonin let out a howl as an intense force seemed to try to crush his very brain. He tumbled off his mount before Jarod could grab him, striking the ground hard enough to jar his bones. Leaping down after him, the night elf tried to help the wizard rise.

Horrific pounding filled Rhonin's head. The sounds of

battle faded in the background. Through bleary eyes, he saw Jarod speaking, but no voice reached him.

Harder and harder the pounding grew. Through his agony, Rhonin understood that he had been attacked by some spell, yet this one had hit with more stealth than any in the past. Briefly the wizard thought of the Nathrezim, whose power had animated the dead, yet this did not feel like their work.

The agony became overwhelming. Rhonin struggled against the crushing sensation, but already knew that he was losing. He was near to blacking out and, if that happened, he feared he would never wake again.

In the midst of the attack, an emotionless voice echoed in his thoughts, *You cannot stand against me, mortal.*

The wizard needed no one to tell him who spoke. As Rhonin's strength at last failed and the blackness took him, the demon's name echoed through his fading senses.

Archimonde . . .

Jarod Shadowsong quickly dragged the still body back behind the lines. The night elf frantically studied Rhonin for some wound, but found nothing. The human was completely untouched, at least on the outside.

"Sorcery," he muttered. Jarod grimaced. A person of little talent in that direction, he had a healthy respect for spellcasters. Anything that could affect Rhonin had clearly originated from a powerful source. To him, that meant only the most powerful of the demons they so far faced, the one called Archimonde.

The fact that Archimonde had found the opportunity to seek out the wizard disturbed the captain very much. Archimonde should have been frantically busy trying to keep order among his retreating forces. Everywhere Jarod had looked, the Burning Legion had been close to crumbling. Lord Stareye's plan had proven a grand success—

The night elf's eyes widened.

Or *had* it?

Brox held on as tight as the others as Korialstrasz flew them toward their destination. The orc had lived in the time when the red dragons had been ruled by his people, but he had never flown on one himself. Now he reveled in the sensation and for the first time truly sympathized with the dragons who had been enslaved. To be so free, to live in the skies, only to be forced to die like dogs for the will of another . . . it was a fate to make any orc shudder. In fact, Brox felt some kinship with the dragons, for, in truth, his people had been slaves of a sort also, their most basic instincts twisted into something grotesque by a demon of the Burning Legion.

Once, Brox had simply wanted to die. Now, he was willing to face death, but death with purpose. He fought not just to defend his people in the far-off future, but to defend all whom the demons sought to crush. The spirits would decide if his life needed to be sacrificed, but Brox hoped that they would wait long enough for him to strike a few more decisive blows . . . and, especially, see that this quest was fulfilled.

The hills gave way to mountains, which at first reminded him of those near his home. However, the mountains soon changed and with them changed something in the air. The landscape turned desolate, as if life was afraid or unwilling to be in this place. Korialstrasz had mentioned an ancient evil and the orc, perhaps more attune to the world than most, felt that evil permeate everything. It was a foulness worse than that spread by the demons and made him want to reach for the ax strapped to his back.

The dragon suddenly descended between a pair of dank,

sharp peaks. Korialstrasz effortlessly glided through the narrow valleys, seeking a proper landing place.

He finally landed in the shadow of a particularly sinister mountain, one that reminded Brox of a monstrous warrior raising a heavy club for a strike. The harsh upper edge of the peak added to the already-prevalent feeling of being watched by dark powers.

"This is as close as I dare fly," the dragon informed his passengers as they dismounted. "But I will still follow along for a time."

"We aren't far," Malfurion commented. "I remember this area."

Krasus eyed the same peak that had so caught the orc's attention. "How could one not? A very appropriate abode for Deathwing."

"You've said that name before," the druid said. "And Rhonin, too."

"It is how we know the Earth Warder where we come from. His madness is well documented, is it not so, Brox?"

The veteran warrior grunted agreement. "My people also call him *Blood's Shadow* . . . but, yes, Deathwing is known to all living creatures, much to their dismay."

Malfurion shuddered. "How do we avoid being noticed? I only escaped detection because of what Cenarius had taught me, but we can't all journey to the Emerald Dream."

"Nor would there be any point," replied Krasus. "We could not touch the Demon Soul from that plane. We must be in this one. I know him best. I should be able to guard us from any warning spells. However, that will mean it will be up to you and Brox to do the rest."

"I'm willing."

"I, too." The orc hefted the magical ax. "I will cleave the black one's head from his neck if I must."

The mage chuckled, if briefly. "And there would be song to sing, would there not?"

At first, Korialstrasz led the way, the dragon making the finest defense of all, even in Brox's eyes. However, before long, the path grew narrower, until finally it was all the leviathan could do to squeeze through.

"You shall have to remain here," Krasus decided.

"I can climb up and around the mountains—"

"We are too close. Even if we manage to avoid the spells, I would not put it past Deathwing to post sentinels. They would see you."

Against this logic, the dragon could not argue. "I await you, here, then. You have but to summon me at your need." His reptilian eyes narrowed. "Even if it is to face *him.*"

At first, the loss of Korialstrasz made a marked difference in the mood of the party. The trio moved on with more care, watching every corner and shadow. Malfurion pointed out more and more landmarks, indicating just how near they had come to their goal. Brox, who now led the way, stared at every rock in their path, determining whether or not it hid some foe.

Day gave way to night and although now Malfurion could see better, they paused to sleep. The druid felt certain that they were nearly at the lair, which made rest an anxious time even for Brox.

As the orc settled in for first watch, Krasus admonished him. "We take our turns fairly, this time. We will need all of us at our peak of strength."

Reluctantly agreeing, the graying orc hunkered down. His sharp ears soon registered the even breathing of his companions, a sign that slumber had quickly taken them. He also registered other sounds, although few in comparison to most places he had visited during his hard life. This was truly an empty land. The wind wailed and now and then bits of rock crumbled free from some mountainside, but, beyond that, there was almost nothing.

In that stillness, Brox began to relive the last days of his first war against the demons. He saw his comrades cheerfully speaking of the carnage they would cause, of the enemy who would fall to their axes. Many of them had expected to die, but what a death it would be.

No one had expected the events that followed.

For long after, Brox had believed that he was haunted by his dead companions. Now, though, the aging fighter knew that they did not condemn him, but rather stood at his side, guiding his arm. They lived through him, every enemy dead another honoring their memories. Someday, it would be Brox who fell, but, until then he was their champion.

That knowledge made him proud.

Long used to such tasks as he performed now, Brox knew exactly how much time passed. Already half his watch was over. He contemplated letting the others sleep, but was aware of Krasus's warning. For all the orc's experience, he was an infant compared to the mage. Brox would obey . . . this time.

Then, a sound that was not the wind caught his attention. He focused on it, his expression hardening as he recognized what it was. Chattering, high-pitched voices. They were far away, only a chance shifting of the wind enabling him to hear them. The orc quickly straightened, trying to identify exactly where the speakers were.

At last, Brox eyed a small side passage some hundred paces or so to the north. The voices had to come from somewhere further in. With the silence of a skilled hunter, he left his post to investigate. There was no need as of yet to wake his companions. In this unsettling place, it was still possible that what he heard was only an effect of the wind blowing through the ancient mountains.

As he neared the passage, the chattering ceased. The orc immediately paused, waiting. After a moment, the talk continued. Brox finally had a fair notion of just what he was listening to and that only made him more cautious as he continued on.

With practiced ears, the orc tried to count the speakers. Three, four at the most. Better than that, he could not say.

Other sounds assailed him. Digging. There would be no dwarves here.

Brox crept up slowly and silently to where the unknown party had to lurk. Clearly, whoever they were, they did not expect others in the region, which gave him a distinct advantage.

A small light illuminated the area just ahead. Brox peered around a bend . . . and beheld the goblins.

Compared to an orc, they were tiny, bony creatures with big heads. Other than their sharp teeth and small, pointed nails, there was little about them that seemed any threat. However, Brox understood just how dangerous goblins could be, especially when there was more than one. They were cunning and quick, their wiry frames able to dart past a larger opponent with ease. One could not trust a goblin to do no harm unless that goblin was dead.

Malfurion had mentioned goblins—scores of goblins—working on something for the black dragon. They had even apparently been integral in Deathwing's creation of the Demon Soul. Brox could only assume that these were a part of that group, but, if so, what were they doing out here?

"More, more!" muttered one. "Not enough for another plate!"

"The vein's tapped out!" snapped a companion who was

almost identical to the first. To a third, he argued, "Gotta find another, another!"

The digging came from a small tunnel in the nearest mountain. The goblin version of a mine. Even as Brox watched, a fourth creature joined the others. In one hand, he held a covered oil lamp and behind him the newcomer dragged a sack almost as large as his body. Goblins were small but extremely strong for their size.

Unlike the others, he seemed in a good mood. "Found another small vein! More iron!"

The rest brightened. "Good!" said the first. "No time to go hunting! Let the others do it!"

Brox's first instinct was to go charging in, but he knew that was not what Krasus would want. The orc eyed the goblins. They looked as if they would be busy for some time. He could return to the mage and tell him what he had found. Krasus would know the right thing to do, be it capture the goblins or avoid them completely—

A heavy force battered him on the back of the skull, sending the orc to his knees. Something landed on his back, clutching his throat. Again, Brox was struck hard on the back of his head.

"Intruder! Help! Intruder!"

The high-pitched voice cut through the fog of his pain. Another goblin had come up from behind. Goblin fists were not that large, so Brox could only assume that he had been hit with either a hammer or a rock.

The orc attempted to rise, but the goblin continued to pound at him. Blood trickled down Brox's head to his mouth. The taste of his own life fluids stirred the warrior to urgency. Still kneeling, he rolled over.

There was a squawk and then the heavy orc landed on something that squirmed. The beating finally halted. Brox continued rolling and felt the goblin lose the last of his grip.

As he pushed himself up, the warrior heard other goblin voices near him. What he assumed was another rock hit his shoulder hard. Brox heard metal drawn and knew that the goblins had knives.

He blindly reached for his ax, but could not find it. Before the orc could clear his sight, a shrieking figure leapt on his chest, almost throwing him back. With arm and legs, the goblin clutched him tight while trying to bury a blade in his eye.

As Brox battled to keep the knife from him, a second attacker landed on his shoulder. The orc grunted as a blade edged his ear. Managing to reach up, Brox tore the creature from his shoulder and threw him as far as possible. As the goblin's scream trailed off, the fighter sought again to pull the one away from his chest.

He almost had it done when both his legs were seized. Brox raised one foot, bringing it down hard. With immense satisfaction, the orc heard bone crunch. The grip on that leg ceased. Unfortunately, when he repeated the maneuver with the other, the goblin there shifted position while still holding tight.

The one on his chest managed to sink his knife into Brox's shoulder. The fiendish creature giggled as he raised the weapon.

Enraged, the orc swung a meaty fist, hitting the goblin square in the side of the head. The giggle cut off, replaced by a short gurgle before the goblin went tumbling away.

But, again, Brox received no reprieve. A new attacker crashed into his stomach, driving the air from his lungs. Brox fell back. The only benefit to his disaster was marked by a squeal from the goblin on his leg. Half-crushed by the weight of the warrior's limb, the creature lost his hold.

A second goblin leapt atop the fallen orc, beating at him

with a rock. This was hardly the noble death in battle Brox had imagined for himself. He did not recall any orc in any of the great epics being brought down by goblins.

Then the pair on his chest shrieked as a red light threw them across the area. One collided with another goblin, ending in a tangle of limbs, while the second smashed hard against the rocks.

"Make certain that we have them all!" the orc heard Krasus demand.

Shaking his head, Brox managed to focus in time to see the two tangled goblins suddenly sink into the once solid ground. Their cries were cut off the moment their heads vanished beneath.

Another of the creatures, either smarter or more arrogant than the rest, threw a rock with unerring aim at the side of the mage's head. Already aware that it was too late, Brox still opened his mouth to warn Krasus—and watched the rock not only not strike the slim figure, but bounce back with such velocity that when it hit the goblin, it cracked his skull.

The hair on the back of the orc's neck rose. Reacting instinctively, Brox swung behind him. The goblin about to stab him in the back tumbled to the earth.

Krasus remained fixed, eyes now shut tight. Brox gingerly got to his feet, trying not to make any sound that would disturb the spellcaster.

"None escaped . . ." Krasus murmured after a moment. His eyes opened and he studied the carnage. "We caught them all."

Locating his ax, the orc bowed his head in regret. "Forgive me, elder one. I acted like an untrained child."

"It is over, Brox . . . and you may have given us a shortcut to our destination." His hand glowing, Krasus touched the warrior lightly on the shoulder, healing Brox's wounds as if they were nothing.

Relieved that he had not entirely shamed himself, Brox looked at the mage in curiosity. Malfurion, too, eyed Krasus, but with more understanding.

"They know how best to reach the dragon's lair," Krasus explained, hand glowing again. "They can show us the way."

Brox gazed around. Of the goblins he could see, all appeared dead. Then he saw the one who had struck the rocks rise awkwardly. At first, the weary orc wondered how the creature had survived such an impact—and realized swiftly that he had not.

"We are the servants of Life," Krasus whispered with clear distaste, "which means we know Death equally well."

"By the Mother Moon . . ." Malfurion gasped.

Muttering a prayer to the spirits, Brox stared at the animated corpse. It reminded him too much of the Scourge. Without realizing it, he kept his ax tight in case the goblin should attack.

"Rest easy, my friends. I am only resurrecting the memories of his path. He will walk it, then that will be the end of the matter. I am no Nathrezim, to relish in the binding of corpses to do my will." He gestured at the dead goblin, who, after performing a haphazard turn, began shambling north. "Now, come! Let us be done with this distasteful business and prepare ourselves for entrance into the sanctum of the dark one . . ."

Krasus calmly walked behind his macabre puppet. After a moment, Malfurion followed. Brox hesitated, then, recalling the evil that they all faced, nodded approval at the mage's necessary course of action and joined the others.

SEVEN

Archimonde watched his warriors forced back on all fronts. He watched as they died by the dozens on the blades of the defenders or ripped apart by the night elves' feline mounts. He noted the scores more perishing under the brute force of the other creatures who had allied themselves with the host.

Archimonde watched it all . . . and smiled. They were without the wizard, without the druid and the mage . . . even without the brawny, green-skinned fighter whose base fury the demon found admirable.

"It is time . . ." he hissed to himself.

Jarod continued to try to wake Rhonin, but the wizard would not respond. The only response that the human had given thus far had been to open his eyes, but they were eyes that did not see, did not even hint of a mind behind them.

But still he tried. "Master Rhonin! You must stir! Something's amiss, I know it!" The captain sprinkled water over the red-haired spellcaster's face. It trickled off with no effect. "The demon lord's up to something!"

Then, a peculiar noise caught his attention. It reminded

Jarod of when he had used to watch flocks of birds landing in the trees. The fluttering of many wings echoed in his ears.

He looked up.

The sky was filled with Doomguard.

"Mother Moon . . ."

Each of the flying demons carried a burden in their arms, a heavy pot from which smoke trailed. The pots were far larger and heavier than any night elf could have borne and even the Doomguard appeared hardpressed to keep them, but keep them they did.

Jarod Shadowsong studied the swarm, watching how they flew as hard as they could for the defenders' lines . . . and then went beyond. Below, it was doubtful that many even noticed them, so ferocious was the fighting. Even Lord Stareye likely saw only the dying demons before him.

The noble had to be warned. It was the only thing that made sense to Jarod. There was no one else. Krasus was gone.

Seizing Rhonin's body, the captain dragged it over to a large rock. He positioned the wizard on the opposing side, away from the view of the battlefield. Hopefully, no one would see the robed figure there.

"Please . . . please forgive me," the soldier asked the unmoving form.

Jarod leapt onto his mount and headed for where he had last seen the noble's banner. But just as he left the area where he had secreted Rhonin, the foremost of the Doomguard suddenly hovered over the night elves. The captain saw the first one tip over his pot.

A boiling, red liquid poured down on the unsuspecting soldiers.

Their screams were awful. Most of those upon whom the deadly rain had fallen dropped writhing. From the single pot, nearly a score of night elves had been burned and maimed, some mortally.

And then the other winged demons began turning over their own containers.

"No . . ." he gasped. "No!"

A deluge of death washed over the defenders.

Rank upon rank of soldiers broke into utter chaos as each fought to protect themselves from the horror. They had stood up to blades and claws—dangers that could be battled with a weapon—but against the scalding horror unleashed by the Doomguard, there was nothing to be done.

The cries ringing in his head, Jarod urged his mount to its swiftest. He sighted Stareye's banner, then, after a few tense moments, the noble himself.

What Jarod saw gave him no heart. The slim night elf sat atop his cat, his expression aghast. Desdel Stareye sat as if dead in the saddle. He watched the destruction of his grand plan with no obvious intention of doing anything to try to salvage the situation. Around him, his staff and guards stared helplessly at their commander. Jarod read no hope in their faces.

Managing to maneuver his night saber closer, the captain pushed past stunned guards and a noble with shaking hands to reach the commander. "My lord! My lord! Do something! We need to bring down those demons!"

"It's too late, too late!" babbled Stareye, not looking at him. "We're all doomed! It's the end of everything!"

"My lord—" Some inner sense caused Jarod to look sky-ward.

A pair of demons hovered above, their pots still filled.

Seizing the noble's arm, Jarod shouted, "Lord Stareye! Move! Quickly!"

The other night elf's expression hardened and he pulled

his arm away in disdain. "Unhand me! You forget yourself, captain!"

Jarod stared incredulously at Stareye. "My lord—"

"Away with you before I have you clapped in irons!"

Knowing he could do nothing to convince the noble otherwise, Jarod reined hard, forcing his mount away.

It was all that saved him.

The torrent that washed over Stareye and the others seared flesh and melted metal. In its death throes, Stareye's night saber threw his sizzling body off. The noble landed in a monstrous heap, his arrogant features now a mangled horror nigh unrecognizable. His companions and guards fared little better; those that were not horridly slain lay twitching, their bodies ruined, their screams enough to chill the soul.

And Jarod could do nothing for them.

The Doomguard flew overhead all but untouched by the defenders. Sporadic fire from an archer here and there brought down a few, and some perished in manners that clearly had the touch of the Moon Guard on them, but there was no cohesive effort. Jarod found the lack of organization stunning, then recalled that Stareye had replaced all of his predecessor's officers with his own sycophants.

More incomprehensible, there were even some elements of the night elf forces not yet in play. They anxiously stood by, awaiting commands that would never be given. Jarod realized that they did not know that Lord Stareye was dead and likely thought the noble would be calling upon them at any moment.

He quickly rode up to one contingent. The officer in charge saluted him.

"How many bows do you have?" Jarod asked.

"Threescore, captain!"

Hardly enough, but at least a start. "Get every bow set! I want them trained on those Doomguard now! The rest create a defensive square for them!"

The other night elf gave the order. Jarod looked around desperately for something else to use. Instead, another rider came racing up to *him*. The newcomer saluted in a manner that indicated immediately that Jarod was the first thing resembling an officer that he had seen.

"The wedge is flattened, the line barely holding by us!" He pointed behind himself to a location near the middle. "Lord Del'theon is dead and we've only a subofficer in charge! He sent me to find out someone to strengthen us!"

By this time, the troops that Jarod had taken over had already arranged themselves. Even as the captain considered what to do about the new problem, he saw almost a dozen Doomguard drop from the sky. It gave him a slight hint of hope, at least.

To the newcomer, he finally suggested, "Ride to the tauren! Tell them Captain Shadowsong asks of the people of Huln for some warriors to come with you and strengthen the wedge!" Jarod recalled something else, "Ask also for their their best archers . . ."

When he had finished, the other night elf, his own expression slightly less distraught, rode off to obey. Jarod barely had time to refocus his thoughts before two more came. The captain could only guess that he had been seen organizing resistance and that someone had foolishly believed he spoke in the name of the dead Stareye.

But despite knowing better, Jarod could not simply turn them away. He listened to their needs and battled to find some solution, however temporary.

To his surprise, one of the Moon Guard arrived shortly after. Although clearly one of the senior spellcasters, the robed figure looked relieved to confront Captain Shadow-song.

"The archers are slowing the damage the winged fiends have been causing! We've been able to reorganize, though three of our number are dead and two more are incapacitated! We are trying to deal with those above and the warlocks in the distance, but to do so we'll need more protection!"

Jarod tried not to swallow. Hoping to avoid showing the sorcerer his uncertainty, he pretended to glance further down the left flank. There he saw several rows of soldiers milling about as they tried to reach the oncoming demons. The press of bodies in front of them prevented those in back from being of any benefit and, in fact, often shoved the ones ahead into the blades of their foe.

He pulled one soldier from the square. "You! Ride with him over there and take a squad from those ranks! Tell the rest to keep back a step and shore up the front lines as needed!"

On and on the demands came. They never allowed Jarod to catch his breath. There came a point when even the Earthen and the other allies began requesting his assistance. Jarod, never able to find someone of greater authority, ever answered their questions and prayed that he had not sent innocent lives to the slaughter.

At any moment, the captain expected to see the horde overwhelm his people, but somehow, the night elves held. The combined efforts of the Moon Guard and archers at last proved too decimating for the winged demons and they fled back, many still with the pots full. The host's casualties had been high, but as matters quieted a little, Jarod hoped that something he had done had kept them from being higher yet.

When the captain finally had the opportunity to return to Rhonin, it was with half a dozen subordinates in tow. He had not asked for them; various officers in the host had insisted they stay with Jarod in case he needed to alert them to some need. The former Guard officer found their presence unsettling, for they treated him as if he were on par with either Ravencrest or Stareye. Jarod Shadowsong was no noble and certainly no commander; if the host had managed to recover from the near disaster, it was due mainly to the fighters themselves.

To his tremendous relief, the wizard was alive and untouched. Unfortunately, he still did not seem to see or hear anything despite looking as if awake.

Jarod tried once more to give him water, but to no avail. Frustrated, he turned to one of the soldiers and snapped, "Find me one of the senior Moon Guard! Hurry!"

Yet, it was not one of the sorcerers who came back with the rider, but rather a pair of figures clad in the armor of the Sisterhood of Elune. Worse, the senior priestess was none other than Maiev.

"When I was told that the officer in command needed a spellcaster, I never dreamed he was speaking of you, little brother!"

Captain Shadowsong had no time for his sister's dominant tone. "Spare me the wit, Maiev! The wizard's caught in some spell that I think one of the master demons cast! Can Elune help free him?"

She eyed him curiously for a moment, then knelt beside Rhonin. "I've never dealt with one of his kind, but I assume he's similar enough to us that the Mother Moon will grant me the chance. Jia, assist me. We shall see what we can do."

The second priestess stepped over to Rhonin's other side. The two raised hands to chest level with the palms out, then

pressed their fingertips together. The moment the priestesses touched one another, a faint, silver glow arose from
their hands. It quickly spread along their arms and around
the rest of their bodies.

Maiev and her companion began chanting. Their words
made no sense to Jarod, but he knew that the Sisterhood of
Elune had a special language of their own that they used to
commune with the lunar deity.

The glow surrounding the females flowed over the wizard. His body jerked slightly, then relaxed.

Another rider joined the group. "Where's the commander?"

Several of the past messengers had called Jarod by that
very title despite his constant insistence that they do no such
thing. Angered by the interruption at so delicate a time, he
spun around and blurted, "You'll keep your mouth shut and
wait until I tell you it's the right time to speak—"

The mounted figure's eyes widened. Only at that point
did the captain see the gold and emerald trim on the shoulders or the emblem on the breast plate.

Jarod had insulted a noble.

But instead of taking offense, the rider nodded in apology
and quieted. In an attempt to hide his shock, Jarod quickly
turned back to watch his sister's work.

Maiev was sweating. The second priestess shook. Rhonin's
body quivered and his already-pale flesh looked as white as
the moon.

The wizard jolted to a sitting position. His mouth opened
wide in a silent scream—and then, for the first time since
being struck down, Rhonin blinked.

A groan escaped the human. He would have slumped
back against the rock, possibly striking his head, but the captain acted, managing to thrust a hand in between.

With a sigh, the wizard closed his eyes. His breathing grew regular.

"Is he—?"

"He's free of the demon's hold, brother," Maiev replied somewhat shakily. "He will rest as long as he needs." She rose. "It was a hard struggle, but Elune was generous, praise be."

"Thank you."

Again, his sister eyed him with curiosity. "No thanks are necessary from *you* of all people. Come, Jia. There are many in need of healing."

Jarod followed Maiev's departure, then turned his attention back to the noble. "Forgive me, my lord, but—"

The rider waved off his words. "My troubles can wait. I failed to see that you sought aid for the foreign sorcerer. I am Lord Blackforest. I know you, don't I?"

"Jarod Shadowsong, my lord."

"Well, Commander Shadowsong, I, for one, am grateful you didn't perish along with Lord Stareye and the others. There were reports you tried to save him even in the end."

"My lord—"

Blackforest ignored his interruption. "I'm trying to gather some of the others. Stareye's strategy was clearly inept, may the Mother Moon forgive any slight toward the dead. We hope to come up with something better—if we're to survive. You'll want to be there, of course. To guide matters, I assume."

This time, Jarod could not speak. He nodded, more out of reflex than anything. The noble apparently took this as determined agreement and gratefully nodded back.

"With your permission, then, I'll have things arranged at my tent and begin gathering the rest." Blackforest nodded once more, then turned his mount around and rode off.

"Looks—looks like—you've come up in the world," a voice rasped.

He glanced down to see Rhonin conscious. The wizard still looked pale, but not so much as before. Jarod quickly bent down and gave him water from a sack. Rhonin eagerly drank.

"I'd feared that the spell had done damage to your mind. How fare you, Master Rhonin?"

"I feel as if a regiment of Infernals are battering my skull from the inside . . . and that's an improvement." The human sat up straight. "I gather there was trouble after I was struck down."

The captain told him, keeping it as brief as possible and downplaying his role. Despite that, however, the wizard looked at Jarod in obvious admiration.

"Looks like Krasus was right about you. You did more than save the day, this time. You likely saved the world, at least for the moment."

Cheeks darkening, the night elf vehemently shook his head. "I am no leader, Master Rhonin! All I did was try to survive."

"Well, nice of you to help the rest of us survive while you were at it. So, Stareye's dead. Sorry for him, not so sorry for the host. Glad to see some of the nobles have come to their senses. Maybe there's hope yet."

"Surely you don't think I'm going to meet with them?" Jarod had a vision of Blackforest and the others surrounding him, their eyes all staring. "I'm only a Guard officer from Suramar!"

"Not anymore . . ." The wizard tried to rise, finally signaling his companion to help him. As he straightened, Rhonin met Jarod's gaze. The human's unique eyes seized his. "Not anymore."

•   •   •

Korialstrasz had not yet learned the patience of his elder counterpart, Krasus, and so it was that he began to fidget. The red dragon knew well that it would be some time before the party would return—assuming that they *did* return—and although he tried to find peace during his wait, he could not. There were too many things running through his thoughts. Alexstrasza, the Burning Legion, the implications of Krasus's presence, and more. He also recalled too well the punishment he had taken at Neltharion's paws. Now his other self was fast approaching the sanctum of that fiend and there was more than a little concern that Krasus might fall prey to the Demon Soul.

In frustration, the red giant began scratching at the mountainside with one talon. Massive chunks of stone and earth that were no more than pebbles to the dragon dropped into the valley below. This, however, entertained Korialstrasz only for an hour. More agitated than ever, he started eyeing the dark sky and wondering if perhaps it was safe to take to the air for a few minutes.

A low roar echoed through the mountains.

All frustration thrust aside, a now alert Korialstrasz slipped down from his perch, planting his huge body on the side of the peak. He peered up, seeking the source of the sound.

A dark form slowly flew overhead. A small black dragon. The pace at which the other leviathan flew marked him as a sentinel.

Korialstrasz quietly hissed. Had the other simply been flying off somewhere, there would have been no cause for worry. However, that the black prowled this particular region meant danger to the plan.

Yet, he was crossed up as to whether he should remain

hidden or seek out the guardian. If the others had not been noticed, then attacking the black might prove a fatal mistake. The sentinel could escape and warn his master. Then again, if left alone, the other dragon might discover Krasus and the rest, anyway, on his return flight.

Korialstrasz clutched the mountainside tight as he attempted to come to some quick conclusion. If the black flew too far away, the red might not be able to catch up to him—

The rock face under his claws gave way.

Caught unaware, Korialstrasz tumbled from the mountain as the entire side collapsed. The dragon instinctively spread his wings and righted himself, suffering only a few hard pelts from the massive avalanche he had inadvertently caused. He shook his head, clearing his tangled thoughts.

The roar in his ears was the only warning he had before the black struck him from behind.

Despite being slightly smaller, Korialstrasz's attacker hit with powerful fury. The red was thrust toward the jagged ground at a ferocious speed. His left wing scraped painfully against the rocks.

Korialstrasz managed to stretch one forepaw against another peak, digging his claws deep. His momentum tore tons of rock from the other mountain, but slowed his descent enough to give him time to think. The red dragon tipped to one side, startling his foe and causing the black to lose hold.

As the second dragon tumbled back, Korialstrasz righted himself. He tried to rise up again, but his adversary still had one pair of claws on his back. The added weight made the strain terrible, but Korialstrasz would not give in.

Flapping as hard as he could, he twisted in mid-air. Using his tail, the red swung his rival against the nearest peak.

The black collided hard, sending a storm of rock below.

His claws came free, but not before tearing off several scales. Korialstrasz roared. He felt blood trickle down his leg.

For a moment, both giants forgot the battle as they recovered from their injuries. Then, Korialstrasz's foe made a lunge for his neck. The larger dragon got his wing up in time, literally batting away the black.

The strike knocked the last bit of fight out of Neltharion's servant. With a last defiant roar, the ebony leviathan veered away from Korialstrasz.

"No!" Now that they had joined in battle, he dared not let the other dragon flee. The sentinel would alert his master, who would, in turn, suspect that more than a single red dragon lurked in the vicinity.

The black was smaller and, therefore, very swift, but Korialstrasz was sleek and cunning. As his adversary slipped around a passage, Korialstrasz took a different route. He had spent enough time staring at the landscape while he waited to know where some of the different valleys remerged.

Through the mountains, he flew. Ahead, the left side of a fork offered an enticing turn, but Korialstrasz knew that it was the one favoring the right that would lead him back to his quarry.

In the distance, he heard the hard flapping of his enemy's wings. The red dragon grew concerned. He should have passed the other by this point, but the sound gave indication that the black one was instead widening the gap.

Pushing himself to his limits, Korialstrasz neared the point he had been seeking. Only a short distance more. He could not hear the flapping, but felt certain that he had finally gotten ahead.

He crossed back into the other valley—

There was a near collision of wings. Both dragons roared, more from surprise than fury. Korialstrasz spun around twice and the black dragon rammed sideways into a small peak, shattering the top.

But momentum was now with the smaller of the two. The black pushed ahead, regaining precious air.

Shaking his head and damning his poor luck, Korialstrasz pursued. He *would* catch the other dragon, no matter what it took. Too much had already been lost in this struggle . . .

His determination hardened, Korialstrasz roared once more and continued the chase.

But in pursuing the obvious, the red leviathan had missed something smaller below. Eyes watched—those who had eyes, that is—as the two huge beasts vanished in the distance.

"An impressive aerial display, don't you think, Captain Varo'then?"

The scarred night elf snorted. "A fair enough fight, though too short."

"And not enough bloodshed for you, I'd wager."

"Never enough," responded Azshara's servant. "But more than enough prattle, *Master* Illidan. Is *this* proof we're close at last?"

Illidan casually adjusted the scarf across his ruined eyes. For him, the battle between two such titans had been far more interesting, for these great creatures were of magic origins and so the sky had been filled with astonishing energies and brilliant colors. Malfurion's brother had come to admire his new senses, they revealing to him a world such as he had never realized existed.

"I'd think that obvious, captain, although don't you find it interesting to have not only a black dragon but a red one near here? Why do you suppose the second was in this area?"

"You said it yourself. This is a place where the beasts live."

The sorcerer shook his head. "I said this was where we'd find the lair of the huge black one. That red was here for a specific reason."

Varo'then's marred face grew uglier as he realized just what his companion meant. "The other dragons want the disk! Makes the only sense!"

"Yes . . ." Illidan urged his mount along, the officer following. Behind them marched the demon warriors. "But they'd be so easily caught. You saw how they were beaten." He considered further. "I think I recognized the markings on that red."

"What of it? All those beasts are the same!"

"Spoken like a Highborne." Illidan rubbed his chin as he mused. "No, I think that *is* the one I've met . . . and if that's so, we might just have some familiar company ahead."

EIGHT

Malfurion watched the goblin wend his way through the narrowing cracks and while he understood that Krasus had needed to animate the body, it still unnerved him. Even the mage's reassurance that this was a spell little used and even less desired by his kind did not completely assuage the night elf.

Yet, he gave no outer sign of his emotions save to stand as far as he could from the creature. Curiously, the goblin's movements grew more adept as time passed, almost to the point where he seemed to have actually come back to life.

To the druid's surprise, it was Krasus who first mouthed what the others had been long thinking.

"How much farther?" muttered the pale, robed figure. "This abuse of the tenets of life disgusts me more and more . . ."

As if in answer, the goblin suddenly bent over. Malfurion glanced at Krasus, thinking that perhaps the mage had become so sick of what he had been doing that he had finally just released the body from the spell. However, the contemplative expression his companion wore said otherwise.

"Watch . . ." Krasus murmured. "Watch . . ."

The animated goblin touched a stone lying near the base of the mountain. To Malfurion's eyes, the stone appeared to be just a random one that had no doubt fallen from the peak some time back.

Yet, as soon as the creature turned it slightly to the right, the entire rock face shimmered—and more than half of it disappeared.

Brox let out a grunt. Krasus nodded.

"Very cunning," he remarked. "Look, where once there was stone, to the left is now a narrow passage cut through the peak itself."

They followed their macabre guide for several more minutes, then Krasus suddenly had the goblin come to a halt.

"Listen . . ."

Somewhere far away, they heard the chitter of goblin voices and the constant hammering of metal.

The druid stiffened. "We've reached it."

"And so we can put an end to this obscenity . . ." Krasus waved his hand and the goblin turned. The animated figure crawled over a rock, vanishing from sight. A moment later, the dragon mage made a cutting action. "He will be found . . . but after we are through here."

Krasus started forward, but Malfurion suddenly seized his arm. "Wait," the druid whispered. "You can't go in there."

He was rewarded with a rare glimpse of the mage caught off guard. Krasus stared deep. "You have a reason for saying this at such a late hour?"

"I didn't think of it until a short time ago. Krasus, of all of us, he'll notice you easiest. You're one of his own kind. He'll be expecting the dragons to try to steal the Demon Soul away from him."

"But my kind is most susceptible and so we would be

more likely to stay far from it. Besides, I have shielded myself well."

Nodding, Malfurion continued, "And your kind also has the most to lose while the disk is still his. It behooves the dragons to at least try . . . and that's what the Earth Warder will think, too. Inside, he'll surely be on guard for any dragon magic, especially such shields."

"And he is an *Aspect* . . ." The slim figure pursed his lips. Malfurion expected Krasus to eloquently explain why the night elf's thinking was incorrect, but, at last, the robed mage replied, "You speak the truth. We would try and he would expect us to try. I know him well. It is something I should have considered earlier, but I suspect I wanted so badly to ignore it. I am fortunate enough to have come this far, but his lair will surely be arranged so as to trap any dragon other than his own."

"As I thought."

"Which does not mean that you and Brox will have it any easier," Krasus reminded him. "Yet, the audacity of two of the lesser races sneaking through his very sanctum might slip by him, if just barely."

"Brox should stay with you."

"No, the orc is better suited to assisting you. There are many physical dangers, least of which are far more goblins than what we've come across. You will need to concentrate on securing the Demon Soul and, while I will assist as much as I can from out here, someone must watch your back inside."

"No one will harm him," rumbled Brox. He hefted the ax and grinned. "Make me a good song, elder one?"

Krasus gave a rare smile. "I will begin composing it the moment we are rid of this place."

Unable to come up with any other argument as to why he

should enter alone, Malfurion accepted the orc's company. In truth, the night elf was glad to have him. Brox's sturdy demeanor and powerful arm made stepping into the dragon's lair a little less daunting.

A little.

But Malfurion knew that it had to be done and he believed that he had the best chance. It was no sense of ego that drove him, only some feeling that all he had studied somehow made him the proper choice.

It was decided that Brox would initially lead the way, with Malfurion taking over when he began to recognize his surroundings. Brox harnessed his ax for the beginning, the passage too narrow for proper use of the huge weapon. Instead, the orc drew a long dagger, which he wielded with clear expertise.

"I will keep watch from here," Krasus promised as they departed. "I can at least do that without the black one noticing."

It was fortunate for them that the goblins used the tunnel to bring raw materials in or else even Malfurion would have had trouble fitting inside. As it was, Brox had to keep his arms close to his body most of the time. The orc held the dagger in front of him, watching and listening.

The sounds ahead grew more incessant. Malfurion hoped that such a racket would work to their advantage. If the goblins were distracted by the noise they created, they might not notice the pair.

A dim light ahead finally illuminated the curving tunnel. Brox visibly tensed. Malfurion put a hand on his shoulder.

"If I'm correct," the druid whispered. "When we entered the caverns, the passage that the dragon took should be to the left."

Brox grunted understanding and led on. Their path grew brighter and the noise began to reach manic levels.

The sight that met their eyes was even more chaotic than what Malfurion had earlier witnessed. There were at least twice as many goblins as before and all scurried about as if their very lives depended upon it . . . likely the truth. Several worked to break down huge piles of raw ore, while others tossed fuel into the towering furnaces. Through a system of massive pots on moving chains, an unceasing flow of molten metal poured into gargantuan molds. Beyond that, vast vats of water awaited those molds that had already been filled. Sweating goblins bathed in steam worked to secure one mold already set in a vat.

Far to the pair's right, two massive plates already forged lay discarded, previous attempts that had failed. There were fine cracks in the metal, making them useless for whatever task the dragon desired them.

"I still don't understand what they want with all this," muttered Malfurion. "Does the dragon plan a suit of armor for himself?"

The orc's brow crushed together. "With that one, could be anything . . ."

Tearing himself from the enigma, the night elf studied their left. Sure enough, a path ran along the edge toward a gargantuan passage, the same one he recalled Neltharion using.

"There! We follow along there!"

Brox nodded, but kept Malfurion from stepping out of the tunnel. "Goblins below. Must wait."

The creatures in question toiled at removing rubble left over from the ore. The druid studied the progress of the work and quickly realized that the goblins would be there much too long.

"We need them away or distracted, Brox . . ."

"Spell, maybe."

Malfurion considered the contents of his belt pouches,

then studied the cavern. There were a couple of things that might just work—

But as he reached into one pouch, the monstrous voice of Neltharion shook the huge chamber. "Meklo! I have returned! This next shall work or I will dine on every miserable one of your kind . . . with you as my appetizer!"

From the far side of the chamber, the aproned goblin whom Malfurion had seen previous suddenly came running. He kicked several of those working, urging them to greater speed, then trotted toward the tall passage. All the while he muttered to himself what Malfurion's sharp ears thought were more calculations.

But even before Meklo could reach the tunnel, from out of it burst the black dragon.

An oath escaped Brox—who had not seen how the transformation had even more consumed Neltharion—but, fortunately, it was drowned out by the giant's bellowing.

"Meklo! You misbegotten get of a worm! My good patience is at an end! Have you the new plates or not?"

"Two! Two, my lord! See? See?" He gestured to where several workers toiled to remove a pair of the gargantuan pieces of metal from their molds. Despite the water vats, they still sizzled with residual heat, enough to burn someone badly.

"Stronger than the last, I hope! They failed miserably!"

His head bobbing up and down, the grizzled goblin declared, "The finest blending of metals! Stronger than steel! And imbued with the energies you presented, they'll last up to any strain even though they will feel as light as a feather!"

As if to emphasis this last, the goblins working on the first of the plates easily carried it about even though Malfurion would have expected that they would need ten times their number.

Neltharion eyed the plate with eagerness. His breath quickened as the still-red metal passed near.

"All we need do is set it in the water tank for a short time, then—"

"NO!" burst out the Earth Warder.

The goblin quivered. "B-beg pardon, my lord?"

Eyes manic, the dragon continued to stare at the plate. "I want it sealed on *now!*"

"But the remaining heat will only add to the stress on you! The bolts already have to be hot out of necessity! It would truly be prudent to wait—"

The ebony leviathan stomped the floor with one paw—coming within inches of Meklo. "Now . . ."

"Yes, my Lord Neltharion! At once, my Lord Neltharion! Move you sluggards!" Meklo blurted the last at the goblins still trying to maneuver the plate.

As they turned about, the dragon headed toward a large, open space against the far wall. While Malfurion and the orc watched in curiosity, the leviathan settled down, exposing his right flank in the process. The great, gaping rips continued to burn with fire.

"Secure it!" Neltharion roared. "Secure it!"

"What do they mean to do with that?" the night elf muttered.

Brox shook his head, as bewildered as him.

"Get the bolts ready, the bolts ready!" Meklo ordered. "As hot as possible!"

Two crews of a dozen goblins began maneuvering a huge pair of tongs into a furnace. As the druid watched, they plucked from it a massive bolt at least as large as the orc.

"Hammer crew! Ready the machine!"

A groaning noise came from the right. A score of goblins pulled what at first looked like a peculiar catapult toward the dragon. Yet, this machine had no cup, but rather a gigantic metal head that was flat on one end. There were chains and pulleys attached to it whose purposes Malfurion could not in the least fathom.

"The plate!" Neltharion's impatience grew. "Set it in place, I say!"

With frantic effort, the goblins obeyed. They swayed back and forth several times as they neared the dragon's flank— not because of the panel's weight, but rather Neltharion's breathing, which apparently made the spot they sought shift more than the tiny creatures could handle. Finally, at a signal from Meklo, they leaned forward and let the plate fall against the scaled hide.

The two onlookers stepped back in shock as metal and flesh collided. A searing sound echoed through the cavern. The terrible rip underneath caused the plate to shake, but it did not slip off.

"It's holding so far!" Meklo announced to all. "Quick! The first of the bolts!"

Malfurion could scarce believe what he was witnessing. "They—they're actually going to seal it to his very flesh! That's madness! Madness!"

Brox said nothing, his eyes narrowed, his hand clutching the dagger so tightly that his knuckles were white.

The Earth Warder had a look almost like bliss. His great mouth was twisted into a reptilian smile and his crimson eyes were half veiled. His chest rose and fell faster and faster in anticipation.

Those goblins working the tongs brought the gigantic bolt toward one of the several holes located around the edge of the plate. At a quick glance, the night elf counted at least a dozen such holes. Were each intended for a bolt that would be driven deep through the scales?

Again, the rocking motion of the dragon's body caused the goblins some difficulty. On their third try, they managed to catch one of the upper holes. The bolt slid partway in, the creatures using the long tongs to keep it there as best as possible.

Meklo immediately waved to the other crew. "Get the hammer in place! Ready it for immediate striking!"

With more grunts and groans, the goblins pulled the device in front of Neltharion. The giant's half-veiled eyes watched eagerly as the dragon's servants adjusted the machine's position.

Meklo leapt atop it with an agility surprising for his age, then peered down at the bolt. He had the crew correct slightly before leaping off.

"Pull!" the goblin leader called.

The same group that had guided the machine now seized the chains and tugged on them in various fashion. How exactly the goblins' creation worked was beyond the druid, but the results of their actions was not.

The flat end of the massive metal head came down hard on the bolt.

The collision sent forth a bone-shattering sound. The bolt sank in deep, almost to its own head.

Neltharion roared, but whatever pain was in his cry was mixed with clear satisfaction.

"Again!" the dragon roared. "Again!"

Meklo climbed up, studied where the bolt lay, and once more had his underlings move the machine. Satisfied, he leapt off, crying as he landed, "Pull!"

The other goblins tugged on the chains. The various pulleys turned here and there—and the hammer came down again.

Neltharion's cry this time drowned out the actual strike. The bolt sank deeper.

"It's in!" the chief goblin called out.

The only response to his words was a tremendous laugh by the black dragon.

"Hurry on with the next bolt!" Meklo ordered. "Hurry on with it, I say!"

In the tunnel, Malfurion, still shivering, dropped against the wall. "He means to have *all* those plates attached to his body! Why? Why?"

"Defense . . ." replied the orc. "Strong, but light. You saw that." Brox shrugged. "Also maybe to keep from ripping apart . . ."

"But the pain! You saw how deep that one went! And the plate itself . . . it's still hot, too!"

"He is mad . . . but maybe his madness will help us, druid."

He had Malfurion's interest. "What do you mean?"

Brox pointed into the cavern. "The eyes of the goblins . . ."

At first, the druid was not certain as to what the orc referred, but then he noticed that every one of the creatures had halted in what he was doing to watch the astounding events unfold. They could scarcely be blamed for doing so, yet, it did indeed offer the pair the chance for which they had been looking.

"We need to time it for when they get the next bolt ready," Malfurion realized.

"Aye. That'll be soon, too, druid."

Already the goblins with the tongs had returned to where the bolts were made. They seized one and brought it to the furnace. Even from where Malfurion stood, he could feel the heat from within and it did not surprise him when the creatures quickly removed the bolt, which now glowed red-hot.

"Must be ready," Brox urged.

They watched as the goblins brought the bolt toward Neltharion. The dragon only had eyes for the work being done upon him. He looked at the bolt as if at a lover.

"Hurry . . . hurry . . ." the Earth Warder rumbled.

As the bolt was raised up to a location on the opposite end of the plate, Malfurion and Brox braced themselves. Much too slowly, the piece of metal neared the hole . . .

As it slipped partway in, they started forward. Switching to his ax, Brox led the way, the orc ready should some goblin happen to enter the cavern from the great passage. Below them, Meklo barked at those working the machine. The creaking of the device as it was moved covered any noise made by the intruders.

They had nearly made it halfway along the path when the goblins got their creation in place. A sudden silence filled the chamber, causing Malfurion and his companion to freeze.

The druid kept one hand by the pouch he had chosen earlier. If the goblins noticed them, he had items within for one spell that would, he hoped, keep the creatures and their master busy while the pair fled.

But Meklo began shouting orders again and things resumed as hoped. As the hammer was readied, first the orc, then the night elf, reached the end of the pathway.

From behind them, the lead goblin's high-pitched voice once again called, "Pull!"

The crack of the hammer vibrated in Malfurion's head as he and Brox rushed down the passage. The foul images of what the dragon was having done to himself reverberated even more. Madness had truly consumed Neltharion and the name by which Krasus and Rhonin especially called him seemed far more apt.

Deathwing.

Brox slowed down, allowing Malfurion to catch up. "Druid . . . the way here is yours now."

The night elf already recognized parts of the passage, enough so that he felt he could indeed locate the disk's hiding place. That hardly meant that the pair were well on their way to success, for the lair of the Earth Warder would certainly have other dangers.

Behind them, there came another clang, followed by the chilling laughter of the black leviathan. The last especially urged Malfurion to greater swiftness.

It took far longer than he expected to reach the first turn. Malfurion had not taken into account either the dragon's much longer stride or his own ability—when in dream form—to easily glide with enough speed to keep up with the beast. That meant that their journey was going to take much more time.

He told this to the orc, who, typical of him, merely shrugged and replied, "Then, we run faster."

And so they did. Even then, it seemed forever before the first turn and even longer before the second. Yet, Malfurion took heart from the fact that he recognized more and more features. They were by now at least midway to their goal . . .

Brox suddenly grabbed the night elf's shoulder, throwing him to the side of the tunnel. Malfurion started to speak, but the warrior shook his head.

The druid heard thundering steps, the cause of the orc's concern. As the pair pressed themselves into the curved wall of the towering tunnel, a murky form stepped from another passage into theirs.

It walked on two legs and had a shape vaguely akin to the two intruders. Protrusions jutted out from all over its body and it walked with a peculiar gait. The head was distorted and at first, Malfurion could see no eyes.

As it drew nearer, the night elf nearly gasped.

The creature was formed from rock, but not in the manner by which either the Earthen or the Infernals were. Rather, what stood before them looked as if someone had piled boulders one on top of another, forming a crude statue of sorts. Yet, despite its appearance, it moved quickly enough for Malfurion to realize that, if it saw them, they would be hardpressed to escape.

The stone figure paused, seeming to scan the area. It did indeed have eyes, if two black gaps in what passed for its head counted. They looked with special interest toward where the duo hid . . . then moved on to study another part of the path.

The guardian—it could be nothing else—took two more steps, which brought it directly even with the druid and the fighter. As tall as any dragon, it dwarfed the night elf. Watching one blocky foot rise and fall, he imagined being crushed flat.

For several anxious moments, it studied its surroundings. Malfurion began to grow certain that it suspected their presence, but at last the giant moved on, heading in the direction from which the two had come.

When it was far from sight, the druid and his companion crept out of their hiding place.

"Do you think it'll come back?" Malfurion asked.

"Yes . . . so we must hurry."

They continued down the winding passages, the night elf pausing more than once to collect his bearings. Once, the two went several yards down one tunnel, only to have Malfurion discover that he had gone the wrong direction.

At last, however, they came across a narrow cavern that Malfurion could never forget. He paused at the entrance, stunned that they had finally reached their destination.

"It's up there." The night elf pointed up at the false protrusion. "Right where that sticks out. Just to the left of that crack."

Brox clearly did not see it, but as he harnessed his ax, he said, "Will take your word, druid."

There remained, however, the difficulty of reaching it. Again, what had been so easy to deal with when in his dream form was now high, high up. The Demon Soul's hiding place required a sturdy—not to mention, dangerous—climb.

In the background, they could still hear the hammering and the dragon's occasional roars. Urged on by that, the pair began climbing. Malfurion, being more nimble, at first took the lead, but Brox's strength and endurance soon had them moving at more or less the same pace.

"There—there's a small cave just below and to the left of the spot," the druid called. "We can use—use it for rest."

"Good," grunted the green-skinned warrior.

Neither looked down, aware how that could throw them off balance. The tiny cave, likely just large enough to hold both of them, beckoned.

Without warning, a familiar voice filled his mind. *Beware the trolls!*

It took the night elf a moment to register the mental warning from Krasus. That the elder spellcaster had kept a link with him did not surprise Malfurion, but the mage's warning made absolutely no sense. Trolls? What did he mean?

A slight powdering of dust sprinkled his face. His eyes stinging, Malfurion blinked it away.

Through watering eyes, he saw a long, cadaverous head with ears akin to those of a night elf and a shock of hair dangling over the forehead. Two yellowed tusks jutted up from his jowls. A black, glowing gem had been embedded in the middle of the forehead, no doubt Deathwing's method of keeping such guards under his sway. The creature was much taller than a goblin, even a bit taller than Malfurion. His ruddy, dark gray skin blended in well with the rock face.

"Hello, supper . . ." sneered the troll. He reached down with the clear intention of pushing Malfurion off the wall.

The druid pulled back as best he could, the troll's sharp nails coming within a hair's breadth of his face. Malfurion tried to steer around the cave, but the troll grabbed hold of the rock face and, much like a spider, came crawling down after his prey.

He heard an angry growl from Brox and saw, out of the corner of his eye, that another troll was coming up from underneath the orc's position. Worse, a third and fourth had emerged from other holes, one heading for each of the intruders.

"You'll make a pretty splat, supper . . ." the first troll taunted. "Eat your brains raw and cook your liver for something special!"

He snatched at Malfurion again, this time managing to get a hold of the druid's wrist. With amazing strength, the troll attempted to tear him free.

None of the spells the night elf had been taught seemed of any use to Malfurion. He fought hard to maintain his remaining grip, digging his fingers in so hard he was certain he would scrape off all the flesh.

Then, a shriek from below distracted the troll. Brox had put his dagger to good use, burying it in his own attacker's shoulder. The troll toppled off the wall, falling to his death. Unfortunately, he took the orc's blade with him.

With a snarl, the one who had seized the druid's wrist tugged even harder. As Malfurion battled to hold on, he noticed the second of his foes coming up underneath, no doubt intending to knock the night elf's foot loose. There would be little chance for Malfurion to maintain his hold if that happened.

The druid noticed a small beetle moving along the wall just above where the troll clung. Malfurion quickly concentrated, praying that his grip would last long enough.

As he hoped, the beetle turned and headed toward the night elf's fiendish adversary. More important, others began coming out of the rock, all of them congregating underneath the troll.

At first, Malfurion's foe did not notice anything amiss, but then the cannibalistic creature began to squirm uncomfortably. He tried to ignore what was happening, but finally it proved too much of an annoyance. With a frustrated hiss, the troll released his grip on Malfurion and began swatting at the insects now crawling on his chest.

Malfurion swung his fist. He only grazed the troll on the arm, but it was enough. Already forced to an awkward position by the beetles, the last of the troll's grip readily gave way.

With a cry, the creature slipped. Luck was with the druid, for the troll collided with his companion below. Unable to withstand the weight crashing down on him, the second troll also lost his hold.

Malfurion looked away as they struck the floor, his gaze turning to the orc.

"Go!" roared Brox, maneuvering against the last of the trolls. "The disk! Get it!"

After a moment's hesitation, Malfurion reluctantly obeyed. He had seen Brox fight demons under worse circumstances. The orc could handle the remaining troll.

Be wary . . . came Krasus's voice. *I have removed some of the protective spells, but there are others with which you must deal!*

The druid already sensed them. Some were fairly obvious, others well-hidden. He studied the nature of each's creation and, through that, either removed or nullified them. It surprised him that this part of his quest should be so swiftly accomplished. Malfurion had expected more from Deathwing.

There was another scream, a troll scream. The night elf did not even bother to look, for he already heard Brox grunting as the orc ascended.

The false front awaited Malfurion. He probed it with his mind—finding new spells, but nothing he could not counter.

Glancing down, he saw that Brox had reached the cave that they had originally sought. The orc peered inside.

"Wind . . . maybe way out, druid."

Anything that would shorten their time here was welcome. Nodding, Malfurion returned his attention to the false front. They had been fortunate so far that the distraction caused by Deathwing's mad work had buried the sounds of the trolls' deaths, but fortune would not smile on the two forever . . .

He delved past the last of the protective spells, then tugged at the false rock. It was heavy, as he had expected, but he managed to pull out the side nearest to him enough so as to be able to slip inside.

"I'll be quick!" he called.

Brox nodded.

Malfurion had expected darkness within, but what greeted him instead was a brilliant light that at first burned his sensitive eyes, then, somehow, soothed them.

And when his eyes adjusted, the night elf saw that but a few scant yards from him lay the Demon Soul. It rested upon a regal, red cloth the size of a ship sail, nestled in it like a newborn infant. The disk was so small that even Malfurion could wield it in one hand. It looked rather plain despite the magnificent glow radiating from it. Yet, knowing what power dwelled within, the night elf treated the dragon's creation with the utmost respect and caution.

The druid studied the forces in play around the Demon Soul and saw none that would endanger him. Clearly, Deathwing believed his prize so safe here that he had not bothered with any further spells inside.

Malfurion leaned over the disk. So much power in something so little. It had seemed larger in the dragon's paw, yet, he knew it had not changed size.

"Druid!" he suddenly heard Brox cry. "Something comes! The stone one, I think!"

With visions of the monstrous golem rushing through his head, Malfurion wasted no time, scooping up the disk in one easy motion.

Only then did he realized his terrible error.

What sounded like the screams of hundreds of dying dragons filled the chamber. Malfurion fell to his knees as the cries momentarily overwhelmed him. He felt as if the essence of every dragon who had contributed to the Demon Soul's creation now screamed for release—but knew that what he actually heard was a last, cunning alarm secreted around the disk in so subtle a fashion as to be invisible to his most acute senses.

And as the first cries died away, a worse sound echoed throughout the caverns.

The furious, frenzied roar of Deathwing.

NINE

The pain was a pleasure to Neltharion, for each bolt hammered into his scaled hide meant one step closer to godhood. With the armor and the disk, he would be invulnerable to any threat . . .

"Hurry!" the dragon demanded again. "Hurry!"

The goblins almost had the hammer machine in place. Meklo clung to the device, directing the last adjustments before the new strike—

And then a sound that the Earth Warder thought never to hear resounded through the caverns, a sound that so horrified the leviathan that he kicked out without thinking, sending the machine, Meklo, and the rest of the goblin crew flying.

"My disk! My Dragon Soul! Someone tries to steal it!" He let out a fearsome roar that sent the rest of the goblins retreating from the massive work chamber.

Neltharion rose. Only partially secured, the third of his metal plates dangled back and forth as he spun toward the passage. The black giant's feet and tail sent tables, forges, and molds scattering across the cavern. Fires broke out and one furnace exploded, bombarding everything with burning missiles.

To Neltharion, none of the chaos and destruction mattered. Someone had dared attempt to take that which was most precious to him. He would not permit it! They would be caught and they would be slain . . . but slowly, agonizingly. It was the least that they deserved for such an affront.

That any intruder had gotten past all his various traps, guardians, and spells utterly outraged the Earth Warder. This had been a concerted effort and one that had to have been attempted by the other dragon flights. He would make them all suffer, as he had done to the blues.

Roaring again, the dragon hurried into the tunnel.

He comes! Krasus warned needlessly. *He comes!*

Then, the link between the pair was unexpectedly severed. Malfurion feared that something had happened to Krasus, but he knew that he could not concern himself with his friend. What mattered most was to escape with the Demon Soul.

"Druid! Come! Hurry!"

He slipped the disk into a pouch, the light fading as Malfurion sealed the bag. Climbing out, he saw Brox waiting anxiously by the nearest edge of the first troll's cave. Moving swiftly, the night elf made his way to the other opening. Brox pulled him inside. Allowing Malfurion no time to catch his breath, the orc dragged his companion deeper into the cave.

"May be a way out! Wind may mean exit."

The troll's lair lay littered with bones and refuse. Malfurion tried not to look at the former, even if they were likely from goblins.

But their hopes for a path to freedom were quickly dashed. The two other chambers that they found led nowhere and the air current that Brox had felt came from small cracks.

"It would make sense that the dragon wouldn't leave such

a route open even to his enslaved trolls," the night elf muttered. "We're trapped . . ."

They heard heavy footsteps outside, but not the kind that a dragon would make. Malfurion peered around the edge of the chamber and made out the hulking form of the stone golem as it passed.

"Deathwing can't be far behind . . ." No other title suited the black dragon anymore, not after what the druid had witnessed.

"We stand and fight, then," Brox replied stoically. "Let them see we have no fear."

The disk . . . use the disk . . .

Malfurion started. The voice vanished so quickly that he had no time to identify it, but it obviously had to be that of Krasus. The night elf still hesitated, though, aware of the dark powers of the Demon Soul. He had seen what wielding the disk had done to the dragon; might it not affect him in some similar manner?

A roar shook the cave. Rocks fell from the ceiling, some of them large enough to cave in a night elf's skull. There was no more time left to think . . .

"Druid, what do you plan?" Brox asked anxiously as he saw Malfurion bring out the Demon Soul. Its light filled the chamber and, unfortunately, spread well beyond. If the golem did not know where they were before, certainly it knew now . . . and so, very soon, would Deathwing.

"It's our only hope . . ." Malfurion raised the disk toward the largest of the air passages. He had no idea how the Demon Soul functioned, so he simply tried to imagine it creating for them an opening large enough for the pair to escape.

Nothing happened.

You must meld with it . . . let it be you and you it . . .

Again, the link vanished, but at least now the night elf

had a clue. Focusing on the disk, Malfurion delved into it with his thoughts.

Immediately, he felt its unnerving nature. This was not an object that belonged of the mortal plane. The forces that Deathwing had summoned came in great part from *elsewhere*. The druid almost withdrew, but knew that he dared not.

Meld with it, Krasus had said. Malfurion tried to open himself up to the Demon Soul, let its power touch his own.

And just like that . . . he succeeded. The strength flowing through the night elf filled him with such confidence that it was all he could do to keep from marching out to confront Deathwing, the golem, and every other dragon in the lair. Only the knowledge that his own death would surely mean the end of hope for those he cared about prevented Malfurion from doing that.

The orc studied him warily. "Druid . . . are you well?"

"I'm fine," he nearly snapped. Taking a deep breath, Malfurion gave Brox an apologetic look, then refocused the Demon Soul on the air passage.

"Open the way . . ." the night elf whispered.

The glow around the disk brightened . . . and suddenly the rock above melted away to vapor. It left no rubble, no trace whatsoever. The Demon Soul burned away stone and earth without any effort. Although they could not see the magical forces in play, the duo marveled at the effects. Further and further up went the new tunnel, disappearing from sight.

"It'll continue until the path is completely cleared," Malfurion said, although how he knew that, he could not say. "We should start up."

What felt like thunder shook their tiny cave. Brox quickly looked around the corner. "The stone one's trying to dig in!"

They wasted no more time. Malfurion leapt up into the magically-created passage, with Brox at his heels. The mountain continued to quake from the malevolent guardian's efforts.

Worse, the two had only managed a few steps when they heard the dragon's rumbling voice. "Where are they? I will peel the flesh from their bones, drive pins through ever nerve! Away!"

The last word was followed by a tremendous crash, which Malfurion could only assume was the golem being shoved aside by its master.

"This mountain will be your tomb!" Deathwing bellowed into the cavern.

There was a great sound—like a geyser that a younger Malfurion had once seen erupting—followed by a horrific increase in the temperature.

"Get in front of me!" the druid cried. As Brox leapt past, he pointed the Demon Soul behind them and threw his entire will into the sinister disk.

A savage gust of icy air shot down the tunnel . . . meeting only a short distance away a fiery flood of molten earth racing up. The monstrous flow slowed to a crawl . . . then halted less than a yard from Malfurion.

Gasping, the night elf scrambled back. Brox, eyes wide, carefully helped Malfurion up the path. The orc appeared overawed by the forces his comrade had wielded, overawed and not a little concerned.

"Be careful with that, druid. I trust not such might in so misleading a form."

"I—I agree wholeheartedly." And yet, it had felt exhilarating unleashing such power. Perhaps Malfurion had been wrong; perhaps he should have turned back to face the black dragon. Had he defeated Deathwing, one of the major threats to Kalimdor would have been removed. After that, the Burning Legion would hardly have seemed like so terrible a danger. With the Demon Soul, Deathwing had handled them quite easily.

The magicks of the disk continued to amaze them as they climbed. All along the way, they found the ground beneath them molded for proper footing. Thanks to that, the pair more than doubled their earlier pace.

"I feel wind," Brox uttered carefully. "Stronger wind."

Their hopes raised, they pushed on harder. Malfurion heard a sound which he at first took for hissing, but then realized was the very wind the orc had mentioned.

"There!" the night elf rasped. "The opening!"

Indeed, the Demon Soul had done exactly as asked. They emerged on the sloping edge of the mountain, a cool yet welcome breeze greeting their exit from the hellish lair.

They were not safe, yet, however. Sooner or later, Deathwing would realize that they had gotten outside. He and his flight would come in pursuit.

"Best put that away again," the aging warrior suggested. "The glow will be seen."

Malfurion did not bother to mention that Deathwing might be able to sense the disk even when it was in the pouch. Still, at least putting it away would give them a little better chance. His fingers reluctantly bidding the Demon Soul farewell, the druid tied the pouch tight.

Once more, it was Brox who led the way. The orc tested each step down the snowy slope, more than once finding spots where they would have ended up tumbling to their deaths. For now, Brox kept his ax secured. One stumble could cost him the valuable weapon.

Fortunately, the need for the dragon's metalwork had meant that Deathwing had made use of caverns located lower in the mountain. While the way was dangerous, they at least did not have to try to descend an entire peak. Malfurion had hopes that they would reach the bottom well before first light.

But their luck seemed to again sour when a great form high above swooped past. Brox and Malfurion immediately fell into the snow, trying to cover themselves up as the dragon flew by.

It was indeed Deathwing and perhaps the only thing that had saved the two was the dragon's own madness. Deathwing searched the area in a manic anger, disgorging massive shots of molten earth at the various peaks as he passed. Each struck with such force that whole parts of mountains went flying off, huge chunks raining down on the landscape. He did not seem to be probing the area with his magical senses or else surely he would have noticed them by now.

Malfurion raised his head. "I think he's flying to the—"

Deathwing abruptly veered, coming back their direction.

"Move!" growled Brox.

They leapt up from their hiding places, making for a large outcropping ahead. Over his shoulder, the night elf saw the rapidly-growing form of the huge black. It was impossible to tell from the dragon's expression whether or not he had seen the pair, but he was certainly coming far too close for comfort.

As they leapt around the outcropping, the druid heard the same horrific sound that presaged each of the molten blasts.

"Here!" The orc pointed at an overhang. A lip on one side gave them some protection, but would it be enough?

The mountainside exploded.

The outcropping vanished utterly, the fragments everywhere. The temperature rose so high that snow melted.

Great chunks of ancient ice slid off, crashing below. Sizzling puddles dotted the side of the peak.

Deathwing fluttered above the area, eyeing the devastation. The great beast moved in closer, then snorted in disgust. With a savage roar, he turned around and headed away again, this time winding around the mountain that housed his lair.

Behind what remained of the lip and half-buried in dirt and wet snow, Malfurion and Brox dug themselves free. The night elf coughed several times, then immediately checked the pouch. When his fingers touched the familiar shape of the disk, he sighed in relief.

Brox was not so cheery. "Deathwing'll be back, druid. Must be away from here before then."

Shaking off residual mud, they started down again. Every so often, they heard the dragon's outraged roar, but the black leviathan did not make a reappearance. Nevertheless, the pair did not lessen their pace.

As they neared the bottom, the night elf peered into the valley below. "I don't recognize where we are. I think we're far from Krasus." He closed his eyes. "I can't sense him, either."

"The elder one may be shielding self, with the black one out and angry."

"But *we* have to find him, somehow."

They agreed to wait until they were at the mountain's base before worrying any more about it. Krasus was likely better off than they were.

The valley was a place of perpetual dark, the tall peaks keeping it in shadow. The night elf led the way, but Brox kept close. They were near enough to Deathwing's domain to have to be concerned about goblins.

They needed to wind around to the left to reach where

they had separated from Krasus, but after only a few yards that direction, the duo found themselves confronted by the edge of an overlapping mountain. Malfurion considered using the Demon Soul, but suspected that such a spell would certainly attract Deathwing's attention. Besides, each time the druid used the disk, it proved harder to put it away again.

"It looks like if we head around the other way, it might just lead us all the way around," suggested Malfurion.

"Agreed."

Their new path forced them to climb over some of the rubble left by the dragon's fury, but, fortunately, there were gaps here and there that worked to their advantage.

Another roar warned them of Deathwing's return. Malfurion and the orc pressed themselves against the mountain base, watching as the giant flew directly overhead. Deathwing scanned the region carefully, but still missed them. They remained hidden until the dragon was well out of sight.

"Odd that we've only seen him. Where are all the other dragons?"

Brox had an answer immediately. "They find the disk; they may try to become leader."

So it was the black's paranoia that now served the two fleeing figures. Deathwing did not dare let another of his flight find the Demon Soul first. Even from what little Malfurion knew of its power, it might have very well been enough for a lesser dragon to defeat the powerful creature.

They quickly moved on, but again the path played tricks with them. Despite their best efforts, the night elf and the orc were forced farther away from their goal.

The druid grew frustrated. "I should just use the damn thing to bring us to Krasus!"

"And the black one will come right behind."

"I know . . . it's just—"

A monstrous, armored figure collided with the orc.

At the same time, a lupine creature the size of a night saber leapt at the druid. From its back thrust a pair of vicious, wriggling suckers that immediately sought for the spellcaster's chest.

A felbeast.

The clang of weapons quickly informed Malfurion that Brox would be of no immediate assistance to him. The druid struggled as the horrific demon atop him tried to snap off his head. Malfurion nearly choked, so overwhelming was the stench of the felbeast's breath.

Row upon row of yellow fangs filled the night elf's gaze. Drool from the monster splattered him, each drop burning like acid. Malfurion used one hand to keep the full weight of the creature off of him, while with the second he batted away at the two hungry suckers.

One, however, finally slipped past his defenses. With the sharp teeth lining the inside of the sucker, it adhered to his flesh.

Malfurion cried out as he felt it begin to drain him of his power. It mattered not whether a spellcaster was a sorcerer, wizard, or druid, the magic that they used quickly became a part of them. By draining it out of its victims, the felbeast also devoured their life force. Given time to finish its unholy meal, the felbeast would leave only a dried husk.

The night elf had no time to consider spells. Even as the pain multiplied, he fumbled for a pouch—*any* pouch.

Taking advantage of his distraction, the demon managed to get the second sucker adhered. Malfurion nearly blacked out, but knew that doing so would mean his terrible demise.

His fingers grazed one bag—the disk's bag—and voices began whispering in his head.

Take it, use it, wield it . . . they said. *Your only hope, your only chance . . . take the disk . . . the disk . . .*

One of them reminded him of the voice that he had earlier thought to be Krasus. Malfurion desperately gripped the pouch, squeezing the Demon Soul out into his hand.

Immediately, he felt his confidence grow. The night elf glared at the fiendish visage above him.

"You want magic—I'll give you magic!"

He touched the Demon Soul to one of the tentacles.

The felbeast's eyes bulged. Its body swelled like a sack suddenly filled to bursting. In desperation, it removed the suckers from Malfurion's chest.

A moment later, it exploded.

Gobbets of demon flesh splattered Malfurion, but he scarcely noticed. Rising to his feet, the druid used the disk's power to instantly clean away the filth. He looked around and saw Brox still in combat against not one, but two Fel Guard. One was wounded, but clearly the orc was still at a disadvantage.

Malfurion casually pointed the Demon Soul at the one he could most clearly see.

A streak of golden light shot out, enveloping the demon warrior. He roared—then dissolved into a pile of dust.

The other Fel Guard hesitated. That was all the opening that Brox needed. The orc's enchanted ax cut deep into the demon's chest, armor and all.

As the second attacker fell, Brox spun about. Malfurion, a very satisfied smile on his face, started toward his companion.

"That went well," he commented.

But Brox did not look so pleased. His eyes shifted to the disk.

The gaze filled Malfurion with sudden distrust. The voices returned, stronger than ever.

He covets the disk . . . he would have it for himself . . . it belongs to you . . . only you can use it to put the world in order . . .

"Druid," the orc said. "You shouldn't use that anymore. Evil, it is."

"It saved both our lives just now!"

"Druid—"

Malfurion stepped back, holding up the Demon Soul. *"You* want its power! You want to take it!"

"Me?" Brox shook his head. "I want nothing from it."

"You lie!" The voices urged him on, telling him what to say. "You want to take over the Burning Legion from Archimonde and his master! You want them to conquer Kalimdor for you! I won't let that happen! I'll see the world in flames before I let you do that!"

"Druid! Do you hear yourself? Your words . . . there is no reason to them . . ."

"I won't let you have it!" He pointed the disk at the orc.

He must be destroyed . . . they all must be destroyed . . . any who would desire the disk . . . who would take it from you . . .

Brox stood steadfast. He did not charge the night elf, did not even raise his ax in attack or defense. He simply watched and waited, leaving his fate in Malfurion's hands.

And, at last, the druid realized what he had been about to do. He had been about to slay Brox just to keep the Demon Soul.

In disgust, Malfurion dropped the sinister disk and backed away from it. He looked again at his companion, seeking some manner by which to properly apologize to Brox for what had nearly happened.

The graying warrior shook his head, indicating that he placed no blame on the night elf.

"The disk," he growled. "It is the disk."

Malfurion did not like the notion of touching it again, but

they had to take it with them. Krasus would surely know how best to handle the black dragon's monstrous creation. All they needed to do was find him.

Locating a loose piece of cloth, Malfurion bent down to retrieve the Demon Soul. He knew in his heart that the cloth was no true protection against its enticements, but it was all he could do. To fight it—and the insidious voices that seemed to follow the disk—the night elf tried to concentrate on those dearest to him. If he fell victim to the Demon Soul, they would all pay with their lives. First and foremost, Tyrande, already a victim, appeared in his mind. Malfurion doubted very much that wielding the Demon Soul would somehow save her. Instead, it was more likely that the druid would end up slaying her as he nearly had Brox.

He gave thanks to Cenarius, whose wise, gentle teachings had helped give him the strength to turn from the voices. The Demon Soul was an abomination to the natural world and, therefore, an abomination to the druidic path.

"We've got to flee this place, Brox," he said, straightening. "There's no telling just how many more demons might be in this area—"

His eyes widened as grotesque hands formed from the hard ground at his feet. With astounding speed, they seized Malfurion's ankles, pinning him in place.

The orc let out a growl and started forward to help him. Brox, however, barely took a step before his own feet were similarly grabbed. Undaunted, he swung at one hand holding him, shattering it. That, though, gave him only a single step before two new ones resecured his freed limb.

Meanwhile, Malfurion found himself caught between using the Demon Soul—which still lay wrapped in his palm—and calling upon the natural forces which Cenarius had taught him to use. That hesitation cost him, for a veil of darkness abruptly covered his eyes and what felt like an iron clamp bound his mouth shut. The Demon Soul slipped from his startled grasp, clattering on the ground.

He heard Brox roar with outrage and the sound of the ax beating at stone. Then, there was harsh thump and the orc grew frighteningly silent.

A heavy breathing that Malfurion recognized as that of night sabers first warned the druid that their attackers drew near. The Burning Legion, though, did not use the panthers. As far as he recalled, only his own people did.

Someone from the *palace?*

"You let them live. Why?" asked a voice that was indeed that of a night elf, but had the emotion of a demon.

"These two will be of great interest to our lord . . ."

Malfurion started at the second voice. *Could it be?*

He heard something land lightly on the ground, followed by footsteps coming toward him. There was a scraping sound as the nearby figure picked up what could only be the dragon's foul creation.

"Not much to look at," the one standing near Malfurion commented. Almost as an afterthought came the words that verified the druid's worst fears. "Hello, brother . . ."

TEN

Krasus cursed when he sensed the disaster erupting in the black dragon's lair. He had tried his best to detect every intricate spell Deathwing had cast over the Demon Soul's hiding place and knew that Malfurion had done likewise, but, despite everything, they had been outwitted.

Worse, his link to the druid and the orc had been severed and not by any magic cast by the black dragon. Some force in its own way as terrible as Deathwing's had come between the mage and his companions . . . and Krasus believed that he had some inkling as to just what it was.

The Old Gods existed only as legend even to most dragons, who had been born in the dawn of the world. Krasus, through his eternal inquisitiveness—or, as Rhonin put it, his eternal *nosiness*—knew them to be much more.

As the tale went, the three dark entities had ruled over a bloody chaos of which even the demon Lords of the Burning Legion could not imagine. They had ruled over the primal plane until the coming of the world's creators. There had been war of cosmic proportions and, in the end, the Old Gods had fallen.

The three had been cast down into eternal imprisonment, the place of their confinement hidden from all and their powers bound until the end of time. That should have been the final line of the saga, but now Krasus suspected that the Old Gods had somehow found a manner by which to reach out to the mortal plane and seek that which would free them.

It all begins to make sense, the mage realized as he climbed over the rocky landscape in search of his friends. *Nozdormu . . . the rip in Time, the coming to the era of the night elves and the Burning Legion . . . the Well of Eternity . . . and even the forging of the Demon Soul . . .*

The Old Ones were creating the key that would open the gates of their prison . . . and if that happened, even Sargeras would find himself pleading for the peace of death.

Rip Time apart and they would unmake their prison. Perhaps they even plotted to reverse their own earlier defeat. It was difficult for him to guess exactly the extent of the Old Gods' plans, for they were as much above him as he was to a worm. Still, at least their initial goal was understandable.

I must warn Alexstrasza! Krasus instinctively thought. The Aspects were the most powerful creatures on all the mortal plane. If anyone had a chance against the Old Gods, it was them. He cursed the madness that had turned Neltharion the Earth Warder into Deathwing the Destroyer. Combined, surely all five of the Aspects represented a force capable of defeating the elder beings. If not for Neltharion—

Krasus slipped, nearly falling from the ridge he had currently been navigating. How labyrinthine were the plots of the Old Gods! *They* were the ones who had turned the Earth Warder! They were the ones who had twisted Neltharion's mind—and with more than one intention! The Old Gods had made of him a puppet who would aid their escape, but they had also divided—and thereby weakened—their one potential nemesis. Without Neltharion, the other four Aspects were not nearly as much a threat.

Worse, they also had Nozdormu occupied, no doubt another layer of their planning. Krasus paused, falling back against the mountainside. It was too overwhelming. The dark elders had spent too much time and effort. Set too many pawns in place and covered their machinations too well. How could anyone—let alone, *him*—undo their malevolent designs?

How?

So caught up was Krasus in such overwhelming realizations that he failed to notice the massive, black shadow until it had long enshrouded the region around him.

Deathwing filled the sky. "YOU!"

The monstrous dragon exhaled.

Had it been any other, the chase would have ended there with a small pile of charred bones quickly engulfed by a steaming torrent of molten earth. But, because it was Krasus, who knew Deathwing far too well, the mage reacted in time . . . just barely.

As Deathwing's manic fury spilled down upon him, the robed figure brought up a wall of pure golden light. The black dragon's blast pounded the seemingly-delicate shield without mercy . . . and yet the latter held. Krasus strained, fought to keep his balance, and sweated from effort. Every fiber of his being screamed for him to give in, but he did not.

Finally, it was the winged terror above who paused, but only to summon up another horrific discharge. That, however, was all the hesitation that Krasus needed.

The focus of Deathwing's ire raised his arms—and vanished.

He could not face the dread behemoth one against one.

The outcome of such a struggle was all too obvious. Even at his strongest, Krasus was merely a consort to an Aspect, not actually one of the five great dragons. Valor was a worthy thing, but not in the face of such impossible odds.

The mage reappeared near the mountain south of the one from which he had fled. Collapsing against a rock, Krasus gasped for breath. The effort of deflecting his adversary's assault *and* transporting himself by spell had taken much out of him. In truth, he had expected to materialize much farther away from the other dragon.

"I'll find you!" called the black leviathan, his shout echoing. "You'll not escape me!"

The one thing Krasus knew was in his favor was that Deathwing had grown so wild with anger that he did not focus his powers as he should have. The mage felt his adversary's magical probe of the surroundings, but it was cursory, sweeping by so fast and wide that the one it hunted was able to shield himself easily.

Forcing himself up, Krasus wended his way down. The nearer to ground level, the better he would be.

What had happened to his companions, the mage could not say. He felt certain, though, that they had escaped Deathwing, or else the black would not have bothered with him. Clearly Deathwing still hunted for his precious disk and now believed Krasus had it.

So much the better. If it cost him his life so that the others could bring the Demon Soul back, so be it. Rhonin would know what to do.

He scrambled down the mountainside, even exhausted as he was moving far more nimbly than any night elf or human. All the while, Krasus listened for Deathwing, noting with expert ears where the raging titan flew.

At one point, Deathwing flew directly overhead, but the

robed figure quickly flattened against an outcropping and the winged giant passed him by. Deathwing loosed random shots at the landscape, unaware that his own fury continued to work against him.

Then, the dragon did what Krasus had feared he might. Apparently deciding that the area had been scrutinized well enough, Deathwing banked and started heading back toward his mountain sanctum. Krasus doubted very much that the black had given up searching so soon . . . which meant that Deathwing now hunted the Demon Soul elsewhere.

Fearing for Malfurion and Brox, Krasus eyed the departing form and concentrated.

From every direction, the rubble caused by some of the black's previous blasts flew up, bombarding Deathwing. Massive chunks, some as large as the dragon's head, struck hard. Deathwing gave out a startled roar as he veered madly toward a mountain, only just at the end avoiding a collision.

Krasus turned and ran.

The cry thundering from behind gave ample proof that Deathwing had taken the bait. Krasus did not bother looking behind him, his senses already warning the mage as to the black's swift coming.

Everything had to be timed right for what Krasus planned. He had to nearly feel the foul Aspect's breath on his neck . . .

"I will burn you to ash!" bellowed his monstrous foe. "Burn you to ash!"

Deathwing did not fear harming his precious creation, the Demon Soul designed to withstand such horrific elements. The irony was that it would be a scale from the dragon's hide that would prove the weakness of the disk . . . a physical part of Deathwing the only thing that could destroy his monstrous toy.

Krasus had considered finding some manner by which to cause the Demon Soul's destruction here in the past, but he feared that such an act might be too much for the already-stressed time line to take. Better to let the dragons have it as he planned and hope that history followed its proper course—assuming that was still possible.

Deathwing drew closer . . . closer . . . The black clearly wanted to make certain of his blast.

Any moment now, the mage thought, tensing and preparing his own action.

He heard the telltale sound of his pursuer about to unleash another wave of molten earth.

Krasus gritted his teeth—

There was a gushing sound . . . and the area where the robed figure had been was drowned in steaming lava.

The Earth Warder rose high into the air, his laughter well-matching his madness. He circled the region, now lit up by the blazing, orange rock. Raw magical forces that were an inherent part of the fiery mass he had disgorged made it impossible to locate the disk, but Neltharion could wait.

He savored the horrific demise of the mysterious dragon mage, the pet of Alexstrasza's who had nearly upset his plans early on. It was a shame that there would be nothing left of the creature, for the black would have liked to carry some reminder with which to present his fellow Aspect before he made her his concubine. Neltharion had sensed the closeness of the two, almost as if this Krasus had been as favored as her consorts, especially the insipid and irritating Korialstrasz.

Still, all that truly mattered was that the creature was dead and the disk would be his again. He simply had to be patient. The Soul was surely near him, buried under the magma and awaiting reunion with him.

. But then . . . a nagging little thought disturbed his reverie. Neltharion considered the guileful ways of his quarry and how he and his companions had managed to steal away the disk in the first place.

The dragon dropped lower, trying to sense his beloved creation through the chaotic energies only just beginning to die down. He could still not sense the disk, but it *had* to be somewhere in there. It *had* to be . . .

Krasus materialized some distance away, the overbearing heat of Deathwing's attack still with him. He sprawled on the ground, aware that once again he had not gotten as far away as he would have liked.

It was his hope that the black thought him dead now, the Demon Soul buried with him. As a dragon himself, Krasus was aware of the energies each of his kind emitted during attacks and believed that Deathwing's would delay the Aspect from searching for the night elf and orc. Each precious minute would further the pair's chances of success.

As for Krasus himself, now that his foe thought him no more, he could rest long enough to gather the strength to transport himself to his companions. The mage gave thanks that his plan had worked, for he doubted that he would have had the ability to do much else if Deathwing had discovered the ruse. In fact, Krasus suspected that, at the moment, he would have been fortunate if he even retained the power to light a candle, much less defend himself against an insane Aspect.

Depleted, the robed figure lay stretched out against the rocky soil. The first rays of light stretched up over what little of the horizon he could see. In this benighted place, they would do little but mark the vague differentiation between eve and day. Yet, Krasus welcomed them, for as one of the red flight, he was a being of Life and Life flourished best in the sun's light. As his eyes adjusted to the new illumination, the mage finally allowed himself to relax, at least for a moment.

And that was when the deep voice from above rumbled triumphantly, "Ah! I have found you after all!"

Hunger began to gnaw at Tyrande's stomach, not a good sign at all. The Mother Moon had sustained her for a long time, but there was so much need for Elune throughout Kalimdor that she could not concentrate so much on a mere priestess. Priestesses expected always to make the sacrifice first, should the need arise.

Tyrande felt no betrayal. She thanked Elune for all that the deity had done. Now it would be up to too-fragile mortal flesh, but the training of the sisterhood would help her.

Each eve, at the time when the sun set, one of the Highborne would bring a bowl of food. That bowl and its contents—some gruel that Tyrande suspected was the old leftovers from her captors' own meals—sat untouched on the floor near the sphere. All Tyrande had to do was tell one of her captors that she was hungry and the sphere would magically descend. It would then allow the ivory spoon always accompanying the bowl to pass with its contents through the barrier.

Considering that the Lady Vashj wanted her dead, Tyrande was doubly grateful that she had not eaten anything so far. Now, however, the cold, congealing substance in the bowl looked very appetizing. A single bite was all that the priestess would have needed to maintain her strength for another day; the full bowl would have aided her for a week, maybe more.

But she could not eat without another's assistance and

she had no intention of asking. That would be a sign of weakness the demons would surely exploit.

Someone unlocked the door. Tyrande quickly glanced away from the food, not wanting to give away any hint of her deteriorating state.

With a grim expression, a guard swung open the door. Through it came a Highborne whom the captive had not met before. His gaudy robes were resplendent and he clearly was aware of his handsome features. Unlike many of his caste, he had a rather athletic build. Most arresting, though, were his pale, violet skin and, especially, his hair— auburn with streaks of *gold* in it, something Tyrande had never seen. Like all Highborne, however, he wore a look of complete disdain, most prominently when addressing the guard.

"Leave us."

The soldier was only too willing to depart the sorcerer's presence. He locked the door behind him, then marched off.

"Holy priestess," the Highborne greeted, with only a hint of the condescension he had granted the guard. "You could make this situation much less uncomfortable for yourself."

"I have the Mother Moon to comfort me. I need and desire nothing else."

His expression shifted subtilely, but in it Tyrande caught a glimpse of something that she almost thought remorse. It was all that she could do keep from being startled by this. She had assumed that the Highborne had all become slave-like minions of the demon lord and Azshara, but her companion revealed that this might not be so.

"Priestess—" he began.

"You may call me Tyrande," she interjected, trying to open him up. "Tyrande Whisperwind."

"Mistress Tyrande, I am Dath'Remar Sunstrider," the Highborne returned, not with a little pride. "Twentieth generation to serve the throne . . ."

"A most illustrious lineage. You've reason to be proud of it."

"As I am." Yet, as Dath'Remar said this, a shadow momentarily crossed his face. "As I should be," he added.

Tyrande saw her opening. Dath'Remar clearly wanted something. "The Highborne have always been the worthy keepers of the realm, watching over both the people and the Well. I'm sure that your ancestors would find no fault in your efforts."

Again, the shadow came and went. Dath'Remar suddenly looked around. "I came to see if I could urge you to eat something, holy priestess." He picked up the bowl. "I'd offer more, but this is all they permit."

"Thank you, Dath'Remar, but I'm not hungry."

"Despite what *some* may desire, there is no poison nor any drug in here, Mistress Tyrande. I can assure you of that." The well-groomed Highborne brought the tip of the spoon up to his mouth and ate a little of the brown substance. Immediately, he made a face. "What I can't assure you of is the *taste* . . . and for that I apologize. You deserve better."

She considered for a moment, then, deciding to take a desperate chance, said, "Very well. I'll eat."

Reacting to her words, the sphere descended. Dath'Remar watched, his eyes never leaving the priestess. Had her heart not been elsewhere, Tyrande would have found the Highborne very attractive. He had little of the foppishness that she had seen in so many others of his caste.

Scooping up a spoonful, Dath'Remar brought the food toward Tyrande. The utensil and its contents shimmered slightly as they pierced the green veil surrounding her.

"You must lean forward a bit," he instructed her. "The sphere will not permit my hand to pass through."

The priestess did as requested. Dath'Remar had spoken true when he had said that the food lacked much in taste, but Tyrande was nonetheless secretly happy to have it. Suddenly her hunger seemed to grow tenfold, but she was careful to hide this from her captor. The Highborne might be sympathetic to her situation, but he still served the demon lord and Azshara.

After the second mouthful, he dared speak again. "If you would only cease resisting, it would go so much easier. Otherwise, they'll eventually tire of having you around. If that should happen, mistress, I fear your fate would not be a pleasant one."

"I must follow as I believe the Mother Moon intends me to, but I thank you for your heartfelt concern, Dath'Remar. It is warming to find such in the palace."

He cocked his head to the side. "There are others, but we know our place and so don't speak unwisely."

Watching him carefully, Tyrande decided that it was time to press deeper. "But your loyalty to the queen is without question."

The tall figure looked affronted. "Of course!" Then, growing more subdued, he added, "Though we fear her judgments not as it has been. She listens not to us, who understand the Well and its power so thoroughly, but rather to the outsiders. All our work has been cast aside simply for the task of bringing into the world the lord of the Legion! There was so much we strove to attain, I—"

He clamped his mouth shut, finally realizing the tone of the words spilling from it. With grim determination, Dath'Remar silently fed her. Tyrande said nothing, but she had seen enough. The Highborne had come here more for himself than her. Dath'Remar had sought a confession of sorts so that he could relieve himself of some of the turmoil going on in his mind.

Before she knew it, the bowl was empty. Dath'Remar started to put the container back, but the priestess, seeking a few more moments, quickly asked, "Might I also have some water?"

A small sack had been brought in with the meal, but, like the food, Tyrande had never touched its contents. With an eagerness that hinted of his own desire to not yet put an end to their encounter, Dath'Remar quickly grabbed the sack. Opening the end, he brought it toward her, only to have the barrier keep the sack from her lips.

"Forgive me," he muttered. "I had forgotten."

The Highborne poured some of the water into the bowl, then, as he had with her meal, fed her a spoonful. Tyrande took a second before daring to speak again.

"It must be strange working beside the satyrs, who were once as us. I must confess to being a bit unsettled by them."

"They are the fortunates who have been elevated by the power of Sargeras, the better to serve him." The answer came so automatically that the priestess could not help feeling that Dath'Remar had repeated it many times . . . perhaps, including, to himself.

"And you were not chosen?"

His eyes hardened. "I declined, though the offer was . . . *seductive*. My service is to the queen and the throne first and foremost. I've no desire to be one of those th—one of them."

Without warning, he put away the bowl and spoon. Tyrande bit her lip, wondering if she had guessed wrong about him. Still, she had little else with which to work. Dath'Remar Sunstrider represented her only chance.

"I must leave now," the robed figure declared. "I've already stayed too long."

"I look forward to our next visit."

He vehemently shook his head. "I'll not be returning. No. I'll not."

Dath'Remar spun from her, but before he could depart, the priestess uttered, "I am the ear of Elune, Dath'Remar. If there's ever anything you'd like to say, it is my role to hear. Nothing goes beyond me. Your words will be known to no other afterward."

The sorcerer looked back at her, and although at first he said nothing, Tyrande could see that she had affected him. Finally, after much hesitation, Dath'Remar answered, "I will see what I can do about bringing you something more palatable next time, Mistress Tyrande."

"May the blessings of the Mother Moon be upon you, Dath'Remar Sunstrider."

The other night elf dipped his head, then departed. Tyrande listened to his footsteps fade away. She waited then for the guards to check on her, but when they returned, they simply took up their positions, as usual.

And at that point, for the first time since her captivity, Tyrande Whisperwind permitted herself a brief smile.

ELEVEN

To an orc, blood was the ultimate tie. It bound oaths, commanded allegiances, and marked the true warrior in combat. To taint a blood bond was one of the worse crimes imaginable.

And now the druid's brother had done just that.

Brox eyed Illidan Stormrage with a loathing he had granted few other creatures. Even the demons he respected more, for they were but true to their nature, however perverse and evil it was. Yet, here was one who had fought beside Brox and the others, who was twin to Malfurion and, therefore, should have shared his love and concern for his comrades. Illidan, however, lived only for power and nothing, not even his closest kin, could change that.

Had his arms not been tightly bound, the orc would have gladly sacrificed himself tackling the sorcerer and snapping his neck. Whatever faults he considered himself to have, the orc would have never willingly betrayed others.

As for Malfurion, the druid stumbled alongside the graying warrior. Their arms tied behind their backs and ropes around their waists tugging them after the night sabers, the pair could barely keep up. Illidan's brother had an even worse disadvantage, for the treacherous twin had not yet removed the spell of blindness. Eyes covered by small black shadows that no light could pierce, Malfurion continued to flounder and fall, scraping and cutting himself constantly and even once nearly smashing his head on a rock.

From the blindfolded sorcerer, there came no sign of regret. Each time Malfurion tripped, Illidan merely tugged on the rope until the druid managed to right himself. Then, the guards behind the prisoners would prod them forward and the trek would continue.

Brox eyed his ax, now hanging from the cat ridden by the scarred officer. The orc had already marked this Captain Varo'then as the other prime target, should circumstance enable Malfurion and him to free themselves. The demon warriors were dangerous, true, but they lacked the devious cunning Brox saw in the other night elf. Even Illidan was second in some regards. Still, if the spirits blessed him, Brox would slay them both.

Then, if it was at all possible, something would have to be done about the Demon Soul.

Curiously, it was not Illidan who carried it now. But moments after the sorcerer had retrieved it from his brother, the captain had walked up to the treacherous twin, stretched out a gauntleted hand, and demanded Illidan give it over. Even more curious, Malfurion's brother had complied without so much as a word of protest.

But such mysteries could not concern the green-skinned fighter. He only knew that he had to slay the pair, then take the Demon Soul from Varo'then's body. Of course, to do that, all the orc had to do first was break free of his bonds and likely battle his way through the demons.

Brox snorted in self-derision. The heroes in the epics always managed to accomplish such things, but it was doubtful that he would. Captain Varo'then had a clear talent for tying rope. He had secured his prisoners all too well.

On and on they trudged, leaving the lair of the black dragon further behind. However, Brox did not travel with the confidence of Illidan and the captain. He was certain that Deathwing would find them. It was a puzzle that the giant had not appeared already. Had something distracted him?

Eyes widening, he suddenly grunted at his own ignorance. Yes, the orc finally realized. Something had. Something . . . or, rather, someone. *Krasus.*

Brox understood well the sacrifice the mage might be making. *Elder one, I wish you well. I will sing of you . . . for what little time I still live.*

"Ungh!"

Brox looked just in time to see Malfurion fall again. This time, though, the druid managed to twist. Instead of landing on his face, he did so on his side. The action saved him from a bloody nose, although clearly Malfurion had still shaken every bone in his body.

Try as he might, the orc could do nothing to aid the fallen night elf. Gritting his teeth, he glared at Illidan. "Give him his sight! He'll walk better, then!"

The sorcerer adjusted the scarf over his own eyes. Brox had seen just enough to know that something terrible had happened to them.

"Give him his sight back? Why should I?"

"The beast has a point," Captain Varo'then abruptly interrupted. "Your brother slows us down too much! Either let me slit his throat here and now or give him eyes so that he can see the trail!"

Illidan gave him a sardonic smile. "Such tempting choices! Oh, very well! Bring him forth!"

Two of the demons pushed Malfurion forward at the

points of their weapons. To his credit, the druid straightened as best he could and marched defiantly toward his twin.

"From *my* eyes to yours," Illidan murmured. "I grant you what I no longer need."

He pulled up the scarf.

The hair on the back of the orc's neck stiffened as he saw for the first time what lay underneath. Brox uttered an oath to the spirits. Even the monstrous guards next to him shifted uneasily.

The shadows faded from Malfurion's own orbs. He blinked, then saw Illidan. The druid, too, gaped in horror at what had befallen his brother's eyes.

"Oh, Illidan . . ." Malfurion managed. "I'm so very sorry . . ."

"About what?" The sorcerer contemptuously replaced the scarf over the ungodly sockets. "I've something much better now! A sense of sight you could only dream of attaining! I've lost *nothing*, do you understand me? Nothing!" To the officer, Illidan disdainfully commented, "He should be good to travel now. We can even pick up the pace, I think."

Varo'then smiled, then gave the command to continue on.

Malfurion stumbled toward the orc. Brox guided the night elf to a more staid pacing, then muttered, "Sorry I am about your brother . . ."

"Illidan's chosen his path," the druid said in a much more gentle tone than the orc would have used.

"He betrays us!"

"Does he?" Malfurion stared hard at his twin's back. "Does he?"

Shaking his head at his companion's wishful thinking, the orc gave up.

They moved on, the shrouded day aging. Their captors

rode with little concern, but Brox kept glancing back at the mountain chain, certain that Deathwing would make his appearance at any moment.

"Tell me, sorcerer," the scarred officer suddenly said after more than an hour of silence. "This disk. It does everything you've told us?"

"Everything and more. You know what it did to the Legion and the night elves . . . and even against the dragons."

"Yes . . ." The orc could hear the avarice in Varo'then's voice. Only now did he notice the way the captain's hand kept caressing the pouch containing the Demon Soul. "All true, eh?"

"Just ask Archimonde, if you like."

Varo'then's hand pulled from the pouch. The soldier had enough sense to respect the power of the great demon.

"It should be powerful enough to transform the portal to Sargeras's desire," Illidan continued. "The rest of the Legion will then be able to enter Kalimdor . . . with Sargeras himself at their head."

Malfurion gasped and even Brox grunted in revulsion. They looked aghast at one another, well aware that no force would be able to withstand both the demon lord and his full host.

"Must do something . . ." Brox quietly urged, testing his muscles against the ropes and, regrettably, finding the ropes still the stronger.

"I have been," the druid whispered back. "Since Illidan gave me my eyes back. I couldn't concentrate before that because I kept falling . . . but now that's no problem."

Making certain that the demons still paid them no mind, Brox growled, "How?"

"The cats. I've been talking with them. Convincing them . . ."

The orc's brow furrowed and he recalled how Malfurion had mentally spoken with animals in the past. "I'll be ready, druid. Is it soon, you think?"

"It's been harder than I thought. They—they've been tainted by the Legion's presence, but . . . I think . . . yes . . . be ready. They should act any moment now."

At first, there was no obvious sign of success . . . but then Captain Varo'then's mount balked. The captain kicked at the animal, but the night saber would not move.

"What's the matter with this damned—"

Varo'then got no farther, for the panther abruptly reared. Caught by surprise, the officer rolled off the creature's back.

Illidan started to look over his shoulder, but then his own mount did as the first. However, the sorcerer was better prepared and although he slid from his seat, he was not toppled.

"You fool!" Illidan blurted, although to who, it was impossible to say. "You stupid—"

Brox acted the moment the cats turned on their riders. He ran toward Captain Varo'then's mount, seeking his ax. The night saber obliged him by turning its flank toward the orc . . . surely a command given by Malfurion.

Spinning around, Brox presented his bound limbs to the ax head. The ever-sharp edge severed the ropes easily and only nicked the warrior's right arm.

Brox seized his weapon. "Druid! To me! We can ride this beast out—"

But the night saber bounded past him. With its head, it rammed a Fel Guard seeking to run Malfurion through. The other demons back away, momentarily uncertain what to make of the mad situation.

The cat, meanwhile, began gnawing on Malfurion's ropes. Gazing at Brox, the night elf shouted, "Never mind me! The pouch, Brox! The pouch!"

The orc looked to where Varo'then had landed. The palace officer sat rubbing his head, the pouch holding the Demon Soul still dangling from his belt. He did not seem aware of the nearby presence of Brox.

Raising his ax high, the orc charged the captain. However, the scarred night elf recovered quicker than Brox hoped. Seeing the huge green form barreling at him, the slim fighter immediately rolled away. As he came to his feet, Varo'then drew his sword.

"Come, you lumbering brute," he taunted. "I'll carve you up and feed you to the cats . . . if they can stomach you!"

Brox brought down the ax . . . and had he struck the elf, Varo'then would have been cut in twain. The captain, however, moved like lightning. The orc's weapon cleaved the hard earth, leaving a trench more than a yard long.

Varo'then leaped forward, jabbing at his foe. The sword cut a crimson line across Brox's left shoulder. Brox ignored the stinging as he hefted the ax for another attempt.

Out of the corner of his eye, he saw Malfurion direct the riderless night saber at the Fel Guard. The first demon retreated, uncertain as to whether to attack Varo'then's mount. That hesitation cost him, the huge panther bringing down the armored figure a moment later and tearing into his throat.

Brox tried to spot Illidan, but the need to keep track of his own adversary made that impossible. He hoped Malfurion was watching his brother. One spell by the sorcerer and they were doomed.

He roared as Captain Varo'then managed a nastier cut on the same shoulder.

The night elf grinned. "The first rule of war is to never be distracted . . ."

In response, the orc swung his ax in a fearsome arc which

narrowly missed decapitating the soldier. Varo'then, his demeanor now more serious, backed away.

"Second rule," growled Brox. "Only fools talk so much on the battlefield."

His body suddenly tingled. Brox's movements slowed down, each action growing more and more ponderous. It felt as if the very air around him solidified.

Sorcery . . .

Malfurion had not dealt with Illidan, just as the veteran warrior had feared. The familial bond had made the druid hesitant and now that hesitation would cost them.

Captain Varo'then's grin returned. He moved with more confidence toward his slowing foe. "Well! I usually don't like things so easy, but, in this case, I'll make an exception." He pointed his sword at Brox's chest. "I wonder if your heart's in the same place as mine . . ."

But as he approached, a dark shadow enveloped both of them. Brox wanted to look up, but his movements had slowed so much now that he knew that the night elf would gut him before he could lower his head again. If this was to be his death, the orc wanted to stare his slayer in the eyes as a warrior should.

But Queen Azshara's servant was not looking at the orc anymore. He, it was, who now gazed high into the heavens, his mouth twisting angrily.

"Away from him, miscreant!" bellowed a voice from above.

As a helpless Brox watched, Varo'then, eyes wide, leapt away from the orc. A mere eyeblink later . . . and the area where the treacherous night elf had stood was bathed in flame.

Most astounding to Brox, the fire came with such precision that he barely felt the heat. That puzzled him further, for he had assumed, rightly, that a dragon soared over-head . . . and surely not just any dragon.

Deathwing.

But if it had been the sinister black, he would have scarcely avoided endangering Brox. With that in mind, the orc could only imagine one other dragon with such interest in the party . . . Korialstrasz. In all the chaos since escaping Deathwing's lair, he had forgotten the red, but, it seemed the red had not forgotten Malfurion and him.

"Be ready!" shouted Korialstrasz. "I come!"

Brox could do little, but he braced himself as best he could for what he knew would come, relying on Korialstrasz's skills.

A moment later, the great claws wrapped around his body and he was torn into the air.

The rush of wind in his face, Brox felt his limbs unstiffen. Either by the red's action or some quirk of circumstance, Illidan's spell had lifted.

He also noticed for the first time that Malfurion hung in the leviathan's other paw. The druid looked exhausted and also a bit upset. Malfurion pointed down at the ground far below, shouting something to both the orc and the dragon.

Brox finally made out his words. "The disk!" Malfurion cried. "They still have the disk!"

The orc started to respond, but Korialstrasz suddenly arced, heading back toward the site of the struggle. The dragon dove toward the party, eyeing each figure.

"Which one?" the giant roared. "Which one?"

He need not have asked. Captain Varo'then, his hand al-ready in the pouch, pulled free the Demon Soul. Brox re-called the troubles Malfurion had first suffered trying to make the disk work and hoped that the scarred officer would have the same problem.

And it seemed that fortune was with them, for Varo'then raised the disk with evil intent clearly in mind . . . but the Demon Soul did nothing.

Roaring, Korialstrasz closed on the captain. Varo'then's expression grew dismayed.

But then, against all logic, the disk flared bright. Another voice called from above the dragon's head, "Away! Quickly, or else we are all—"

What struck the red was clearly but a fraction of the Demon Soul's might, but it was enough. Brox himself felt the repercussion of the shock wave that hit Korialstrasz dead on. The dragon quivered, moaned . . . and ceased flapping his wings.

The leviathan veered back toward the peaks. The ground rushed up. Brox began reciting the names of his ancestors, calling on them to ready themselves for his coming.

The unyielding side of a granite mountain filled his gaze . . .

"What did you do?" Illidan snapped.

"I used the disk . . ." Captain Varo'then replied, his tone initially filled with awe. Then, awareness returned and he studied both the piece and his companion. "You were right! It's everything you said and more! One could become an emperor with it . . ."

"And one could be flayed alive by Sargeras for even thinking such."

The temptation crossing the officer's face vanished. "And rightly should they be, sorcerer. I trust you've not entertained such a foolish notion."

Malfurion's twin smiled ever so briefly. "No more than you would, dear captain."

"The queen will be most pleased by the results of our

quest. The Soul secured, its power proven on a full-grown red dragon, and the end of two of those most responsible for the delays thus far."

"You could have used the disk differently," the sorcerer pointed out, "and saved the pair for questioning."

Varo'then scoffed. "What could they tell us that we need to know now? This—" He thrust the disk toward Illidan. "—is all that is required for victory." The other night elf leaned forward, his mouth bending down cruelly. "Unless you've some remorse concerning your brother? Some disloyal regret?"

Adjusting his scarf, Illidan snorted. "You saw how I treated him. Does that look like brotherly love?"

"A point well taken," his companion said after a time. The captain thrust the disk back into the pouch. As he did, his brow furrowed slightly.

"Something else wrong, captain?"

"No . . . just thought . . . there were voices . . . no . . . nothing." He did not notice Illidan's studious expression, which vanished the moment the officer looked at the sorcerer again. "I think it nothing. Now, come. The cats are under control again. We need to get the disk back to Zin-Azshari as soon as possible, don't we?"

"Of course."

Varo'then secured his animal and mounted. Illidan did likewise, but, as he climbed up, he took the moment to briefly look back at the mountains.

Look back and frown bitterly.

They should have been back by now, so Rhonin thought as he stared in the direction that Krasus and the others had ridden. They should have been back. Somehow, he knew something had gone wrong. When the night sabers had returned with the elder mage's note, the human's hopes had risen. Korialstrasz should have enabled the party to make much quicker time. They should have reached their destination long ago and surely Krasus would have wasted no time in attempting to secure the Demon Soul.

Yes, something had gone terribly wrong.

He mentioned none of this to Jarod, who had his own mountain of troubles. It was not that the meeting in Blackforest's tent had gone awry; on the contrary, just by being himself, Shadowsong had cemented his position as commander. At some time during the last battle, the former Guard captain had reached a point where he could not stand by and let foolish orders, whatever the caste of their source, pass as wise council.

When another noble had suggested a flanking maneuver that would have likely ended with the host fragmented, Jarod had started in, explaining why such would only create a debacle that would destroy the night elves. That he had to make this clear to what should have been the most learned of his race astounded the human. In the end, Jarod had managed to turn every noble there into his loyal followers, so relieved were they to have someone who appeared to have an instinctive grasp of tactics.

Rhonin had, at first, assumed that he would have to secretly guide Jarod, but the young night elf *did* know what he was doing. The wizard had seen Jarod's kind before—born with an ability the greatest learning could not surpass—and gave thanks to Elune and whatever other deity might have been responsible for granting the defenders someone to take Ravencrest's place.

But with the quest for the disk in jeopardy, would even Jarod be enough?

Jarod joined the wizard. The reluctant leader of the host

wore a newly-polished set of armor given to him by Blackforest, one that bore no crest, but did have red and orange arcs running down both sides to the waist. The cloak was likewise colored and flowed about him like a possessive lover. He now also had a crested helmet, the fiery tail—made from dyed night saber hair—dangling below his neck.

Behind him came his ever-present retinue, subofficers and liaisons for the varying noble leaders. Jarod paused to wave the group away from him before finally speaking.

"Once, I'd have dreamt of no greater honor than to rise to a rank of privilege and wear the fine garments appropriate to my new station," Jarod remarked dourly. "Now, I just feel like I look like a buffoon!"

"You won't get much argument from me," Rhonin admitted. "But it impresses the lot, so you'll have to make due with it, at least for now. When your authority's stronger, you can begin dispensing with the trappings, piece by piece."

"I can hardly wait."

The wizard led him farther away. "Cheer up, Jarod! It won't do if your people see their new hope looking so bleak. They might fear for their chances."

"I fear for our chances, especially with me in command!"

The human would not permit him such talk. Leaning close, Rhonin snapped, "Thanks to you, we live! Yes, that includes me, too! You *will* come to terms with this! We've heard nothing yet from the others, which means that you, I, and those dying in battle may be the only hope for Kalimdor . . . the only hope for the future!"

He did not elaborate, for it would have been beyond even the erstwhile officer to come to grips with the truth . . . that Rhonin was from a period perhaps ten thousand years later. How could the wizard explain that he fought not only for those who lived, but for those *yet* to be born, including the ones he loved most.

"I never asked for this . . ." protested Jarod.

"Neither did the rest of us."

The night elf sighed. Removing the garish helmet, he wiped his forehead. "You're right, Master Rhonin. Forgive me. I'll do whatever I can, even if I can't promise it'll be much."

"Just keep doing what you're doing . . . the right thing. You turn into another Desdel Stareye and we're all lost."

The new commander gazed down at his finery, sneering at its impeccable state. "Little enough chance of that, I promise."

That brought a smile to the wizard. "Good to hear—"

A horn blared. A battle horn.

Rhonin looked over his shoulder. "That's coming from far down the right flank! There shouldn't be any Legion force there! They could never get around without us knowing it!"

Jarod clamped on his helmet. "But it appears that they have!" He waved the soldiers back over to him. "Mount up and bring me my own cat! The wizard's, also! We need to see what's happening over there now!"

They brought the animals with an efficiency that Rhonin had not noted under the leadership of Stareye. These soldiers truly respected Jarod. It was not merely that he now had the backing of so many important if impotent nobles. Word had already spread of his deeds and how he had taken the reins in the moment when everyone else had believed the cause lost.

As the captain—no, *former* captain, the spellcaster had to remind himself—mounted, a new transformation seem to overcome him. A grim determination spread across his once-innocent countenance. He urged his night saber on, quickly pushing ahead of Rhonin and the others.

The horn sounded again. The wizard noted that it was a night elven horn. One of Jarod's first commands and the one that had proven he had the nobles' backing was to blend the host and its allies better. No longer were Huln's and Dungard's people off to the one side. Now, each element of night elf military had its own contingent of outsiders whose skills augmented, not detracted. Even the furbolgs had their part to play, strengthening wedges and using their clubs to crack the skulls of any Fel Guard who tried to reach the valued sorcerers and archers further back.

Many of the changes were simple or subtle and it amazed Rhonin that he had not thought of them himself. However, now something had come to truly test the revamped host. A ploy no one could have expected from Archimonde.

Yet, as they neared, it was not quite a battle that they confronted, but rather a confusion. Night elves sought to bring weapons into play, but the tauren and Earthen that Rhonin saw appeared to have no interest in playing any part in their own defense. They stood idly by as their allies frantically tried to fill the gaps that they created by their inaction.

"What by the Mother Moon are they doing?" Jarod demanded to the air. "They'll undermine everything! I finally had the nobles convinced of their necessity."

Rhonin started to answer, but just then he became aware of something far beyond the line. The enemy was even closer than he could have imagined. The wizard made out hulking forms, winged creatures, and a vast variety of ominous shapes that he, who had faced the Legion in the future, still could not identify.

Oddly, they moved almost at a walking pace and from them Rhonin heard no bloodcurdling calls. There were giants among them, too, giants that dwarfed any demon of which the wizard was familiar. The winged forms did not remind him of Doomguard and although there were other flying horrors among the Burning Legion, he could not recall any matching those approaching.

Jarod reined his night saber to a halt near a tauren that turned out to be none other than Huln. "What's the matter? Why aren't you fighting?"

The tauren leader blinked and looked at Jarod as if the questions made no sense. "We will not fight these! It would be unthinkable!"

A pair of Earthen nearby echoed his words with stern nods. Jarod at first looked dismayed, then his expression turned resolute.

"Then, we will fight them ourselves!" he growled, riding past the tauren.

But Rhonin had grown very suspicious concerning the reasons for the allies' reticence. "Wait, Jarod!"

"Master Rhonin, not you, too?"

The oncoming horde was now close enough that the wizard could make out some individual features . . . enough to verify for him that he had been correct in calling the night elf back.

"They're not the Legion! They've come to join us, I'm sure of that!"

He was even more certain when he saw that which lead them, a towering creature moving on four swift legs and atop whose shaggy head was a rack of magnificent antlers. The gargantuan being was followed closely by scores of creatures resembling satyrs in that their upper torsos were like those of night elves, but their lower bodies were instead those of fauns and they were all young, beautiful females. They seemed almost as much plant as animal, their skin covered in sleek, green leaves. While more delicate-looking in some ways, there was that about their demeanors that made him suspect that any foe would regret confronting them.

Already caught up in their preparations, the soldiers paid this figure no mind. Rhonin realized that a catastrophe of great proportions would quickly take place if he did not put a stop to things.

"Jarod! Ride up with me, quick!"

With the night elf in tow, the crimson-tressed wizard urged his mount past startled soldiers. Jarod caught up to him, shouting, "Are you mad? What are you doing?"

"Trust me! They *are* allies!"

The figure in the lead suddenly loomed over them. Startled, Rhonin barely reined in time.

"Greetings, Rhonin Redhair!" boomed the antlered being. The female figures eyed the wizard with curiosity. "We come to join the fight for our precious realm . . ." He studied Jarod Shadowsong. "Is this the one with whom we must coordinate our actions?"

The human glanced at his companion, who sat openmouthed. "He is. Forgive him! I find myself a little astounded by your coming as well . . . Cenarius."

"Cenarius . . ." muttered Jarod. "The forest lord?"

"Yes, and I believe he's brought some august company with him." Rhonin added, peering beyond the mythic guardian.

It was as if the tales of his childhood had come to life . . . and, indeed, perhaps that was the most apt description. Rhonin and the night elf gazed up—often *high* up—at giants known only from the dreams of mortals. For all his height, the forest lord was dwarfed by some of his companions. A pair of twin, bearlike creatures like veritable mountains flanked Cenarius, one eyeing Rhonin with particular interest. Beyond them and only slightly smaller, a being resembling a wolverine with six limbs and a serpentine tail eagerly surveyed the distant battlefield. His breath came in hungry pants and his massive claws raked the ground, creating massive grooves.

Towering over almost everything else was a humongous, tusked boar with a mane of sharp, even deadly thorns. A name came unbidden from Rhonin's early studies . . . *Agamaggan* . . . a demigod of primal fury . . .

Some were not so overwhelming, but were no less stunning. There was a beautiful yet dangerous-looking bird woman around whom flocks of avians abounded. A tiny red fox with a sly yet gnomish visage scurried between the legs of the giants and darting around many of the demigods were minute, sword-wielding men with butterfly wings . . . pixies of a sort.

A shape pure white flashed by at the edge of the wizard's gaze. He immediately sought out the source, but found nothing. Yet, an image remained burned in his thoughts, that of a huge stag with antlers that seemed to reach the heavens . . .

And on it went. Male figures with hooded faces and whose flesh—what little there was visible—was oak bark. Hippogriffs and gryphons fluttered in the air and creatures resembling giant stick bugs with humanoid forms swayed patiently in the wind. Further on, there were scores of *other* unique figures, some of whom the wizard would have been hard-pressed to describe even while staring at them—but all of whom bore marked resemblance to some particular aspect of the natural world.

And even from where he stood, Rhonin could sense the energies surrounding each, the natural forces of the world embodied by those created first to protect it from harm.

"Jarod Shadowsong . . ." the wizard managed. "May I introduce to you the demigods of Kalimdor . . . *all* of them."

"At your command," Cenarius added respectfully, his front legs falling to a kneeling position. Behind him, the others followed suit in their own manner.

The new leader of the host swallowed, unable to speak.

Rhonin took a quick look behind himself. Everywhere, soldiers, tauren, furbolgs, Earthen, and more watched the tableau in awe. Most now recognized that these newcomers were beings of tremendous age and power . . . all of whom were now acknowledging Jarod as the one from whom they would take their cues in battle.

Cenarius rose, eyeing the night elf as one did an equal. "We await your word."

And to his credit, the former Guard captain straightened, replying, "You are all very welcome, elder one. Your strength is greatly appreciated. With any luck, we have a chance, a good chance, of surviving."

The forest lord nodded, his eyes looking beyond Jarod to the other mortal defenders. A determined expression steeled Cenarius's bearded countenance. "Yes. You have it right, Lord Shadowsong . . . we have a *chance* . . ."

TWELVE

As Malfurion stirred from unconsciousness, pain struck him over what seemed every inch of his body. It was almost enough to send him back to the darkness, but a sense of urgency pushed him on. Slowly, the druid began to register sounds and, just as significant, the lack of sounds.

He opened his eyes and was greeted by the soft shadow of night. Thankful for once to avoid the glare of daylight, Malfurion pushed his aching form up to a sitting position, then surveyed the region.

He let out a gasp.

Some yards beyond and half-buried in a crater no doubt caused by the collision, the dragon Korialstrasz lay still.

"He—he lives . . ." managed a rumpled figure rising like a specter from the grave. "I—I can readily assure you of th-that."

"Krasus?"

The mage stumbled toward him, looking more gaunt and pale than ever. "Not . . . not the circumstances I had planned for our reunion."

Taking hold of the elder spellcaster, Malfurion guided

him over to a rock and made Krasus sit. "What happened? How do you come to be here?"

Taking a deep breath, the robed figure explained how he had led the black dragon on a chase, trying to buy time for the night elf and the orc. As he spoke, Krasus seemed to recover much of his strength, something the night elf attributed to the other's amazing background.

Then, Malfurion recalled mention of their other comrade. "Brox!" he blurted, looking around. "Is he—"

"The orc lives. I think his hide and skull even stronger than a dragon's. He came to me just as I stirred. I believe he is out trying to locate food and water, our own destroyed in the crash." Krasus shook his head and continued, "We may also thank Korialstrasz for our relative health. He did what he could to protect us—including a hasty spell—at cost to himself." The mage said the last proudly.

"Shall I try to heal him as I did once before?"

"No . . . the last time, you drew upon the strength of a healthy land. Here, you might have to draw too much on yourself. He would understand. There is another way." Krasus did not explain what it was, though, instead saying, "As to how the two of us came to be together, Korialstrasz found me as I lay recuperating from a narrow escape from the black one. He had slain a guardian of Deathwing's, then feared—rightly, as it turned out—that something had gone wrong with our plan to steal the disk."

With Krasus astride, they had taken a circuitous route to avoid both Deathwing and any other sentinels he might have stationed, then had followed as best they could the telltale trace magic Krasus detected from the Demon Soul. Unfortunately, they had not found the pair until after those from the palace had captured them and taken the disk.

"That was your brother with them, was it not, Malfurion?"

The druid hung his head. "Yes. He . . . I don't know what to tell you, Krasus!"

"Illidan bears their taint," the mage said pointedly. "You would do best to remember that and remember well." There was something in his tone that hinted of more knowledge in respect to Malfurion's twin, but Krasus did not elaborate.

"What do we do now? Do we go after the Demon Soul?"

"I think we must . . . but first, you need to tell me everything you can about what transpired before my arrival."

Nodding, Malfurion detailed his and Brox's capture, the taking of the malevolent disk, and the arduous journey. Each time it was necessary to mention Illidan, Malfurion nearly choked.

Krasus listened stone-faced, even when the night elf described as best as he could recall for what purpose they hoped to utilize the Demon Soul. Only when Malfurion had finished did the mage respond.

"It is an even more foul scenario than I had imagined . . ." he muttered, half speaking to himself. "They will have planned this . . . and yet . . . and yet, in it there may be some hope . . ."

"Hope?" Malfurion could hardly see any hope in what he had told the other.

"Yes . . ." Krasus rose. Steepling his fingers, he rested his chin on them as he considered further. "If we can only make them *listen*."

"Who?"

"The Aspects."

The night elf was incredulous. "But we can't! They've shut themselves away, even from you! If Korialstrasz were conscious, then—"

"Yes," interrupted the dragon mage. "And it is Korial-strasz who, in part, may aid us in bringing them out . . . if I know She Who is Life as I do."

His words made little sense to Malfurion, but the druid had gotten used to that somewhat. If Krasus had some plan in mind, the night elf would do whatever he could to help.

The rattle of loose rock presaged Brox's return. Unfortunately, the orc returned empty-handed.

"No stream . . . no puddle. No food . . . not even insects," the warrior reported. "I have failed, elder one."

"You have done as best as you could, Brox. This is a dismal land, even so far from Deathwing's domain."

At mention of the black scourge's new name, Malfurion tensed. "Do you think that he might still come after us?"

"I would be astounded if he did not. We must attempt something before that happens." Krasus peered over his shoulder at the unmoving form of Korialstrasz. "I give thanks that this Captain Varo'then used the Demon Soul in haste, or else we would all be ash. Korialstrasz can recover—and I know that—but, it is up to us to make contact first. And by us, I mean *you*, night elf."

"Me?"

As Krasus's eyes narrowed, Malfurion noticed for the first time how reptilian they were. "Yes. You must walk the Emerald Dream again. You must find its mistress, Ysera."

"But we've already attempted that since the dragons were driven off by the Demon Soul and she's refused to respond."

"Then, this time you must tell her that Alexstrasza must know that Korialstrasz is dying."

Aghast, Malfurion looked at the huge body, but Krasus immediately shook his head. "No! Trust me . . . I would be the first to fear that. Just tell Ysera. She cannot but help alert She Who is Life of this."

"You want me to *lie* to the mistress of the dream realm?"

"There is no other choice."

Thinking about it, the druid saw that his comrade made sense. Only a warning of such magnitude might gain one of the Aspects' attention. They would not think Malfurion so foolish as to risk their wrath with a false story.

There remained only the question as to what would happen when the dragon discovered that he *had* lied.

But Malfurion could not think about that. He trusted in Krasus's judgment. "I'll do it."

"I will try to watch over you. Brox, I leave it to you to protect both of us, if necessary."

The orc bowed. "My honor, elder one."

As he had done in the past, Malfurion sat with legs folded and cleared his mind first of all outside disturbances, then worked on easing the aches of his body. As the pain receded, he focused on the mythic realm.

Even despite his present condition, the night elf discovered it easier than ever to enter the Emerald Dream. The only unsettling sensation was a warmth at the points where the two small nubs on his forehead were located. Malfurion wanted to reach up and touch them in order to see if there had been any change, but knew that his first priority was finding Ysera.

He considered searching for her across the elemental landscape, then realized that, being who she was, all he had to theoretically do was call out to her. Whether or not the Aspect responded was another matter entirely.

Lady of the Emerald Dream, Malfurion called in his mind. *She of the Dreaming . . . Ysera . . .*

The druid sensed no other presence, but knew that he had to continue. She was here, somewhere . . . or everywhere. Ysera *would* hear him.

Ysera . . . I bring dire news for She Who is Life . . . the consort of Alexstrasza . . . Korialstrasz . . . is dying . . . Malfurion pictured the scene, trying to give the one he sought to contact some notion as to where the male dragon lay. *Korialstrasz is dying . . .*

He waited. Surely *now* the mistress of the dream realm would appear. How could she not at least investigate such potential tragedy?

Time was a nebulous thing in the Emerald Dream, but it still passed. Malfurion waited and waited, yet of the green dragon, he sensed nothing.

There came a point when at last he knew that to hope any longer would simply prove folly. Deflated by his failure, the druid returned to his body.

Krasus's anxious gaze met his own. "She responded?"

"No . . . there was nothing."

The mage looked away, frowning. "But she should've responded," he muttered half to himself. "She knows what it would mean to Alexstrasza . . ."

"I did as you said," the druid insisted, not wanting Krasus to find fault with his effort. "Said everything as you suggested."

The robed figure patted him on the shoulder. "I know you did, Malfurion. Of you, I have the utmost faith. It is a—"

"Dragon!"

Brox's warning cry came just before the behemoth materialized through the clouds. Malfurion focused on those clouds, hoping that he could urge them to some effort against the attacker.

But not only was it not a black dragon who approached, its very appearance made Krasus laugh heartily. Both the night elf and the druid gazed with some concern at their senior comrade.

"*She* comes! I should have realized that *she* herself would seek to discover the truth about such dire news!"

A crimson dragon the size of Deathwing hovered overhead. As Malfurion studied her, he recognized certain traits and knew that he had seen this particular giant before.

Alexstrasza, the Aspect of Life, landed anxiously next to the body of Korialstrasz. Even despite her reptilian appearance, the night elf recognized the all too common traits of fear and concern.

"He cannot be dead!" she bellowed. "I will not permit it!"

Krasus strode up next to the prone male, displaying himself before the red female. "And he is *not*, as you can so plainly see, my queen!"

Her consternation changed to confusion and then to anger. Alexstrasza thrust her head down toward the tiny mage, her maw coming within arm's length of his body.

"You of all who know me know what a bitter jest that was! I feared that—that you—and he—"

"Not for the lack of the Demon Soul's trying," he returned. "If its current wielder had not been so unversed in its usage, you would see four dead here."

"You will explain yourself in a moment," the dragon snapped. "But first I must see to him."

She leaned over Korialstrasz, spreading her wings wide so as to encompass the male's entire form. As she did, a golden radiance surrounded the great Aspect, one that quickly enveloped Korialstrasz as well. A gentle warmth touched Malfurion, easing his troubled mind. It occurred to him that here was a being as much a part of his calling as Ysera, possibly more. Druids worked with the natural life forces of the world and who better represented that than Alexstrasza? "He has suffered much," the dragon stated, her expression softening. "The Demon Soul, as you have rightly declared that abomination, caused him great harm . . . but, yes, he will recover completely . . . given the opportunity, that is."

The golden aura receded. Turning her massive head to the sky, Alexstrasza let out a great roar.

To the party's surprise, two more gargantuan reds dropped through the clouds. They circled once, then alighted near opposite ends of Korialstrasz. Once near, they still proved to be smaller than their queen, but on par with the unconscious male.

"Your command, my queen?"

"Take him back to the lair and place him in the Grotto of the Shadow Rose. He will mend better in mind and soul there. Treat him gently, Tyran."

The larger of the two newcomers bowed his head respectfully. "Of course, I shall, my queen."

"You will find there will be some more memory loss," Krasus interjected, not at all overawed by the presence of so many dragons. But then, he was one, also, Malfurion had to remind himself. "Those shall never be recovered," the mage added.

"Perhaps that is for the best," she returned, gazing at the tiny figure with the utmost fondness.

"As I thought."

Krasus stepped back as the two males—Alexstrasza's other consorts, apparently—carefully seized Korialstrasz, then took to the air. The Aspect, meanwhile, turned her full attention to the cowled figure. The fondness had become mixed with annoyance.

"It was not a particularly pleasant trick you played! Ysera alerted me immediately and although it was against my better judgment, I immediately came to investigate—as you *knew* I would!"

"If I have been remiss," Krasus answered, bowing deep. "I accept your anger and your punishment."

The huge dragon hissed. "You have me here and you speak of the Demon Soul in another's grip! How does this all come to pass?"

Without preamble, the mage went into the tale. Alexstrasza's expression changed several times and some of her anger faded. By the end of the story, disbelief dominated her emotions.

"Into the sanctum of Neltharion himself! It is a wonder that any of you live!" She cocked her head as she studied Krasus. "But, from you, I am growing less surprised by such actions. It is only a shame that after so much effort, the disk ends up in the clutches of those as monstrous in their own way as the Earth Warder has become."

"Yet, this seeming disaster offers us potential for salvaging at least some part of Kalimdor, my queen. The greatest goal they have is to bring into our world their master, Sargeras . . ."

"And they will use the Demon Soul to do that!"

"Yes . . . which means that they can wield it for no other purpose during that attempt." Krasus met her gaze defiantly. "The dragons will have nothing to fear from it. This is the moment when the Legion will be at its most vulnerable . . ."

"But the disk—"

"This is the one chance when you might seize it, as well," he pointed out. "And if you cannot destroy it, you can certainly bind it so that Deathwing will never be able to wield it again."

"Deathwing," she growled. "So appropriate for him now. There is no more Neltharion, no more Earth Warder. Truly, he is Deathwing . . . and you are right, this is our one chance to make certain that his foul creation troubles us no more."

Although it clearly slipped past Alexstrasza's attention, Malfurion noticed Krasus's expression briefly darken. In some manner, the mage had not been entirely honest with the dragon. The night elf said nothing, trusting that whatever secret Krasus held back, he held it back for good reason.

"Malygos will be of no use to us, I regret to say," the gigantic red murmured. "And the Timeless One is still missing, but his flight stands with us. Ysera's flight and mine will fly united, also . . ." Alexstrasza nodded. "Yes, it is possible. You are correct. I will speak with her and the consorts of Nozdormu. I should be able to convince them."

"Quickly, I hope."

"I can only promise to try." She spread her wings, but before the dragon could take off, Krasus signaled again for her attention. "You have more to say?"

"Only this. The Old Gods seek to use the disk, too, and they manipulate the Legion."

Her eyes widened so much that Malfurion was taken aback. Alexstrasza caught herself, then demanded, "You are certain of this?

"There is question . . . but, yes."

"Then I must make doubly certain of convincing the rest. Is that all or do you have another surprise?"

Krasus shook his head. "But it is paramount that we return to the host and try to convince their commander to coordinate with the flights. All can still easily go awry if we do not. Can you aid us in our journey? I fear my powers untrustworthy at this time."

The queen considered. "Yes, I have something I can quickly do. Stand far back, all of you."

As Krasus and the others quickly obeyed, Alexstrasza once more stretched her wings. At the same time, the golden radiance returned a hundredfold stronger, yet, now it concentrated most behind the dragon. So bright was it that Alexstrasza's shadow lay well-defined before the trio, covering the landscape where once Korialstrasz had lain.

The dragon queen uttered words that made no sense to Malfurion save that he felt the power that each syllable contained. Alexstrasza cast a spell of terrible potency . . . but for what purpose?

The ground before the night elf rumbled. Brox grunted, eyeing the earth as if it were a foe. The hard surface started to rise . . .

And with a grinding sound, one vast piece broke free. Something about it struck the druid as familiar, but, only when another, similar portion tore loose farther away did Malfurion understand.

They were *wings*. The rising earth perfectly matched the outline of the Aspect's shadow. Even as the rock wings flapped once, another, more sinewy section joined them in life—and immediately opened its maw to unleash a cry identical in tone to that earlier uttered by Alexstrasza.

A stone replica of the dragon queen pulled itself free of the ground.

In all ways, it looked like a perfect carving of the great red, save in color. Even the eyes bore the same wisdom, the same care, that he had seen in hers.

The two giants stood side by side, the reproduction watching the original. The glow faded from Alexstrasza and she focused on Krasus.

"She will do for you as I would do for you."

The mage looked humbled. "I am not worthy of you, my queen."

Alexstrasza snorted. "If you were not, I would not be here."

The stone version raised its—her—head in what was recognizable as mirth, then also looked down at Krasus.

"I go now to convince the others," the red added. "I feel certain that all will be as we hope."

"Beware! Deathwing will still desire his abomination!"

She gave him a knowing look. "I am familiar with him of old. We will keep him from interfering."

With that, Alexstrasza leapt into the air. She circled over the party once, her gaze upon Krasus in particular. Then, with a last sweep, the Aspect soared up into the clouds.

"If only I could tell her . . ." the cowled figure whispered.

"Tell her what?"

Krasus frowned as he eyed the druid. "Nothing . . . nothing that I dare change." His expression shifted back to determination. "We have the means by which to return swiftly to our comrades! Let us not waste it . . ."

But Malfurion was not finished. "Krasus . . . who are 'The Old Gods' of whom you spoke?"

"A terrible evil. I will say no more, but know this. To defeat the Legion is to defeat them . . ."

Malfurion doubted it was all that simple, yet the night elf chose not to pursue his questioning any further . . . at least for the time being.

The stone dragon bent low as the three approached. Malfurion marveled at the fluidity of the creature, the grace with which such a thing could mimic true life. It showed the power of the Aspect, that she could create such a wondrous imitation of herself.

With Krasus in the lead, the trio climbed atop near the shoulders. Once aboard, the size difference between Alexstrasza and Korialstrasz became even more apparent.

"You will find that the scales will shift as readily as on a true dragon," Krasus explained. "Slip your feet in behind them to secure yourself better, then hold on as you generally do. She will be faster than Korialstrasz."

Their mount waited until all three had settled in, then, with a roar worthy of the dragon queen, she flapped her heavy wings and took off. Krasus had not been exaggerating. Even before the golem leveled out, she had already flown some distance.

The miles quickly raced by as they flew. The night elf gazed over the stone leviathan's shoulder, still not used to flying, especially so *high*.

"Couldn't we have followed Illidan and the others and taken the disk back?" he asked the mage.

"Even if we had caught up with them, it is most likely that we would have suffered a similar, if not more lethal, fate than previous. If they are not well into the Legion-held lands already, I would be surprised. As frustrating as it is for me to say this, our chances greatly improve once they deliver the Demon Soul to the palace."

Malfurion grew silent. Everything that Krasus said made sense, but the very notion of just letting the demons have the disk—if only to distract them for a time—repelled the druid immensely.

Yet, it did not repel him as much as the fact that it was his own brother who had personally made such a dire event possible.

You have pleased me very much . . . the voice from within the portal grated. *So very much . . .*

Illidan and Captain Varo'then knelt before the fiery hole, Malfurion's brother revealing none of his thoughts as he listened to the demon lord's praise. He and Azshara's underling had left the rest of their party behind once they had entered the ravaged regions conquered by the Legion. Illidan had not wanted to dare a spell transporting them until that point, for he highly respected the black dragon's own skills. The Earth Warder might have seized upon their spell and brought them to him, not a fate at all enticing.

The duo had materialized in this very chamber before the startled gaze of Mannoroth, the high-ranking demon's disconcerted expression a bonus for not only the sorcerer but apparently Varo'then, too. However, before Mannoroth's surprise could fully transform to outrage, Sargeras had reached out from the beyond to demand if his servants had accomplished their mission.

Informed that they had, Sargeras now lavished praise on them. Such only further frustrated the demon lord's lieutenant, but his devotion—and fear—of Sargeras obviously outweighed any animosities. However, clearly trying to gain some bit of glory for himself, Mannoroth immediately rumbled, "Very well done, indeed, mortals!" He stretched out one meaty paw toward Varo'then. "I'll take that now so that I can prepare the spell for the portal."

Although he showed nothing on the outside, Illidan's heart jumped. Now, of all times, the sorcerer had no desire to give over the disk to a demon. Still kneeling, he gazed up at both the waiting giant and the portal. "With all due respect, Lord Mannoroth, the intricate magicks of the dragon's creation are better wielded by myself, who now understands them best thanks to our master's gift."

To emphasize his point, Illidan raised up the scarf. Even Mannoroth grimaced at the sight.

"He makes a valid point," the captain interjected. "But as the current bearer of the disk, I respectfully suggest it is the great one who shall decide who wields it in order to strengthen the portal."

Both the sorcerer and the demon glanced with annoyance at the soldier, who stared straight into the abyss and paid neither any more attention.

"Of course, it's Sargeras who decides," Malfurion's twin quickly agreed.

"None other," echoed Mannoroth.

There can be but one wielder, the demon lord's voice declared. *And that one shall be . . . me . . .*

His pronouncement caught all of them offguard, but, especially Illidan. This was not—this could not *be*—the outcome. Everything hinged on his manipulating the disk.

Almost the instant he thought that, Illidan immediately checked the mental shields that he had built around his innermost thoughts. Secure in the knowledge that Sargeras could not have possibly detected anything, he focused on this new problem. There had to be some way . . .

"With all due respect, great one," the sorcerer dared interrupt. "The portal is a night elven creation and so in the manipulation of it with the disk—"

The portal is no longer a concern . . . not now that I have the dragon's toy . . .

The words reverberated in the heads of each. Illidan, Captain Varo'then, and Mannoroth stared uncomprehendingly at the monstrous gap. Even the Highborne, who continuously strained to keep the portal together, almost paused, so stunned were they.

The disk shall open the way, as planned, but through a medium more trustworthy than this pathetic little hole . . . The gap pulsated. *One more powerful, more certain to hold when bound with the power of you have brought me . . . I speak, of course, of the Well itself . . .*

THIRTEEN

Jarod Shadowsong did not feel like a legend, but the eyes of everyone he passed gazed at him as if he was one. His reputation, already built up far beyond what it deserved for his minuscule successes on the battlefield, had grown a hundred times greater with the coming of such mythic beings as Cenarius and the other ancient protectors of the world. The story of the intentional public acknowledgment of him as commander by Cenarius had been retold over and over throughout the camp until some variations had him clad in gold and accepting the forest lord's service by knighting the latter with a gleaming, magical sword. Despite the outrageousness of such tales, few among the defenders seemed to scoff at them. Even the council of nobles eyed the low-caste officer with something resembling reverence.

There was no one Jarod could talk to about his concerns, either. Rhonin was the closest thing to a confidant, but the human kept insisting that the night elf live with the changes in his life.

He dared not even go to the priestesses and seek some sort of confession by which to unburden himself of his anxieties. With Maiev all but high priestess, word would certainly get back to his sister . . . and that was the last thing the officer wanted.

For one of the few times since having command thrust upon his back, Jarod rode alone through the camp. He had told his adjutants that he would not be long and so there was no need for them to follow. Besides, everyone already knew who he was. All they had to do was ask and he would easily be located.

He received constant salutes and more than a few grateful expressions. Some sisters of Elune working among the wounded looked up at his pacing, even they nodding respectfully. Thankfully, Maiev was not one of them.

One slightly shorter priestess adjusted her helmet, saw him, and immediately came running. Jarod reined his mount to a halt, fearful that she bore some message requiring a meeting with his sister but aware that he could hardly turn tail.

"Commander Shadowsong! I was *hoping* to see you again!"

Jarod scrutinized the priestess's face. Attractive, although a little younger up close than he had first supposed. The face was familiar, but where—

"Shandris . . . it's Shandris, isn't it?" The orphan that Mistress Tyrande had taken under her wing before her kidnapping.

Her eyes widened appreciatively at his remembrance of her. Jarod suddenly felt very uncomfortable under that intense gaze. Shandris was a year or two away from being old enough for a suitor and while he was not that many years ahead of her, it was still a gulf the size of the Well of Eternity.

"Yes! Commander, have you heard anything about her?"

Now, he recalled their last conversation . . . and each one previous. Her missing rescuer had been a focal point of each and every one of their encounters. Jarod had been polite with her, but never could give her the answer she sought. There had been no attempt to rescue the high priestess. How *could* there be? She had surely been taken to the palace and, if so, had likely been slain shortly thereafter.

But Shandris refused to believe that Tyrande would not return. Even when Malfurion, the most logical one to attempt to rescue her, had gone off on his mission, Shandris had half believed that when he returned, the druid would somehow have Tyrande with him. Jarod had kindly tried to convince her otherwise, but the young female had a stubborn trait worthy of a tauren. Once she set her mind on something, she kept to it—which was also why when the novice had first begun to look at him with personal interest, the soldier had started to worry.

"Nothing. I'm sorry, Shandris."

"And Malfurion? He's back?"

He frowned. "There's been no sign of him, either, little one, but I must remind you, his mission leads him elsewhere. What he and the others attempt means more to our people than even rescuing the high priestess means to you and, especially, the druid. You know that."

"She's not dead!"

"I never said that she was!" he snapped back. "Shandris, it would be a dream of mine for her to be rescued, but even Mistress Tyrande would understand why that's not come to pass!"

Her expression froze for a moment, then softened. "I'm sorry! I know you've got so much to do! I shouldn't bother you with this, Jarod."

Oblivious to her use of his first name, the former Guard

captain tried to placate her. "I've always time for you, Shandris . . ."

Her eyes took on a sudden glow that warned him that he had taken his placating one step too far. Again, the novice looked at him in a manner females did not generally look at Jarod Shadowsong.

"I really must go now, Shan—" But the rest of what he planned to say died on his lips, for the all-too-familiar cry of the battle horns sounded just then and Jarod knew that, this time, they were no mistake actually announcing the arrival of welcome additions. No, these sounded from the front lines and the roar that followed accented all too well the fact that the bloodshed had started once more.

As he turned his mount, a slim hand touched his knee. Shandris Feathermoon called, "Commander! Jarod! May the blessings of Elune be upon you . . ."

Despite himself, Jarod smiled gratefully, then urged his beast on. Although he did not look back, he felt with complete certainty her eyes on his back.

Reports came at him left and right the moment he reached his tent. There were demons on the southern ridge, others coming over the river to the north. The main horde pressed the center, a massive wedge of their own already cutting into the defenders' lines without any sign of slowing.

"The scouts report a second massing just behind the first!" shouted a rider just arriving. "They swear it's as large, even *larger*, than the main body!"

"How many of the damned monsters are there?" growled a noble. "Haven't we made a dent in their army yet?"

The answer came not from Jarod, but rather Rhonin, and it was not an answer any of them wanted to hear. "Yes, we have . . . but it's a very, very small dent."

"By the Mother Moon, outsider, how can we possibly win, then?"

The wizard shrugged and gave the only response he could. "Because we must."

They all looked to Jarod. Trying not to swallow hard, he looked over the party, then, in his sternest voice, said, "You all know what you need to do at your positions! We need this new wedge broken up! Let's get to it!"

He surprised even himself with how determined he was. As the others dispersed, the night elf turned to Rhonin. "I think they're saving that second massing for when that wedge breaks through!"

"Send the tauren in," suggested the wizard.

"Huln's people are needed where they are." Jarod tried to think, but, unfortunately, the only notion he had was one he could not imagine implementing. Yet . . . "I must find Cenarius!"

And, with that, he ran off.

It was time to end this farce.

So Archimonde thought as he used his senses to survey the battle. The news had come to him that a thing of power had been delivered to his lord, the disk utilized by the mad dragon to create such admirable carnage. Sargeras himself felt certain that this disk would open the way for him. Having seen it—and coveted it for the battlefield— Archimonde could well believe his lord correct.

But if the entrance of Sargeras into Kalimdor was now an imminent event, it behooved the demon commander to make certain that the world was ready . . . and that meant that he had to present Sargeras with a victory. His lord had to see that Archimonde could be trusted, as always, to deliver a conquered world.

And so, with the swiftness and cunning that had made him the one to ever sit at the hand of Sargeras, Archimonde had devised a new battle plan that would ensure the final annihilation of the miserable creatures defending this backwater realm. There would be no escape, no last minute reprieve. He knew that he now pitted himself against a much untried, untested adversary whose only virtue was that he had a grain more sense than the buffoon commanding prior. This new leader had momentarily entertained Archimonde with his good fortune, but good fortune was nothing in the long term.

I will bring you a new trophy, my lord, he thought to himself, already imagining the wailing survivors brought in chains by the hundreds to the lord of the Legion. *I will bring you much sport,* Archimonde added, imagining the horrible, tortured demises Sargeras would grant each prisoner.

I will bring you this world . . .

The demons' wedge continued to cut through despite the night elves' best efforts to halt it. Even the assistance of the Earthen and other races already mixed among the defenders did nothing to even slow it.

A line of Infernals formed the point of the wedge, barreling through with monstrous efficiency. They were guarded well by Eredar, who created around them a shield that let no mortal weapon through. Even Earthen war hammers made only a spark and that but a moment before their wielders were crushed under the massive onslaught of the stone demons.

While those in the center attempted in vain to at least hinder the wedge, the demon horde doubled its onslaught on those just beyond the edge of the Infernals' charge. Already shaken up, the soldiers there fell easy prey.

Slowly at first, then with much more certainty, the Burning Legion began to cut the host in two. No one doubted that if they succeeded, the day—and the world—would be lost.

Rhonin and the Moon Guard did what they could, but they were mortal and suffered exhaustion more than the Eredar and other spellcasters of the Legion. Worse, they had to watch out for their own lives, for Archimonde focused on them more than ever.

A night elven sorcerer to Rhonin's right suddenly shrieked and shriveled as if all moisture had been sucked out of his body. A second passed in the same gruesome manner before the wizard could register the first death.

Then, Rhonin felt an intense dryness spreading within his own body. Gasping from instant dehydration, he barely managed to throw up a shield against the spell.

One of the Moon Guard caught him as he fell, dragging the stricken wizard from the battle.

"Water . . ." Rhonin called. "Bring water!"

They brought him a sack, which he emptied without a drop spilt. Even then, Rhonin felt as if he had not drunken a thing in more than a day.

"Kir'altius is dead now, too," reported the sorcerer who had come to his aid. "It happened too swiftly to do anything . . ."

"Three here . . . how many elsewhere?" The crimson-haired spellcaster grimaced. "We've no choice! We can't do anything for the soldiers if we're all dying like this . . . and yet, if we're occupied, the Legion's sure to break through the last lines!"

The night elf with him shrugged helplessly. They both knew that there was nothing that they could do change the situation.

"Help me up! We have to create a matrix! It might be enough to at least shield ourselves better! Maybe then we can—"

From behind him sounded horns calling the host to battle. Rhonin and the sorcerer looked back in puzzlement, they, like everyone else, aware that every night elf was already on the front line.

And then . . . there came a charge like none witnessed in the life of Kalimdor. It consisted of no cavalry, no regiment of hardened soldiers. There was only one night elf even among them and that was Jarod Shadowsong, leading the charge astride his cat.

Rhonin shook his head, scarcely able to accept the sight. "He's leading the guardians of Kalimdor against the wedge!"

Cenarius followed closely behind the night elf, the two bear lords—Ursoc and Ursol, if Rhonin remembered correctly—behind him. Above them flew what from Krasus's account had to be Aviana, Mistress of Birds. After that came a being like a winged panther with hands almost human and beyond that a reptilian warrior with a shell reminiscent of a turtle's. They were but the first wave of several score beings, many of whom Rhonin could not even recall having seen earlier. The wizard knew none of the names or titles, but he sensed better than others their full power focused on the oncoming demons.

And sensing that power, the spellcaster smiled in hope.

"We need to ready the Moon Guard!" he commanded. "Forget the wedge! Concentrate only on the Legion's spell attacks!" Rhonin grinned wider. "Damn that Jarod! Only he'd be naive enough to order demigods into battle behind him and get away with it!" Then, his mood darkened as he recalled all that the Legion threw at the defenders. "I hope even they're going to be enough . . ."

• • •

"Forward!" shouted Jarod needlessly. His view filled with Infernals and other demons. He silently gave himself to Elune and prepared to die. All he hoped was that his insane act would somehow stave off the enemy's advance long enough for some miracle.

The Infernals were the embodiment of primal force. They were creatures that existed only to crush, pummel, or crash through whatever obstacles—living or not—lay in their path. The spells of the warlocks and other dark sorcerers of the Legion made them a force nigh unstoppable.

Until, that is, they collided with Jarod's charge.

The shield spell of the Eredar was nothing to Cenarius and his kind, for they had been wielding the natural magic of their world since nearly its birth. They tore through the shield as if it were air . . . then did the same to the Infernals behind it.

Agamaggan it was who sped past the rest, the boar proving far more impenetrable than the stonehard demons as he plowed up both the ground and them in one sweep. Great tusks skewered Fel Guard, then tossed the remains aside. Doomguard fluttered up ahead, trying to lance the gargantuan boar, but those that attempted to get through the deadly forest of thorns covering Agamaggan's back instead ended up impaled.

Dead demons still hanging from his mane, the demigod swung around, bowling over other Infernals. The Infernals scattered in utter confusion, this not at all the delicious devastation that they generally wrought. Their rout in turn created further bewilderment among the Fel Guard, who had never faced a situation where their advance force had been so utterly brought to ruin.

Doomguard whipped them on, but all the Fel Guard did was to continue to be crushed under the demigod's hooves or be mangled atop his tusks. Agamaggan welcomed all such foolhardy foes with a gleeful snort. His eyes burned bright as he cleared the path before him, leaving an awful spectacle of his might behind him. The warriors of the Burning Legion lay piled high. Agamaggan paused only when he had so many corpses caught on his thorns that it proved time to shake a few off. The boar shook like a wet dog, flinging ragged pieces of demons left and right. His coat cleared for more, the demigod lustily returned to his entertainment.

Yet, despite such a horrific debacle, the demons kept coming. Jarod's sword cleaved through the head of the first demon to survive Agamaggan's passing. Cenarius seized another Infernal, raised the struggling monster high over his head, and *threw* him back among his brethren. For the first time, Infernals discovered what it was like to be rammed by one of their kind. The force with which the demigod tossed his missile sent his targets tumbling back into others, creating a chain reaction that went on several lines deep.

The twin bears were much more direct. With heavy paws, they raked across the demons' ranks, bowling aside Infernals and Fel Guard as if brushing leaves off their arms. Several felbeasts leapt through the crumbling wedge and adhered themselves to the foremost of the pair. He laughed and tore off the Legion's hounds from his torso one by one, breaking their backs and sending the corpses flying into the deeper ranks of Archimonde's warriors.

The wedge disintegrated. Doomguard flew in from above to hold back the chaos, but from the sky there came what seemed every bird in all the land. The demons spun about in panic as tiny finches and gigantic raptors tore at their flesh. And among the birds flew their mistress, Aviana, her delicate face now transformed into that of a hungry predator. The demigod's talons ripped through wings, sending Doomguard spiraling to their deaths. Others she seized in an inescapable grip, then used her sharp beak to tear out their throats.

A bearded warrior clad in brown leather and but half the height of a night elf rode into the fray atop a pair of white wolves he guided by the reins in one hand. In his other, the laughing figure wielded what first appeared a sickle. This he threw among the demons with as equally deadly an effect as any other weapon there, if not more so. The spinning sickle flew through the Legion, beheading one demon and cutting open the chest of another before returning to the hand of its master. Over and over this was repeated, the squat warrior reaping a bloody harvest each time.

The demons faltered as they had previously only under the onslaught of the black dragon's disk. This was a foe on par with any that they had ever faced and even their fear of Archimonde briefly evaporated. Fel Guard began to do the unthinkable . . . turn from a battle.

But those first to make that mistake did so at the cost of their lives. Archimonde brooked no retreat, not now, not ever, save as it suited his strategy. The demons upon whom he turned his wrath *melted*, their armor and flesh sliding off their bones like soft wax. Their shrieks became gurgling sounds and in seconds all that remained were bubbling puddles with a few fragments floating within.

The message was clear enough for those who would have followed their path . . . death came in many forms, some more terrifying than others. Daunted, the fleeing warriors turned back to face the demigods, the former's strength now fueled by Archimonde's dark incentives. Aware that one way or another they would perish, the demons fought without regard to safety.

Their manic fighting at last had its effect on Jarod's astounding force. The blades of a score of Fel Guard finally proved too much for the wolverine guardian Rhonin had earlier seen. Yet, as his life force drained from a hundred deep thrusts, he still tore apart each of his attackers, be it by tooth or claw. When this first of the demigods finally fell, his burial mound consisted of Legion bodies piled higher than his head.

There were others that soon joined him, chief among them the Mistress of Birds. Guided by the will of Archimonde, Doomguard with lances fought their way through the flocks toward the one they sought. Two dozen demons perished along the way, but too many more achieved their goal, surrounding the guardian of all winged creatures of Kalimdor and piercing her with their long, barbed spears.

But even the blood of the demigoddess fought for her, dripping down the lances of her slayers and pouring onto their hands. As she fell, lifeless, her assassins tore at their own hides, her blessed blood now infesting their unholy bodies. In the end, the Doomguard died to a one, rending themselves to pieces trying to escape what they could not.

Lances and blades now stuck out of the hides of both bears and Cenarius had wicked cuts all over his body. Every other demigod bore similar marks of the Legion's brutal strength, but still they pushed on.

With them came the night elves, the tauren, the furbolgs, the Earthen . . . every mortal race that had become part of the host. All sensed that now was the defining point of Kalimdor's struggle.

•　　•　　•

But Rhonin feared that the defining point still favored the Legion. Even with the world's guardians at the forefront, the host had made no actual inroads. If the defenders could not utterly defeat the Burning Legion with such allies, what hope was there?

"We still need the dragons . . ." he muttered as he repelled a warlock's attack. Three more sorcerers had died before he and the Moon Guard had recovered enough and even though the spellcasters now held their own again, they did little other than keep their counterparts occupied.

"We still need the dragons . . ." Rhonin repeated almost like a mantra. But there had been no word from Krasus and even the wizard, who knew well the mage's tremendous skills and cunning, began to wonder if perhaps his former mentor had indeed perished in the lair of Deathwing.

Then a huge, dark shape soared over the battle and Rhonin's worst fears were realized. Deathwing was here! That could only mean that Krasus and the others *were* dead and now the black sought to wreak vengeance upon all his imagined enemies.

But as the huge, winged beast turned back, the wizard noted a peculiar thing about it. The dragon was not black, but a dusky *gray*, like rock. There were also many differences in its face and form, differences that, for some reason, had a familiarity to Rhonin. It almost reminded him of another dragon from his days fighting the orcs. It almost looked like—like—

Alexstrasza?

The gray dragon landed among the demons, crushing several underneath. With one wing, it swept aside a dozen more. The giant let out a roar and seized a mouthful of the enemy, crushing them between its jaws before letting their bodies drop.

Only then did Rhonin see that the dragon had no gullet.

It was *literally* made of stone.

With ruthless abandon, the great golem tore through the Legion. Seeing what it alone could do, the wizard again wished for the true dragons to return.

Then, it occurred to him to wonder just what had brought this false Alexstrasza to the host's aid.

"Krasus?" he blurted, turning around. "Krasus?"

And there, just coming up over a ridge, strode the tall, pale form he knew so well. Beside Krasus walked Malfurion and Brox, both clearly weary, but intact.

Cautiously breaking off from the battle, Rhonin ran to meet the others. He almost hugged them, so grateful was he to see such familiar faces.

"Praise be, that you're all alive!" He grinned. "The Demon Soul! You've got it!"

No sooner had he spoken then Rhonin saw that he was wrong. He looked from one to the other, trying to read the story from their eyes alone.

"We had it," Krasus replied. "But it was stolen by agents of the Legion . . ."

"Including my brother," added Malfurion, shaking his head at Krasus, who had clearly wanted to avoid telling Rhonin that part. "It's no use to hide that! Illidan's thrown his lot in with the palace!" The druid shook from frustration. "The palace!"

"But . . . that dragon! What does that mean . . . and where's Korialstrasz? You said in your message that you'd met up with him!"

"There is no time for that! We must prepare!"

"Prepare for what?"

Brox suddenly pointed his ax past the others. "Look! The stone one!"

They followed his gaze to see the animated effigy of Alexstrasza aswarm with demons. They chopped at it—her—much the way the Earthen had earlier the one Infernal. Others attacked her legs with blades, chipping away as best they could at the false dragon's foundation.

The wizard could scarce believe what was happening. "Why doesn't she fly away?"

"Because the time of her enchantment is almost at an end," Krasus remarked with clear sadness.

"I don't understand . . ."

"Look. It happens already."

The golem's movements grew sluggish, this despite the fact that the damage done to the body had to be superficial at worst. The stone dragon managed to shake her wings free of several of the demons, sending them flying far into the sky. However, that effort proved her last major one.

"What's happening, Krasus?"

"She was meant to bring us here at the desire of the one of whom she is only a shadow. But shadows fade, Rhonin, and her task is done. We can give thanks that enough remained for her to do such damage as we have witnessed."

Despite the clinical tone of his words, the mage's eyes gave indication of a regret far deeper. Rhonin understood. To Krasus, even seeing this effigy of his beloved queen and mate suffer was a strain.

The false dragon roared mournfully. Demons now practically covered the entire body save the head. The left legs defiantly straightened, but from the right ones there was no movement.

"It's over—" Krasus began.

Then, without warning, the false Alexstrasza leaned into her right. Her wing on that side folded in and her left rose into the sky.

Midway up, all animation ceased. The eyes of the golem grew lifeless.

And under the stress of so much weight, the right wing collapsed. The demons atop the statue clung helplessly as the dragon queen's creation tipped over . . . and crushed every demon still hanging onto the back.

Krasus's chest swelled with pride. "Every inch worthy of my queen, even *if* only her shadow!"

Dust rose from where the gargantuan statue lay. Even as they watched, the legs and the left wing joined the right in collapsing. Demon warriors scattered as huge chunks of rock fell among them.

"What now, though?" demanded the human. His hopes had grown with the arrival of his companions, but if they had neither the disk nor this magical construct as reward for their efforts, then their entire journey had been for nought.

He was not encouraged by Krasus's next words. "What *now,* young Rhonin? We fight as we have fought and we wait. We wait for my good queen to rally my kind and bring them to the fight. The Demon Soul is going where it will be, for a time, no threat to them. They will *have* to act."

"And if they don't? If they hesitate too long, as before?"

His former mentor leaned close so that only the wizard would hear. "Then Sargeras will have at last the means by which to enter Kalimdor . . . and once he has entered our world, the demon lord will unwrite the history of ten thousand years."

FOURTEEN

The storm raged over the Well of Eternity, the black waters whipping into a frenzy. Waves higher than the palace crashed on the shore. A howling wind tossed any loose debris through the air like deadly missiles.

Lightning illuminated the coming of the party from the towered edifice. Even the queen herself—accompanied by her handmaidens, of course—had journeyed with, although she was borne on a silver litter carried by Fel Guard.

Mannoroth led the way, followed by Illidan and Captain Varo'then. A number of Highborne sorcerers and satyrs—the two groups purposely separate from one another—followed in their wake and, behind them, came a contingent of the palace guard. At the end of the grand procession marched twin ranks of demon warriors a hundred strong each.

Mannoroth stood at the edge of the Well, stretching forth his brutish arms and drinking in the chaos beyond. Through the "gift" granted him by Sargeras, Illidan marveled at the forces in play above and within the vast body of water. Nothing he had experienced so far, not even the power of the demon lord, compared to that which the sacred Well contained.

"Truly, we never tapped more than a shadow of its greatness," he murmured to the captain.

Varo'then, blind to such glory, merely shrugged. "It'll now serve us well by bringing to us our Lord Sargeras."

"But not immediately," the sorcerer reminded him. "Not immediately."

"What does that matter?"

They grew silent as the winged demon turned. He reached out to the officer, grating, "The disk! It's time!"

Expression masked, Varo'then removed the Soul from his belt pouch and handed it over. Mannoroth momentarily eyed the dragon's creation with open avarice, then likely thought better of trying to keep it for himself. Glaring at the Highborne and the satyrs, the tusked demon snapped, "Take your places!"

The spellcasters wended their way over fragments of homes and broken bits of bone. The carnage that had taken much of Zin-Azshari had spread even to the very edge of the Well. Illidan learned that a few defiant night elves had tried to make a stand here on the shore, hoping that their nearness would enable them to draw better from the source of their people's magic. That hope had not panned out and the demons had gleefully torn them apart on this very spot.

The irony was, at least to Malfurion's twin, that they had been correct in their assumption, if not the execution of their plan. He could see the myriad ways in which to manipulate the Well's immense potential and understood more than ever what the lord of the Legion intended.

The sorcerers and satyrs formed the pattern dictated by Sargeras. Mannoroth studied their positions carefully, threatening into their proper places those who had erred. When at last the scaled behemoth was satisfied, he stepped back from the group.

"Do I understand we won't see our Lord Sargeras just yet, dear captain?" Azshara languidly asked from her litter.

"Not at this time, no, Light of Lights . . . but it shall not be much longer. Once he has the way stabilized, he will step through."

Eyes veiled, she nodded. "I trust I will be notified of his arrival, then."

"What can be done will be done," Varo'then promised.

Illidan wondered if the queen truly believed that she would become the consort of the demon lord. He doubted very much such a notion fit into Sargeras's designs.

But thought of Azshara's desires faded quickly as he watched the spellcasters begin. A crackling ball of blue lightning formed within their pattern. Now and then, a tiny bolt would dart toward one figure or another, but although the Highborne or satyr in question started slightly, they never faltered in their task.

Muttering filled the air, each voice speaking minutely different words of power. The combination of their distinctive incantations began to summon forth energy from the Well. Illidan watched as those energies, as individual as their summoners, coalesced around the sphere. With each addition, the bolts cast off by it grew brighter, stronger . . .

Then, within the sphere . . . the all-too familiar gap appeared.

The spellcasters had reopened the portal to the Legion's nether realm close to the Well of Eternity so that Sargeras could better draw upon the latter. Illidan sensed the sudden nearness of the demon lord's presence.

Let it be cast out . . . the voice in all their heads commanded.

"Do it!" reinforced Mannoroth, looming over the night elves and satyrs.

As one, those making up the pattern ceased their muttering and clenched their fists.

The sphere—and the portal within—soared out over the storm-tossed waters, quickly vanishing from sight.

Now . . . the disk . . .

Illidan's heart leapt. He wanted to grab the dragon's creation from Mannoroth, but common sense kept his countenance still and his hand by his side. There would be no taking the Dragon Soul—or *Demon Soul,* as he had heard his brother call it—at this time.

But at another opportunity, however . . .

As before, Illidan immediately buried such thoughts. Fortunately, even Sargeras was likely far too intent on the events at hand to pay any attention to the sorcerer's duplicitous intentions, even had Illidan's mind been unshielded.

He watched intently as Mannoroth held the disk high. The winged demon muttered words lost in the wind.

Green fire surrounded the golden piece. The *Demon Soul*—yes, that name was far more appropriate, Malfurion's brother decided—rose above Mannoroth's palm . . . and then, like the sphere containing the portal, flew out over the churning waters of the Well.

"Is that *all?*" Azshara asked somewhat petulantly.

Before the erstwhile Captain Varo'then could soothe her, the wind abruptly died. The storm, too, appeared to pause, although the dark, menacing clouds continued to twist and turn like a thousand serpents coiling around one another.

Illidan it was who sensed first what was coming. "I'd recommend that your highness have her bearers retreat up to the top of the ridge down which we earlier came."

To prove that he meant what he said, the sorcerer turned and started back. The captain glared at him, as if suspecting some ruse, then ordered his own soldiers to do the same.

With a graceful wave of her hand, the queen had her Fel Guard follow suit.

A sound like the roar of a thousand night sabers issued forth from somewhere near the center of the Well. Illidan glanced over his shoulder at the black waters, his pace doubling.

The sorcerer and satyrs finally fled, their task no longer demanding that they stay so near the shoreline. Only Mannoroth remained, the demon again stretching forth his arms as if to embrace a lover.

"It begins!" he roared almost merrily. "It begins!"

And a wave as large as any dragon swept over the area where the demon stood.

The entire shoreline vanished under a relentless, ripping tide that did not flow inward, but rather *sideways*. Ruined structures were washed away as if they were nothing. The horrific waves washed over the land again and again, more and more stripping it bare. Stone obelisks were torn from their foundations and paved pathways scattered in chunks. The dead, who had remained unburied, were taken to a deeper, darker place beyond Zin-Azshari where Illidan knew that they would find no better rest than before.

As he finished climbing the ridge, the sorcerer saw at last what was truly happening to the Well and even he stood stunned at the magicks wielded so easily by the distant Sargeras.

A vast whirlpool now engulfed the entire body of water.

He could not, of course, view its full extent, but the very fact that it stretched from the shore of the capital for as far as he could see in *any* direction gave ample evidence of its mammoth proportions. Illidan saw that, for once, the frenzied energies of the Well now moved in uniform purpose . . . and all were drawn toward the center.

Below and awash in the forces at the edge of the Well, Mannoroth laughed. Fearsome waves that continued to rip away chunks of stone and earth larger than the demon did not even bother the winged being in the least. Mannoroth drank in the glory of his lord's power, urging Sargeras on with shouts.

Secure on shore, Illidan dared probe deeper into the spell. His higher senses brought him seemingly bodily over the water, moving him along so swiftly that he soon left all land behind. At the same time, the sorcerer's mind also soared higher, taking in a better overall picture of what Sargeras had wrought.

He had guessed right when he had believed that the whirlpool encompassed the whole of the Well of Eternity. Even yet only able to see a portion of the entire panorama, it was already obvious to the night elf that no part of the Well had been left untouched.

Then, a shimmering light ahead caught his attention. Stretching his senses to their limits, Illidan took in the Demon Soul itself floating high above the surface. The simple-looking disk radiated a golden light that focused most on the waters below. Illidan already knew enough about the Demon Soul to understand that Sargeras wielded it as no one other than the black dragon could have, possibly more so. Even from the distant realm where he waited, the lord of the Legion manipulated the incredible power of the disk perfectly in conjunction with the primal forces of the Well.

But where was the portal? Try as he might, Illidan could not sense it around the Demon Soul. Where, then had Sargeras—

Cursing his ignorance, the sorcerer looked down into the center of the maelstrom.

Looked down . . . and stared into a pathway beyond reality, a pathway to the realm of the Burning Legion.

Illidan had thought that most of the demons had passed through already, but he saw now that what had come had been but a fraction. Endless ranks awaited in the beyond, savage, tusked warriors hungry for destruction. They spread on forever, as far as he could tell, and among them were fiends such as he knew Kalimdor had yet to experience. Some were winged, others crawled, but all were filled with the same intense lust for blood as those he had faced.

Then . . . Illidan sensed the demon lord himself. He felt only the least bit of Sargeras's presence, but it was more than enough to make the night elf flee from his glimpse of the nether realm. What Illidan had previously experienced of Sargeras's will had been, he realized belatedly, the tiniest mote of what there truly was. Here, where the lord of the Legion physically existed, no shield could possibly keep the demon from knowing all that Malfurion's brother thought.

And if Sargeras knew what Illidan planned, the sorcerer's fate would make that which had befallen the citizens of Zin-Azshari a pleasant and peaceful way to die . . .

"What ails you, spellcaster?" grated Varo'then's voice.

Illidan forced himself not to shake as his mind returned to his body. "It's . . . overwhelming . . ." he said honestly. "Just overwhelming."

Even the captain did not argue with him there.

Mannoroth plodded up the ridge, his four trunklike legs making craters in the already much-damaged ground. His monstrous orbs held a fanatical look such as Illidan had never seen in the demon prior. Although he had been drenched in the Well, the fearsome figure was completely dry. Such was the truth of the Well, for although it resembled liquid, it was far more.

"Soon . . ." Mannoroth nearly cooed. "Soon, our lord will pass through into Kalimdor! Soon he will come . . ."

"And then he will remake Kalimdor into paradise!" Azshara breathed from atop her litter. "Paradise!"

The demon commander's eyes grew fiery with anticipation, anticipation . . . and something else that Illidan quickly focused upon. "Yes . . . Kalimdor will be remade."

"How soon?" the queen pressed, her lips parted and her breath quickening. "Very soon?"

"Yes . . . very soon . . ." Mannoroth answered. He trudged past her, heading back to the palace. "Very soon . . ."

"How wonderful!" Azshara clapped her hands together. Lady Vashj and the other attendants mirrored her glee.

"We're done here, then," snarled Captain Varo'then, who seemed caught between his desire for Sargeras to arrive and his jealousy against any being who would steal the queen's emotions from him. "Back to the palace!" the officer commanded the soldiers and demon warriors. "Back to the palace!"

The Highborne and the satyrs needed no such commands, most already following Mannoroth. Only Illidan lagged behind, his thoughts torn between what he thought he had read in the latter's words and expression and the glimpse the sorcerer had managed of the demon lord's realm.

Malfurion's brother looked back at the roaring whirlpool that was now the Well of Eternity . . . looked back and, for the first time, felt his extreme confidence in himself slightly shaken.

Tyrande was aware that something was taking place, something of tremendous magnitude, but what it might be, she certainly could not tell from her cell. Elune still provided her with some defense against her captors, but little more. The priestess was blind to what happened in the outside world. For all she knew, her people had been crushed and the Burning Legion now marched unhindered across Kalimdor, razing to the ground what remained of the once-beautiful land.

They had taken the guard from her door, the insidious Captain Varo'then deciding that such were wasted on a prisoner clearly going nowhere. Tyrande could hardly blame the officer for his decision; she had certainly revealed herself to be of no threat to the palace.

The sound of sudden footsteps caught her attention. It was hardly the time to bring her food and water. Besides, since the one time she had accepted both from Dath'Remar, Tyrande had neither eaten nor drunk anything more. The Highborne had begged her on both his successive visits to do so, but she took only what she needed, not wanting to risk becoming accustomed to depending upon those who had imprisoned her.

The door slid open with a short-lived creak. To her surprise, it was Dath'Remar and another Highborne. The latter glanced inside only once, took stock of the prisoner, then slipped back into the corridor.

"Dath'Remar! What brings you—"

"Hush, mistress!" He surveyed the cell as if expecting to find it filled with Fel Guard. Seeing that they were alone, Dath'Remar approached the sphere.

From his robes, he removed the sinister artifact that Lady Vashj had used to briefly free her. Tyrande bit back an exclamation, at first wondering if perhaps the sorcerer intended the same fate for her as Azshara's attendant had.

"Prepare yourself," Dath'Remar whispered.

He repeated the same steps Vashj had. The sphere lowered and the invisible bonds vanished.

Stiff, Tyrande nearly fell. The Highborne caught her in one arm, the artifact held close to her throat.

"My death will avail you little," she told him.

He looked startled, then glanced at the thing in his hand. With utter repugnance, the other night elf tossed it away. "I have not come to perform such a foul deed, mistress! Now, keep your voice low if you wish to have any hope of escaping this place!"

"Escape?" Tyrande felt her pulse race. Was this some new, cruel jest?

Dath'Remar read her eyes. "No trickery! This was discussed long and hard by us! We cannot stand this obscenity any longer! The queen—" He almost choked, clearly caught between his devotion to Azshara and his repugnance for all that had occurred. "The queen . . . she is mad. There can be other explanation. She has turned her back on her people for a being of depravity and carnage! This Sargeras promises a perfect world where we, the Highborne, would rule, but all some of us see is the ruination of everything! What paradise can be built from blood-drenched stone and parched earth? None, we think!"

She was not entirely astounded by his confession. There had been hint of his concerns in their prior conversations. It had originally surprised her that there was any independent thought left in the palace—the demon lord surely desiring absolute devotion—but perhaps Sargeras had finally spread his will in too many directions.

Whatever the reasons, the high priestess gave thanks to the Mother Moon for this opportunity. She felt certain that she could entrust herself to Dath'Remar.

"This is our only chance," the sorcerer emphasized. "The demon lord's minions are out near the Well performing some spellwork. They'll be occupied long enough. The others are waiting below, in the stables."

"The *others?*"

"We can stay here no longer, especially if you are discovered missing. This was decided. I arranged so that most who would leave would not be included in the demons' present task . . . and those who had to be will be honored for their sacrifice for the rest of us."

"May the Mother Moon watch over them," Tyrande whispered. The fates of those others would not be pleasant ones when Mannoroth and his lord discovered the night elves' duplicity. "But what about the guards?"

"There are a few of them among us, but most are the dogs of Captain Varo'then! We will have to be cautious about them! Now come! No more questions!"

He led her out into the corridor where the second Highborne waited. Tyrande hesitated at first, suddenly startled to actually be out of her cell. Dath'Remar, glaring impatiently, pulled her along.

Up a long flight of stairs they rushed, Dath'Remar's companion taking the lead. There were no signs of sentries, which the priestess assumed had to mean that the sorcerers had done their best to clear the path ahead of time.

The stairway ended at an iron door upon whose center had been framed the beatific face of Azshara. Seeing her made Tyrande involuntarily shake, a reaction which stirred a sympathetic look from the two Highborne.

"Through here is the hall that will lead us directly to the stables. The others should have the mounts ready. When the gates open, we charge like the wind."

"What about . . . what about the demons?"

He straightened in pride. "We are the *Highborne*, after all! We are the finest spellcasters in all the realm! They will fall before our might!" Then, with less hubris, Dath'Remar added, "And, likely, many of us will fall as well . . ."

"I sense the way is clear," interjected the second sorcerer, smiling arrogantly. "The distraction spell still holds Varo'then's little curs."

"But not much longer, I suspect." Dath'Remar gently pushed aside the door. Sure enough, the hallway beyond was devoid of the grim-faced soldiers.

"We are nearly at the stables," the other Highborne remarked, his own confidence growing. "You see, Dath'Remar! So much worry about a worthless pack of—"

His words ended in a gurgle as a bolt pierced his neck, the end coming out the opposing side. Blood sprayed Tyrande and Dath'Remar.

As the dead sorcerer tumbled to the floor, several guards filled the corridor.

"Halt right there!" ordered a subofficer with a plumed helm.

In response, Dath'Remar angrily waved one hand to the side.

An invisible force bowled over the guards, sending them flying against the walls like leaves in the wind. The clatter of their striking echoed throughout the hall.

"That will teach them to dare attack a Highborne of the Elite Circle!" he snapped.

"Someone will come to investigate the noise," the priestess counseled.

To his credit, Dath'Remar seemed to acknowledge his overzealous assault. With a grimace, he pulled Tyrande along.

They entered the stables but a short time later, where Tyrande found herself confronted with an amazing sight. She had assumed from her companion's description that there would be a fair number of Highborne, but not so many as she saw before her now. Surely a good third of the caste awaited, including entire families.

"Where is—?" began one female, but, a look from

Dath'Remar immediately silenced her on the subject of the dead sorcerer.

"We heard the struggle above and sensed the shifting of magical forces," added another male. "The demons will have sensed it, also."

"It was necessary." Dath'Remar led Tyrande forward. "You've a swift mount for the priestess, Quin'thatano?"

"The swiftest."

"Good." The sorcerer turned to her. "Mistress Tyrande, we will need you to speak for us when we reach the host. We are aware of the ill-feelings the rest will have toward our kind—"

"We will make them listen!" urged the female Highborne. "We have the power to do so—"

"And likely get ourselves all slain!" growled Dath'Remar. To Tyrande, he added, "You will do this for us?"

"Such a question! Of course, I will! I swear, by the Mother Moon!"

This seemed to satisfy him, if not some of his fellows. Yet, it seemed that everyone here deferred to Dath'Remar Sunstrider when it came to decisions.

"Well enough, then! The word of the high priestess should be sufficient for all!" He indicated the night sabers. "Mount up! We've not a moment more to lose!"

The fleeing Highborne brought little with them, a mark of the urgency. Well-accustomed to the fineries of life, Tyrande would have expected them to have nearly brought their entire homes.

Another sorcerer handed the reins of a sleek, lean female panther to the priestess. Hanging from the animal's side was a long, sturdy sword no doubt stolen from Captain Varo'then's soldiers. Nodding her gratitude for this welcome gift, she climbed up and waited.

Dath'Remar looked to make certain that everyone was ready, then pointed at the two huge, wooden doors leading out. "We ride together! No breaking off! Those that do shall suffer the consequences of their carelessness. The demons are everywhere. We must fight and ride at the same time, possibly for days." He straightened. "But we are the *Highborne,* the foremost wielders of the Well's bounty! With it, we shall tear open the path ahead and leave in our wake the bodies of those who would seek to prevent our passing!"

Tyrande kept her expression neutral. Even the Highborne had to know that many would die and die brutally. She silently prayed to Elune to guide her in aiding her new companions. These Highborne sought redemption for their part in bringing the Legion to Kalimdor; Tyrande would do whatever necessary to see to it that they were given the opportunity to receive that forgiveness.

Dath'Remar pointed at the entrance. "Let the way be open!"

The huge doors exploded outward.

"Ride!"

Tyrande urged her mount after his.

The first of the Highborne burst through the shattered doors, their night sabers leaping over the wreckage with ease. The corpses of a few demons littered the immediate area, apparently caught up in the devastation.

"Mannoroth and the others should still be at the Well!" shouted Dath'Remar. "Therein lies our hope of success!"

Mention of the Well brought Illidan into Tyrande's thoughts. How she wished that he was among these trying to escape the demon lord's evil rather than embracing it.

The sinister mist pervading Zin-Azshari did not slow the riders, the Highborne likely very familiar with it by now. The priestess focused on following her rescuers and waiting.

Waiting for the first threat to their flight.

And when it came, it came in the form of felbeasts, who leapt upon riders in the middle of the pack, bringing down two and nearly eviscerating another. The demons' tentacles adhered to the bodies of the victims, draining them with gusto.

A female spellcaster threw what at first appeared a tiny stick. However, by the time it reached its target, it had stretched out into a full lance, which pierced the felbeast in the chest.

The other demonic hounds perished in similar fashion, the last of them fleeing off with loud, dismayed howls. Dath'Remar sent a bolt of lightning down on the survivors, obliterating two and sending their body parts raining down on the fleeing Highborne. A third felbeast escaped.

"We are surely known now!" the sorcerer snarled. "Faster!"

A deep, mournful horn blared. Moments later, several others from far ahead of the party responded. Tyrande prayed fervently to Elune, aware that the night elves would very soon be fighting for their lives.

"Sarath'Najak! Yol'Tithian! To me!" The pair in question rode up beside Dath'Remar. Each raised a fist ahead and began chanting.

A sharp, continuous flash of crimson energy formed before the lead riders. Even Tyrande sensed the tremendous forces summoned from the Well.

Then . . . out of the mist materialized a wall of gargantuan, tusked warriors framed by the greenish flames radiating from their armored forms. The Fel Guard poured toward the renegades with weapons nearly as long as Tyrande.

But the first to meet the crimson barrier *burned*. Their own flames took on the same cast as the sorcerers' creation, then engulfed the demons. Monstrous warriors shrieked and fell to the wayside. In only a heartbeat, nothing remained of those stricken save a few scorched pieces of armor.

But the demons continued to press and soon they surrounded the escapees. Individual sorcerers began casting their own spells, with mixed success. They could not concentrate on every demon present and those that managed to slip past wreaked havoc on the night elves. A female went down as her mount, its throat severed, collapsed beneath her. Before she could rise, the Fel Guard who had slain her cat beheaded her. Another Highborne was stripped from the saddle, his body impaled through the back before being tossed without care under the trampling paws of the night sabers.

One huge warrior managed to slip in behind Dath'Remar. Gasping, Tyrande drew her blade and prayed for Elune to guide her hand.

The sword took on the pale, silver glow of her patron. It cut through the demon's armor as if through air.

With a grunt, the Fel Guard started to turn toward Tyrande—and the top half of his body slid off. The demon crumpled, the priestess's blessed strike so fine that its victim had not at first realized that he was dead.

Unaware of his near-fatal brush, Dath'Remar shouted something to his two comrades. Tyrande could not see what they did, but the shield that they had created not only spread farther afield, but also shifted to an intense blue.

There was a crackling sound and the first demon to run into the new spell flew back as if tossed by a catapult. He crashed among his fellows, his body crumbling to dust.

This new spell proved far more effective. Slowed down by the demons' initial onslaught, the escaping Highborne now regained speed. Yet, behind them they left more than a dozen of their number, most ripped apart by the savage blades of the Burning Legion. Riderless night sabers, their backs soaked in blood, kept with the pack.

A younger Highborne female near Tyrande screamed, then rose up and vanished into the mist. A second later, her scream cut off with a terrible finality and her broken body dropped among the fleeing figures.

Night elves began looking up and around in consternation. Tyrande looked over her shoulder—and saw, too late, the clawed hands that seized an older male and dragged him up out of sight.

"Doomguard!" she shouted. "Beware! Doomguard in the mists above!"

Another pair of claws came down near her. Tyrande slashed. She heard a savage growl and the Doomguard retreated . . . minus one hand.

Two robed spellcasters raised their arms. What seemed like a halo formed first over them, then spread out over much of the rest of the party.

But before they could finish whatever spell they sought to unleash, an explosion rocked them. Their night sabers reeled and the two Highborne were thrown.

From the center of the explosion arose an Infernal. How the demon had fallen among the riders without being either seen or detected, Tyrande did not know, but, at the moment, that hardly mattered. The Infernal began rampaging among the night elves, crashing into full-size panthers without so much as losing a step.

Even as that happened, two more Highborne were stolen from their seats by Doomguard above. The priestess looked to Dath'Remar, but there was no help or guidance from that direction. The lead sorcerer was already hard-pressed to keep back the thickening ranks of Fel Guard, who appeared to be trying by sheer numbers to overwhelm the spell he and the others had concocted. With each step, the escape slowed and by Tyrande's estimation, it would not be long before the Highborne came to an utter halt.

Pulling up, she raised her sword to her face and called again upon the powers granted her by the Mother Moon. Whether or not she survived, Tyrande could not stand idly by while others perished.

"Please, Mother Moon, hear me, Mother Moon . . ." the priestess muttered.

The glow about her blade spread to her, at the same time intensifying. Tyrande thought of the cleansing light of the lunar deity, how, under it, everything was revealed for what it was.

The silver aura flared bright.

Under Elune's light, the mist melted away. Demons on the ground and in the sky found nothing shielding them. More important, they suddenly cringed and looked away, unable to withstand the divine illumination.

And in faltering, they opened a way for the riders.

"There, Dath'Remar!" Tyrande shouted. "Ride that way!"

He did not have to be encouraged. Dath'Remar and his two comrades blazed the path the priestess's prayer had revealed. Mostly blinded, the few demons before them proved minor obstacles readily crushed.

"Ride through! Ride through!" the leader of the Highborne encouraged. Their attackers fell away, none strong enough to resist the light.

Her heart emboldened, Tyrande enthusiastically followed with the rest. The glow about her extended some distance beyond the fringes of the group. She thanked Elune over and over again for this miracle . . .

But, just as Tyrande herself cut past the Legion's lines,

clawed hands seized her, ripping the priestess from her night saber. With a startled cry, she flew up and away from her companions.

Straining, Tyrande looked into the contorted visage of a Doomguard. The demon's eyes were all but shut and his ragged breathing indicated just how much the illumination around her pained him.

Without hesitation, she cut at the armored figure. Her blow landed sideways, but it startled her attacker. One hand lost its grip. Tyrande had no opportunity to look down to see how far away the ground was. She could only pray that Elune would cushion her fall.

With grim determination, the priestess drove her blade through the Doomguard's chest.

His jerking movements tore the sword from her grip. The last bit of the demon's hold vanished.

Tyrande clutched his dead body, hoping to pull it under her before she hit the earth. Unfortunately, in his death throes, the Doomguard twisted out of her reach.

She shut her eyes tight. Her prayers were to her goddess, but her last focused thoughts were on Malfurion. He would blame himself for her death, if that was now to be, and she wanted no such burden upon his shoulders. What happened to her would be fated by the gods, not his actions. Tyrande understood that Malfurion had done all he could, but that the fate of their people far outweighed her meager self.

But if only she could have looked into his face once more . . .

Tyrande struck the ground . . . and yet, the collision was not at all as she expected. It barely even shook her, much less broke all her bones and split open her skull.

Her fingers touched dirt. She *had* landed . . . but, if so, why was she still in one piece?

Rolling to a sitting position, Tyrande looked around. The aura about her had faded, leaving her surrounded by mist and alone save for the broken bodies of night elves and demons.

No . . . not alone. A tall, so very familiar figure emerged from the resurging mist and, at sight of him, her cheeks flushed.

"Malfurion!"

But almost the instant that Tyrande uttered the name, she knew that she had chosen the wrong one.

Illidan, his mouth fighting a frown, leaned over the fallen priestess. "Stupid little fool . . ." He reached down a hand. "Well? Come on with me . . . if you'd like to live long enough to see me save the world!"

FIFTEEN

Above the center of the Well of Eternity, the Demon Soul flared bright. Within the abyss formed by the Sargeras's spell, forces set in play by both the Soul and the Well churned, slowly building up into the creation of a stable portal. From his monstrous realm, the lord of the Legion prepared for his entrance into this latest prize. Soon, so very soon, he would eradicate all life, all existence, from it . . . and then he would go on to the next ripe world.

But there were others waiting in growing expectation, others with dire dreams far older than even that of the demon lord. They had waited for so very long for the means to escape, the means to reclaim what had once been theirs. Each step of success by Sargeras toward strengthening his portal was a step of success for them. With the Well, with the Demon Soul, and with the lord of the Legion's might, they would instead open up a window into their eternal prison.

And once open, there would be no sealing it again.

The Old Gods waited. They had done so for so very long, they could wait a little longer.

But only a little . . .

• • •

And with the entrance of Sargeras surely imminent, Archimonde threw everything into the battle. He stripped warriors from all other directions, knowing that the defeat of the host would be the defeat of the world.

The host, in turn, fought because it had no choice but to fight. Night elves, tauren, and others knew only that to give in meant to bend their necks to demon blades. Fall they might, but not without giving everything they could.

Malfurion struggled to do his part. His spells summoned whirlwinds that carried aloft warriors and beasts, then dropped them from deathly heights. Seeds cast by him into those winds sprouted full-grown in the demon bellies, ripping their hosts to shreds. The lifeless corpses then dropped down upon the Legion, causing further havoc.

Deep below the earth, Malfurion found the burrowers, the worms and such, who had managed so far to hide from the evil. Urged on by him, they churned away at the ground, making it unstable. Tusked warriors suddenly sank beneath as if in quicksand, while others, bogged down, fell easy prey to archers and lancers.

In the sky, the demons held sway, but they held it with much cost. Jarod had archers almost fully concentrating on the Doomguard and their like. Whatever the carnage caused by the winged furies, many paid for it with bolts bristling out of their necks.

The Moon Guard fought valiantly against the Eredar, the Infernals, and, worse, the Dreadlords. The night elves were strengthened not only by Rhonin and Krasus, but also the shamans of the tauren and furbolgs. The shamans worked in much more subtle manners, but their results were proven by warlocks who fell over dead or simply vanished.

And yet, there were always more demons to replace those who perished.

Brox stood at the forefront with Jarod and Kalimdor's legendary guardians, the orc seeming as astounding a creature as the beings by whose side he fought. Brox laughed as he had not since that day of battle when he and his comrades had expected to die valiantly. Indeed, the graying warrior expected to die now, but still his ax proved the superior, cutting through foe after foe as if it hungered for demon flesh. It was not merely the magic instilled in the weapon that caused such damage to the enemy, but the skill with which the orc wielded it. Brox was a master of his art, which was why his chieftain, Thrall, had chosen him in the first place.

Then, a pack of felbeasts caught one of the bears by surprise, leaping atop their victim and quickly bringing down the giant. Before their gargantuan adversary even hit the ground, a score more joined the first pack. Their suckers immediately adhered to the furred body and the monsters drank lustily of the guardian's inherent magic . . . and, thus, life.

The fallen one's twin roared angrily when he saw what had happened. Pummeling aside Fel Guard, he threw himself upon the horrific leeches. One by one, the demigod tore them away from the unmoving form, ripping off heads and breaking backs in the process.

But when he had reached his twin, it was immediately evident that rescue had come too late.

Raising his head high, the forest guardian roared his pain, then turned on the ranks of demons and began rampaging through their lines as if they were made of paper. Despite lances and other weapons constantly pincushioning him, he dug deeper into the Burning Legion, swiftly leaving behind his other companions until he could no longer even be seen.

Brox and Jarod, closest to the front, heard his last, unrepentant roar . . . and then noted grimly the silence that followed.

Bodies lay littered for as far as the eye could see and it was not uncommon for combatants to duel one another standing atop the corpses of their predecessors. Demigods fought besides night elves who fought beside tauren who fought beside furbolgs, Earthen, and more and all wore the same grim expressions.

It was Cenarius who still led Kalimdor's epic guardians and he tore at the demons with a violence that shocked even Rhonin and Krasus. His gnarled talons stripped through armor and flesh, spilling the monstrous warriors' innards upon the field. The forest lord fought as if one possessed and with the death of each fellow guardian, his efforts grew more terrifying, more relentless. He seemed determined to make up for all those who had fallen, no matter the cost to himself.

And fall they continued to do. With Fel Guard clutching him like hounds worrying their prey, the great boar, Agamaggan, finally teetered. He rammed into several felbeasts, tossing them up or goring them with his tusks, but then, at last, the weight of so many demons proved too much. The demigod dropped to his knees, where his tenacious adversaries began chopping in earnest at his torso. The huge beast shook off some of those clinging to him, but that proved his last effort. Blood dripping from a hundred deep wounds, he groaned . . . and then stilled. Even after, the savage attacks on his body did not cease, the demons so caught up in their butchery that they did not yet realize that they had slain him.

This latest death spurred Cenarius yet further. He fell upon the demons hacking away at the boar's mangled corpse, crushing their throats or impaling them on the other

demigod's thorny mane. Such was his fury that at last he became the prime focus of the Burning Legion's onslaught.
The invisible hand of Archimonde guided the most powerful
of demons toward the forest lord.

Already battling for their own survival, there was nothing
Krasus or any of the others could do. More and more the
fearsome warriors surrounded Malfurion's mentor until
even Cenarius's antlers could barely be seen.

Then . . . just as it seemed he, too, would fall, there was
again the flash of white once seen by Rhonin. A gargantuan,
four-legged form struck the swarm of demons head on. A
rack several times more massive than that of the forest lord
threw fiery warriors by the score from the faltering
Cenarius. Huge hooves crushed in hard skulls or caved in armored chests. Teeth snapped off limbs or ripped open
throats.

And only at last did the astounding creature come into
focus. There, towering over the weakened Cenarius, a magnificent, pure white stag held the demons at bay. So much
did his coat gleam that the minions of the Burning Legion
were half-blinded, making them easy prey for the massive
animal.

Again and again, the stag used his antlers to clear the
bloody field before him of foes. Nothing, not even Infernals,
could slow his efforts. He cleared the Burning Legion not
only from the area of the fallen forest lord, but even from
that of other defenders nearby.

Brox and Jarod suddenly found themselves under the
overwhelming gaze of the stag. Words did not pass from the
gigantic creature to them, yet, somehow they knew that
they were to drag Cenarius back from the battle. This they
did even as a new wave of horror charged forward. Yet, before the stag, nothing long stood. Row upon row of demon

rushed up with weapons drawn, only to be torn to shreds moments later.

But if the Legion's blades could not bring down this new champion, the horde had other, more sinister tools at their disposal. From the sky there abruptly came black lightning, which burnt and baked the ground around the stag. In the lightning's wake erupted dark, green fires that scorched the pristine coat of the demigod. Charred earth rose up and, forming clawed hands, seized the four legs tight.

Then, the ranks of demons parted . . . and through the ominous gap strode Archimonde himself.

With each step toward the stag, Archimode swelled in size until he stood as tall as his adversary. In contrast to his manic warriors, the demonic commander remained stone-faced, almost analytical. He held no weapon, but his clenched fists radiated the same monstrous fire that burned around the stag.

The demigod shook, breaking away the earthy claws. Then, with a challenging snort, the demigod lowered his antlers and met the archdemon.

Their collision was marked by thunder and a tremor that toppled fighters for some distance around. Demons and night elves alike fled the awesome fury of their duel. Where the stag's hooves struck the harsh ground, sparks flew up into the heavens. Archimonde's own feet dug deep, creating ravines and tossing up new hills taller than his warriors.

Bloody scars traced the paths of the demon's claws in the stag's hide. Sharp, glistening dots from which burst green fire showed where antlers had pierced Archimonde's seemingly impervious skin. Demon and demigod wrestled and no other living creature dared come in their path.

Further back, Jarod and Brox, joined midway by Dungard

the Earthen, brought the stricken Cenarius to where Krasus stood. Risking an attack by the Eredar, Krasus pulled himself from the battle to investigate the forest lord's condition.

" 'Tis some bad wounds he's suffered," muttered Dungard, taking out his pipe.

"He is badly struck," the mage agreed after running his hands across Cenarius's chest. "The poison that is a part of all demons affects him much more than most, possibly because of his affinity to Kalimdor itself." Krasus grimaced. "Still, I *think* he will live . . ."

At that moment, the demigod muttered something. Only Krasus knelt close enough to hear his words properly and when the robed figure looked up, he wore an expression of sorrow.

"What is it?" asked Jarod.

But before Krasus could answer, from the battlefield came a terrible cry. As they all turned toward its source, they witnessed Archimonde with one arm around the giant stag's neck, his other hand twisting his foe's muzzle to the side. Already the stag's head turned at an awful angle, hence the cry.

Krasus leapt to his feet. "No! He must not!"

It was already too late. The demon, his expression still indifferent, tightened his hold further.

A tremendous cracking sound echoed through the region, one that, for just a brief moment, caused all other noises to cease.

And in Archimonde's grip, Cenarius's valiant rescuer fell limp and lifeless.

With an almost flagrant detachment, the archdemon tossed aside his adversary as one might discard a piece of refuse. He then wiped his hands and gazed at the stunned defenders.

Suddenly, creeping vines rushed up from the otherwise lifeless soil, seizing Archimonde's limbs and squeezing tight. Undaunted, Archimonde tore off one set of vines, but as he attempted to throw them away, they instead wrapped around his wrist. At the same time, others grew to take the place of those removed.

Malfurion Stormrage stepped forward, facing the distant demon with eyes as dead as when he had first told the others of Tyrande's kidnapping. A static aura surrounded him and he constantly muttered over a small piece of what Krasus was the first to recognize as a leaf similar to those of the vines.

Archimonde's expression never shifted, but his movements became more frantic. The vines now covered three-quarters of his immense body and appeared all but certain to drape the rest imminently.

Perhaps realizing this, the archdemon ceased his attempts to remove the strangling plants. Instead, eyes narrowed, he freed his arms enough to bring his hands together.

And as Archimonde clasped his fingers . . . the Legion's terrifying commander vanished in a blaze of green flame.

Malfurion gasped. The druid went down on one knee, shaking his head.

"I've failed him . . ." Brox and the mage heard him mutter. "Failed my shan'do when I most shouldn't have . . ."

The orc and the Earthen looked to Krasus for some explanation. The robed figure pursed his lips for a moment, then, quietly explained, "The great Green Dragon, the Aspect called Ysera, is the mother of Cenarius, the forest lord."

Dungard, who had been puffing on his pipe, furrowed his brow, then said, "My people always thought it to be Elune who birthed the forest lord . . ."

"The true tale is quite complicated," replied Krasus.

Brox still said nothing, aware that there was more to come.

"His father . . ." the mage continued, "his father is the ancient woodland spirit, Malorne . . ."

After a moment, the orc finally asked, "And so?"

"Malorne . . . also called the White Stag."

Dungard almost dropped his pipe. A sharp intake of breath marked Brox's sudden understanding. He looked out to where the huge, torn body of the beast lay sprawled ignominiously among the other dead. The father had come to save the son at cost of his own life, something any orc easily understood.

"I failed him . . ." Malfurion repeated, forcing himself up. He glanced at Krasus. "From you, I learned that Ysera was my shan'do's mother—which was surprise enough—but I already knew the truth concerning Malorne. Cenarius made it known to me during my studies that he was seed of the White Stag . . ." The night elf clenched his fist. "And when I saw what Archimonde had done to the father of he who's been like a parent to me, I wanted nothing more than to squeeze the life out of the fiend."

Krasus put a comforting hand on the druid's shoulder. "Have heart, young one. You have briefly driven Archimonde from the battle, no light thing . . ." The mage's eyes narrowed as he glanced past his companion to the field of carnage. "It at least buys us time . . ."

Malfurion shook himself from his sorrow. "We're losing, aren't we?"

"I fear so. With all we throw against them, the demons still prove too strong. I had been certain—had thought—" Krasus spat. "I dared turn Time on its head, did everything despite my own warnings . . . and the results are nothing but calamity after calamity!"

"I don't understand . . ."

"You need understand only this—unless the dragons come and come soon, we shall fall, if not by the blades of the Burning Legion, than by a darker, more ancient evil that manipulates even the dread Sargeras! You know of that which I speak! You felt their awful presence! You know what they would wish of this world! They—"

A howl erupted from Krasus.

"What—" began the druid.

Krasus bent low to the ground. The others watched in horror as his limbs began to turn to stone.

"Eredar!" shouted Malfurion. He felt his own limbs begin to contort in what he knew presaged the same dire fate as that striking the mage. "Brox! Seek out Rhonin—"

But the orc was in no better state than the night elf. Wounded though Archimonde had to be, it was clear to all that he had orchestrated this insidious spell that struck only them. Sargeras's lieutenant knew well that to slay Krasus and his band would be to put an end to the last major hurdle preventing the Burning Legion's victory. Even Jarod lay stricken.

Then, just as each felt the growing stone constrict their lungs and force out their last breath, they heard in their minds a feminine voice that both comforted and steeled them. *Fear not,* it said, *and breathe easy . . .*

As one, Krasus, Malfurion, Brox, and Jarod gratefully inhaled. At the same time, they noticed the rising of the wind and the tremendous shadow passing overhead.

"She has come!" roared Krasus, lifting his hands to the heavens. "*They* have come!"

The sky filled with dragons.

They were red, green, and bronze, the flights of Alexstrasza, Ysera, and the absent Nozdormu. The two Aspects dominated the array, their tremendous wings alone spanning distances several times that of the dragons next nearest in size.

As one, the leviathans dove down toward the demons, who were still focused on their earthbound foes.

"Jarod!" called Krasus, spinning on the host's commander. "Get those horns roaring so loud and so long that there will be no mistaking their intent! The day can still be ours!"

Jarod seized the nearest night saber and rode off. As he vanished in the distance, the dragons began their attack in earnest.

A line of crimson giants opened their mighty maws and unleashed an inferno. Fire swept over the Legion's front lines, several hundred demons burnt to ash in the blink of an eye.

Bronze dragons swept over the demon ranks . . . and as they passed, the monstrous warriors moved in reverse. Yet, while Time had turned about for them, it had not for those behind. Chaos ensued as a collision of titanic proportions created utter mayhem among Archimonde's fighters.

One of the bronzes fell—twisted beyond recognition—as the Eredar and Nathrezim sought to hold back this imposing attack. But their spells faltered and their focus turned on one another as the flight of Ysera hovered above. The closed, dreaming eyes of the green dragons put nightmares into the minds of the susceptible spellcasters. Warlocks looked at one another and saw only the enemy about them.

They reacted accordingly. Eredar slew Eredar and Nathrezim gladly joined in the slaughter. Trapped in the dark daydreams created by the greens, the demons were merciless against their own kind and even Archimonde could not rouse them from their lethal mistake.

Back behind the mayhem, Alexstrasza descended to

where Krasus and the others awaited her. Ysera began to do the same—but then, to the astonishment of those who knew of her, the Aspect's eyes opened wide at the horrific sight that lay in the midst of the battlefield. Beautiful, glistening, jade orbs drank in the vision of the white, antlered corpse.

Malorne's corpse.

The dragon let out a wail—not a roar, but a very *pitiful* wail—and flew to where the giant stag lay. The demons still in the area fell victim to her immediate outrage. Ysera snapped up several, crushed others, and sent the rest flying with a slap of one massive wing.

When there was no one else upon which to vent her sorrows, She of the Dreaming descended next to the stag and rested her chin upon his broken head. Her body shook from what could only be sobs.

"We had known we would be late . . ." Alexstrasza managed, eyeing her counterpart with much understanding. "But not so late as this . . ."

"Cenarius still lives," Krasus pointed out. "She must be made aware of that."

With a nod, the Aspect of Life momentarily shut her eyes. A moment later, Ysera lifted her head and looked their way. The two giants gazed at one another, then Ysera fluttered up from Malorne's body.

The others stepped back as she landed next to the unconscious Cenarius. With remarkable delicacy, Ysera took the prone forest lord into her forepaws.

"They will suffer such nightmares that whatever they have for hearts will explode . . ." she grated. "I will bring upon them demons of their own, who will drive them mad until all they can think about is death . . . but I will not permit them to wake long enough to achieve it . . ."

She would have gone on—and also made good her

promise—but Krasus dared interrupt. "Render onto the Legion what fate it deserves, She of the Dreaming, but recall that the fate of Kalimdor—that which Malorne and Cenarius fought well for—still hangs in the balance! Sargeras seeks entrance into the mortal plane . . . and the Old Gods seek to manipulate the demon lord for their own escape!"

"And well aware we are of this," Alexstrasza interjected before a still-distraught Ysera could snap back at the mage. "What is it that must be done?"

"The struggle must go on here, but it also must come to Zin-Azshari . . . and the Well. It will take both dragon and mortal, for there are many elements to confront there."

"Tell us what you plan." Ysera almost objected to her sister's acquiescence, but Alexstrasza would brook no delay from even her. "You know him! You have but to see within him to understand that he must be listened to!"

The emerald dragon finally bowed her head. "So long as the demons suffer."

"We will *all* suffer," the cowled mage went on. "If we do not stop the portal from reaching full bloom . . ." Krasus faced the direction of far-off Zin-Azshari. "A thing that cannot be too far-off, if what I sense means anything . . ."

Sargeras felt Archimonde's hidden dismay. The demon lord was disappointed with his most trusted servant—who had never failed before—but there would be time to punish Archimonde later. The portal was nearly finished. Sargeras wondered why it had taken so long for him to consider this plan. It had all proven so *simple.*

Still, in the long run, such things did not matter. All that did was that soon *he* would step into Kalimdor and when that happened, not all the dragons in that world would be able to save it from him . . .

•   •   •

They felt the nearness of their freedom quickly approaching. How ironic that it would be one who had once been one of the hated Titans who would prove the instrument of their release! It had taken the combined might of many Titans to even force them into captivity; after their triumphant return, there would be little effort needed to eradicate this single, arrogant creature and turn his warriors to serving *their* cause.

The portal strengthened. The time when to usurp it fast approached. Most amusing, the pathetic little beings who fought the fallen Titan's warriors thought that they could take back the disk. Even now, the imprisoned entities could sense the dragons—the Titans' hounds—approaching the Well.

They would be in for a very fatal surprise.

SIXTEEN

A storm raged over the Well, one that from even such a far distance Malfurion could detect all too easily. It was no normal storm, not even in the sense of those that frequented the mystical waters. This one touched upon powers that were not a part of the mortal plane, powers all too akin to those unleashed by the Burning Legion.

The Burning Legion . . . and something more.

The druid did not quite understand just who or *what* the Three were even after having been touched by their ancient evil. In truth, Malfurion did not *want* to know more. What had insinuated itself into his mind during the quest into Deathwing's lair had been enough to make him determined that such beings could never be allowed to enter Kalimdor . . . if that was any more possible to achieve than stopping the entrance of the lord of the Legion.

He glanced up and around him at the hope of his world. A dozen dragons, Alexstrasza and Ysera at their head. Another female who represented the bronzes followed close behind. Three others of each flight flew in their wake, all of them consorts of one of the Aspects, including this Nozdormu spoken of earlier by Krasus.

The mage himself rode astride the giant red's shoulders, seeming to drink in the wind as they sailed. Knowing him for what he was, Malfurion suspected that Krasus tried to imagine himself as one of the dozen leviathans, his own wings sending him coursing through the heavens.

Brox rode the bronze leader and Rhonin one of Alexstrasza's mates. The red Aspect's senior consort—Tyranastrasz—oversaw the dragon efforts against Archimonde, but the rest were with her, save the stricken Korialstrasz. As for Malfurion, the night elf had the honor to have as his mount Ysera. She had, in fact, insisted upon his being the one she carried.

"You are his pride," she had told the druid, speaking of Cenarius, "and for what you sought to do for him and Malorne, I owe you this . . ."

Unable to articulate any worthy reply, Malfurion had simply bowed before her, then climbed up near her shoulders.

And off they had flown, as simple as all that, to face the terrible might of the demon lord and those manipulating him.

As simple as that . . . all knowing that they might very well perish.

Yet, for Malfurion, it was even more complex than that. At this point, he had little fear concerning his own death—any sacrifice he made worth it to stop such menace—but there were others on his mind as well. Somewhere near their destination, somewhere near or within vast Zin-Azshari, he hoped to find Tyrande and Illidan.

He still could not forgive himself for what had befallen Tyrande and could not blame *her* if she could not find it in her heart to forgive him, either. He had let her fall into the Legion's clutches, a most unthinkable fate. No, if, as he hoped, Tyrande lived, Malfurion expected nothing but hatred and contempt from his childhood friend.

What he expected from himself if he came across his *brother*, the druid could not even imagine, but something would have to be done about Illidan.

Something . . .

"Illidan, please! You must listen to me!" Tyrande blurted as the sorcerer dragged her along with him. It was not her first such outburst, but she hoped that this time he might heed her words. "This is not the path you should take! Think! By embracing the power of the Legion, you more and more draw yourself toward their evil!"

"Don't talk nonsense! I'm going to save Kalimdor! I'll be its beloved hero!" He turned on her. "Don't you understand? Nothing else has worked! We fought and fought and the Legion just keeps coming! I finally came to realize that the only way to deal with demons was to understand them as only they can understand themselves! We must use what they were against them! That's why I came here and pretended to join their ranks! I even fooled their lord into granting me his greatest gifts—"

"Gifts? You call what he did to your eyes *gifts?*"

Malfurion's brother loomed over her, looking at that moment more like one of the demons than any night elf. "If you could *see* as I do, you'd know how amazing the powers are he gave me . . ." With an unnerving smile, Illidan allowed her again to see the pits where once his eyes had been. He paid no mind when Tyrande, just as she had upon her first view of the horror wrought upon him, involuntarily pulled back. Replacing the scarf, he concluded, "Yes, the greatest gifts imaginable . . . and the greatest weapons against the Burning Legion . . ."

The sorcerer pulled her along again and although it was within the priestess's power to struggle free of him, in truth, Tyrande did not exactly wish to leave Illidan. She feared for him, feared for his heart and mind and wanted to do what she could to try to save the misguided spellcaster. The teachings of Elune only in part guided her; Tyrande Whisperwind still recalled vividly the younger Illidan, the Illidan full of dreams, hope, and goodness.

She only prayed that some part of that younger Illidan still existed within this more jaded, highly-ambitious figure eagerly dragging her through a demon-benighted land.

Thinking of the armored horrors she had already fought, Tyrande glanced around as they wended their way through the fallen city. Each moment, the priestess expected one of the monstrous warriors to pop up from among the ruins and attack. Surely, Mannoroth knew of Illidan's treachery by now.

Perhaps noticing her glances or even reading her thoughts, the black-clad sorcerer slyly informed Tyrande, "The spellwork over the Well has Mannoroth's full attention and he thinks little of me as it is. I've cast the illusion that I've returned to my quarters and am meditating." He grinned wide. "Besides that, the flight of several of the Highborne— the priestess of Elune with them—has also taken their focus elsewhere."

In the distance, they heard Legion horns again sounding the chase. Tyrande prayed to Elune to watch over Dath'Remar and his comrades. They had a long, long way to ride and so many demons to fight through.

Oblivious to her concern for the Highborne, Illidan grinned and added, "Yes, this should give me just enough time for what I planned!"

"And what is that?" Even as she asked, Tyrande saw in the

distance the black, foreboding waters. "Why are we headed toward the Well?"

"Because I intend to turn Sargeras's portal into a full-fledged maelstrom, one that will *suck* the demons back out of Kalimdor and into their nether world! I'll utterly reverse the effect of the dragon's disk! Think of it! With one spell, I'll save not only our people, but *everything!*"

His expression shifted, now almost seeming hopeful of her approval. However, when Tyrande did not immediately show such emotion, Illidan quickly became his harsher self again.

"You don't believe I can do it! Maybe if I was your precious Malfurion, you'd be jumping up and down, clapping your hands at my cleverness!"

"It isn't that at all, Illidan! I just—"

"Never mind!" He peered around the stormy landscape, seeking something. His monstrous gaze alighted on a fallen tree home. The angle of the dead oak meant that they could climb inside and get a perfect view of the Well of Eternity. "Just Perfect! Get in there!"

Practically tossed forward, the priestess wended her way into the ruined domicile. The sorcerer followed right behind, all but shoving her as they went.

As she climbed into the overturned structure, Tyrande's foot kicked something.

A skull.

She found herself standing amidst a pile of bones from at least five or six figures. No skeleton was complete and most of the bones had long, telling scratches and gouges in them. Tyrande shuddered, hoping that the felbeasts had feasted on dead carcasses, not living, helpless victims, but from experience fearing the worst.

"You can pray over them once I've saved all of us," Illidan

remarked disdainfully. "Just ahead looks like the best—"

A monstrously-familiar form leapt out of the shadows.

It took down Malfurion's twin before he could react. Tyrande screamed, then immediately called upon the power of Elune.

But before she could do anything, the felbeast, its tentacles already seeking Illidan's chest, howled painfully. The demon hound writhed as the sorcerer calmly rose. Illidan's right hand held both suckers together.

"I could use the magic you've been gorging yourself on . . ." he commented almost blithely to the creature.

The night elf planted his left palm against the suckers. However, unlike times past, this felbeast showed no interest in trying to drink from its intended victim. Instead, it fought—however futilely—to pull its vile appendages back.

Illidan's left hand glowed an eerie green that Tyrande recognized as the same color as the horrific flames surrounding the demons. Malfurion's twin inhaled—and Tyrande watched in horror as the demon literally crumbled to dust from end to front, whining to the last. Its very essence was sucked into the sorcerer's palm.

As the horrific vision unfolded, Illidan's aspect became something frightening to behold. Even though he had replaced the scarf over his eye sockets, she could see the terrible fires burning within. The sorcerer wore a wide, almost drunken grin and around him flared green flames as potent as those surrounding any demon. Illidan seemed to swell—

Then, the flames abruptly died away and the sorcerer instantly returned to his normal appearance. He wiped clean his hand, then kicked a little at the ash that was all that remained of the felbeast. Smoothing his hair, Illidan gave Tyrande another confident smile. "Well! Shall we proceed?"

The priestess hid her shock as best she could. This was no

longer the Illidan with whom she had grown up. This figure reveled in carnage as much as the demons themselves did. Worse, that he could so eagerly accept into his body the taint of the Legion stirred within her a disgust that Tyrande had never experienced.

Mother Moon, guide me in this! Tell me what to do! Can I still save him?

"Up here," her companion ordered. "I can focus on the center of the Well from that point on the roof."

Moving past the bones, they climbed up to what had once been an elegant roof terrace. Broken rails originally shaped from living wood lay scattered on the ground below and a pearl statue of Azshara—still amazingly whole—lay tangled in the dead foliage of the tree that had supported the house.

Illidan propped himself against what had once been the mosaic floor. Bits of the forest pageantry that decorated it still remained, revealing bits of fanciful animals, bucolic scenery, and lush trees.

Queen Azshara's beatific countenance still made up the center. Malfurion's brother rested his head against her full, if now cracked, lips.

"Nearly time," he murmured, speaking to himself more than her. From a pouch on his belt, Illidan removed a long, narrow vial. Although the crimson glass hid exactly what was within, Tyrande sensed just enough about its contents to feel her anxiety rise.

"Illidan . . . what's in that bottle?"

His shrouded gaze did not shift from the container. "Just a bit of the Well itself."

"What?" His words, said so lightly expressed, shook her to the core. Illidan had dared *take* from the night elves' source of power? "But—no one—it's forbidden—even the Highborne would never think—"

The sorcerer nodded. "No . . . even *they* wouldn't. That is so interesting about our people, wouldn't you say, Tyrande? Surely, though, the notion occurred to *someone* before me . . . perhaps that's where our legends of our greatest spellcasters comes from. Maybe they secretly borrowed from the Well for a special casting or two! Probably did." Illidan shrugged, his countenance stiffening again. "But even if no one else ever did, I don't see any reason why I should hold back. It just came to me, as if out of the blue. Take some of the Well for myself and there will be nothing too great for me to achieve!"

"But the Well—even a drop of it—" Tyrande had to make him see sense! Dabbling with the waters of the Well in such a way courted disaster on par with his acceptance of the Legion's dark magic.

"Yes . . . imagine what forces this entire vial contains . . ." Had Illidan still had true eyes, they would have lit up with anticipation of the results he expected. "Should be enough to enable me to save the world!"

But the priestess was not so convinced. As an acolyte of Elune, Tyrande was far more aware of the Well's legends and history than Illidan could possibly be. "Illidan . . . to use the Well against itself in such a way . . . you could be opening the doors to utter chaos! Remember the tale of Aru-Talis . . ."

"Aru-Talis is only that. A myth."

"And is the gaping crater, so many generations overgrown now by new life, also a myth?"

He waved off her warning. "No one knows what happened to that city or even if it really existed! Spare me your stories of wisdom and fear . . ."

"Illidan—"

The scarved face contorted in growing anger. "I want you to be quiet . . . *now*."

"—" No sound escaped Tyrande's mouth despite her best attempt to create even the slightest noise. Even when she coughed, it was in utter silence.

Standing again, Illidan eyed the center of the Well. The storm had grown so intense that the ruined tree home now shook from the rising winds. Over the waters, unsettling, almost ghostly lights flashed.

The priestess shook her head. It bothered her that, despite Illidan's own confidence in his abilities, they had not been noticed. Surely Mannoroth was not so blind as Malfurion's twin believed. Yet, other than the hound, they had come across no demons save a pair of Fel Guard early on that Illidan had misdirected with a simple wave of his hand.

Illidan touched a finger to the stopper, which only now Tyrande saw was a tiny, crystalline facsimile of the queen from head to foot. Azshara spun around three times as if dancing for the sorcerer, then the stopper popped off. Illidan caught it with ease.

"Watch, Tyrande . . . watch while I do what your precious Malfurion could not . . ."

And he promptly poured the contents over himself.

But the waters of the Well did not act like normal waters, at least not where Illidan was concerned. They did not drench him and, in fact, only momentarily even made him damp. More ominous, wherever the waters touched Malfurion's twin, he briefly shimmered an intense black. Then, the unsettling aura sank within the sorcerer, filling him much as the felbeast's stolen energies had earlier.

"By the gods . . ." he whispered. "I knew I would feel something . . . but this . . . this is *wonderful.*"

The priestess vehemently shook her head, but her silent protest was lost on Illidan. She started toward him, only to discover that he had also sealed her feet in place.

Mother Moon! she thought. *Can you not help me?*

But there was no sign that Elune responded and Tyrande could only continue to watch Illidan.

He stretched his arms toward the Well and began muttering under his breath. Now the black aura returned, concentrating itself in his hands and intensifying more with each second.

Beneath the scarf, his eye sockets glowed like fire. The material even looked as if it had begun to singe.

But as Illidan began his spell, Tyrande's own highly-attuned senses felt another presence stir. The priestess sought again to give warning, but Illidan faced away from her.

She felt the invisible presence enshroud the unsuspecting sorcerer and, as it did, Tyrande realized it was not the touch of *one* being, but rather *several*.

And as that awful knowledge sank in, so, too, did the sensation that the entities were of a nature as dark as—no!—*darker* than even that she had felt when touched by the foul mind of Sargeras.

It astounded her that Illidan did not also sense them. Tyrande, certain that somehow this was yet another vile element of the Burning Legion, waited for Malfurion's brother to be horribly struck down.

But, instead, she noted in amazement that the mysterious entities now *augmented* Illidan's spell, transforming it into something far more formidable than it would have been. The sorcerer laughed as his work drew near to fruition, Illidan clearly certain that all the effort was his and his alone.

The priestess suddenly understood that the lack of encounters along the way to the Well had not been entirely due to Illidan's cunning.

More frantic now, she prayed over and over to Elune for aid. Illidan had to be warned that he was being duped. She was certain that his grand spell would somehow only trigger a worse disaster.

Mother Moon! Hear my pleas!

A blessed warmth filled Tyrande. She felt the spell that Illidan had put on her suddenly fade away. Her hopes rose anew.

"Illidan!" the priestess immediately cried out. "Illidan! Beware—"

But even as he started to look her way, the sorcerer brought his palms together . . . and a beam of black light burst forth, racing out into the storm-rocked heavens above the Well of Eternity.

Tyrande felt the presences withdraw. Worse, as they faded away, she also sensed their immense satisfaction.

Her warning had come too late.

Sargeras felt the last vestiges of resistance suddenly fall away. The portal that he desired began to fully form. Soon, he would gain entrance into this life-befouled world . . .

Krasus jolted.

"What is it?" called Alexstrasza.

The cowled figure eyed the tiny vision of Zin-Azshari lying far ahead . . . and the colossal tempest spreading out over the Well of Eternity. He shuddered. "I fear we have even less time than I calculated . . ."

"Then, we must make even greater speed!" With that, the huge red dragon beat her wings harder yet, her muscles straining from effort.

Peering behind them, Krasus saw the other dragons follow suit. Everyone sensed that, more than ever, time was against them. The mage silently swore. This should not have happened. Even his own kind had taken far too long to debate the merits of what should have been obvious. If they had only listened . . .

Yet, Krasus could also not help thinking that, if he and his comrades failed, the doom befalling not only the night elves but unborn generations ahead would be in tremendous part his fault. He himself had hesitated to toy with Time, then, when the decision had finally been made to do so, he it was who had suggested attempting no pursuit of Illidan's band. Of all who had crossed its path, Krasus knew most the cursed way of the Demon Soul. If he had tried to track down those who had taken it from Malfurion, then perhaps there would have still been a chance to retrieve the disk.

But that was neither here nor there. What mattered now was to make amends, to still return history to its former course.

"We must be prepared!" he called out to Alexstrasza. "Even though we will bypass the palace, neither the Highborne nor Mannoroth can be taken lightly, even by our ancient line! They will attack from Azshara's stronghold! Nor must we forget what else seeks use of the portal the Well and the Soul create! They will also do everything within their power to keep us from the disk."

"If sacrifice ourselves we must to save Kalimdor, then we but fulfill our sacred duty!" she responded back.

Krasus gritted his teeth. The future he knew so well was still a possible thing, but just as likely was one—supposing that they succeeded—where any or all of them perished here. For himself, that was something he could accept. To see his beloved queen die, though . . .

No! She will not! The mage prepared himself. Whatever it

took, he would do his best to see that Alexstrasza lived . . . even if without him.

The dragons came upon the outskirts of Zin-Azshari and Krasus, who had expected the carnage wrought by the Burning Legion's initial entrance into the mortal plane, was still highly repelled by all he saw. Memories of that second war, when Dalaran and other nations had fallen before the demons and their dread allies, stirred.

Below, endless ranks of demons looked up at their coming and roared challenge. The dragons ignored most, the Fel Guard and their like bound to the ground and, therefore, of little threat. Of more interest were the Doomguard, who came up in great numbers, fiery lances and blades at the ready.

Alexstrasza watched a massive group converge on them, then, pulling her head back, she released a fount of flame.

Cries arose and burning Doomguard plummeted. With that single breath, the crimson leviathan had cleared the sky of almost a hundred demons.

"Gnats . . ." she muttered. "Nothing but gnats . . ."

Then, one of the green dragons in the back roared in surprise as he was pummeled by several huge, round missiles. Krasus did not have to see them close to know that they were Infernals. Even the scales of a huge dragon were not entirely impervious. The wounds the green suffered were superficial, but repeated strikes would eventually take their toll.

"Let us make some use of these foul creatures!" Ysera hissed. She focused her closed eyes upon the next wave.

The new band of Infernals slowed. They continued to descend, but far from their intended targets. Krasus calculated their new path and smiled grimly. The palace was about to learn firsthand of the sort of devastation that they had permitted into Kalimdor.

But Krasus's earlier warning of the dangers that both the Highborne and Mannoroth represented proved all too prophetic in the moments following, for suddenly the stormy sky unleashed a barrage of horrific, black bolts. Caught in the center, the dragons and their riders were forced to break formation just in the hopes of surviving.

Not all did. Perhaps slowed by the earlier barrage of Infernals, the green male hesitated. More than a dozen bolts struck him hard. Lightning scorched through his left wing, then seared him horribly in his tail and chest.

But although the lightning ceased, the worst was yet to come. Each of the wounds burned bright, and, as Krasus watched, their damage rapidly spread along the dragon's body. Weakened further, the green made an all too easy target for more of the Highborne's lightning. Six more bolts caught the male as he fought to stay aloft. The dragon roared in agony, his death knell echoing in Krasus's ears.

The green dropped from the sky.

His huge form hit the Well's dark waters hard. Yet, even for so gigantic a creature, the dragon's collision was as a pebble to the swirling maelstrom. Barely a ripple marked the green as he sank into the foreboding lake.

A foreboding rumble filled their ears.

"Hold on tight!" commanded Alexstrasza, turning.

A new, frenzied attack swarmed the dragons. Black lightning shot down everywhere and, this time, no dragon survived unscathed. Even Alexstrasza shook as one bolt caught her on the right hip.

"It does not burn!" she exclaimed. "It is so very cold! It chills to the bone!"

"I will see what I can do for it!"

"No!" She glanced back at him. "We must preserve our strength for attack—!"

The Aspect of Life abruptly banked, barely avoiding a pair of bolts that would have struck not only her dead-on, but Krasus as well. All over the heavens, dragons twisted about in a macabre ballet. Krasus looked about and saw that all his companions still held tight. He had feared that the necessity of avoiding the magical lightning might make it impossible for the dragons to keep their riders aloft, but even under such circumstances, the ancient leviathans kept watch over their charges.

But this could not go on forever. Eyes narrowed, Krasus peered toward the center of the Well. Yes . . . he could detect the Demon Soul. He could also sense that the portal was nearly complete.

"To the center!" the cowled spellcaster shouted. "We have little time!"

Alexstrasza immediately veered that direction. Krasus leaned forward. As vast as the Well of Eternity was, it still proved only a few beats of Alexstrasza's vast wings to bring them within sight of their objective.

Sure enough, there, high above the gaping maw of the maelstrom, the Demon Soul floated almost serenely. Surrounded by an unholy black aura, it was unaffected by the fearsome magical storm.

"It will be protected!" Krasus reminded her.

"Ysera and I will work in conjunction with Nozdormu's prime consort!"

He nodded. "Rhonin and I will watch for reaction from Sargeras or the Old Gods!"

The riderless dragons withdrew to watch for attack from Zin-Azshari. The three female dragons encircled the sinister disk, their previous encounter with it making all extremely wary. Alexstrasza looked once at her counterparts, then nodded.

From each burst forth a golden light.

Their spells touched the Demon Soul simultaneously, enveloping it. The foul aura about it was smothered by their power. The disk began to tremble . . .

Without warning, their spells were suddenly repelled. The backlash was so terrible that all three dragons were tossed backward for some distance. It was all that their riders could do to maintain hold.

Barely clinging to his queen, Krasus shouted, "What is it? What happened?"

Alexstrasza managed to right herself. Her eyes stared wide at the Demon Soul, now some distance off. "The Old Gods! I *felt* them! But from within the disk! The Demon Soul not only bears a part of our existence, but *theirs* as well!"

The news did not entirely surprise Krasus. Yet, clearly their addition to the disk's creation did not hinder the Elder Gods as it did the dragons. They obviously hoped to wield it, something that the other dragons could not do. Deathwing had evidently crafted it differently where they were concerned . . . if he had even realized their intrusion.

"Can you penetrate their spellwork?"

"I do not know . . . I honestly do not know!"

Krasus swore. Once again, he had underestimated the Three.

He saw Rhonin trying to signal him. The wizard pointed in the direction of Zin-Azshari. Krasus turned his gaze toward the fabled city—

—And watched as more than a score of shadowy abominations, each as large as a dragon, soared toward them.

SEVENTEEN

Azshara had been primping herself.

Oh, it was not that she was not already perfection incarnate—even *she* knew that much—but that for once the queen had found someone worthy of more effort.

My Lord Sargeras is arriving! At last, one fit to be called my husband!

Not for a moment did Azshara question the sanity of her convictions. She who had mesmerized her subjects was herself mesmerized by the lord of the Legion.

At that moment, a tremor shook the palace. It was not the first to do so. Pulling herself from the splendid view in the mirror, the queen spun around. "Vashj! Vashj! What is responsible for that awful racket?"

Her chief handmaiden came rushing in. "A feeble attempt by rabble to stop the inevitable, so reports Captain Varo'then, oh Light of Lights!"

"And what is the dear captain doing about this insult to my ears?"

"Lord Mannoroth has given to him and his hand-picked soldiers appropriate mounts. The captain is already on his way to deal with the miscreants."

"So, all is proceeding as it should? There will be no delay of our lord's arrival?"

Lady Vashj bowed elegantly. "None that Lord Mannoroth foresees. The rabble batter uselessly at the spell."

"Splendid . . ." Queen Azshara went back to admiring herself in the mirror. There was really nothing else she could do to further enhance her beauty. The silken gown trailed behind her over the marble floor, its gossamer design leaving very little unrevealed. Her luxurious hair was piled high and glittering star diamonds—illuminated by their own inner light—decorated it in strategic locations.

Another tremor struck, this one much nearer. Azshara heard cries from the direction of her handmaidens' quarters and saw cracks spread across the wall there.

"See if anyone is injured, Vashj," she commanded. As the latter moved to obey, the ruler of the night elves added, "And if so, please relieve her of her duties and send her back to her family. I will accept nothing but utter perfection from those who would surround me."

"Aye, Light of Lights!"

A distasteful frown greeted Azshara as she looked again to the full-length mirror in the opposing wall. The queen immediately imagined greeting her Lord Sargeras. That brought back the smile.

"There . . . now we just have to wait a little longer . . ." She continued to survey herself, dreaming of the world that she and her new mate would create. A world as perfect as her.

A world *worthy* of her.

Malfurion shook his head, trying to clear it of the vertigo he had suffered during Ysera's tumble. It amazed him that he even had a head left to shake, considering that more than once the druid had been hanging by his hands over the gaping hole at the center of the darksome Well.

"What happened?" he asked, not realizing that he repeated Krasus's own query.

Ysera told him much the same as Alexstrasza had the mage. The night elf listened with sinking heart. To come so close, only to have their hopes dashed so quickly . . .

Then, he, like Rhonin and Krasus, saw the horrific forms rising up from the city. Malfurion saw that soldiers rode astride the abominations, which resembled bats formed from shadow. He knew without a doubt that Captain Varo'then would be leading the sinister band.

Sure enough, a moment later, the druid made out the familiar figure of the scarred officer. Sword out, Varo'then shouted something to those behind him. Immediately, the soldiers broke up into three groups, one for each flight. Only then did Malfurion see that he had terribly underestimated their numbers. There had to be at least three beasts for every dragon.

Alexstrasza wasted no time. The red dragon unleashed a stream of fire—which went through the foremost monster and continued on, finally fading. Even the soldier riding the beast looked unfazed.

"That's impossible!" Malfurion gasped.

"Impossible . . . yes . . ." Ysera's eyes moved back and forth rapidly beneath her shut lids. "There is . . . a fault in our perspective of these fiends . . ."

"What do you mean?"

"That they are not quite as they appear to be nor are they *where* they seem."

Yet, if that was the case, Varo'then and his soldiers made for very tangible illusions. Two of the shadow creatures fixed onto Brox's mount, tearing at her wings. The bloody scores that they made in her hard, scaled hide were proof enough as to their deadliness. Yet, when the bronze sought to strike back, her attacks went for naught.

Ysera, too, fell prey to them. One flew past her throat, raking it with curved, black claws that were a part of the wing. Blood dripped from the red wounds. Ysera snapped at the wing, but her bite found only air.

"I know where they must be!" growled Ysera, for one of her rare times losing her patience. "But when I wish to strike, they are no longer there!"

To make matters worse, one in particular now fixed upon Malfurion and the Aspect . . . the beast carrying Captain Varo'then himself.

"I thought I spied you!" sneered the scarred night elf. "As slippery as your brother! I warned them! I knew he couldn't be trusted!"

Malfurion had no opportunity to ask what Varo'then meant by his words, for the next second the captain and his unholy mount were upon the druid and the dragon. A fetid smell engulfed Malfurion and even Ysera wrinkled her nose. Intangible to their attacks this horror might be, but its stench was so powerful that the druid felt as if struck by a fist.

A mocking laugh was all that warned Malfurion of the captain's lunge. Varo'then's blade stretched impossibly, darting for the other night elf's unprotected chest.

Tipping to the right, Malfurion avoided the sword, but nearly lost his grip. As he clutched tight, Varo'then attacked him again.

Ysera could do nothing, for the inky form of the bat creature all but enveloped She of the Dreaming. At the same time, a second monster snagged the dragon's hind legs.

Something that Cenarius had taught him suddenly came

to mind. Reaching into a pouch, the druid removed a small, prickly seed. Unlike those he had used against the Burning Legion in the past, this one had points too delicate to wreak any havoc on the foe. However, they were especially adept at sticking to anything with which they came into contact.

He tossed out two to the heavens and through his casting the two became four, then became eight, sixteen, and doubled accordingly in rapid succession. Within a heartbeat, hundreds filled the air, then thousands. They did not, as they should have, cling to the dragons or Malfurion's comrades, for that was not the druid's desire. Rather, he sought to use them to find out the truth about their adversaries.

The first ones passed through the bat creatures, but, curiously, others began sticking to empty space. More and more quickly followed suit. Shapes began to form, shapes creating quite a revelation.

The secret of the shadow bats finally lay revealed. The monstrous mounts of the soldiers shimmered constantly, disappearing from sight every few seconds and reappearing elsewhere almost instantly. To fight them would still prove tricky, but now the defenders had a far better idea of where to strike and that was all that they needed.

Perhaps because the bronze female was part of the Aspect of Time's flight, she reacted quickest. With great gusto, the dragon seized upon one bat who materialized just within reach. Her swiftness astounded Malfurion, as did her savageness. She ripped through what passed for a stout neck on the creature, then sent it and its frantic rider hurtling into the black void below.

"Damn!"

At the angry epithet, Malfurion looked over his shoulder to find Captain Varo'then almost upon both his and Ysera's back. The scarred night elf thrust and this time managed to scrape the druid's leg. His thigh stinging, Malfurion threw the first thing that he could pull from a pouch.

His adversary sneezed—and so did his hideous mount. Taking advantage of the distraction, Ysera dove into the monster, biting and tearing with such abandon that no semblance of her superior intellect remained apparent. She was pure beast, fighting with the same primal fury as her foe.

But the shadow creature was not defenseless. Its claws were still as sharp as the dragon's and its long fangs looked more than able to pierce hard scale. With a strange keening cry, it met Ysera eagerly.

At first, the two riders could do nothing but hold on for their lives. Malfurion tried to concentrate on a spell, but the jarring movements of the two combating behemoths made that impossible.

Ysera batted with her tail at the second creature near her hind legs. A lucky strike sent the beast flying back, giving the dragon, at least for the moment, a more even combat with Varo'then's mount.

The captain had sheathed his sword and now drew a dagger. Suspecting that Varo'then was quite skilled at tossing such a blade, Malfurion kept low. The officer grinned darkly, patient despite their dire situation.

Ysera's body jerked. The druid looked down and saw that the second beast had returned . . . and a third followed close behind. He shouted a warning to the dragon.

With a roar, the green leviathan used her incredible wings to throw herself from her opponent. The act caught both the monster and Varo'then by surprise. It also enabled Ysera to turn on her second attacker. Wings still, she dropped upon the bat and rider, catching both under her immense girth. Her claws ripped to shreds the seed-coated wings and she bit deep into the squat neck.

With a harsh squeal, the monstrosity went limp in her claws. Ysera immediately discarded the carcass, letting it fall toward the Well. Of the soldier, Malfurion could see no sign and the druid had to assume he had been slain when first the dragon had landed atop the pair.

As the green leviathan pulled away in order to orient herself, the night elf caught brief glimpses of the others. Three bat creatures harassed Brox and the bronze. Even as Malfurion watched, the orc buried his ax in the shoulder of the nearest with remarkable effect. The enchanted weapon cut through whatever bone and sinew there was and exited the other side.

The monster veered off awkwardly, barely able to stay aloft. The bronze, however, did not let it escape. She breathed once at the fleeing figures . . . and both rider and mount transformed from menace to decayed corpses that a moment later crumbled to dust. The mad wind quickly scattered the decomposing fragments over the dark waters.

But if several of the bats were gone, so, too, were some of the dragons. Only one other green male still flew and one of the bronzes was also missing. Others among the survivors had bleeding wounds that, with what they had suffered from the lightning barrage, had to be be debilitating.

But, worse, Malfurion knew that so long as they had to deal with their foes, they could do nothing about the Demon Soul and the portal. Already, the vast maelstrom below had taken on a noticeable greenish hue at its edges, one too akin to the flames of the Burning Legion to be coincidence.

"The Demon Soul!" he shouted. "We have to do something about it! The portal's nearly complete!"

"I am open to suggestions, mortal—if you can also tell me how to be rid of these pests at the same time!"

A fiery burst briefly illuminated their surroundings.

Malfurion caught the last vestiges of a burning bat dropping into the Well. Directly above it flew Alexstrasza and Krasus. The druid could sense the mage's handiwork in the devastation. Given time, the band *would* defeat Varo'then's fighters, but by then it would be too late. Even if it would not be, they had already seen that the combined might of Ysera and Alexstrasza was not enough to break the defenses surrounding the disk. Something else would have to be done . . . but *what?*

Dragons and bats continued to swoop past. The odds were more even than before, but still not enough to enable them to concentrate at all on the Demon Soul. The shadow bats continued to harass each of the dragons. One of the reds, already dripping from several bites, fell under assault by a pair of the fiends. Another bronze bit through the wing of her assailant, but the monster had its fangs deep in her shoulder. Rhonin and Krasus continued to cast spells of varying success and Brox cut expertly at whatever foe came within reach.

An ebony form darted past. Malfurion thought it one of the bats, but then saw the familiar, reptilian outline of a dragon. He glanced away—then, jaw dropping—looked back again.

It was indeed a dragon . . . but a dragon as black as the demonic creatures that they fought and with iron plates bolted to his hide.

Deathwing . . .

They had thought that they could keep his beloved creation hidden from him. They had dared think that he would not eventually find out where it had been taken. Their audacity enraged him. Once Neltharion had his glorious disk back, he would punish *all* of them. The world would be better off with no one but dragons . . . and only dragons who understood matters as he did.

Called by the Soul, Neltharion had flown across the swirling Well totally oblivious to what was happening. Everything else was of secondary importance. All that existed for the black dragon was the disk.

He flew past both Ysera and Alexstrasza, giving them but cursory glances. With the disk, he would bring them down, then add them to his consorts. Their power would add to his, as was only right.

The Soul floated serenely ahead, as if waiting patiently for him to rescue it. Neltharion's monstrous visage stretched into a wide, anticipatory grin. They would soon be reunited . . .

Then a force struck the black with such might that Neltharion was tossed back among the combatants. He collided with one of the bat creatures, sending its rider screaming to his death. Neltharion roared in outrage at the unexpected attack. Seeking a focus for his intense anger, he seized the stunned bat and tore it to shreds. When that did not assuage him, he turned his baleful gaze on the disk, searching with his heightened senses for that which held him from his prize.

The spellwork he detected around the Soul was intricate, very intricate . . . and vaguely familiar in some aspects. Yet, Neltharion could not put together the voices in his head with that which now confronted him. Even when those same voices now began urging him away from his desire, the dragon could not conceive that he had been someone's dupe.

Neltharion shook his head, driving away the voices. If they spoke against taking the disk, then they were no more to be trusted than Alexstrasza and the others. Nothing—absolutely nothing—mattered other than retrieving the Soul.

And so, the huge black dove in again.

But, like before, he was repelled as if nothing of consequence. The dragon fought not merely the power wielded by the voices, but also that of the lord of the Legion. With a roar mixing outrage and pain, Neltharion spun far beyond the battle, finally coming to a halt at the very northern edge of the Well. Fighting his agony, the furious giant glared at the storm-wracked center.

He would not be rejected again. Whatever spells his enemies had cast around the Soul, he would tear through them. The disk would be his . . .

And then *all* of them would pay . . .

The Burning Legion struggled against the overwhelming might of both the dragons and the host. Doomguard swarmed the leviathans, seeking to bring them down by lance. Nathrezim and Eredar cast monstrous spells, but they were caught between defending against the dragons and fighting the Moon Guard. The warlocks could not do both. They perished more often than they slew, mostly under the unyielding flame of a leviathan's breath.

Yet, throughout it all, Archimonde revealed no uncertainty. He understood that what happened here now had no relevance save that the mortals and their allies would be distracted until the coming of his Lord Sargeras. Archimonde accepted that he and Mannoroth would be punished for their failure to prepare Kalimdor properly for their master, but that was as it should be. All that mattered now was to play the game a little longer. If that meant the deaths of more Fel Guard and Eredar, then so be it. There were always more, especially waiting to march in behind Sargeras.

But that did not at all mean that Archimonde simply

watched and waited. If he was to be punished, he would vent some of his well-hidden fury on those who had caused it. The giant demon raised his hand, pointing toward a bronze dragon hovering above the Legion's right flank. The dragon had been systematically ripping apart warriors below, digging through them the way a burrowing animal would soft earth.

Archimonde made a grasping gesture. The distant dragon suddenly quivered . . . and then every scale *tore* from its body. Blood spilling from everywhere, the flayed giant bellowed in shock, then dropped among its victims. Demon warriors immediately flowed over the unprotected body, thrusting with their weapons until the dragon lay lifeless.

Unsatisfied, Archimonde looked for another victim. How he wished the night elf, Malfurion Stormrage, had been among the host. The druid had cost him much in their previous encounter, but Archimonde sensed that Malfurion was one of those who had flown toward the Well. Once Sargeras came through, the druid would suffer a far worse fate than even Archimonde had planned for him.

Still, there were so many others upon which to vent himself. Expression cold and calculating, the archdemon fixed upon a band of the bullmen he had heard called tauren. They had the potential to become splendid additions to the Legion's ranks, but this particular group would never survive to see that glorious day . . . or the end of their world, either . . .

They were winning . . . they were winning . . .

The dragons had made the difference. Jarod knew that. Without them, the host would have fallen. The demons had come across the one force that they could not defeat. True, some dragons had perished—one just in a most grisly manner—but the host pushed forward and the demons fought in more and more disarray.

Still, he was bothered. The demons' confusion was no trick this time, that he knew. Yet, he would have expected something more from Archimonde. Some masterful regrouping. Archimonde, though, seemed to be attempting nothing more than a holding action, as if he awaited something . . .

The night elf cursed himself for a fool. Of *course*, Archimonde awaited something . . . or rather *someone*.

His lord, Sargeras.

And if the archdemon believed that the arrival of the Legion's master was still imminent, that did not bode well for those who had gone to take the Demon Soul and seal the portal.

For a moment, Jarod's nerve failed him, but then his expression hardened and he fought with even more fervor. It would not be due to any lacking on his part if the defenders failed. His people—his *world*—would certainly fall if the host faltered now. Jarod could only hope that Krasus, Malfurion, and the others would somehow still succeed in their mission.

Overhead, dragons continued to soar past in search of the enemy or to aid those in the host under the most stress. To the commander's right, Earthen chopped their way through demoralized Fel Guard. A furbolg battered in the skull of a felbeast.

It all looks so hopeful, Jarod thought, aware that it was anything but. He saw a band of Huln's people slicing their way through the opposition. With them rode a party of the priestesses of Elune and Jarod noticed his sister, Maiev, at their head. It did not at all surprise him to see her up at the front. Although he quietly worried for her, there would be no dragging her from the battle. He had concluded that

Maiev was trying to prove herself to the rest of her sect so that they would correct what she clearly thought an oversight and make her high priestess. Whether or not such ambition was permitted in the moon goddess's order was debatable, but Maiev was Maiev.

Astride the third night saber he had ridden this day, Jarod gutted a tusked warrior. His own armor hung ragged on him, so damaged had it gotten from the blows of his adversaries. There were at least half a dozen wounds spread out over his body, but none, thankfully, life threatening or even overly-draining. Jarod could rest when the battle was over . . . or when he was dead.

Then . . . cries broke out from the direction of the tauren. The night elf watched in horror as several of Huln's kind burned as if some virulent acid had been poured over them. Their hair sizzled and their flesh melted away in clumps.

The priestesses tried to aid them, but a surge of Fel Guard barreled over the foremost females. The demons cared not whether an adversary was male or female. They impaled tauren and beheaded priestesses with utter savagery.

Jarod knew that he should stay where he was, but Maiev, whatever her faults, was his only family. He cared for her far more than he dared show. Quickly making certain that his own area would not fall victim once he departed, the commander forced his mount around and headed for the horrific scene.

A few tauren still stood, some of them badly injured but able to wield their spears and axes. They and the survivors of Maiev's band stood all but encircled by demons. Even before he had ridden halfway, Jarod watched two more of the defenders perish under the onslaught.

Then, Maiev slipped. A looming Fel Guard swung at her. She managed to deflect his attack, but just barely.

With a howl, Jarod rode his mount into the struggle. His cat took down the demon attacking his sister. Another demon slashed at him, instead catching the animal on the shoulder. Jarod ran his blade through his foe's throat.

The demons suddenly focused on Jarod. It had not occurred to him that they might know who he was, but their determination suggested just that. They ignored other viable targets just to reach the commander.

His night saber took down two more, but then suffered several deep wounds from lances. On foot, Jarod would have a great disadvantage over so many towering figures, yet, there was nothing he could do. Three more lances finished the noble animal and it was all Jarod could do to leap off or be trapped underneath its carcass.

He landed in a crouching position next to his sister, who, for the first time, seemed to realize the identity of her would-be rescuer.

"Jarod! You shouldn't have come! They need you!"

"Stop commanding for once and get behind me!" He shoved his sister unceremoniously to the rear just as two horned figures closed on him. Despite his good fortune so far, Jarod Shadowsong had little belief that his small sword would be any match for their two massive blades.

But as he readied himself for his final battle, a horn sounded and the area was suddenly aswarm with soldiers and tauren. Huln crashed into the two demons, beheading one and crushing in the chest of the other before the pair could realize that they were under assault. A cloaked figure rode past, one Jarod belatedly recognized as Lord Blackforest.

There could only be one explanation for their sudden arrival. They had seen Jarod riding into struggle . . . and believed in him enough to come to his aid.

The reinforcements shoved back the Burning Legion, buying Jarod and Maiev time. He dragged her further from the fight, the remaining sisters following close behind.

Jarod made her sit on a rock. Maiev, eyes speculative, studied her younger brother.

"Jarod—" she started.

"You can reprimand me later, sister!" he snapped. "I won't stand behind while those who followed me face the enemy in my name!"

"I was not going to reprimand—" was as far as the priestess got before he was out of earshot. With his sister at least temporarily secure, Jarod concerned himself only with his comrades. Even Blackforest, one of the most prominent of the nobles, fought hard. He and his ilk had managed to learn from Lord Stareye's mistakes. This was a battle for survival, not a game for the amusement of the high castes.

Coming up on Huln, Jarod lunged at a demon seeking the tauren's side. Huln noticed the action and gave the night elf an appreciative snort.

"I will carve your name on my spear!" he rumbled. "You will be honored by generations of my line!"

"I'd be honored just to live through this!"

"Ha! Such wisdom in one so young!"

A female dragon of Alexstrasza's flight swooped down, laying a cleansing blast of red flame that forever doused many green ones. The action further eased the situation for Jarod's contingent. The commander of the host began to breath just a little easier.

But a second later, the same dragon went careening back beyond the night elves' lines, her chest a sizzling mass of ruined scale and torn innards. The earth shook as she collided with it and a furtive look by Jarod gave him ample enough evidence to know that she would not fly again.

And in the wake of the leviathan's death, a dozen soldiers also flew back, their bodies charred. Demons, too, tumbled, as if whatever attacked did not care who perished so long as nothing stood in its path.

Huln put a protective arm across Jarod's chest. "What comes is no Infernal or the work of the Eredar! I believe it seeks—"

Then a massive wind tossed fighters from both forces aside as if they were nothing. Night sabers were no less immune, Blackforest and his mount thrown with the rest. Huln managed to stand his ground a second longer, but even the stubbornness of a tauren could not hold against the incredible gale. He went flying past, the warrior striking at the wind in frustration as he vanished from sight.

Yet . . . Jarod Shadowsong felt *nothing*, not even a breeze.

And so he found himself alone when the giant strode out of the dust raised by the wind, the giant with dark skin and intricate tattoos that even the unskilled Jarod could sense radiated sinister magical forces.

"Yes . . ." mused the figure, eyeing the night elf up and down. "If I cannot have the druid, I shall amuse myself on what pathetically passes as the hope of this doomed host."

Jarod readied his blade, aware that he had no hope against this opponent but finding himself unwilling to surrender to the inevitable. "I await you, Archimonde."

The archdemon laughed.

EIGHTEEN

Brox was only a simple warrior, but he knew when a battle was going bad. It was not that he and the others could not defeat these armored night elves and their fiendish mounts, but that each second wasted so brought the portal nearer and nearer to completion. Already, a sinister green aura had formed around the gullet of the whirlpool. The orc understood magic well enough to know that soon the passage would be strong enough for whatever evil desired to come through, be it Sargeras or the "Old Gods" Krasus had mentioned.

A barbed lance flashed by his head, scraping away a few bits of skin but otherwise doing the hardened orc no harm. The scowling soldier wielding it steered his shadow bat to the side, hoping to get in past the bronze dragon's claws for another thrust at the green warrior.

The dragon caught hold of the shadow bat. The two struggled, upsetting the night elf's aim. Instead of impaling Brox, he caught the orc at the shoulder. Brox growled as the barbed head tore a thick piece of flesh from the spot. Despite the pain, he managed to lean forward and chop the lance in two.

With a curse, the soldier drew his sword. However, Brox, throwing caution to the wind, rose from his seat and *leapt* at his opponent.

He landed in a crouching position, gripping one of the bat's ears for support. The outrageous act so startled the night elf that he sat openmouthed as, with one hand, the orc buried his ax in his foe's armored chest. The soldier collapsed, tumbling off the back of his mount.

But Brox's impetuous action nearly cost him his own life. He had thought to use the bat's back to leap back atop the dragon, but the creature's hide proved oddly slick. As he let go of the ear, the orc lost his footing. Still gripping his ax tight, he slid toward the tail, following the night elf's corpse.

The burgeoning gateway far below filled Brox's eyes. He sensed the evil swelling within—

Then, a pair of claws caught him just as he fell free and Rhonin's voice shouted, "We've got you, Brox!"

The red dragon acting as the wizard's mount twisted so as to allow the orc to climb atop. Rhonin gave the orc a hand up, letting the graying warrior slide in behind him.

"That was just a little foolhardy even for an orc, wasn't it?"

"Maybe so," Brox admitted, thinking of the portal. Brave as he considered himself, he was grateful that he had not fallen into it. The further away he got from it, the better.

The wizard suddenly stiffened. "Watch out! Here come two more!"

The shadow bats converged on their position. Rhonin's hand flared bright as he readied a spell. Brox hefted his ax, prepared to be as much help as he could. He welcomed the new adversaries, if only because they took his mind off the portal.

The portal and an evil that stirred fear even in an orc.

• • •

The sight of Deathwing rebuffed by the spell surrounding the disk both astounded and disheartened Malfurion. If even the black dragon could not penetrate the dark magic, then what could the druid and his companions hope to do?

But Malfurion had no more opportunity to worry about the disk, for, at that moment, a menacing form dropped upon Ysera. The green dragon roared as the bat's fangs sank into her shoulder near the spine. The night elf slid to the side, trying to avoid being buried under the beast.

A sword cut at his head, narrowly missing his ear.

"Slippery little fool!" hissed Varo'then, once more wielding his favored weapon. Azshara's officer thrust again, this time nicking Malfurion on the cheek. Varo'then drew the sword back for another strike. "The next one'll take your head!"

The druid thrust his hand into a pouch. He knew what he sought and prayed he would find it. The familiar feel reassured him and he pulled out the seeds.

Captain Varo'then adjusted his position. The evil grin spread wide. The demons had found a perfect subordinate in the sadistic soldier.

As the blade came down, Malfurion threw the seeds into the bat's maw.

The monster convulsed immediately. The sword point, fixed on the druid's throat, instead cut a bloody but shallow line across his collarbone. Malfurion grunted from the pain, but held on.

A fiery glow erupted from within Varo'then's mount. The captain tried to maintain control, but to no avail. The bat flailed around, shrieking.

A moment later, it burst into flames.

Malfurion had used the seeds' inherent heat during earlier battles. However, with only a few left, he had not thought to wield them up here, where they might not be utilized well. Only because the shadowy creature had been right on top of him had the night elf managed to make certain that all reached their target, the throat.

The fiery spectacle was so bright that Malfurion had to look away. He heard Varo'then shout, but the words were lost.

With one last shrill cry, the incinerated beast dropped from sight.

Gasping for breath, Malfurion clung to Ysera. The dragon could do nothing for her rider, for another of the bats already had her attention. The druid held on as tight as he could while he tried to regain his composure. The pain from his wounds stung terribly and the knowledge that the disk was still untouchable drained him further.

A sharp pain coursed through his calf.

Malfurion cried out. He nearly lost his hold. Blood trickled into his boot as he wildly kicked at the source. He turned watery eyes toward his leg and the cause of his agony.

Captain Varo'then clutched tightly to Ysera's lower back, the scarred soldier grunting as he made his way up a scale at a time. The cause of Malfurion's new pain—the officer's curved dagger—was clenched between Varo'then's teeth. Malfurion's blood dribbled unnoticed down the other night elf's pointed chin.

How Varo'then had managed to snag hold of Ysera as his burning mount had dropped, Malfurion did not know, but once again he had underestimated the officer. He kicked again as hard as he could, but the captain easily avoided his foot. While it was all Malfurion could do to hold on as Ysera fought, the more battle-hardened Varo'then moved with practiced skill toward his foe. His narrowed eyes sized up

Malfurion like a fat animal ready for the slaughter . . .

The druid reached for a pouch—and, at the same time, Varo'then's left hand came up.

"Aaugh!" A crimson flash blinded Malfurion. Too late he recalled that the captain had some minor talent with sorcery. Not enough to be a true threat in that manner, but certainly enough to put his enemy off-guard while the officer moved in for the kill.

Malfurion put up his free hand, an act which likely kept him from being slain. A heavy, metallic form fell upon him— Varo'then's armored body—and the druid felt the other night elf's hot breath in his face.

"The Light of Lights will reward me greatly for this!" the captain uttered maniacally. "Mannoroth fell afoul of you! Archimonde fell afoul of you! Such an insipid creature and you outwitted them both! Lord Sargeras's grand commanders! Ha! I'll not only again be her favored for this, but *his* as well! Me! *Lord* Varo'then!"

"Sargeras means to destroy Kalimdor, not remake it!" Malfurion blurted, trying to make his foe see sense.

"Of course! I realized that long ago! Pfah! What do I care for this little patch of dirt? So long as I can serve the queen and command warriors in her name, I care not where I do it! Who knows, perhaps for this Sargeras will make *me* his supreme commander! For that and the adoration of Azshara, I'll gladly see Kalimdor a cinder!"

Varo'then's madness truly consumed him. Malfurion suddenly grew outraged that one of his own kind could so blithely speak of the end of all things, especially the cherished world that had birthed their kind. It went against everything Cenarius had taught him and what Malfurion had always believed.

"Kalimdor is our blood, our breath, our very existence!"

the druid shouted, his fury rising. "We are as much a part of it as the trees, the rivers, and the very rocks! We are its children! You would be slaying the mother that birthed us!" His forehead started to burn.

"You *are* pathetic! We live upon a tiny rock that's one of many rocks! Kalimdor is nothing! Through the Legion and my queen, I will cross a thousand worlds, all of whom will be crushed under our feet! Power, druid! Power is my blood, my breath, do you understand?" Captain Varo'then twisted his dagger-wielding hand out of Malfurion's grasp. "But if the coming death of Kalimdor troubles you so, I'll grant you the favor of sending you to the afterlife to be there to welcome its shade firsthand!"

But Malfurion's anger had reached its limits. Eyes on fire, he stared into Varo'then's own. "You want *power*? Feel the power of the world you would betray, captain!"

It flowed through the druid as naturally as his blood. He felt it rush from its source . . . Kalimdor. The world itself was not sentient, but it was a living thing, nonetheless and, through Malfurion, it at last struck back.

From the druid erupted a soft, blue light that hit Varo'then full in the chest.

With a cry, Malfurion's attacker was battered from his mount. Dagger knocked from his flailing grip, the captain helplessly soared up high over the Well of Eternity. The light not only now bathed Varo'then, it burned right through him. His flesh, his sinew, his organs, and his skeleton were all visible beneath his glowing armor. The officer's screaming head was a skull under transparent skin.

Varo'then had rejected everything about Kalimdor . . . and now, through Malfurion, Kalimdor rejected everything about him. Still enveloping the captain, the light made an arc over the center of the Well, then descended sharply toward the gullet of the whirlpool. As it did, it suddenly faded.

Like an Infernal dropping upon the victims of Suramar, what was left of Captain Varo'then plummeted into the solidifying portal.

As suddenly as it had come, the power surging through Malfurion ceased. He felt a loss and yet, at the same time, a comfort that the world had not yet become entirely defenseless. Still dangling from Ysera's back, he eyed Varo'then's ultimate destination.

"Let us see if the lord of the Legion still rewards you after *this*, captain . . ."

A jolt nearly sent him falling after Varo'then. Ysera had a bat in each forepaw and although the dragon had just ripped out the throat of one, the second had torn through her wing.

Malfurion struggled to a more stable position, then took from another pouch a tiny bit of salve he had earlier mixed. The salve had been made from selected herbs, but although the druid had tested it on the battlefield, he was not at all certain that it would be strong enough to aid such a giant as Ysera.

Yet, from the moment Malfurion rubbed it on the base of her wing, the results prove far more than he could have anticipated. The tiny amount of salve spread beyond where he touched, quickly covering the entire appendage. The rips in Ysera's wing quickly and completely mended, not even scars remaining to mark the savage wounds.

"I feel invigorated!" roared She of the Dreaming as she tore apart the second of the creatures. Ysera turned her head to Malfurion. Despite the shut lids, he felt the intensity of her gaze. "Cenarius has taught you well—" She suddenly stopped. Her eyes flickered open, if just for a second. "But perhaps *much* of the credit must still go to your natural tie to that which you wield. Yes, much, indeed . . ."

The druid realized that her brief glimpse had been focused at the top of his head. He reached up . . . and discovered that the nubs now thrust out a good three inches.

He had begun to grow antlers just like those of his shan'do.

Before this newest revelation could take hold in his mind, a fearsome roar shook the area, drowning out even the storm.

Out of the storm clouds dropped Deathwing.

The black leviathan hurtled himself once more at the impenetrable spells. His body erupted continually where plates had not yet sealed the tears in his hide. His eyes were wide with utter rage. He flew toward the Demon Soul with a swiftness that took Malfurion's breath away.

The air around the disk abruptly crackled, flashes of yellow and red giving warning as to the power bound to the dragon's stolen creation. Malfurion sensed new forces at play, power instilled into the spell matrix in order to amplify its hold on the Demon Soul.

Deathwing struck the matrix head-on. The sky around him exploded with raw energy that should have seared the insane Aspect to death, but, although his flesh and scales clearly burned, Deathwing nevertheless pushed forward. He roared defiantly at the mighty forces set in array against him. His mouth twisted into an insane, reptilian grin that grew with each push closer to his goal.

"There are no boundaries to his obsession . . ." Ysera said, marveling at the other Aspect.

"Do you think he might actually make it?"

"The true question is . . . do we wish him to?"

Scales tore from the black's already savaged body. The crackling bolts now focused fully on the giant, scorching him again and again. Yet, although he would now and then flinch under their intensity, Deathwing did not slow.

A red dragon flew past Malfurion and he saw both Rhonin and Brox astride. In a voice amplified by a spell, the wizard called, "Krasus warns that we have to be prepared! He thinks that Deathwing may yet manage to break the spell! We have to be ready to take on the black the moment that happens!"

"Deathwing . . ." Ysera muttered. "Seeing him now, how true that name rings . . ." To Rhonin, she roared, "We shall be ready!"

They would have to strike immediately and in concert. It was the only chance they had . . . and only a slightly better one than attempting to take the disk from the spell themselves. The night elf did not like their chances, but he would summon whatever he could of Kalimdor into him.

Aware that this might be the last hope for everything he loved, his heart instinctively went to Tyrande. Not Illidan, but Tyrande. He wanted to speak to her one last time, to know that she might live . . . even if he did not.

Malfurion?

The druid nearly slipped from Ysera's back. At first he believed the voice in his head only illusion or perhaps some sinister ploy by the dark powers against which they fought, but, in truth, Malfurion sensed that this could be none other than Tyrande who contacted him now.

He recalled how she had been the one who had helped summon him back when he been unable to return to his body. Her link to the druid was far greater than he could have ever imagined and in the instant that he thought that, Malfurion sensed that she had noticed it, also.

Malfurion! she repeated with more hope. *Oh, Malfurion! It is you!*

Tyrande! You live! Are you—have they—

The priestess was quick to reassure him. *The Mother Moon*

watched over me, praise be, and I was aided by Highborne seeking return to our people! I know that you did what you had to do! But listen! Your brother—

My brother . . . No sooner did she mention Illidan, then the druid sensed that presence once so much like his own very near Tyrande. So near, in fact, that they had to be *touching.*

Brother—began Illidan.

You! Something surged within Malfurion, something that he realized he had to check immediately. Yet, despite his best efforts, the druid was not completely successful.

Malfurion! came Tyrande's plaintive call. *Cease! You'll kill him!*

He had no idea exactly what it was he was doing to Illidan, but Malfurion concentrated, trying to draw back what he had released. To his relief, he felt Illidan recover quickly.

Never . . . never knew you had that in you . . . brother . . . While the tone held consistent with Illidan's usual condescension, there lay in his mind a more stunned knowledge that the sibling he had felt weak was not.

You've much to answer for, Illidan!

If we all live, I will face my accusations . . .

His words held merit. What use was there to condemn Illidan if they were all to perish? Besides, Malfurion realized he wasted valuable power on his brother.

Putting thought of Illidan aside, the druid touched Tyrande again. *You're well? He's done nothing to you?*

Nothing, Malfurion. I swear by Elune . . . but we hide now in the ruins near the Well and dare not even attempt to cast a spell! The demon Mannoroth has warriors everywhere! I think they suspect where we are despite both Illidan's sorcery and my prayers . . .

He wanted to go to her, but, once again, that was not possible. Malfurion swore. *If we can succeed in—*

But before he could relay more, Deathwing unleashed a horrific bellow. The raw emotions in the dragon's cry shattered the links with Tyrande and Illidan and erased from Malfurion's thoughts any other matter.

He found himself looking upon a dragon tortured beyond comprehension but yet who was so obsessed with what he sought that no pain could daunt him. Some of the plates sealed to the black were nearly slag and several portions of his body had been stripped clear of scale. Revealed underneath was raw flesh burnt or ripped away. The leviathan's wings were torn in several places and it amazed Malfurion that the mad Earth Warder could still fly. Deathwing's claws were gnarled and ruined, as if he had been scratching at some impervious object.

Then, Malfurion saw how near the black hovered from his prize.

"By the creators!" Ysera roared. "He will let nothing stop him!"

The druid silently nodded, then realized how dire her words truly were. It looked as if, at any moment, Deathwing would do the impossible . . . and then it would be up to those hoping to steal the disk from him to do the same.

Away . . . away . . . demanded the voices that had once encouraged the dragon in everything he did. Now, they, like all the others, had proven themselves to be treacherous. Truly, there was no one Neltharion could trust but himself.

"I *will* have it! The Soul is mine! No one else's!"

He sensed their outrage that he would not obey them. They savagely attacked his mind even as through other means they fueled the Burning Legion's spells that also battled him. Never had the black dragon suffered so, but it would all be worth it. Even though he only inched forward, he still made progress. The disk was almost within his grasp.

Away... they repeated. *Away*...

Under their outrage, however, Neltharion also noted growing anxiety, even *fear*. The voices, too, saw that he had almost reached the his creation. Perhaps they understood that when it came back into his possession, he would punish *them* along with all the rest.

Then, another factor came more into play. The demon lord reached out from his own realm, magnifying the horrific forces already bound into the spell matrix. Neltharion bellowed again as the torture he had suffered previous proved but a fraction of what he now felt.

But, if anything, it only drove him on. Mouth stretched back in a dragon's version of a death grin, the leviathan laughed loud at all those who would deny him his right. He laughed and pushed the final few yards to the disk.

"It is mine!" he roared in triumph. "Mine!"

His paw wrapped around the Demon Soul.

"It must be now!" Krasus warned Alexstrasza. "It must be now, if we are to—"

The world exploded.

Or so, at least, it seemed to the cowled figure. A mad cornucopia of colors overwhelmed Krasus. He heard Alexstrasza roar in surprise and agony. A tremendous force buffeted the two. Krasus tried to hold onto his queen, but it was too much of a strain for the mortal form he wore.

He was thrown.

Things hurtled past him. A squealing, charred shadow bat. A small form that might have been its rider or one of his own comrades. Several pieces of dragon scale, their own color burnt away.

Krasus rolled over and over, unable to slow his momentum despite attempted spells.

We have lost! he managed to think. *Surely, this is the end of all!*

Then, a huge paw scooped him up and he heard Alexstrasza's hoarse voice cry out, "He has done it! He **has** done it!"

Through his tears, the mage managed to peer at Deathwing and the Demon Soul.

The black dragon roared at the top of his lungs as he ripped the disk free of the spell. Deathwing's body blazed and it amazed Krasus that even a being as powerful as the Aspect could survive such damage. The leviathan raised his creation high, laughing triumphantly despite his clear agony.

And then, from the depths of the Well, a black force shot out and struck Deathwing head-on.

It threw the dragon back, hitting him with such ferocity that he was hurtled far, far beyond the vast Well. Far beyond even the shore. A tumbling Deathwing flew from sight into the clouds . . .

In his wake, the Demon Soul—lost from his grip—plunged toward the whirlpool.

"We must seize control before either Sargeras or the Old Gods can restore it to the portal's matrix! I think that, despite Deathwing's spell on it, I can hold it, at least long enough for our purposes! But we must reach it first!"

"I will try my best . . ." gasped Alexstrasza.

Only then did Krasus see how much his queen had been burnt by the forces unleashed by Deathwing's mad actions. The Aspect of Life could barely keep aloft.

But another massive dragon suddenly flew past them, a familiar green leviathan with a most unique night elf astride.

"Malfurion . . ." Krasus murmured, eyeing the druid, who

now sported a small pair of antlers akin to those of his teacher. "Yes, it *has* to be he who attempts it . . ."

Yet, that did not preclude any effort by the others. Alexstrasza did not slow despite her wounds and from Krasus's right flew Rhonin and Brox on the red male. The bronze female also followed, but without a rider, she could not do anything but watch over the others.

Malfurion's dragon moved in on the plummeting disk, the Demon Soul leaving a bright, golden trail as it dropped. Krasus watched as the druid opened his palm . . . then unerringly caught the foul piece. The night elf clutched it to his chest.

And from within the portal came a monstrous roar that shook the dragon mage's very soul. He peered down, staring in dismay at a horrific green storm brewing in the center.

Sargeras was trying to cross through the nearly-completed gateway.

As a warrior, Brox knew well his limits. This was now a time of wizards and sorcerers. There were no foes with blades and axes up here, not anymore.

Malfurion gazed at the dread device, his eyes wide and unblinking. Brox understood the disk's seductive power and quickly shouted past Rhonin, "Druid! You must not trust it so! It is evil!"

The night elf glanced up, then gave his comrade a determined nod. Brox exhaled in relief—an exhalation that became a choking sound as he, like the rest, heard the fiendish cry erupting from the Well. It was the cry of an angered god.

The cry of Sargeras, lord of the Burning Legion.

"The demon lord seeks to enter Kalimdor!" the crimson male roared. "The portal is all but complete! He may be able to succeed . . . and, if he does, we are all lost!"

Brox stared at the green tempest below. It was contracting, coalescing into a smaller, almost perfectly octagonal gap. "What happens? The gateway shrinks, not grows!"

"Sargeras must further seek to strengthen his chances by localizing the spell! Once through, he will have no trouble stretching it wide again. If anything, he has his chance of success more likely!"

Horrified, the orc pulled his gaze from the monstrous storm . . . and saw that their situation was even more dire. From Zin-Azshari there now rose hundreds, perhaps, *thousands*, of winged forms. "Look! There!"

The demon Mannoroth had allowed Captain Varo'then and his soldiers to attack the party when all it had seemed was needed had been a delaying tactic. Now, though, with what the black dragon had done, the plan had clearly changed. Mannoroth surely realized that there was a true danger to the Legion. He had therefore summoned every Doomguard and other winged demon available to deal with the world's defenders.

Brox itched to sink his ax into the oncoming swarm, but he knew his efforts would be laughable compared to those of Rhonin and Krasus. True, he could ride along as the red male and the wizard fought them, but what good would that do?

Alexstrasza and Krasus, being further back, had already turned to confront the horde of aerial demons. The red male began arcing away from the center of the Well. That left the wielding of the Demon Soul and the sealing of the portal to Malfurion . . . providing that he was somehow given the time needed. Even Brox could sense the sinister energies building up within the condensed portal. Sargeras had nearly succeeded . . .

The orc could think of only one thing to do. A part of

him spoke called it madness, yet, another part insisted it *had* to be done.

"Farewell, wizard!" he roared. "It is my honor to have fought beside you and the rest!"

Rhonin glanced back at him. "What're you planning to—"

Brox leapt.

The red dragon attempted to snatch Brox, but the giant's astonishment made him react far too slowly. The orc fell past his claws, dropping relentlessly toward the center of the Well of Eternity . . . and the blazing storm now reaching its peak.

Howling with anticipation, Brox felt the wind tear at his face as he descended. His grip on his ax so tight that his knuckles had turned white. He grinned just as he had that day when he and his comrades had stood ready to protect the pass at cost of their lives.

As Brox neared the portal, his perspective shifted. He saw movement within. Ranks and ranks of demons, all preparing to follow their lord into the mortal plane. Demons stretching into Forever. Of Sargeras himself, Brox saw no sign, but he knew that the demons' fearsome master had to be very, very near.

And then . . . the orc passed through the gateway.

NINETEEN

Malfurion did not see Brox leap, the night elf already consumed by what lay before him. Now that he had the disk, it occurred to the druid just how daunting his task was. Malfurion had hoped one of the others, especially Krasus, would be the one to seize the Demon Soul, but their underestimation of the spell and the black dragon's shocking intrusion into events had turned everything upside down. Now, it was all up to him and he had no idea exactly what to do.

At that moment, he sensed Tyrande in his thoughts again. Instinctively reaching out, Malfurion sensed with horror that she was in danger.

Tyrande! What—?

Malfurion! There are demons everywhere! Illidan and I believe that Mannoroth is trying to get you through us!

He quickly sought the link that he still shared with his twin. His initial contact with Illidan shocked Malfurion, so full of bloodlust was it. Through his brother, the druid felt Illidan strike out at the Burning Legion, the bodies of fiery warriors piled high before the black-clad spellcaster.

Illidan suddenly became aware of his presence. *Brother?*

Illidan! Can you flee?

We are surrounded and Mannoroth no doubt eagerly awaits my use of a spell to spirit us to safety! He would quickly usurp it, bringing us to his loving arms . . .

Malfurion shuddered. *I'm coming! I'll help you!*

But even as he said it, the druid knew that he could not leave the Well. The portal had to be destroyed, even if it meant *sacrificing* his twin and Tyrande.

How Malfurion prayed for a return to the old days, before the Legion. The days when he and his brother would have fought side by side. When they had been youths, he and Illidan had been able to overcome all obstacles because they had been as one.

Would that it could be so one more time, the druid desperately thought. *Would that I could stand next to Illidan and he next to me and together we dealt with this evil . . .*

Only too late, did Malfurion notice the Demon Soul flare.

A peculiar feeling of displacement hit him. His eyes momentarily lost focus. Groaning, Malfurion shook his head . . . and discovered that he now stood next to Illidan in the ruins of Zin-Azshari.

"Malfurion?" gasped Tyrande. She reached out to touch him, but her hand went through the druid.

Yet, when Malfurion put out a hand toward his twin, he felt solid flesh. Illidan flinched, startled.

Malfurion blinked . . . and once again he rode above the Well of Eternity.

Only, this time . . . Illidan sat beside him.

The sorcerer gazed at Malfurion from behind his scarf with both suspicion and barely-concealed awe. "What've you *done*, brother?"

The druid eyed the Demon Soul and recalled his desire. The foul disk had granted it.

He and Illidan were in both places simultaneously.

So be it. Whatever its evil, the Demon Soul had given him the chance he needed. "Stand with me, Illidan!" Malfurion challenged. "Stand with me here—" The scene shifted back to Zin-Azshari. "—and here!"

To his credit—and with an old, familiar grin—Malfurion's twin immediately nodded.

In the mist-befouled city, the brothers stood shoulder-to-shoulder as the demons poured over the rubble trying to reach them. Scores perished as Illidan created yard-long swords from black energy and Malfurion channeled the forces of nature into a storm whose raindrops melted armor and demon flesh. Tyrande stood with them, the priestess of Elune calling upon the pure light of her mistress to blind, even burn, the approaching monsters.

And all while this happened, Malfurion and Illidan also sat astride Ysera, struggling with the spell holding the portal together. That Sargeras had not yet stepped forth puzzled both, but they did not question their momentary reprieve.

Yet, even with the Demon Soul, they accomplished nothing. Already the sky was filled with Doomguard, all seeking those who would keep their master from Kalimdor. Krasus, Rhonin, and the dragons destroyed them by the dozens, but still their numbers appeared undiminished. Of Brox, there was no sign, but the druid could not truly concern himself with the orc just now.

Ysera deflected attack after attack, but Malfurion understood that she could not defend them forever. Yet, despite both his and Illidan's attempts to use the Demon Soul against the portal, they continued to fail.

Then, the answer came to him. Malfurion looked into his brother's shrouded eye sockets. "We're doing this all wrong! We're using the disk to enhance our spells!"

"Of course!" snapped Illidan. The scene around them momentarily shifted back to Zin-Azshari, with the sorcerer gutting a Fel Guard. "How else to wield it?"

Their surroundings again became the Well and the demon-filled sky. The druid looked at Deathwing's unholy creation. He loathed what he was about to suggest. "The Demon Soul is still part of the spellwork! Instead of drawing from disk, we should be *giving* to it! We should be working *through* the disk, not treating it like a sword or ax!"

Illidan opened his mouth to argue, then shut it immediately. He saw the sense in his twin's words.

Again, Malfurion's view became Zin-Azshari. He immediately sensed a new force among the demons in the city, one moving with dire purpose toward the ruins where the brothers and Tyrande sheltered. It had a familiar taint . . . and stench.

"Satyrs!"

The goat creatures bounded over the other demons, each of the former night elves already preparing spells. They laughed madly and some even bleated.

But as the abominations converged on the trio, Malfurion once more found himself astride Ysera. The constant shifting distracted him and he suspected that, one way or another, he and his brother's ability to be in two places would soon cease.

"Join with me, Illidan! Do it!"

Despite their enmities, the sorcerer did not hesitate. Their minds linked, fusing almost completely. Malfurion sensed his twin's ill-conceived plans to make himself the hero of Kalimdor and recognized immediately how the sinister forces that had almost seduced the druid into claiming the disk for his own had used Illidan's arrogance to add their own spells into the mix.

He had forgotten the Old Gods, as Krasus called them.

So, they had not abandoned their efforts; Sargeras's portal still held the key to their freedom. More than ever, the druid understood that he *had* to use the Demon Soul if they were to destroy the gateway.

Be ready! he commanded Illidan.

Malfurion called upon the inherent energies of Kalimdor, the same forces that had helped him cast out the venomous Captain Varo'then. Now, he would have to demand of them a far greater sacrifice. This would take more than that he had used to save a dragon from death, as the druid had naively done for Krasus and Korialstrasz. In asking of his precious world such power, there was a chance that the druid might bring upon his home the very fate the Burning Legion had planned for it.

As he called upon Kalimdor and asked it to grant him its strength once more, he felt Illidan draw upon the energies of the Well itself. Once both had achieved their desire, the brothers bound the two forces together—making them one—and fed the results into the Demon Soul.

Both Malfurion and Illidan jerked as their magicks melded with that within the disk. The druid momentarily returned to Zin-Azshari . . . just as a satyr leapt upon Tyrande. Without regard for himself, the druid slashed at the horned creature with a sword created from a jagged leaf. The satyr's head went rolling—

And, once again, Malfurion's focus shifted back to his position over the Well. Gritting his teeth, he forced his senses back into the Demon Soul.

He and Illidan became a part of the disk. They *were* the Demon Soul . . .

They flowed toward him, an endless river of utter evil seeking his death.

"Come!" roared Brox, kicking aside the severed limb of another demon foolish enough to get within reach of his ax. He stood atop a mound of dead flesh, his many kills. The orc's body was awash in his own blood, but a strength such as he had not felt in years filled the graying warrior.

A chaotic fury surrounded the lone guardian, the madness of the realm of the Burning Legion. There seemed no ground, no sky, only an insane swirl of fiery colors and untamed energies. Had he not been so completely focused upon his adversaries, the orc suspected that he surely would have been driven insane by now.

Behind him, the portal burned with evil purpose. The green flames danced as if demons themselves and seemed to draw the Burning Legion like the proverbial moth. Brox had expected that he would be overcome immediately, but not only had he so far survived, he had kept not even a single demon from reaching the gateway.

How much longer he could last, the aged warrior did not know. For as long as the portal existed, he hoped. The enchanted ax gave him an edge, one that Brox had utilized to good advantage, but the weapon was only as good for as long as his strength lasted.

A movement of black at his right caught the orc's attention. Instinctively, he shifted to meet it—

And was battered horribly by a force that made the might of the demons before him seem as nothing. Brox's shoulder cracked and he felt several of his ribs collapse into his organs. Sharp, agonizing pains ripped through him.

He tried to rise, but again the veteran warrior was battered relentlessly. His legs were crushed and his jaw broken on the right. Brox tasted his own blood, a not unfamiliar thing. One eye was bruised beyond opening and it was all the orc could do just to breathe.

But his one remaining hand still gripped the ax. Overcoming everything, Brox swung, hoping to hit his attacker.

The blade encountered an obstruction, and, at first, Brox's hopes rose. However, the squeal that immediately followed informed the badly-injured orc that he had only caught an eager felbeast trying to close in on easy prey.

Such a pity . . .

Despite the words, there was certainly *no* pity in the terrible voice thundering in his head. A vast shadow blanketed the orc.

Such a pity to waste such a delicious ability for carnage . . .

With a strained roar, Brox managed to right himself. The ax came spinning around.

This time, he knew that it was no mere demon hound he hit.

A resounding bellow of outrage deafened the injured warrior. Through what remained of his good eye, Brox caught sight of a titanic, horned figure in molten black armor whose thick mane and beard appeared to be composed of wildly dancing flames. The orc could not make out the giant's features well enough, yet somehow knew them to be both wondrously perfect and terribly awful at the same time.

Then, the titan raised one arm and in it Brox beheld a long, wicked sword the upper half of whose blade had been broken off. What remained was jagged and still very capable of slaying.

Through broken teeth, the orc began a death chant.

The jagged tip impaled him, bursting through his spine. Brox's body quivered uncontrollably and the light in his eyes dimmed. The ax slipped from his limp fingers.

With a sigh, the orc at last joined his comrades from the past.

• • •

"There're too many of them!" Rhonin shouted.

"We must do what we can! Malfurion must be given time!" Krasus responded from Alexstrasza's back.

"Can he do anything?"

"He is a part of Kalimdor itself! He must be able to! He stands the best chance! Believe it!"

Rhonin said nothing else, merely nodding and sending a score more demons to whatever hell existed for them in the afterlife.

The noise without and even within had grown incessant. Queen Azshara no longer had any patience. Clad in her finest so as to present the great Sargeras a most wonderful spectacle, the Light of Lights strode into the hall, followed by her demon guards. Night elven sentries stood nervously at attention as she passed.

"Vashj! Lady Vashj!"

Azshara's chief attendant came rushing from the opposite direction, quickly prostrating herself before her monarch. "Yes, my mistress! I am here to obey!"

"You are here to answer questions, Vashj! I was assured that nothing was amiss, but, if anything, it sounds so highly chaotic in and around the palace! My sensibilities are offended! I want order restored, is that understood? What will our Lord Sargeras think?"

Vashj kept her face all the way to the exquisite marble floor, each square of which bore the stylized profile of Azshara. "I am but your humble servant, Light of Lights! I have tried to ask of Lord Mannoroth some news, but he ordered me away with threats of peeling my flesh from my bones!"

"Impertinent!" Azshara looked in the direction leading to

the tower where the Highborne and demons worked. "We shall see! Come, Vashj!"

With her anxious companion in tow, the queen wended her way up. It was a sign of her displeasure that she had not first summoned the rest of her attendants so as to make a more glorious entrance. For this journey, Vashj and her bodyguards would just have to do.

At the doorway, a pair of Fel Guard and two felbeasts attempted to block her entrance. "Move aside! I command you!"

The hounds whined, obviously desiring to obey, but the two monstrous warriors defiantly shook their heads.

Azshara looked back at her own retinue. Smiling at the demons who had accompanied her, she commanded, "Please remove these from my sight."

Her guards moved without hesitation against their comrades. They had been around the queen long enough to fall prey to her wiles. Outnumbered, the demons blocking the way fell quickly, as did the hounds. One of her own perished in the process, but what was a guard compared to the desires of Azshara?

When the corpses had been cleared from her path, the queen stepped forward. Vashj opened the way, then slipped behind Azshara.

The chamber was a beehive of activity. Gaunt, sweating sorcerers worked frantically under the baleful gaze of Mannoroth. Satyrs, Eredar, and Dreadlords also struggled with spells, the results of which obviously took place beyond the palace walls.

Undaunted by what was clearly a monumental strain on the part of the spellcasters, Azshara approached the gargantuan demon. Mannoroth, sweating not a little himself, did not notice her presence at first, a slight the queen only barely forgave.

"My Lord Mannoroth," she began frostily. "I find myself disappointed with the lack of order taking place before the arrival of Sargeras—"

He spun on her, his toadlike visage filled with astonishment at her audacity. "Little creature, you'd do well to leave here now! My patience is at an end! For even interrupting me at this juncture, I should rip off your head and devour your innards!"

Azshara said nothing, merely gazing imperiously at the demon.

With a hiss, Mannoroth reached one meaty hand toward her. His intention was clear; he had no further use for the night elf's existence.

But though he came close, Mannoroth faltered at the end. It was not because of any sudden notion that Sargeras might still desire the silver-haired creature to live. Rather, Mannoroth discovered that here was a force against which only his lord and Archimonde would prove superior. Try as he might, the demon would have found it easier to throttle himself than the queen.

He finally drew back, caught between his sudden unease around one he had highly underestimated and the present danger to the portal.

"For the sake of our Lord Sargeras," Azshara regally declared. "I shall forgive your outburst . . . this time."

Hiding his unease, Mannoroth quickly turned from her. "I've no more time for this! The portal must be protected . . ."

He did not see her brow arch. "The portal is in danger? How?"

Grinding his yellowed fangs together, the demon rumbled, "The desperate acts of a few last rabble! All will be well . . . but only if there are no more interruptions!"

Azshara pursed her lips at his offensive tone, but saw the sense of his words. "Very well, Lord Mannoroth! I shall return to my quarters . . . but I expect this incident to be settled swiftly so that Sargeras will finally come to me. We are done here, Vashj."

The queen of the night elves departed with regal flair. Mannoroth glanced over his shoulder as she stepped from sight, the demon still incredulous. Then, recalling himself, Mannoroth quickly went back to the task at hand. The rebels would be crushed and the way kept open for the lord of the Legion. Already, he could feel Sargeras nearing the gate, which held despite the stealing of the dragon's disk by the druid and his friends.

Soon . . . very soon . . .

Malfurion and Illidan continued to battle the demons in the ruins. At the same time, they continued to let flow into the disk their very selves. Illidan sought to push full force into the situation, but, fortunately, Malfurion kept his twin in check. This had to be done in a calculated manner, even if seconds were as valuable as one's last breath.

Then . . . at last they were ready to strike.

But as he began the final spell, Malfurion felt a tremendous evil touching his mind, an evil that was not Sargeras. Voices whispered in his head, promising him everything. He could rule Kalimdor, have Tyrande as his queen and the Burning Legion as his army. All would bow to his greatness. He had but to make a slight alteration to his casting.

The druid fought back the whispers, aware of what their speakers truly desired. He pushed on with the spell—

Only to have Illidan suddenly seek to do what the voices had desired of Malfurion. Where the druid had overcome their seductive words, the sorcerer had fallen victim.

Illidan! Malfurion thrust his thoughts at his twin in a manner akin to physically striking him. He felt the dark hold over Illidan break. His twin gasped . . .

I am myself again, Illidan assured him a moment later.

Although not entirely trusting, Malfurion continued with their task. They had little time left. It was a wonder that the demon lord had not already entered. Worse, although the entities had been repulsed, if the portal stayed open, Malfurion had no doubt that they would somehow still follow Sargeras into the mortal plane.

Aware of what would befall Kalimdor then, Malfurion cast the spell. Whatever damage it did, it would be as a light breeze in comparison.

A dead silence filled the air. It was as if no sound existed in all the world. The wind stilled and even the storm-tossed Well emitted not even the least rumble of thunder.

Then . . . a great howl shook the Well, Zin-Azshari, and, possibly, all the rest of Kalimdor. A terrible gale picked up behind Malfurion, but Ysera quickly compensated for it. The new wind rose with a fury matching anything the druid had ever come across before. Caught unaware, the other dragons flew about wildly at first, then, amazingly, righted themselves as if the gale had vanished.

That was hardly the case for the Doomguard and their ilk. The winged demons fluttered about uncontrollably, unable at all to battle against this new and fearsome wind. Several collided, cracking skulls and shattering limbs, but although many demons perished, the wind was so powerful that their limp corpses did not drop but instead spun around over the Well as if performing some macabre dance.

The gale swelled tenfold, a hundredfold, and yet for the dragons and their riders, it was little more than a breeze. Not so for their frantic foes. By the hundreds, the Doomguard swirled around and around and around . . .

And then were sucked inexorably toward the portal.

Those with breath left to them howled and screamed and gnashed their teeth, but they were as dust to the blast. From every direction, the monstrous warriors plummeted relentlessly toward the gateway through which their brethren waited to emerge.

"It's working!" shouted Illidan with a triumphant laugh. "It's working!"

But Malfurion did not ease up, for he felt resistance pressing against the spell. Whether the work of the lord of the Legion or the Old Gods, he could not say at this point. All the druid knew was that if he weakened, all he had achieved would be lost and his world with it.

The unnatural wind continued to grow, sucking demons out of the sky and into the vortex at the center of the Well. Within seconds, the heavens had been cleansed of the Legion's foulness, and yet, the gale did not let up.

Malfurion, still in two places at the same time, now watched in awe as the horde converging on the spot where he, his twin, and Tyrande still stood suddenly slowed in panic. Huge Fel Guard and monstrous hounds began clutching at the ruined earth. A savage Infernal managed two steps toward the trio, then, even the massive demon could go no farther.

Limbs and tail flailing, the first felbeast flew off into the air, its whine pitiful as it vanished over the Well.

It was followed swiftly by another felbeast, then several of the gargantuan warriors. The dam opened wide then, demons by the scores suddenly pouring upward in some bizarre reversed rain. They flowed unceasingly over the black waters and, as they did, Malfurion noted how their bodies grew more fluid, almost insubstantial.

A sense of vertigo shook him and the night elf nearly lost control of the spell. His view of Zin-Azshari vanished. Quickly turning to his side, Malfurion saw that Illidan no longer sat beside him. He still felt the link between his twin and himself, but it was more tenuous.

The druid maintained his concentration. He felt the natural forces of the world feed through him. The trees, the grass, the rocks, the fauna . . . all sacrificed a part of themselves to give him the strength he needed. Malfurion vaguely understood that what he did now went far beyond what Cenarius had taught him and far beyond anything that the night elf had done before. Illidan's magic continued to bind with his, adding its might, too.

He cried out abruptly as what felt like a thousand needles buried themselves in his mind. There was no mistaking Sargeras in this attack. The demon lord's presence filled him, attempted to consume the druid from within.

Malfurion strained, fighting back some bit of the agony. Kalimdor continued to feed him, to give him all it could. It entrusted Malfurion with its future, its fate. He was its guardian now, more so than Cenarius, Malorne, or even the dragons. It was up to him and him alone.

Alone . . . against the Burning Legion and the Old Gods.

"Work, you dogs!" Mannoroth bellowed at the sorcerers and demons. "Harder!"

One of the Highborne momentarily slumped forward. Like the rest, he was almost skeletal. The once-extravagant robes now draped him like a colorful funeral shroud. He coughed, then noticed too late the humongous shadow over him.

"My Lord Mannoroth! Please, I only need—"

With one hand, the demon seized him by the head, crushing the skull and its contents to a bloody pulp. Mannoroth shook the dangling body for the benefit of the cringing night elves and warlocks. "Work!"

Despite their emaciated states, the spellcasters immediately doubled their efforts. Even then, Mannoroth found no satisfaction. He tossed the grisly remnants aside and moved to the pattern. He would have to rejoin the effort if he hoped for it to succeed.

But as he shoved aside those in his path, a peculiar sense of displacement touched him. Mannoroth's movement grew sluggish and when he looked at one of the Eredar, he saw that the same was happening to the warlock. The night elves seemed less affected, but even they moved slower and slower.

"What—is—happening?" he demanded of no one and everyone.

Heavy tail slapping against the floor, Mannoroth tried to return to the spellwork, but as he raised his still blood-soaked hand, his eyes widened. The scaled hide had a translucent appearance. The demon could see his own sinew and bone and even they no longer looked completely substantial.

"Not possible!" the winged behemoth rumbled. "Not possible!"

The tower wall facing the Well of Eternity shattered outward.

A great force tugged at the demons. Those nearest the jagged gap almost immediately followed the massive chunks of stone out over the black body of water, quickly vanishing in the distance. Heavily-armored warriors were lifted as if as light as a feather.

The pattern broke. Despite their fear of Mannoroth, the night elves fled what was clearly catastrophe. Having reached their own limits, the Eredar attempted to follow the sorcerers, only to be swept up in the same awful wind that had ripped away the Fel Guard. With wild howls, the warlocks vanished through the hole.

At last, there remained only Mannoroth. His incredible strength and bulk working for him, the winged demon held his own against the hungering gale. Mannoroth's brutish orbs fixed on the decaying pattern. He started for the center. Enough magic remained in it so that with his own power he could create about him a protective shield in which he could wait out this attack.

Each step proved ponderous, but Mannoroth forced himself forward. One trunklike limb entered the pattern, then another. His wings beat madly, giving him what little push they could. The demon's third foot entered . . . and, with a triumphant grin spreading across his horrific countenance, Mannoroth planted the fourth there as well.

Raising his clawed hands high, he summoned the magic of the pattern around him. Even moving his arms proved nearly unbearable, but the gigantic demon managed.

A fiery, green dome formed around him. The suction ceased. Mannoroth turned to face the shattered wall and laughed hard. Against lesser demons the wind might prove superior, but he was *Mannoroth!* Mannoroth the Flayer! Mannoroth the Destructor! One of Sargeras's chosen—

The flames of the shield bent toward the broken wall . . . and to his dismay, the demon watched as his protection was sucked away.

As he attempted to turn from the wall, the wind seized hold of him. A backward-flying Mannoroth gaped as he was plucked from the floor with ease. The demon roared his frustration as he slammed into the broken stone, sending more huge chunks of the wall tumbling outside.

He managed to grab hold and, for a brief moment, hope

filled Mannoroth. But the strain on his thick fingers and heavy claws was too much. His nails scraped uselessly against the stone as he was finally torn from the tower.

Still roaring, Mannoroth was cast out over the Well of Eternity.

TWENTY

Blood trickled down Jarod Shadowsong's face. His left arm was broken, of that he was certain. What was not so certain was whether any of his vital organs had been damaged by the hammering blows that had caved in his breast plate in several places. He had a little trouble breathing, but, for the moment, at least he could stand . . . somewhat.

Struggling to raise his sword, Jarod again faced his adversary.

Archimonde looked none the worse for wear. Jarod had left no mark on the sinister demon, had not even managed to *touch* Archimonde once, save at the receiving end of one cruel hit after another.

What made it all worse was that Jarod understood quite well that the towering demon was merely toying with him. Archimonde could have slain his tiny foe a dozen times over, but the creature was taking a sadistic pleasure in slowly battering the night elf into oblivion. Still, Jarod knew it would not be much longer before Archimonde unleashed the fatal blow. There was only so much more he could do to the beaten soldier.

And yet, some inner force made Jarod stand ready for more punishment.

They stood alone on this part of the battlefield, although there were those in the distance on both sides watching the tableau unfold. The demons, of course, surveyed the sight of their commander thrashing the night elf with horrific glee and constantly yelled their encouragement to Archimonde. Jarod's own followers no doubt saw just how pathetic the former guard captain truly was. They likely wondered how they could have ever seen him as their hope.

A fierce wind swept up, raising dust. Jarod squinted, trying not to be blinded. Archimonde slowed as he approached, the demon expressionless. Jarod imagined that dark giant was plotting how best to pummel his victim.

But if he was to die, the night elf decided that he would do so at least giving the appearance of trying to fight on. Gripping his sword tight in both hands, Jarod let out a cry and charged Archimonde.

Through the rising dust, he caught the demon smiling slightly at his audacity. However, as Jarod neared, that smile slipped away and, to the desperate officer's surprise, Archimonde *stiffened*.

The powerful wind nearly threw Jarod forward. Bearing his teeth, the night elf lunged at his adversary's stomach. It was the only spot he could reach that might—just might—give way to his feeble blade. If he could at least mark Archimonde before the giant crushed him . . .

Dust and tears blurred Jarod's vision, giving the demon an almost ghostly appearance in the process. Archimonde reached a hand toward him and the night elf braced himself for some hideous spell to melt his flesh or turn his bones to oil.

But no such spell came. Instead, crouching slightly, Archimonde took a step *back*. His torso he left completely unprotected.

Jarod thrust, already preparing himself for failure. He had no doubt that either his blade would break off Archimonde's hide or that he would miss entirely.

But he did *not* miss and, to his further astonishment, the sword sank deep into the gigantic demon's stomach. Yet, curiously, there was no resistance whatsoever, almost as if Archimonde was indeed a ghost. Jarod continued pressing, all the while awaiting his own death.

Instead . . . Archimonde went flying back as if struck hard. However, he did not land, as might have been expected, but rather *kept* flying. Arms and legs flailing, the demon commander rose up into the air and only then did Jarod realize that it was the wind that had Archimonde.

All composure finally abandoned Archimonde's expression as he hurtled higher and higher into the heavens. His face contorted into a grotesque mockery more apt for a creature of his evil. The demon let out a cry of fury . . . and then vanished from sight over the horizon.

Even before the weary officer could register that he had survived his incredible duel, he saw that the wind now assailed the *entire* Legion. Demons struggled to keep their positions, but like the dust they were taken up and tossed about. Monstrous hounds leaping forward instead rolled backward, bouncing first over the landscape before soaring after Archimonde. The Fel Guard were plucked one by one from the lines and even though many stood face-to-face with the defenders, not one night elf, tauren, or other creature of Kalimdor joined their astounding fate.

Infernals dropping from the sky abruptly veered off, their flights now mirroring that of their lost commander. One even came within inches of the soil before reversing direction.

The dragons, oddly, were also barely touched by the mad elements. After some minor adjustments, they regained their balance, then, wisely retreated to the ground. There, they, too, watched the Legion's downfall unfold.

The sky filled with writhing, snarling demons, all struggling in vain to return to the ground. Below them, gaping fighters stared with weapons lowered as the threat to their land, to their world, was simply torn away before their very eyes. Even the corpses of those demons long slain joined the ones above, adding to the spectacle.

" 'Tis a miracle!" someone shouted from behind Jarod. He glanced over his shoulder to discover that several of those who had earlier been tossed back by Archimonde had begun to return. Many continued to watch the sky, but a number of others eyed Jarod as if he alone was responsible for the stunning turn of events.

The ranks of the demons were stripped from Kalimdor line after line until soon a barren wasteland spread out before the defenders. Not one demon remained. In fact, not even one *piece* of any demon remained.

More than a few night elves dropped to their knees in relief. However, despite what had happened, Jarod had the unsettling feeling that the struggle was not quite at an end. It could not be so easy . . .

"On your feet, all of you!" he roared. With his good hand, he seized a dumbfounded herald and commanded, "Sound the horns! I want order in the host again! We have to be prepared to move!"

A priestess of Elune came to his side and inspected his arm. As she did, Jarod continued to collect his thoughts.

"Are we giving chase?" a noble called, looking too eager for Jarod's taste.

"No!" the commander snapped back, unmindful of the difference in caste. "We wait for word from the mage Krasus or one of those with him! Only then do we move . . . and whether it's to advance on Zin-Azshari or flee for our lives, we'll need to be ready to do it as fast this wind!"

As they obeyed, Jarod, allowing himself just enough time for the priestess's ministrations, stared once more in the direction the demons had flown, the direction of the capital and the Well.

It could not end this simply, no . . .

Yet, throughout Kalimdor, the Burning Legion was cast from the ground and tossed helplessly toward the Well of Eternity. Their struggles were as nothing against the wind and as Krasus and the rest watched, they massed over the waters like a gigantic swarm of bees before dropping into the maelstrom.

"Is that it? Is it over?" shouted Rhonin.

"It may be . . . and it may be not!" To Alexstrasza, Krasus called, "To Malfurion!"

She nodded, banking in the direction of the druid and Ysera. Rhonin and the red male followed close behind.

Malfurion and his mount hovered over the whirlpool, the night elf awash in the Demon Soul's golden glow. His normally-dark skin looked almost as pale as Krasus's. He glanced at the cowled mage in anxiousness.

"He's still trying to come through!" The druid's face had aged. Lines traced over it and his eyes had sunken in a little. "I don't know if my spell can hold him!"

Krasus gazed down, his heightened senses enabling him to see deep into the Well.

Deep into the portal . . .

And so it was that he beheld Sargeras, lord of the Legion.

Molten armor clad the titan from neck to foot, its black fury so great that it burned the mage's eyes just to look. Fighting the pain, Krasus dared stare into the face of evil, a monstrous distortion of perfection. Once, there had been a handsome, even beautiful being—a being of the race that Krasus knew had created his world. Now, however, the beauty was tainted. The flesh was that of death and the eyes the fiery emptiness of utter chaos. Sargeras's teeth were fangs. Behind him whipped a long, thick tail with jagged scales jutting out at the tip. His hands ended in wicked, curved talons and in one of those hands, he wielded a monstrous sword cracked midway but with a jagged edge still capable of much mayhem.

Krasus choked, horrified at what he discovered next. On the end of that monstrous weapon, a tiny, green body lay impaled.

Brox.

In all the excitement, the mage had forgotten all about the orc. Now, though, Krasus understood why his party had gained precious—very precious—seconds. The orc had sacrificed himself to delay the Legion.

Sargeras stood at the gateway. Despite the incredible forces driving his horde back into his realm, the lord of the Legion pressed forward. Slowly, surely, he reached the portal . . .

But as Sargeras neared, Krasus noted a stunning thing. The demon lord was *injured*, albeit minutely. A small slash mark decorated his right leg, a mark that Krasus's keen eyes recognized as made by an ax.

Brox's ax. Impossible as it seemed, the enchanted weapon had scratched Sargeras. Not enough to cause him any real harm, of course, but that a wound existed at all opened up a unique possibility.

"Rhonin! Alexstrasza! We must act as one! Malfurion! Be prepared! You will have your chance to destroy the portal, but only barely!"

The others followed his lead. Krasus felt his queen and his former protege allow him to guide their power. The red male added his strength as well, as did Ysera. It left Malfurion open to attack, but if this final effort failed, *none* of them could hope to survive.

Eyes alight with power, Krasus focused the party's combined magic at the gateway. The mage trusted to the demon lord's intense concentration for the success of the spellcasters' desperate venture.

In comparison to Sargeras, both Archimonde and Mannoroth were as fleas. The power of a hundred dragons would have been as nothing to him. Had Krasus sought to strike Sargeras directly, either in the chest or head, the results would have been laughable, at least to the demon lord. That Brox had managed his miraculous attack at all said much for the power imbued in the weapon by the druid and his shan'do.

No, instead, the mage poured all that he was given by the others at the tiny, insignificant wound Brox's ax—a piece of Kalimdor's magic itself—had managed.

And then it happened. Krasus sensed Sargeras's concentration weaken just for a moment. Not from pain—that would have been too much hope for—but rather, simply from *startlement*.

Which was what Krasus wanted. "Now, Malfurion!"

Clutching the Demon Soul tight, Malfurion assailed the portal.

Krasus had gambled that the magically-wrought wound would be just sensitive enough to gain the demon lord's momentary attention if it was struck again. All their assembled might had done had been to create a slight irritation, one upon which Sargeras had instinctively focused instead of the gateway.

The mouth of the maelstrom quivered, then lost cohesion. An explosion of energy erupted from the depths of the whirlpool.

The portal started to collapse.

One side after another, the fiery border surrounding it fell in upon itself. Sargeras attempted to reconstruct it, but by then, it had moved beyond even his power to do so. One precious second had stolen the demon lord's victory.

And then a thing happened that Krasus could never have dreamed possible. Sargeras, refusing to believe his defeat, stepped within the crumbling portal itself, trying both to rebuild it and cross through. His desire to do so proved his undoing. As the portal imploded, the demon lord found himself trapped. He could not flee, could not pull back. Dropping his sword, the titan even battered against the gateway with his fists, but to no avail. The corridor between realms shrank rapidly, at last crushing in on him. Sargeras roared and his voice echoed in the heads of all.

I will not be denied! I will not!

But the gateway continued to condense and Sargeras seemed to condense with it. He struggled to keep the way open, the interior of the gate aflame from his titanic efforts.

And then, with the demon lord still shouting his rage and beating at the walls . . . the portal ceased to be.

Sargeras ceased to be.

"It's done!" gasped Malfurion. "It's—"

But his voice died as, despite the gateway's vanishing, the maelstrom in the center of the Well continued to swirl madly. Worse, it appeared to be growing, swelling. Even as the druid watched, the edges ate away at the shoreline of Zin-Azshari.

The night elf glanced over at Krasus. "What's happening?"

Krasus waved off explanations. "We must be away from here! We must get *everyone* as far from the Well as possible!"

Alexstrasza and the others quickly veered away, heading for land. Raw energy crackled in and around the black waters. The whole of Zin-Azshari shook and as the dragons passed over, the mage spied massive faults beyond the city's limits.

"It's begun . . ." Krasus whispered to himself. "May the creators protect us . . . it's begun and there is nothing we can do to stop it . . ."

A new tempest assailed the party, scattering the dragons despite their might. Compensating for this latest storm, the winged leviathans regathered . . . save for one.

Ysera—and thus Malfurion and the disk—was missing.

Krasus quickly scanned the heavens, but of the Aspect, he could see nothing. Not until his gaze turned groundward did the cowled figure see where she had flown.

Back toward the Well of Eternity.

"No!" Even Ysera did not understand what fate was to befall this region. Worse, there was no telling what would happen to the time line if, instead of being carried away, the Demon Soul was lost to the Well's throes. "We must go back! We must get them!"

To her credit, Alexstrasza immediately banked. Rhonin's red male and the riderless bronze began to follow, but Krasus waved them on. Concentrating, he managed to enter Rhonin's thoughts despite the myriad magical forces interfering.

You must go to the host! You must warn Jarod that everyone has to flee as far as they can from the direction of the Well! Flee to Mount Hyjal!

He did not have to explain further, for, of all of them, the human understood best. A child of the future, Rhonin knew what was to come as well as his former mentor did. The wizard leaned forward, speaking to his mount, and, seconds later, the red turned away. The bronze hesitated, then followed.

Krasus watched the landscape as Alexstrasza pursued Ysera's trail. Near what had once been the gates of the city, a deep crevice as wide as his queen's wing now stretched. Some of the structures that had been left standing despite the demons' initial rampage now shook violently and several tumbled over even as the pair soared over.

It is imminent . . . The dragon mage stared ahead, trying to catch a glance of Ysera and the druid. *The Sundering is upon Kalimdor* . . .

A chandelier crashed on the marble floor, the thousand crystals composing it scattering. Several flew with the sharp speed of missiles. One of Azshara's handmaidens fell, a beautiful, glistening shard through her forehead.

The queen, gripping a pillar for support, eyed the bleeding corpse with frustration. She had enough on her mind without one of her servants sullying her presence so. Yet, clearly no one had the wherewithal to clear the body away. The rest of them, even Vashj, ran around in panic as the walls shook and the floor cracked.

Evidently forgetting the laws against touching the queen's person without permission, Vashj seized Azshara's arm. "Light of Lights! We must flee the palace! Something has gone terribly wrong! None of the Great One's warriors remain and the sorcerers have fled the tower! One I stopped claimed a tremendous wind cast out even Lord Mannoroth over the Well!"

Azshara was already aware of the absence of the warriors of the Burning Legion, her personal bodyguard having been ripped from their positions before her very eyes and sucked through a wall in her chamber. Despite the stunning spectacle, though, the queen refused to believe that Sargeras would not in fact still appear and she intended to be ready when that glorious event took place.

Vashj still tugged on her arm. Azshara's infinite patience had its limits. She suddenly slapped her lady-in-waiting.

The others froze where they were, the fact that their surroundings threatened to collapse upon them forgotten. They fully expected their mistress to now execute Vashj on the spot.

Instead, in her most regal voice, Azshara commanded, "You will all remember your places! I expect you to obey the instructions I have given you! We will continue to prepare for our Lord Sargeras's entrance . . ."

To emphasize her point, she strode to one of her chairs. The first tremor had toppled it over, but Vashj quickly righted it, then dusted off the seat with the hem of her own garment.

Nodding approval, Azshara sat. Her handmaidens immediately took up their positions and Vashj poured the queen a goblet of wine, somehow avoiding spilling it despite the continued shaking of the palace.

"Thank you, Lady Vashj," the queen of the night elves said graciously. She sipped a bit, then posed herself in expectation. No matter how long it took for Sargeras to arrive, she would be ready for him. He would step before her and be dazzled by her perfection, as all were.

After all, she *was* Azshara.

As Ysera reached the shore, Malfurion, the Demon Soul pressed against his breast, eyed the grand capital of the night elves with horror. Attuned to the natural forces of Kalimdor, he recognized immediately imminent disaster. Recognized it and realized that he had to act fast.

"My brother and Tyrande! They're still in Zin-Azshari! Please! I can't leave them!"

"You know where they are?"

"I do!"

The massive green dragon nodded. "Guide me, but make it quick!"

They turned off without alerting the others. Malfurion peered across the shoreline. Ysera had flown so swiftly that they had been forced to backtrack some distance, but the druid sensed that they were finally near the other night elves.

There! Tyrande waved to him, the sight of her so wonderful that Malfurion momentarily forgot that he was also here for his twin. Only after recalling that did the druid suddenly note that Illidan was nowhere to be seen.

Ysera landed. As ever, the Aspect gazed around with eyes shut, but Malfurion understood by now that, despite appearances, she could see far better than most creatures.

He leapt off. Tyrande met him, clinging to Malfurion with such intensity that he momentarily could think of nothing else than doing the same. Only when the dragon cleared her throat slightly did the two reluctantly separate.

"Malfurion—" the priestess began.

He put his fingers over her lips. "Hush, Tyrande. Where's Illidan?"

Her eyes widened briefly. She looked over her shoulder. "By the very edge."

With a curse, the druid ran past her. Illidan surely knew that the land was crumbling about him. How could he be so mad?

As he scrambled around a ruined tower, Malfurion nearly

collided with his twin. Illidan somehow managed to stare at him with his covered eye sockets.

"Brother . . . a timely return . . ."

"Illidan! The Well is out of control—"

The sorcerer nodded. "Aye! It's been twisted and turned by too many spells! That fuss we—especially you—made with the Demon Soul was too much! The same spell that sent the Burning Legion back into their foul realm now works on the Well! It's devouring itself and taking its surroundings with it!" He turned back to the black body of water. "Fascinating, isn't it?"

"Not if we're caught up in it! Why weren't you running?"

Illidan wiped his hand. Only then did Malfurion see the slight glimmer of power surrounding it. He also noted the moisture.

"What've you been doing with your hand in the Well, Illidan?"

At that moment, a tremendous tremor sent both night elves to their knees. Illidan shouted, "If you've a way out of here, we should probably use it! I've tried casting Tyrande and myself out of here, but the Well is too much in flux!"

"This way!" Malfurion grabbed his brother by the arm and dragged Illidan back to the others. Tyrande already sat upon Ysera. She aided Illidan up, then Malfurion.

At that moment, a huge form hovered overhead. The druid instinctively expected some demonic horror, then saw that it was none other than Krasus and Alexstrasza.

"The Demon Soul!" the mage shouted. "You have it still?"

The night elf slapped one of the pouches at his waist. He had secreted the disk in it just before Ysera had landed.

Krasus nodded in relief. "Hurry, then! We must fly fast and far! Even the air will not be safe!"

Well aware by now that the mage knew so much more than he had yet admitted, Malfurion held on tight. Ysera rose from the rubble just as another crevice opened up beneath her paws.

"Zin-Azshari is going . . ." the cowled spellcaster cried, "and it is only the beginning!"

The two dragons beat their wings as hard as they could, but they moved as if flying through tar. Malfurion looked behind and saw that the sky above the Well no longer even existed. A huge funnel cloud enshrouded everything. Illidan had spoken much of the truth, it seemed. Between the spellwork of the demons, that of the elder gods, and the defenders' own efforts, the Well of Eternity had been torn asunder once too often.

Had he and his friends saved the world, only to destroy it?

What first he took for deafening thunder rattled the druid. He clutched his ears, waiting for it to pass.

"Look!" cried Tyrande, her lips near enough to him for her voice to still be heard. "The city!"

They watched . . . watched as the ground beyond Zin-Azshari broke apart. A great canyon miles deep opened. The entire capital literally began sliding toward the Well.

"The . . . pull . . . grows . . . greater!" Ysera roared.

The Well was drawing the surrounding regions into its maw, literally devouring Kalimdor. Zin-Azshari now floated in the black waters, an island bobbing about like so much flotsam. Ironically, the palace still stood mostly intact, although the tower where the Highborne had moved after the destruction of their previous sanctum leaned precariously.

Ominous bolts of energy played around the city as it neared the maelstrom's gullet. Unlike much of what the

Well tore loose from Kalimdor, Zin-Azshari headed straight for the center. Malfurion felt Tyrande's grip on him tighten to the point of pain.

"It's going . . ." she whispered. "It's going . . ."

Around her, Azshara's handmaidens screamed. Vashj clung to her leg. The queen held her empty goblet, refusing to accept what was happening to her palace. She was *Azshara*, Light of Lights, supreme ruler of her people! She had not permitted this!

Sargeras would not be coming. Azshara understood that, although she had not said so to her followers. It would not do to let them know that she realized that she had erred. Somehow, the rabble had kept him from coming to Kalimdor . . . from coming to her.

The rumbling grew louder. A darkness in which even night elves could not see suddenly enveloped the palace. The only illumination came from the untamed forces of the Well. Black water began pouring into the palace, washing away two of her servants. Their screams were quickly drowned out.

I am Azshara! she silently insisted, her expression constant. With but a thought, the queen created a shield that surrounded her and those still remaining. *My desires are absolute!*

Her power kept the water at bay, but the pressure of maintaining her shield quickly grew troublesome. Azshara's brow furrowed and beads of sweat—the first sweat of her life—appeared on her forehead.

Then . . . voices whispered from the gloom, voices calling to her, promising her escape.

There is a way . . . there is a way . . . you will become more than you ever were . . . more than you ever were . . . we can help . . . we can help . . .

The queen was no fool. She knew her shield would not last much longer. Then the Well would claim her and her followers and the glory that was Azshara would be lost to the world.

The silver-tressed night elf nodded.

"Ungh!" The goblet fell from her hand. Her body was wracked with pain. She felt her limbs twisting, curling. Her spine felt fluid, as if much of it had instantly melted away . . .

You will be more than you have ever been . . . promised the voices. *And when the time comes, for what we grant you . . . you will serve us well . . .*

The last vestiges of her shield spell failed. Azshara shrieked as the waters overwhelmed her. In the background, she heard other cries as well . . . her handmaidens, the guards, and the rest of the Highborne who still served her.

The Well filled her lungs . . .

But . . . she did not drown.

Krasus, too, watched as the vast city, the epitome of the night elf civilization, was sucked whole into the throat of the maelstrom. He shivered, not only because of the destruction before him, but of the knowledge that he had of the future. The dragon mage had hoped to see Zin-Azshari torn apart before it sank, but that part of history had remained true. The city would sink to the depths . . . and, over the centuries, begin to birth a new horror.

There was nothing he could do about that now. Krasus looked away from the Well, looked away from the devastation spreading rapidly in all directions. Huge chunks of Kalimdor continued to be torn into the Well with no sign of the terror lessening. Already several miles of land beyond Zin-Azshari had vanished. The only good thing was that the Burning Legion had long ago sent fleeing any life that had remained. So far, only parched soil and the bones of the dead fell victim . . . but if the catastrophe did not slow soon, Krasus wondered if anything would remain.

It has to, though! he insisted. *History says it must be so!*

But he knew too well that Time had already unraveled far too much . . . and that he was, in great part, responsible.

Krasus could only pray . . .

TWENTY-ONE

Rhonin thanked the stars that he saw little in the way of life before reaching the host. It would have been impossible for two dragons and a weary wizard to save anyone still so near the region of the Well. The only people he discovered was a large band of Highborne riding for their lives toward the host. Fortunately, they had nearly made it by the time he and the dragons came upon them.

A quick descent and an even quicker conversation revealed the surprising truth. Their leader, one Dath'Remar Sunstrider, told the story of their attempt to flee with Tyrande. Dath'Remar's regret over losing her was clear and Rhonin, who had sensed Malfurion's contact with her, informed the sorcerer that she had survived the escape. He could not promise that Tyrande still lived, although the wizard doubted that Malfurion would let anything happen to the female night elf once he had been reunited with her.

Rhonin and the dragons guided the Highborne to the host, preventing, in the process, any fight breaking out between the two factions. With the bronze dragon guarding the Highborne—for their own safety—the human and his mount sought out Jarod.

They found the commander already astride his night saber and anxiously awaiting word. Rhonin smiled in relief as he realized that the night elves and their allies were already prepared to move.

Still atop the red, he quickly greeted Jarod, then said, "We have to get the host moving! All the way to Mount Hyjal! The portal's been destroyed, but all that spellwork around the Well has caused chaos! It's eating itself up and taking everything around it with it!"

"Gods . . ." But Jarod's shock quickly subsided as his inherent sense of responsibility took over. He summoned a herald who Rhonin realized the former guard captain had kept handy just for such news. "Give the signal to reverse direction!" Calling up two more riders, Jarod added, "Send word to the officers and nobles! We move at swiftest pace to Mount Hyjal! No stopping! Those who need assistance will be granted it, but no one hesitates and no one stays behind! Go!"

"We'll keep watch from above," the wizard said.

"What about . . . what about those who might be other directions?"

Rhonin was grim. "The Burning Legion cleared the way for us there. I would say that any survivors are as far from the Well as we hope to get. We were the strongest resistance, after all."

"We can only hope for the best for those, then."

"And pray for ourselves at the same time."

As if to emphasize that point, a distant rumble caught the attention of both. Both the wizard and the soldier looked in the direction of the sound . . . and saw utter blackness just at the horizon.

"Get them moving, Jarod! Fast!"

The host started toward Mount Hyjal mere minutes later,

but still not swift enough for Rhonin. Each time he glanced back, the darkness appeared to have swollen. The human swallowed, aware just what was happening and wondering if the catastrophe had already taken Krasus and the others.

A short distance into their desperate trek, the night elves and others began to realize their danger. It would have been impossible to keep them ignorant and neither Rhonin nor Jarod had any desire to do so. What did matter was to maintain some order and Jarod Shadowsong proved adept at that. The dragons, too, aided, swooping down and guiding back to the throng those who began, in their panic, to turn off.

Rhonin kept looking back, seeking some sign of Krasus and the others, but finding nothing. The darkness continued to encroach at an incredible pace and the ominous rumble grew more and more strident.

It's catching up to us! The wizard looked ahead. Mount Hyjal stood in the distance, enticingly close and yet still so far.

Would even reaching it be enough? Krasus thought so and Rhonin's recollection of history agreed . . . but so *much* had been altered.

Vereesa . . . I did what I could . . .

The darkness drew nearer. The roar as the ground miles back was torn and sucked into the Well pounded in his head. Below, many started to run and scream . . .

And still there was no sign of Krasus and the others.

Hillsides were ripped away. Entire lands simply crumbled into the churning, hungry whirlpool, quickly vanishing into its center. High above, Krasus watched whole settlements— fortunately long emptied by the war—vanish in a heartbeat. Nothing could stand before the onslaught of the Well's death throes. The carnage caused by the Burning Legion paled . . . no . . . it could not even *compare* to what now took place.

The first hint of Mount Hyjal appeared at the horizon. From high above, the mage could make out the desperate mass of bodies moving toward it. Providing that he had not guessed wrong, they would just *barely* make it to safety.

If there were any survivors of the war in the other directions, Krasus could do nothing for them. He could only again thank the stars that so little of worth remained in the areas over which the demons had marched.

He still had hope that the destruction would soon cease, that in this instance, at least, things would go as history recalled. They had the Demon Soul, an important factor in that, and—

He suddenly had a premonition of danger. Krasus quickly looked back.

A monstrous, black tendril arose from within the gargantuan Well . . . a tendril darting up toward an unsuspecting Ysera and the trio astride her.

The Old Gods! I should have known!

"Turn! The Old Gods still seek the Demon Soul for their use! This is their last chance before they are sealed off again!"

Alexstrasza veered around. Ysera noted their sudden action, but at that moment, the tendril reached her . . . and plucked the druid from the dragon's back.

"Malfurion!" cried Tyrande. The priestess tried to grab him, but he was already well out of her reach.

Frowning, Illidan also stretched a hand toward Malfurion. From his fingertips, a claw of crimson energy formed that immediately sought to snare the druid by the arm. Unfortunately, the claw only made it midway to his twin before abruptly fading, the violence of the Well disrupting the sorcerer's handiwork.

Malfurion gaped in horror as the tendril swiftly drew him back. Alexstrasza beat her wings hard. Krasus concentrated, trying to focus on Malfurion and the disk. At the very least, the dragon mage knew that he had to try to retrieve the Demon Soul. It was not a cold decision; the loss of the druid would be a tremendous one . . . but the loss of the Demon Soul to the dread elders would be calamitous.

Wild, rampaging magical forces battered Krasus and his queen. The spells he sought to cast went awry. The foul tendril brought Malfurion to the Well's gullet.

Then . . . what Krasus had prayed for but had, at this point feared would not pass, saved the night elf. The Well of Eternity had, *finally*, reached the end of its struggles. Now, it no longer devoured Kalimdor, but only itself. With a rapidity against which even the dark entities could not match, Krasus watched the vast, black body fall in upon itself. Even the storm surrounding them sank into it. Alexstrasza flapped furiously, barely able to keep them from following it.

The black waters receded, pouring into the Well's own gullet. The tendril tried to retract faster, but before it could . . . the very last of the Well of Eternity sank down into its own throat.

The tendril faded away like so much smoke. Krasus sensed the malevolent presence of the Old Gods vanish with it.

Flailing, the druid suddenly tumbled loose over a new threat. Below, filling the abrupt void left by the Well's apocalyptic hunger, came the seas of Kalimdor. Great waves a thousand feet high crashed against one another, hundreds of tons of water pouring each second into what had been the middle of the continent.

Krasus watched, awestruck, as the Sundering came to a crashing end and the *Great Sea* formed.

Yet, although taken by the sight, he did not forget Malfurion and the Demon Soul. With the Well had gone the last of its untamed and turbulent energies. Now, Krasus had full command of his power . . .

But before he could use it, a magnificent giant of bronze appeared from nowhere, a huge male dragon who glittered despite the remnants of the gloom still overshadowing the sky.

"Nozdormu!" the mage uttered.

The Aspect of Time swooped down, catching both the night elf and the disk. He soared quickly toward Alexstrasza and Ysera, but his golden gaze was for Krasus alone.

"Just in Time . . ." was all the male rumbled. Then, he flew past them, heading toward Mount Hyjal with Malfurion and the disk still clutched in one huge paw.

The other Aspects immediately banked, following. Krasus watched Nozdormu fly on as if nothing at all had happened to the world.

The mage finally shook his head and, for the first time since being cast into the past, breathed easier.

The survivors of the host did not breathe easier, not yet, for although they began to recognize the end of the danger, they also knew that their world had been forever altered. Many simply stared hollow-eyed at the new sea. The waters were already stilling, the waves beginning to lap *gently* at the ravaged shoreline.

So many had lost loved ones. The repercussions would only just begin materializing over the weeks and months— even years—to come. One of those who understood it best was Jarod Shadowsong. Despite his own shaken soul, he kept on a face of determination for his people. Even the nobles for the most part turned to him in need of reassurance. From those who seemed more steadfast, such as Blackforest, he appointed commanders to oversee the requirements of the host.

Mount Hyjal became a rallying point, for it remained untouched by the war and disaster that had followed. Jarod ordered banners made with the peak as their centerpiece, a new flag for a new beginning.

Aid came to the night elves from the tauren and others less affected by the ruination of Kalimdor. All had suffered, but no one's home had been so utterly destroyed as had that of Jarod's race. He greatly accepted the help of Huln's people and was glad to see that there were few incidents of prejudice from the other night elves toward outside assistance. How long that would last would depend on the future of the refugees. They no longer had their elegant and extraordinary cities—their cities with the huge, living tree homes and magically-sculpted landscapes reserved only for themselves—from which to look down upon all else. In fact, most no longer even had roofs over their heads, the number of tents in very short supply. Jarod had donated his own tent to younger refugees orphaned by the ordeal.

Unfortunately, it did not take long for the first threat to the stability of the host to rear its ugly head. With the Well no more, the rest of the night elves did not fear the Highborne as they once had. Muttering began to grow among the refugees, muttering which intensified the more the Highborne made themselves visible.

"You'll have a new war on your hands," Krasus advised him. "You need to quell this now."

"Some will never forget the horrors wrought upon us by their actions." Jarod's gaze shifted off toward the new waters. Below it lay the ruins of his own lost Suramar. "Never."

The pale figure confronted him. "You *must* put aside the differences, Jarod Shadowsong, if you wish your people to survive!"

Steeling himself, Jarod summoned the nobles and other ranking members of the host. He also called forth Dath'Remar Sunstrider and the seniormost Highborne. The two factions met him under the old banner of Lord Ravencrest, which Jarod used as a substitute until the new ones could be finished. Krasus had suggested this last, both of them aware that the reputation of the late noble was one that had been respected by both the aristocracy and palace alike.

"We are here under protest," Blackforest growled, eyeing the robed figures. His gauntleted hand rested on the pommel of his sword. "And will not long abide such foul company . . ."

Dath'Remar sniffed disdainfully, but said nothing. His opinion of the nobles was clear enough.

"Haven't you learned anything from all this?" snapped Jarod. He gestured toward the sea. "Isn't that enough to put an end to animosities? Do you both intend to finish what the demons began?"

"And what these willingly assisted in!" pointed out another noble.

"We make no excuses for what we did," Dath'Remar returned defiantly. "But we tried to make amends. Did you never wonder why the full portal took so long to come to fruition? We risked ourselves to keep it from doing so under the very eye of the demon lord! We sought to rescue the high priestess of Elune and many of us perished fighting the Burning Legion ourselves!"

"Not enough!"

"May I speak?"

A group of Elune's followers joined the fray, Tyrande Whisperwind and Jarod's sister at the forefront. Maiev looked uncommonly subdued in the high priestess's presence and Jarod could understand that. There was something about the young female that immediately eased his heart.

Everyone bent down on one knee, but Tyrande, an embarrassed frown appearing, gestured for them to rise. Jarod bowed slightly, then said, "By all means, the voice of the Mother Moon may speak whenever she so desires."

Tyrande nodded gratefully, then, to the assembled parties, she said, "Our world will never be the same. That which we were we are no more." Her expression grew solemn. "We are in flux. What our people are to become, I cannot say, but it will likely be nothing akin to what we once were."

Uneasy rumbling rose from both the nobles and the Highborne. The words of the high priestess were not to be taken lightly.

"We have survived this struggle, but, if we do not come together, we may not survive our own evolution. Consider this before you begin resurrecting old enmities . . ."

And with that, Tyrande turned. Maiev eyed her brother with what Jarod realized was confidence in him.

As his sister followed Tyrande, he saw that Shandris Feathermoon had been standing behind her. The departing novice gave Jarod an unabashed smile that made him more uncomfortable than the presence of the nobles and the sorcerers, yet, at the same time added to the lightening of his heart.

Blackforest cleared his throat. Jarod quickly returned to the matter at hand. "You've heard the voice of the Mother Moon and I couldn't agree more with her words. What say you?"

Blackforest opened his mouth, but Dath'Remar managed to answer before the armored aristocrat could utter a sound. "We greatly respect the word of the high priestess and will do what we can to make further amends for our past transgressions . . . if we will be permitted the opportunity by our august companions."

The lead noble let out a grunt. "We will do no less. If the Highborne have seen the error of their ways, we will accept their return to the fold and welcome their effort as we all seek to rebuild our home."

Both answers were spoken with some lingering animosity, but it was the best that Jarod could hope for at this point. There would be confrontations ahead, but perhaps none that would drag his people down to oblivion.

"I thank you all for coming and for seeing reason. Let us now begin to consider how best to take advantage of the miracle that's let us survive."

Several voices from both factions began speaking at once, each trying to come up with better ideas than the others. Jarod grimaced, then started trying to pick out the best ones.

One immediately caught his attention. "Water!" he interrupted. Something that had been reported to him by a scout came to mind. A lake at the very top of Hyjal. It was worth investigating. He decided to do so himself, though, if only to gain some reprieve from all his other responsibilities. "Lord Blackforest! I'd like three volunteers from among you! I've a short excursion in mind . . ." To Dath'Remar, he added, "From your group, too . . ."

As they chose from among themselves, Jarod congratulated himself. The excursion would also be a good opportunity to force the parties to work together. It was a safe, quiet event, but one, because of the importance of water, that would resound well among his people. If the nobles and sorcerers reported the findings together, the rest would see that cooperation *was* possible.

Jarod fought back a smile. Perhaps he was finally learning about leadership after all . . .

• • •

"Malfurion . . ."

The druid tore his gaze from the new sea. "Master Krasus."

The dragon mage grimaced. "Equals need no title between one another. Please, for the last time, I am merely *Krasus.*"

"I will try." Unconsciously, Malfurion took a step back from his friend. "Did you want something?"

"No . . . but *they* do."

A great beating of wings filled the night elf's ears. Dust arose around him and suddenly three gargantuan forms alighted behind the cowled figure.

Alexstrasza. Ysera. Nozdormu.

"You know why we have come," the red female said softly.

Malfurion's hand slipped to the pouch at his side. "You want it. You want the Soul."

"The *Demon* Soul," Krasus corrected. "You forgot to give it over to the Aspects once we landed. The heat of the moment, no doubt."

"Yes . . . yes . . ." The druid's hand thrust into the pouch. His fingers encircled the disk, caressing it in the process. Why did he have to give it up? Had he not proven that he had the right to it? Had he not singlehandedly used it to rid Kalimdor of not one menace, but two?

"Malfurion . . ."

If they felt that they deserved it more than him, why did he not just make them try to take it? Between his own skills and the power of the Soul, he could surely slay them all—

Disgust filled the druid. He quickly drew the damnable disk from its hiding place, then held it out for the mage to take.

Krasus nodded. "I knew you would make the correct decision." Yet, he did not accept the Demon Soul directly, instead pointing to the ground. "Please place it there."

Brow arched in curiosity, Malfurion obeyed. The moment that the disk left his grasp, he felt as if a tremendous weight lifted from his back.

"Step away, please."

When the night elf had obeyed, Krasus faced the three Aspects. "Will your power be enough?"

"It will have to be," replied Nozdormu.

The trio arched their necks, bringing their colossal heads within inches of the Demon Soul.

"We cannot bind it completely," Alexstrasza uttered. "That is beyond even all of us put together. Yet, we can ensure that Neltharion—*Deathwing*—cannot wield it any better than us."

"A wise maneuver, as I said," Krasus responded. Yet, Malfurion sensed again that the cowled figure, the dragon in mortal form, held back important information from even the queen he so obviously adored. What it was, the night elf could not even hazard, but there was a sadness in Krasus's ancient eyes that the mage quickly hid whenever the leviathans glanced his way.

The three giants stared at the tiny object, the simple golden disk that had caused so much calamity. They stared at it . . . and the Demon Soul was suddenly engulfed in a rainbow of energies. Dominating were red, green, and the brilliant bronze of the sandy Nozdormu. The Demon Soul rose several inches off the ground, hovering just before the Aspects. The magical forces unleashed by the dragons circulated around it, in the process turning the disk over and over.

Then . . . one by one, those energies sank into the black

dragon's abomination. Red, then green, then bronze, followed by the myriad colors accompanying each.

The spellwork ceased. The Demon Soul dropped, clattering on the hard ground. It looked unchanged, undiminished.

"Did it work?" he asked.

"It has." Krasus met the druid's eyes. "Malfurion, I ask you to pick it up again."

Loathe as he was to touch the piece, the night elf acquiesced. Oddly, Malfurion discovered that he had no more desire to keep the Demon Soul. Either the dragons had made that so or his will had grown stronger.

The mage glanced at the Aspects, who nodded in unison. To Malfurion, he respectfully said, "There is a place we know. A place the black one would not. With your permission, we will show it to you in your mind . . . and then I ask that you call upon your own skills to send that foul thing there."

Although he felt capable of doing as Krasus asked, Malfurion frowned. "Can't you do it?"

"Before, I alone might have been able to carry the disk, albeit with difficulty. The others, they could not because of Deathwing's handiwork. Now, this new spell has made it impossible for the black one or *any* other dragon to touch the Demon Soul, much less use it. That is why we need you for this."

Nodding, the druid held out the disk. "Show me."

Krasus and the Aspects stared deep. Malfurion shook momentarily as they entered his thoughts.

The image they created was so vivid that he almost felt as if he had visited it himself. Eager to be rid of the Demon Soul, the druid quickly said, "I have it."

With much relief, Malfurion sent the golden disk away.

Krasus exhaled. "Thank you."

The Aspects nodded their heads in gratitude. Then, Alexstrasza looked to the sky. "The clouds . . . they are beginning to part . . ."

Sure enough, for the first time since the Burning Legion had come to Kalimdor, the sky finally started to clear. It began as small gaps here and there, then large, thick clouds broke into much smaller, thinner ones. Those, in turn, became silken wisps easily scattered by soft winds.

Malfurion felt a sudden rising of hope, of renewed life . . . and realized that it was not only his own, but that of the land itself. Kalimdor *would* survive, of that he was certain.

A warmth touched his forehead, a pleasant warmth. He reached up and realized that his antlers had grown more. Now small ones jutted from the main stems.

Ysera, her eyelids shut but her eyes moving rapidly underneath, stretched to her full height, then turned to face her fellow Aspects.

"The world will heal, but there is much more work to do. We should return to the others . . ."

Nozdormu nodded. "Agreed."

Malfurion opened his mouth to thank the dragons for all that they had done . . . then hesitated as a sense of unease swept over him. He looked around suddenly, as if seeking someone. Only after doing so did the druid at last realize just *who* it was he sought so desperately, although the reason why still escaped him.

Where was Illidan?

Rhonin eyed the sea, thinking of all the deaths he had witnessed—both in his own time and in this period—at the hands of the Burning Legion. Many of them had affected him deeply, for, if several had not been friends, they had at least been parts of his life.

He knew that Krasus felt the same, perhaps even more so, for the dragon mage had lived long enough to lose generations of loved ones and companions. The wizard understood his former mentor well enough to realize that the centuries had not made Krasus immune to sorrow. The cowled spellcaster suffered deeply with each death, however much he hid those emotions at times.

And now, there was yet another to add to the losses. Rhonin had never thought to mourn an orc, but he did. Brox had become a stalwart comrade, a noble companion. Only belatedly had the human understood the warrior's sacrifice. The orc had dropped himself through the portal knowing that horrible doom awaited him there, yet, Brox had not hesitated. He had been aware that Malfurion needed time and time the orc had granted the druid.

Rhonin knelt by the edge of the sea, the creation of which he saw in some ways as a tribute itself to Brox. It would not have existed without the orc's action. Undelayed, Sargeras likely would have stepped through the gateway, then slaughtered everyone.

Did Brox bring history back to what it should be or was he part of it all along? the wizard wondered. Perhaps Nozdormu knew, but the Aspect of Time was not about to tell anyone. He had not even spoken of his own ordeal save that it had involved the Old Gods. Now, with the portal gone, even that threat had been removed.

Standing again, the wizard eyed the flotsam still flowing toward the shore. The tide brought in a variety of things, bits of plants, mostly, but also wreckage from the night elves' realm. Shreds of clothes, broken pieces of furniture, rotting food, and, yes, there were bodies. Not many, thankfully, and none at this spot. Jarod had parties scanning the shore, seeking any dead so that they could have swift but proper burials.

It was not just a matter of propriety, but safety, too. The dead might carry with them disease, a very real fear for the refugees.

Something floated near the wizard, bobbing up and down twice before settling just under the surface. Rhonin would have ignored it, but sensed something unusual. The thing had a touch of magic to it.

Stepping into the water, he reached down.

Brox's ax.

There could be no mistaking it. Rhonin had seen the astonishing weapon in action enough times. Despite its tremendous size, the double-edged ax fit perfectly in his grip and felt as light as a feather. It did not even feel wet.

"This isn't possible," he muttered, eyeing the sea suspiciously.

But no spirit arose from the depths to give a reason for the amazing discovery. The wizard looked down at the ax, then at the sea, and lastly at the ax again.

Finally, Rhonin stared off into the direction of the lost portal. An image of Brox standing atop slaughtered demons and challenging more to come to him filled the human's thoughts.

The wizard suddenly raised the ax high in what he recalled from his own time as an orcish salute to fallen heroes. Rhonin brandished it three times, then lowered the ax headfirst.

"They'll sing of you yet," he whispered, recalling Brox's words to both him and Krasus. "They'll pass songs of you down for generations to come. We'll see to that."

Hefting the ax over his shoulder, he went to find Krasus.

TWENTY-TWO

Illidan dismounted, his wrapped eyes surveying the thick forest for any threat. Of course, even had there been one, he had no doubt as to his ability to deal with it. The Well might be gone, but he had learned enough from Rhonin and the Burning Legion to make up for much of its loss. Besides, in a few minutes, even that consideration would be of no consequence.

The sorcerer tied his mount to a tree. Jarod Shadowsong and the others in charge of the host were busy arguing about mundane matters such as food and shelter. Illidan was more than happy to leave such petty things to others. He had come to this place for a far more important reason, one that he felt outshone all others.

He intended to salvage the lifeblood of the night elves.

They were all naive, so Malfurion's twin had decided, if they did not believe that the demons would someday return. Having tasted Kalimdor once, the Burning Legion would be eager for a second bite. Next time, they would strike in a far more terrifying manner, of that he was certain.

And so, Illidan planned to be prepared for that coming invasion.

The pristine lake buried deep atop Hyjal's highest peak had survived the onslaught undiscovered by either the defenders or the demons. A green, idyllic island lay at the very center. Illidan saw it as fate that he had been the one to come across the body of water first. It suited his desires perfectly.

He touched the thick pouch at his waist. The precious contents within called to Illidan. Their siren song assured the sorcerer that he had made the right decision. His people would fall over themselves in their gratitude and he would stand among them as one of their greatest heroes, possibly even more so than Malfurion.

Malfurion . . . his twin was honored by all as if he alone has saved the world. The people gave Illidan some crumb of recognition, but many misunderstood what the sorcerer had attempted to do. Rumors swelled that he had gone to the demons to truly join them and that only his brother had saved his soul from damnation. All Illidan's own efforts went unappreciated. His eyes—his *glorious* eyes—were only seen by the rest as a mark of his supposed pact with the lord of the Legion.

His so-perfect brother spoke pretty words about him to the public, but that only made Malfurion look magnanimous. Even the antlers sprouting from his twin's forehead did not disgust the dainty night elves. They embraced it as a sign of divinity, as if Malfurion now stood as one of the demigods . . . the same demigods who had perished so easily in battle while Illidan had survived and thrived.

It'll all change, though, he told himself, not for the first time. *They'll see what I've done . . . and thank me a thousand times over.*

Anticipation spreading across his face, the sorcerer opened the pouch and removed from it a vial identical to the one that Tyrande had seen him use earlier. In fact, not only was the vial the same, but so were contents.

The Well of Eternity might be gone, but Illidan Stormrage had saved a small bit of it.

It'll work! I know it'll work! He had felt the Well's astonishing properties himself. Even so minute an amount would be potent.

The stopper shaped like Queen Azshara once more danced for him before popping off. Letting the stopper fall to the grass, the night elf held the open container over the lake.

He poured the contents into the water.

The lake shimmered where the drops of the Well touched it. The water, originally a calm blue, suddenly glowed intensely where the drops hit. The change spread rapidly, first cutting across to the island, then around it. In but seconds, the entire lake had taken on a rich azure hue that no one could mistake as other than magic.

To Illidan's heightened senses, the spectacle was even more breathtaking. He had expected a reproduction of the Well, but this was fascinating in itself.

Yet . . . it could still be so much more.

He reached into the pouch and removed a second vial.

This time, the sorcerer simply tore off the stopper and dumped the contents into the lake. As he did, the blue intensified further. Tendrils of raw energy began to play on the surface and Illidan felt a wonderful radiance that he had not experienced since the Well.

His lips parted. He wanted to throw himself into the water, but managed to hold back. His hand slipped to the pouch.

What would a *third* vial do?

He undid the stopper and started to pour.

"What by the Mother Moon are you doing there?"

Illidan had been so caught up in his efforts that he had failed to notice the approach of others. He spun about, the last vial still in his hand, to face a party of mounted figures, Jarod Shadowsong chief among them.

"Captain . . ." the sorcerer began.

One of the Highborne glanced past Illidan. "He's done something to the lake! It—" The spellcaster's expression grew awed. "It feels like the *Well*—"

"Elune preserve us!" bellowed a noble next to Jarod. "He's resurrecting it!"

The commander dismounted. "Illidan Stormrage! Cease this immediately! If not for your brother, I'd—"

"My *brother* . . ." An imperious fury arose, fueled by his nearness to the enchanted lake. Once more, the power surged through him. He was capable of anything . . . "Always my precious brother . . ."

The others dismounted, following Jarod Shadowsong. Their wary expressions made Illidan tense. They wanted to keep him from the lake's power! He eyed the Highborne, who would certainly attempt to usurp it for themselves . . .

"No . . ."

One of the nobles hesitated. "By Elune! What sort of eyes does he have that glow beneath that veil?"

Illidan glared at the Highborne.

Their leader raised a hand in defense. "Look out—"

Flames erupted around the other sorcerers. They screamed.

Jarod and the nobles charged him. Illidan sneered at the paltry threat and gestured.

The ground beneath them exploded. Jarod was tossed back. The lead noble, Blackforest flew high in the air, finally striking a tree with a resounding crack.

"You stupid fools! You—"

His feet suddenly sank into the earth. As he looked down, tree branches wrapped around his body, pinning his legs together and his arms to his torso. Illidan tried to speak, but his mouth filled with leaves that adhered to his tongue. The sorcerer could not even concentrate, for a buzzing echoed in his ears, as if a thousand tiny insects nestled in them.

Gasping, Illidan slumped to his knees. Through the buzzing, he vaguely sensed someone else approaching. The sorcerer knew without a doubt who it had to be . . .

"Oh, Illidan . . ." Malfurion's voice cut perfectly through the buzzing. "Illidan . . . why?"

The druid stared at the lake, its blazing blue color a clear sign of its contamination. No one could drink from it now. Like the Well of Eternity before it, it was now a fount of power, not life.

"Oh, Illidan . . ." he repeated, eyeing his bound twin.

"Dath'Remar is still alive," reported Tyrande, kneeling beside the Highborne leader. "One more also, but the others are dead." She shuddered. "They were burned in their skins . . ."

Malfurion had intended to come alone, only the dragons and Krasus with him, but, like the druid, Tyrande had somehow sensed that Illidan was up to something. With several of her priestesses in tow, she had ridden after the dragons, but had arrived too late.

As had Malfurion.

"Lord Blackforest is dead. The others, I think can be saved," announced another priestess.

"My . . . brother *lives*," managed Maiev. She and Shandris both attended to an unconscious Jarod. He had bruises all over his face and his armor was even more battered now. Dried blood caked several wounds already healing thanks to the prayers of the priestesses.

Jarod's sister rose and her countenance was one terrible to behold. She started for Illidan, at the same time drawing her weapon.

"No, Maiev!" Tyrande commanded.

"He almost slew my brother!"

The high priestess met her. "But failed. His fate is not yours to decide. Jarod will do so." She glanced at Malfurion. "Is that not so?"

He nodded sadly. "It's his right and I'll not argue it." The druid shook his head. "So, this is why he stayed so near the shore of the Well."

"I didn't know that he had gathered more," Tyrande added apologetically.

With a sudden hunch, Malfurion knelt near his brother. Illidan's breathing was even, but he stiffened when he sensed Malfurion near. The druid searched the pouch.

"At least four more vials . . . he would have turned this lake completely into another Well."

"Can anything be done to change it back?"

Krasus had remained in the background, watching the events unfold. Now, however, the cowled mage muttered, "No . . . nothing. What has been done cannot be undone."

Alexstrasza, however, added, "We can do something to make of it a different force. One not as treacherous in nature as the Well became."

The mage's eyes momentarily widened. "Ah! Of course!"

Malfurion forced himself from his brother's side. "And what's that?"

The three dragons glanced at one another, each nodding agreement. Alexstrasza turned back to the night elves. "We are going to plant a tree."

"A tree?" The druid looked to Krasus for some sort of clarification.

But the mage, his own expression guarded, simply answered, "Not a tree. *The* tree."

They quickly turned it into a ceremony so as to lessen the impact of Illidan's misdeeds. The sorcerer was hidden away in order to prevent further trouble and Jarod's sister volunteered to guard him until a final fate could be decided. Jarod, healed by Shandris and Maiev, insisted that, when that time came, it would not be only his choice, but Malfurion's.

Other than Krasus, Rhonin, and the dragons, there were only night elves at the gathering. What the Aspects intended was for their race, which had suffered so much and feared for its continuance. Nobles, Highborne, and representatives of what had once been the lower castes assembled. The rest of the survivors gathered as they could down below, unable to see the spectacle but aware that it would influence the course of their lives.

Malfurion and the rest who had been invited journeyed to the island at the center of the lake. Despite Hyjal's tremendous height, the top of the peak was fairly warm, perhaps even more so now that the lake had become touched by magic.

"It's beautiful," Tyrande whispered.

"Would that it was only that," Malfurion replied morosely. Illidan continued to be in his thoughts. He already had some suggestions as to what to do about his twin and it pained the druid to imagine them being put into action. Yet, Illidan clearly could not longer be trusted. He had slain others out of madness. His notion that the night elves needed a new Well in order to protect themselves against some possible future attack by the Burning Legion was not sufficient reason for his heinous crimes.

Although still creatures of the dark despite having been

forced to adapt to daylight battles, Jarod had agreed with the dragons to assemble at noontime. Alexstrasza explained that the sun's zenith would be essential to what they planned and the night elf was not about to argue with the giants.

Despite the island's reasonable size, only tall grass covered it. At its center, the group positioned itself as requested by Alexstrasza. The dragons took up a prime location near what they said was the *exact* middle, leaving a small place open between them.

The Aspect of Life began the ceremony. "Kalimdor has suffered greatly," she rumbled. As those in the group nodded, Alexstrasza continued, "And the night elves most of all. Your race was not completely innocent in all of this, but the trials and tribulations through which you have passed forgive that."

There were a few uneasy glances toward the Highborne, but no one argued.

The red dragon lowered her palm. In it, nestled like an infant, a single seed similar in appearance to an acorn rested. Malfurion felt a tingle as he stared at it.

"Taken from G'Hanir, the Mother Tree," she explained.

The druid recognized the home of the dead demigoddess, Aviana.

"G'Hanir is no more, having perished with its mistress, but this seed survives. From it, we shall raise a new tree."

Nozdormu dropped one paw to the ground and, with a single swipe, created a hole perfect for planting the seed, Alexstrasza gently placed the seed in it, then Ysera pushed the dirt over the hole.

The Aspect of Life gazed up at the sun. Then, she and the other two dragons bent their heads low over the buried seed.

"I give Strength and Healthy Life to the night elves, for so long as the tree stands," Alexstrasza proclaimed.

From her, a soft, red glow flowed to the mound. At the same time, the sunlight over the mound intensified, spreading all the way across the lake in every direction. Some of the night elves stirred, but all remained silent.

A wonderful warmth spread over Malfurion and he instinctively took Tyrande's hand. She did not pull away, but rather tightened her grip.

And from the mound, there came movement. As if a tiny creature burrowed to the surface, the dirt pushed up and away.

From the seed had sprouted a tiny sapling.

It rose until a yard high, small branches sprouting. Lush, green leaves burst from the branches, creating a delicate canopy.

As Alexstrasza pulled back slightly, Nozdormu spoke, a slight hiss in his voice. "Time will be on the night elvesss' side once again, for I grant them continued Immortality, forever a chance to learn, for asss long asss the tree stands . . ."

From him issued forth a golden bronze aura that joined with the sunlight as the red had. Flowing through the sapling, it sank into the mound.

The tree grew again. As the onlookers gaped, it rose to more than twice the height of a night elf. Its foliage grew dense, green, and full of promise. Branches thickened, showing the health and strength of the tree. The roots began to come up above ground like many legs. A space almost large enough for several seated night elves formed underneath.

Nozdormu nodded, then, like his counterpart, withdrew. There remained only Ysera.

Eyes lidded, the green leviathan studied the tree. Despite its swift growth, it was still dwarfed by the dragons.

"To the night elves, who have lost their hopes, I give forth the ability to Dream again. To Dream, to Imagine, for in that is the best hope of rebuilding, of recovering, of growing . . ." She looked ready to do as the other Aspects had, then paused. Her head swung toward Malfurion. "And to those who follow the path of one held special by me—and mine— I grant him and the other druids to come the path into the Emerald Dream, where, even in their deepest sleep, they may cross the world, learn from it, and draw upon its own strength . . . the better to guide Kalimdor's health and safety throughout the future."

Malfurion swallowed, unable to otherwise respond. He felt the eyes of everyone upon him, but, most of all, felt Tyrande's proud touch.

Ysera looked again to the tree . . . and from her issued a green mist. Like the two before, her offering bound with the sunlight, then settled over the tree.

As the last of it vanished into the soil, the assembled on-lookers felt the ground shake. Malfurion led Tyrande back a few steps and, as if this was a cue, the rest followed suit. Even the dragons moved back, albeit not near as much as the tinier creatures.

And the tree *grew*. It grew twice its previous height, then twice that. It rose higher and higher into the heavens, until the druid felt certain that even those well below the peak could at least see the huge, burgeoning canopy. So massive was the canopy that the entire region should have been bathed in shadow, but somehow the sunlight continued to focus on the area, even the lake.

The roots also expanded, stretching taller and bending to best support the gigantic tree. They spread so high that now it seemed all of Lord Ravencrest's lost Black Rook Hold could have fit underneath . . . and still the roots—the entire tree—grew.

When at last it ceased, even the dragons looked like no

more than birds who could perch upon one of the branches and hide in the foliage.

"Here stands before you *Nordrassil*. The *World Tree* is brought into existence!" intoned the Aspect of Life. "For as long as it stands, for as long as it is honored, the night elves will thrive! You may alter, you may follow different paths, but you will ever be an integral part of Kalimdor . . ."

Krasus suddenly stood behind Malfurion. In a whisper to the druid, he added, "And the tree, whose roots go deep, will keep this lake as it is. The sun will always be a part of this well. The black waters will not run here."

Malfurion took this in with much relief. He glanced down at Tyrande, who met his gaze with an expression that left his cheeks darkening. Before Malfurion realized what was happening, she kissed him.

"Whatever this long future our people have been promised holds," his childhood friend murmured. "I wish to see it with you."

He felt more blood rush to his cheeks. "As I do with you, Tyrande."

Malfurion kissed her back, but as he did, another's face intruded into his thoughts. There would be a period of rejoicing, of spreading the word concerning the Aspects' gifts to their people, but for Malfurion, those events suddenly mattered little. There was still Illidan to deal with.

Tyrande pulled away, her mouth twisted into a frown. "I know what it is that suddenly fills you with sorrow. What must be done must be done, Malfurion, but don't let his crimes steal your heart away."

He took strength from her words. "I won't. I promise you, I won't."

Over her shoulder, Malfurion noticed Krasus and Rhonin quietly retreating from the gathering. He glanced at the dragons and saw that Nozdormu was also missing. Just like that. Somehow, the Aspect had simply vanished without anyone noticing.

There had to be a connection.

"Malfurion, what is it now?"

"Come with me, Tyrande, while no one's looking."

She did not argue. The two night elves followed after Krasus and the wizard.

The voice echoed in Krasus's head. *It hasss been delayed far too long. It mussst be done now.*

Nozdormu.

"Rhonin—"

The human nodded. "I heard him."

They slipped out while the night elves were still babbling over the tree. Krasus would have liked to have spoken with Malfurion a little more, but the mage *was* eager to return home.

Before the ceremony, Nozdormu had come to him. The Aspect of Time had caught Krasus alone. "We owe you a debt, Korialstrasz."

By "we," Nozdormu did not just mean the other Aspects and him. He referred also to his various selves spread through Time itself. Such was his unique nature.

"I did what had to be done. Rhonin—and Brox—too."

"I alssso speak to the wizard at this very moment," the Aspect had commented offhandedly. It was nothing for him to be in two places at the same time, if he so desired. "I tell him, asss I tell you, that I will sssee to it that you reach home."

Krasus had been very grateful. It had pained him to still be around an Alexstrasza who did not know the fate to befall her and the other dragons. "I am—thank you."

The bronze giant had given him a solemn look. "I know

what you hide from her, from usss. It is my fate and curssse to know such things and be unable myssself to prevent them. Know that I now asssk for forgiveness for the wrongs I will caussse you in the future, but I mussst be what I am destined to be . . . as Malygos is."

"Malygos!" Krasus had blurted, thinking of the eggs secreted in the pocket dimension. "Nozdormu—"

"I know what you did. Give them over to me and I will pass them to Alexstrasza. When Malygosss is well enough, he will be presssented with the young. Compared to all elssse that has happened, it isss a sssmall change to the time line and one of which I approve. The bluesss will fly the skies again, even though their numberss will not be great even after ten thousand yearsss. But better sssome, than none."

Krasus had also wished to see his beloved queen once more, but it had been agreed that he might let slip something even she should not know. Now, though, as he and Rhonin stood ready for the bronze dragon's reappearance, the mage regretted not having sought her out, anyway.

Rhonin studied him. "You could still run to her. I'd understand."

The gaunt figure shook his head. "We have twisted the future enough. What will be will be."

"Hmmph. You're stronger than I am."

"No, Rhonin," Krasus muttered with a shake of his head. "Not in the least."

"Are you prepared?" Nozdormu suddenly asked.

They turned to find the Aspect waiting patiently.

"How long have you been there?" snapped the cowled spellcaster.

"Asss long as I chose to be." Foregoing any other answer, Nozdormu spread his wings. "Climb atop. I will take you to your proper period in the future."

Rhonin looked dubious. "Just like that?"

"When the lassst of the Well devoured itself, the Old Gods were again sssealed away. Their reach into the river of Time vanished with it. The tearsss in the fabric of reality vanished. The way forward is now sssimple enough . . . for me."

From the ground, Rhonin lifted up Brox's ax.

"What isss *that* doing here?" asked the Aspect.

Both spellcasters looked defiant. "It comes with us," Krasus insisted. "Or we stay here and meddle more."

"Then, by all means, bring it with."

They mounted quickly, but as they did, Krasus spied a pair of forms hiding in the woods. He sensed immediately who they were.

"Nozdormu—"

"Yesss, yesss, the druid and the priestess. I've known all along. Ssstep out and say your farewellsss, then! We must be gone!"

Although the Aspect took their appearance in stride, Krasus felt far less comfortable. "You two heard—"

"We heard all," interjected Malfurion. "Not that we understand *all.*"

The mage nodded. "We could say little and still cannot say more. Just know this, the two of you. We *shall* meet again."

"Our people will survive?" asked Tyrande.

The mage calculated his words before speaking. "Yes, and the world will be the better for it. And with that, I say goodbye."

Rhonin raised Brox's ax, echoing Krasus's farewell.

Nozdormu stretched his wings again. The night elves immediately backed away. They raised hands toward the pair.

But before they could . . . both the dragon and his riders simply vanished.

TWENTY-THREE

Rhonin awoke to find himself lying in a field of grass.
At first, he feared that something had gone awry,
but then, as he sat up, a familiar and very welcome
sight greeted his eyes.

A house. *His* house.

He was home.

More important, he sighted Jalia, the townswoman who
had been taking care of Vereesa during her pregnancy. She
seemed in a fair state, anxious but cheerful. Rhonin unsuccess-
fully tried to calculate the time passing since he had vanished.
He wondered how old the babies would be by now.

Then, to his horror, he heard Vereesa cry out, "Jalia!
Come!"

Without hesitation, he leapt to his feet and followed after
the woman. For a full-bodied person, Jalia moved quickly.
She raced through the doorway, even as Vereesa called out
again.

The wizard burst through the door a few moments later,
hand already up in preparation to defend his bride and children. He looked around, expecting a home ransacked or
burnt, but found everything in place.

"Vereesa? Vereesa?"

"Rhonin! Praise the Sunwell! Rhonin, in here!"

He ran toward the bedroom, fearful of what he would find. A moan set the hair on his neck standing.

"Vereesa!" Rhonin barged inside. "The twins! Are they—"

"They're coming!"

He stared wide-eyed. His wife lay in the bed, *still* very much pregnant . . . but not for long.

"How—" he began, but Jalia shoved him aside.

"If you don't know how, then you'd best just stand back and let her and me handle it, Master Rhonin!"

The wizard knew better than to argue. He fell back against the wall, ready to be of any help should the need arrive, but saw quickly that Vereesa and Jalia had things well in hand.

"The first one's coming," Vereesa announced.

As he watched and waited, Rhonin thought of all the astounding events he had recently been a part of. He had passed through time, survived the first coming of the Burning Legion, and had aided in the effort to save the world and the future.

But none of that, he discovered, was as miraculous as what he was a part of now . . . and for that he gave thanks that he and the others had succeeded.

And in that time so long ago, Jarod Shadowsong presided over a gathering far more dour than the one on the island. Those who now represented the leaders of the host—and their allies, too—stood ready to hear judgment.

Soldiers prodded along the one on trial. His mouth was wrapped shut with a cloth but bonds of metal now kept his arms behind him and his hands from gesturing. Invisible spells cast by Malfurion and others ensured that there would be no repeat of the terrible incident at the lake.

When he stood in the center of the circle that his accusers had formed, Illidan, monstrous eyes scarved, stared arrogantly at the figure before him. One of the soldiers cautiously removed the gag.

"Illidan Stormrage," began Jarod, sounding nothing like the simple Guard captain he had once been. "Many are the times you fought valiantly alongside others against the evil encroaching on our world, but, sadly, too many are the times you've proven yourself a danger to your own people!"

"A danger? I'm the only one who sees honestly! I was planning for our future! I was saving our race! I—"

"Attacked those who disagreed with you—slaying many— and recreated what should have been best forgotten!"

Illidan spat. "You'll all be praying to me as if I were a god when the demons return! I know how they think, how they act! Next time, they won't be cast out! You'll need to fight them as they fight! Only I have that knowledge—"

"Such knowledge, we're better without." Jarod looked around, as if seeking someone. When he apparently did not find that person, the leader of the night elves sighed and continued, "Illidan Stormrage, as it falls to me, I can think of only one thing to do with you! It pains me, but I hereby declare that you shall be put to death—"

"How *original,*" sneered the sorcerer.

"Put to death in a manner—"

"Jarod . . . forgive me for being late," interrupted a figure behind Illidan. "May I still speak?"

The armored night elf nodded almost gratefully. "This is yours to decide as much as it's mine."

Malfurion walked around his brother. Illidan's face followed him as the druid stepped between the sorcerer and the soldier. "I'm sorry, Illidan."

"Ha!"

"What is it you want to say, Master Malfurion?" urged Jarod.

"There is some truth in what my brother says about the Burning Legion, Jarod. They may come again."

"And you want us therefore to forget his crimes and his danger?"

The druid shook his antlered head. "No." He glanced at his twin, the other half of him, then briefly at Tyrande, who stood at the edge of the circle with Maiev and Shandris. She had stayed with him all the while he had suffered through what should be done. The high priestess supported his decision, not that it eased his ache.

"No, Jarod," Malfurion repeated, steeling himself. "No. I want you to imprison him . . . even if it means he stays so for ten thousand years . . . if necessary . . ."

As the rest of those assembled suddenly broke out into startled muttering, Malfurion closed his eyes and tried to calm himself. He had his suspicions concerning the future, knowing as he did now about Krasus and Rhonin. The druid prayed he had made the right decision.

But only the future would tell . . .

And, lastly . . .

Thrall had not heard from the two he had sent to the mountains to investigate the shaman's vision. They might still be searching, but the orc leader had the suspicion that the truth was far worse. No good ruler, not even of his race, liked to send loyal warriors to their death without something coming from it.

Night had long fallen and most of his subjects were deep asleep. Only he and the guards outside still stirred. Thrall *should* have been sleeping, but his concern over this unsettling quest had grown with each day since Brox's and Gaskal's departure.

The torchlights flickered, creating shadows that moved as if alive. Thrall paid them no mind until he suddenly noticed that one by the door was solid.

The orc immediately leapt up from his stone throne. "Who dares?"

But instead of an assassin—and there were always plenty of those—a wizened orc wearing wolf skins and bearing a totem with the carved head of a dragon on it shuffled forward.

"Hail, Thrall!" the elder figure called in an oddly-strong voice. "Hail, savior of the orcs!"

"Who are you? You are not Kalthar!" Thrall growled, referring to his shaman.

"I am one who brings news . . . news of a valiant warrior, Broxigar."

"Brox? What of him? Speak!"

"The warrior is dead . . . but dead sending many enemies before him! He has again fought the Legion and cut down so many it would take a day just to count them one by one!"

"The Legion?" The orc's worst fears were realized. "Where? Tell me so that I can gather our warriors and fight them!"

The almost hairless elder shook his head, then gave Thrall a grin without teeth. "There are no more demons! Broxigar and those fighting beside him defeated the Legion and it was your warrior who stood at the pass again, even when faced by their master!" The figure bowed his head respectfully.

"Sing songs of him, great Thrall, for he was part of those who saved the world for you . . ."

For a time, the younger orc stood silent, then, "This is true? All of it?"

"Aye . . . and I bring this, all that remains to honor a hero." Despite his seeming infirmity, the shaman brought forth a huge, twin-edged ax. Thrall blinked, somehow not having noticed it earlier.

"I've seen nothing like it."

"It is a weapon crafted by the first druid, formed from the magic of a forest spirit. Fashioned especially for Brox's hand."

"It will have a place of honor," Thrall whispered, gently taking it from the crooked figure. He eyed it in admiration. Light as a feather and, from the look of it, wood from bottom to head—even the blades—but clearly a capable ax. "How is it you have this—"

But the shaman did not answer . . . because he was no longer there.

With a grunt, Thrall rushed through the entranceway. He instinctively gripped the ax, suddenly wary that this had all been some intricate plot to do away with him.

He confronted the two guards stationed outside what passed for his throne room. "Where is he? Where is the old one?"

"There's been no one!" the senior guard quickly answered.

With a frustrated growl, Thrall pushed past them. He hurried out into the open. The full moon well illuminated the surroundings, but still the ruler of the orcs saw nothing.

Not, that is, until he happened to look up at that moon.

And in it, just passing into the night, he saw a huge, winged form.

A red dragon.

• • •

Krasus/Korialstrasz veered in the direction of his flight's lair. Rhonin was with his Vereesa and, through the dragon, the legacy of brave Brox had been brought to the orcs.

Now it was *his* turn to at last go home . . . and see tomorrow what the future would bring.

THE END

ABOUT THE AUTHOR

Richard A. Knaak is *The New York Times* bestselling Fantasy Author of 29 novels and over a dozen short pieces, including *The Legend of Huma, Tides of Blood,* and *Kaz the Minotaur* for *Dragonlance,* and *The Demon Soul* for *WarCraft,* the last published by Simon & Schuster. Born and raised in the Chicago area, he now splits his time between there and the panoramic area of northern Arkansas. His works have been published most recently in Russian, Turkish, Bulgarian, Chinese, Czech, German, Spanish, and more. In addition to his work for *Dragonlance,* he is the author of the popular *Dragonrealm* series, a number of independent novels, and has penned several tales for both *WarCraft* and *Diablo,* based on the worldwide-bestselling games from Blizzard Entertainment. He is also the author of the new manga *Dragon Hunt*—the first in the *Sunwell Trilogy*—and the forthcoming sequel, *Shadows of Ice,* for Tokyopop. Both are also based on the *World of Warcraft* massively multiplayer game.

The thrilling conclusion to his *Minotaur Wars, Empire of Blood,* was just recently released in hardcover. Currently, Knaak is at work on *Ghostlands*—the third in his *Sunwell Trilogy*—and is just concluding his *Aquilonia Trilogy*—*A Silent*

Shadow, The Power of Fury, and *The Lion's Den*—based on the worlds of Robert E. Howard. Fans of his Blizzard work will be delighted to know that he has also completed another exciting *Diablo* novel, *Moon of the Spider,* featuring the necromancer Zayl, and has agreed to write the first epic trilogy for the series, *The Sin War.*

Those wishing to find out more about his projects, or would like to join his e-mail list for announcements, should visit his website at www.sff.net/people/knaak.

As many as 1 in 3 Americans
have HIV and don't know it.

**TAKE CONTROL.
KNOW YOUR STATUS.
GET TESTED.**

To learn more about HIV testing,
or get a free guide to HIV and
other sexually transmitted diseases.

**www.knowhivaids.org
1-866-344-KNOW**

09620